PENGUIN BOOKS

THE LIGHT AND THE DARK

Lord Snow was born in Leicester in 1905, and educated at a secondary school. He started his career as a professional scientist, though writing was always his ultimate aim. He won a research scholarship to Cambridge, worked on molecular physics, and became Fellow of his college in 1930. He continued his academic life in Cambridge until the beginning of the war, by which time he had already begun the 'Lewis Eliot' novels of his *Strangers and Brothers* series. The first volume, *George Passant*, was published in 1940; *Last Things* completes the sequence. (They are all published by Penguins.) His most recent books are a non-fiction book, *Public Affairs* (1971) and a novel, *The Malcontents* (1972).

In the war he became a Civil Servant, and because of his human and scientific knowledge was engaged in selecting scientific personnel. He has had further experience of these problems since the war, both in industry and as a Civil Service Commissioner, for which work he received a knighthood in 1957. His Rede Lecture on *The Two Cultures and the Scientific Revolution* (1959), and Godkin Lectures on *Science and Government* (1960), and his address to the A.A.A.S., *The Moral Unneutrality of Science*, have been widely discussed. He has received many honours, including Honorary Membership of the American Academy Institute, and the Rectorship of St Andrew's University. He was made Parliamentary Secretary to the Ministry of Technology (1964–66) and received a barony (1964).

He is married to Pamela Hansford Johnson.

THE LIGHT AND
THE DARK

C. P. SNOW

PENGUIN BOOKS

Penguin Books Ltd, Harmondsworth, Middlesex, England
Penguin Books Australia Ltd, Ringwood, Victoria, Australia

—

First published by Faber & Faber 1947
Published by Macmillan 1951
Published in Penguin Books 1962
Reprinted 1964 1965, 1968, 1973

—

—

Made and printed in Great Britain
by Richard Clay (The Chaucer Press) Ltd
Bungay, Suffolk
Set in Monotype Bembo

CONTENTS

Contents

PART THREE
THE LAST ATTEMPT

PART FOUR
CLARITY

PART ONE

WALKS AT NIGHT

CHAPTER I

A Spring Afternoon

I SMELT blossom everywhere as I walked through the town that afternoon. The sky was bright, cloudless and pale, and the wind cut coldly down the narrow Cambridge streets. Round Fenner's the trees flared out in bloom, and the scent was sweet, heady, and charged with one's desires.

I had been walking all the afternoon weighed down by a trouble. It was a trouble I was used to, there was no help for it, it could only be endured. It gnawed acutely that day, and so I had tried to comfort myself, walking alone; but I should have said nothing, if Roy Calvert had not asked me direct.

I had turned towards the college, and was still engrossed in my thoughts; it was not until he called out that I saw him moving towards me with his light, quick, graceful stride. He was over middle height, slightly built but strong; and each physical action was so full of ease and grace that he had only to enter a room for eyes to follow him.

'You look extremely statesman-like, Lewis,' he said, mimicking an acquaintance's favourite word of praise. His eyes were glinting a clear transparent hazel yellow, and his whole expression was mischievous and gay. It was often otherwise. In repose, his face became sad and grave, and in a moment the brilliant high spirits could be swept away and he would look years older, more handsome, more finely shaped. And once or twice already I had seen his face, not sad, but stricken and haunted by a wild melancholy, inexplicably stricken it seemed for so young a man.

Now he was cheerful, gay, and mocking. 'Do you need to address your colleagues? Do you need to make something clear to unperceptive persons?'

I said no, and at the sound of my voice he glanced at me sharply. He walked at my side under the trees by the edge of Parker's Piece. When he next spoke, his tone had changed.

'Lewis, why are you unhappy?'

'There's nothing the matter.'

'Why are you unhappy?'

'It's nothing.'

'Not true,' he said. 'I can't get you to smile.'

Then I did smile. To put him off, I asked about a predicament of his own which I had heard about, week by week, for some time past. Roy shook his head and smiled. 'No,' he said. 'You mustn't escape by talking about me. It's very like you. It's the way you protect yourself, old boy. You mustn't. You need to talk.'

I was twenty-nine, and Roy five years younger. I was fond of him in a casual, protective fashion, and I expected to be told of his adventures and have him seek me out when he was despondent. I knew a good deal of his life, and he very little of mine. This was the habit I had formed, not only with him but with most people that I cared for. It had become second nature to listen to confidences and not to offer them. And so I was not used to Roy's insistence, clear, intimate, direct. With another I should have passed it off for ever, but about his affection there was something at the same time disarming and piercing. It seemed quite free from self. To my own surprise, I found myself beginning to talk.

We walked along the back streets to Maid's Causeway, over Midsummer Common to the river, came back to Christ's Piece and then, still intent, retraced our steps. It was bitterly cold in the shade, but we walked slowly: the dense snow-white masses of the chestnuts gleamed in the sunshine: there was a first hint of lilac in the wind. Once, after I had fallen silent and Roy had said 'just so' and was waiting for me to start again, I heard a series of college clocks clanging out the hour, very faintly, for the wind took the sound away.

The story I told Roy need not be set down until I describe my own life; it would not add anything to this account of him. All I need say here is that I told him about my marriage. No one else knew what I told him, though one or two must have guessed something near the truth. I had been desperately in love with Sheila when I was a very young man; when at twenty-six I married her, I still loved her, and I married her knowing that she did not love me and that her temperament was unstable. This was three years before. I went into it thinking I might have to look after her: it had turned out worse than I feared.

'Just so,' said Roy. 'You can't leave her now, can you? You couldn't if you tried. You need to go on looking after her. You need to go on looking after her always.'

'Yes,' I said.

He put his arm round my shoulders.

'You know, old boy,' he said, 'you're not the one I pity. Should you be? I'm extremely sorry, things must be made as easy for you as they can. But you're interested in life, you've got tremendous spirits, you can bear anything. No, it's she whom I pity desperately. I don't see what she has to hope for.'

He was utterly right. I knew it too well. Again we walked under the fragrant trees. 'You mustn't lose too much,' said Roy. I had forgotten by now how young he was, and he was talking as though we had each been through the same darkness.

'As you've just said,' I replied, 'there's nothing to be done. One has to go on, that's all.'

'Just so,' said Roy. 'Life's very unfair. Why should this happen to you?'

Yet I felt he liked me more because it had happened.

I told him one other thing, which helped explain why I had taken a job in Cambridge at all. As he knew, I had been born poor. Through a mixture of good luck and good management, I had done well in the Bar examinations and in my period as a pupil. By the time I married, I was making a fair living at the Bar. But I was overstrained, my inner life racked me more after marriage than before, I wanted to rest a little. Some of my influential friends made inquiries, and soon Francis Getliffe told me there might be an opening in his college for an academic lawyer. At last, after a long delay, the offer was officially made: I accepted it, and was elected late in 1933, a few months before this talk with Roy. The college did not object to my keeping on a consultant's job with an industrial firm, and I spent some days each week in London, where my wife was still living in our Chelsea house. I usually stayed in Cambridge from Thursday to Monday, and slept in my college rooms on those nights, as though I had been a bachelor fellow.

It was since I came to live so much in college that Roy began to call on me. I had met him once when he was a boy (his father was a very wealthy man in the provincial town where I was born), and occasionally in his undergraduate days. I knew he was a member of the college when Getliffe first approached me and I had heard several conflicting rumours about him – that he was drinking himself to death, spending all his nights with women, becoming an accomplished oriental scholar. But it was a coincidence that his rooms should be on the next staircase to mine, and that we should be waited on by the same servant. The first week-end I spent in college he ran up to see me, and since then it was very strange if I did not hear his light step on my stairs once or twice a day.

I had come to the end of what I could tell him: we stood under the trees in the bright sunshine; Roy said 'just so' again to lead me farther, but the clear light reedy voice died away without reply from me, for I had finished. He smiled because he felt I was less careworn, and took me to his rooms for tea.

They were a curious set of rooms, in a turret over the kitchen, right in the middle of the college. From a window on the staircase one could look out over the first court to the front gate, and his sitting-room window gave on to the palladian building in the second court and the high trees in the garden beyond. It was for strictly nepotic reasons that Roy was allowed to live there. He had ceased to be an undergraduate nearly three years before; he would normally have gone out of college then. He was a rich man, and it would have been easy for him to live in comfort anywhere in the town. But he was a favourite pupil of the Master's and of Arthur Brown's, the tutor who arranged about rooms: and they decided that it would be good for his researches if he stayed where he was.

The sitting-room itself struck oddly and brightly on the eye. There were all kinds of desks in a glazed and shining white – an upright one, at which he could work standing and read a manuscript against an opalescent screen, several for sitting at, one with three arms like a Greek pi, one curved like a horseshoe, and one very low which he could use by lying on cushions on the floor. For the rumours about him had a knack of containing a scrap of truth, and the one which to many of his acquaintances sounded the most fantastic was less extra-ordinary than the fact. He had already put a mass of original scholar-ship behind him; most days he worked in this room for seven or eight hours without a break, and he had struck a field where each day's work meant a discovery both new and certain.

The whole room was full of gadgets for his work, most of which he had designed. There were holders for his manuscripts, lights to inspect them by, a small X-ray apparatus which he had learned to work, card indexes which stood up and could be used with one hand. Everything glistened in its dazzling white, except for some van Goghs on the walls, a rich russet carpet all over the floor, and a sofa and armchair by the fire.

A kitchen porter brought us a big tray wrapped in green baize; underneath stood a robust silver teapot, a plate of toast, a dish of mulberry jam, a bowl of thick cream.

Roy patted the shining silver.

'You deserve some tea,' he said. 'Reward for interesting conversa-tion.'

He gave a smile, intimate and kind. He knew now that he had helped bring me somewhere near a normal state. He was sure enough to laugh at me. As I spread jam and cream on a piece of toast and tasted the tart mulberry flavour through cream, butter, burned bread, I saw he had a mocking glint in his eyes.

'Well?' I said.

'I was only thinking.'

'What of?'

'Women.'

'Well?' I said again.

'Each to his métier,' said Roy. 'You'd better leave them to me in future. You take them too seriously.'

In fact, he attracted much love. He had been sought after by women since he was a boy: and he enjoyed making love, and threw it lightly away.

Five o'clock struck, and Roy sprang from his chair. 'Not much time,' he said. 'We must be off. I need you. I need to buy some books.'

'What is it?' I asked, but he smiled demurely and secretively.

'You'll know quite soon,' he said.

He led the way to the nearest bookshop. 'Quick,' he said as I followed through the press of people on the narrow pavement. 'We need to get through them all in half an hour.'

He was playing a trick, but there was nothing to worry about. He was cheerful, settled, enjoying himself. When we arrived at the shop, he stared round with an expression serious, eager, keenly anxious. Then he moved over to the shelf of theological works, and said with intensity:

'There are still some here. We're not too late.' He had taken hold of three copies of a thin volume. The dust cover carried a small cross and the words: *The Middle Period of Richard Heppenstall* by Ralph Udal. 'Who in God's name was Richard Heppenstall?' I asked.

'Seventeenth-century clergyman,' Roy whispered. 'Somewhat old-brandy, but very good.' Then in a loud clear voice he greeted the manager of the shop, who was coming to attend to him.

'I see I've just got here in time. How many have you sold?'

'None as far as I know, Mr Calvert. It's only come in today –'

'That's extremely odd,' said Roy.

'Is it a good book, Mr Calvert?'

'It's a very remarkable book,' said Roy. 'You must read it yourself. Promise me you will, and tell me what you think of it. But you need to buy some more. We shall have to take these three. I'm extremely sorry, but you'll have to wait before you read it. I want one myself *urgently* tonight. I need to send one at once to Mr Despard-Smith. And of course Lord Boscastle needs one too. You'd better put that one down to Mr Lewis Eliot –' He walked the manager away from me, whispering confidentially, the manager responding by wise and knowing nods. I never learned for certain what he said; but for the rest of my time in Cambridge, the manager, and the whole of the staff of his shop, treated me with uneasy deference, as though, instead of being an ordinary law don, I might turn out to be a peer incognito.

I was half-ruffled, half-amused, when Roy rushed me away to another shop.

'I'm buying these books,' he said before I could protest. 'Just lend me your name. I'll settle tonight. Talking of names, Lord B is staying at the Lodge tomorrow' (for Lord Boscastle was a real person, and his sister, Lady Muriel, was the Master's wife).

Breathlessly we hurried from bookshop to bookshop, buying every copy of Udal's book before half past five. Roy sent them as presents, had them put down to my account, asked me to inquire for them myself.

As we left the last shop, Roy grinned.

'Well, that was quite a rush,' he said.

He insisted on paying three pounds for the books that had been put down to me – and, to tell the truth, I did not feel like stopping him.

'I suppose I'm right in thinking that Udal is a friend of yours?' I said.

Roy smiled.

On our way back to the college, he asked:

'Tell me, Lewis, are you extremely tired?'

'Not specially.'

'Nor am I. We need some nets. Let's have some.'

We changed, and he drove me down to Fenner's in the cold April evening. The freshman's match was being played, and we watched the last overs of the day; then Roy bought a new ball in the pavilion, we went over to the nets, and I began to bowl to him. Precisely how good he was I found it difficult to be sure. He had a style, as in most things of extreme elegance and ease; he seemed to need no practice at all, and the day after a journey abroad or a wild and sleepless night would play the first over with an eye as sure as if he had been batting all the summer. When he first came up, people had thought he might get into the university team, but he used to make beautiful twenties and thirties against first-class bowling, and then carelessly give his wicket away.

He was fond of the game, and batted on this cold evening with a sleek lazy physical content. Given the new ball, I was just good enough a bowler to make him play. My best ball, which went away a little off the seam, he met with a back stroke from the top of his height, strong, watchful, leisurely, and controlled. When I over-pitched them on the off, he drove with statuesque grace and measured power. He hit the ball very hard – but, when one watched him at the wicket, his strength was not so surprising as if one had only seen him upright and slender in a fashionable suit.

I bowled to him for half an hour, but my only success was to get one ball through and rap him on the pads.

'Promising,' said Roy.

Then we had a few minutes during which I batted and he bowled, but at that point the evening lost its decorum, for Roy suddenly ceased to be either graceful or competent when he ran up to bowl.

The ground was empty now, the light was going, chimes from the Catholic church rang out clearly in the quiet. We stopped to listen; it was the hour, it was seven o'clock. We walked across the ground and under the trees in the road outside. The night was turning colder still, and our breath formed clouds in the twilight air. But we were hot with exercise, and Roy did not put on his sweater, but knotted the sleeves under his chin. A few white petals fell on his shoulders on our way towards the car. His eyes were lit up as though he were smiling at my expense, and his face was at rest.

'At any rate, old boy,' he said, 'you should be able to sleep tonight.'

CHAPTER 2

Inspection at Dinner

THE next morning, as I was going out of the college, I met the Master in the court.

'I was wanting to catch you, Eliot,' he said. 'I tried to get you by telephone last night, but had no luck.'

He was a man of sixty, but his figure was well preserved, the skin of his cheeks fresh, rosy, and unlined. He was continuously and excessively busy, yet his manner stayed brisk and cheerful; he complained sometimes of the books he had left unwritten or had still to write, but he was happier in committees, meetings, selection boards than in any other place. He was a profoundly humble man, and had no faith in anything original of his own. But he felt complete confidence in the middle of any society or piece of business; he went briskly about, cheerful and unaffected, indulging in familiar intimate whispers; he had never quite conquered his tongue, and if he was inspired by an amusing sarcasm he often was impelled to share it. He asked me to the Lodge for dinner the following night, in order to meet the Boscastles. 'My wife's note will follow, naturally, but I was anxious not to miss you.' It was clear that I was being invited to fill a gap, and the Master, whose manners were warm as well as good, wanted to make up for it.

'We've already asked young Calvert,' he went on, and dropped into his intimate whisper: 'Between ourselves, my brother-in-law never has considered this was the state of life his sister was born to. I fancy she wants to present him with someone who might pass muster. It's a very singular coincidence that we should possess a remarkably talented scholar who also cuts his hair. It's much more than we could reasonably expect.'

I chuckled.

'Yes,' said the Master, 'our young friend is distinctly presentable. Which is another strong reason for electing him, Eliot. The standard of our colleagues needs raising in that respect.'

I was left in no doubt that Roy had been invited to the original party, and that I was a reserve. The Master could not explain or apologize more, for, indiscreetly as he talked about fellows of the college, he was completely loyal to his wife. Yet it could not have escaped him that she was a formidable and grandiose snob. She was much else besides, she was a woman of character and power, but she was unquestionably a snob. I wondered if it surprised the Master as much as it did me, when I first noticed it. For he, the son of a Scottish lawyer, had not married Lady Muriel until he was middle-aged; he must have come strange to the Boscastles, and with some pre-conceptions about the aristocracy. In my turn, they were the first high and genuine aristocrats I had met; they were Bevills and the family had been solidly noble since the sixteenth century (which is a long time for a genuine descent); I had expected them to be less interested in social niceties than the middle classes were. I had not found it so. Nothing could be farther from the truth. They did it on a grander scale, that was all.

On the night of the dinner party, I was the first guest to arrive, and the Master, Lady Muriel, and their daughter Joan were alone in the great drawing-room when I was announced.

'Good evening, Mr Eliot,' said Lady Muriel. 'It is very good of you to come to see us at such short notice.'

I was slightly amused: that sounded like rubbing it in.

I was not allowed to chat; she had discovered that I had an interest in world affairs, and every time I set foot in the Lodge she began by cross-questioning me about the 'latest trends'. She was a stiffly built heavy woman, her body seeming cylindrical in a black evening dress; she looked up at me with bold full tawny eyes, and did not let her gaze falter. Yet I had felt, from the first time I met her and she looked at me so, that there was something baffled about her, a hidden yearning to be liked – as though she were a little girl, aggressive and heavy among children smaller than herself, unable to understand why they did not love her.

Seeing her in her own family, one felt most of all that yearning and the strain it caused. In the long drawing-room that night, I looked across at her husband and her daughter. The Master was standing beside one of the lofty fire screens, his hand on a Queen Anne chair, trim and erect in his tails like a much younger man. He and Lady Muriel exchanged some words: there was loyalty between them, but no ease. And Joan, the eldest of the Royces' children, a girl of eighteen, stood beside him, silent and constrained. Her face at the moment seemed intelligent, strong, and sulky. When she answered a direct question from her mother, the friction sounded in each syllable. Lady Muriel sturdily asked another question in a more insistent voice.

The butler called out 'Mr Calvert', and Roy came quickly up the long room, past the small tables, towards the group of us standing by the fire. Lady Muriel's face lightened, and she cried out: 'Good evening, Roy. I almost thought you were going to be late.'

'I'm never late, Lady Muriel,' said Roy. 'You should know that, shouldn't you? I am never late, unless it's somewhere I don't want to go. Then I usually appear on the wrong day.'

'You're quite absurd,' said Lady Muriel, who did not use a hostess's opening topic with Roy. 'I wonder why I allow you in the house.'

'Because you know I like to come,' said Roy. He knew it pleased her – but each word was clear, natural, without pretence.

'You've learned to flatter too young,' she said with a happy crow of laughter.

'You're suspicious of every nice thing you hear, Lady Muriel. Particularly when it's true,' said Roy. 'Now aren't you?'

'I refuse to argue with you.' She laughed happily. Roy turned to Joan, and began teasing her about what she should do at the university next year: but he did not disarm her as easily as her mother.

Just then the Boscastles entered from one of the inner doors. They were an incongruous pair, but they had great presence and none of us could help watching them. Lord Boscastle was both massive and fat; there was muscular reserve underneath his ample, portly walk, and he was still light on his feet. His face did not match his comfortable body: a great beak of a nose stood out above a jutting jaw, with a stiff grey moustache between them. By his side, by the side of Lady Muriel and Joan, who were both strong women, his wife looked so delicate and frail that it seemed she ought to be carried. She was fragile, thin with an invalid's thinness, and she helped herself along with a stick. In the other hand she carried a lorgnette, and, while she was limping slowly along, she was studying us all with eyes that, even at a distance, shone a brilliant porcelain blue. She had aged through illness, her skin was puckered and brown, she looked at moments like a delicate, humorous, and distinguished monkey; but it was easy to believe that she had once been noted for her beauty.

I watched her as I was being presented to her, and as Roy's turn came. He smiled at her: as though by instinct, she gave a coquettish flick with the lorgnette. I was sure he felt, as I had felt myself, that she had always been courted, that she still, on meeting a strange man at a party, heard the echoes of gallant words.

Lord Boscastle greeted us with impersonal cordiality, and settled down to his sherry. The last guest came, Mrs Seymour, a cousin of Lady Muriel's who lived in Cambridge, and soon we set out to walk to the dining-room. This took some time, for the Lodge had been built, reconstructed, patched up, and rebuilt for five hundred years, and we had to make our way along narrow passages, down draughty stairs, across landings: Lady Boscastle's stick tapped away in front, and I talked to Mrs Seymour, who seemed gentle, inane, vague, and given to enthusiasms. She was exactly like Lady Muriel's concept of a suitable dinner partner for one of the younger fellows, I thought. In addition, Lady Muriel, to whom disapproval came as a natural response to most situations, disapproved with particular strength of my leaving my wife in London. She was not going to let me get any advantages through bad conduct, so far as she could help it.

Curiously enough, the first real excitement of the dinner arrived through Mrs Seymour. We sat round the table in the candlelight, admired the table which had come from the family house at Boscastle – 'from our house,' said Lady Muriel with some superbity – admired the Bevill silver, and enjoyed ourselves with the food and wine. Both were excellent, for Lady Muriel had healthy appetites herself, and also was not prepared to let her dinners be outclassed by anything the college could do. She sat at the end of the table, stiff-backed, bold-eyed, satisfied that all was well with her side of the evening, inspecting her guests as though she were weighing their more obvious shortcomings.

She began by taking charge of the conversation herself. 'Mr Eliot was putting forward an interesting point of view before dinner,' she said in an authoritative voice, and then puzzled us all by describing my opinions on Paul Morand. It seemed that I had a high opinion of his profundity. Joan questioned her fiercely, Roy soothed them both, but it was some time before we realized that she meant Mauriac. It was a kind of intellectual malapropism such as she frequently made.

I thought, not for the first time, that she was at heart uninterested in all this talk of ideas and books – but she did it because it was due to her position, and nothing would have deterred her. Not in the slightest abashed, she repeated 'Mauriac' firmly twice and was going ahead, when Mrs Seymour broke in:

'Oh, I'd forgotten. I meant to tell you straightaway, but that comes of being late. I've always said that they ought to put an extra light on your dressing-table. Particularly in strange bedrooms –'

'Yes, Doris?' Lady Muriel's voice rang out.

'I haven't told you, have I?'

'You have certainly told us nothing since you arrived.'

'I thought I'd forgotten. Tom's girl is engaged. It will be in *The Times* this week.'

The Boscastles and the Royces all knew the genealogy of 'Tom's girl'. For Mrs Seymour might be scatterbrained, but her breeding was the Boscastles' own; she had married a Seymour, who was not much of a catch but was eminently 'someone one could know', and Tom was her husband's brother. So Tom's girl was taken seriously, even though Lord Boscastle had never met her, and Lady Muriel only once. She was part of the preserve. Abandoning in a hurry all abstract conversation, Lady Muriel plunged in with her whole weight. She sat more upright than ever and called out:

'Who is the man?'

'He's a man called Houston Eggar.'

Lord Boscastle filled the chair on his sister's right. He finished a sip of hock, put down the glass, and asked:

'Who?'

'Houston Eggar.'

Lady Muriel and Lord Boscastle looked at each other. In a faint, tired, disconsolate tone Lord Boscastle said:

'I'm afraid I don't know the fellow.'

'I can help,' said the Master briskly from the other end of the table. 'He's a brother-in-law of the Dean of this college. He's dined in hall once or twice.'

'I'm afraid,' said Lord Boscastle, 'that I don't know who he is.'

There was a moment's silence, and I looked at the faces round the table. Lord Boscastle was holding his glass up to the candlelight and staring unconcernedly through it. Roy watched with an expression solemn, demure, inquiring: but I caught his eye for a second, and saw a gleam of pure glee: each word was passing into his mimic's ear. By his side, Joan was gazing down fixedly at the table, the poise of her neck and strong shoulders full of anger, scorn, and the passionate rebellion of youth. Mrs Seymour seemed vaguely troubled, as though she had mislaid her handbag; she patted her hair, trying to get a strand into place. On my right Lady Boscastle had mounted her lorgnette and focused the others one by one.

It was she who asked the next question.

'Could you tell us a little about this Dean of yours, Vernon?' she said to the Master, in a high, delicate, amused voice.

'He's quite a good Dean,' said the Master. 'He's very useful on the financial side. Colleges need their Marthas, you know. The unfortunate thing is that one can never keep the Marthas in their place. Before you can look round, you find they're running the college and regarding you as a frivolous and irresponsible person.'

'What's the Dean's name?' said Lord Boscastle, getting back to the point.

'Chrystal.'

'It sounds Scotch,' said Lord Boscastle dubiously.

'I believe, Lord Boscastle,' Roy put in, seeming tentative and diffident, 'that he comes from Bedford.'

Lord Boscastle shook his head.

'I know his wife, of course,' said Lady Muriel. 'Naturally I have to know the wives of the fellows. She's a nice quiet little thing. But there's nothing special about her. She's an Eggar, whoever they may be.'

'She's the sister of this man you're telling us about,' Lord Boscastle remarked, half to himself. 'I should have said he was nothing out of the ordinary, shouldn't you have said so?'

His social judgements became more circuitous the nearer they came to anyone the company knew: Lady Muriel, more direct and unperceptive than her brother, had never quite picked up the labyrinthine phrases with which he finally placed an acquaintance of someone in the room; but in effect she and he said the same thing.

Mrs Seymour, who was still looking faintly distressed, suddenly clapped her hands.

'Of course, I'd forgotten to tell you. I've just remembered about the post office place –'

'Yes, Doris?' said Lady Muriel inexorably.

'Houston's a brilliant young man. He's in the Foreign Office. They said he was first secretary' – Mrs Seymour gabbled rapidly in case she should forget – 'at that place which looks after the post, the place in Switzerland, I forget –'

'Berne,' Roy whispered.

'Berne.' She smiled at him gratefully.

'How old is your Houston?' asked Lady Boscastle.

'About forty, I should say. And I think that's a very nice and sensible age,' said Mrs Seymour with unexpected firmness. 'I always wished my husband had been older –'

'If he's only a first secretary at forty, I should not think he was going so terribly far.' Lady Boscastle directed her lorgnette at her husband. 'I remember one years younger. We were in Warsaw. Yes, he was clever.' A faint, sarcastic, charming smile crossed her face. Lord Boscastle smiled back – was I imagining it, or was there something humble, unconfident, about that smile?

At any rate, he began to address the table again.

'I shouldn't have thought that the Foreign Office was specially distinguished nowadays. I've actually known one or two people who went in,' he added as though he were straining our credulity.

While he thought no one was looking, Roy could not repress a smile of delight. He could no longer resist taking a hand: his face composed again, he was just beginning to ask Lord Boscastle a question, when Lady Muriel cut across him.

'Of course,' she said, 'someone's obliged to do these things.'

'Someone's obliged to become Civil Servants and look after the drains,' said Lord Boscastle with good-natured scorn. 'That doesn't make it any better.'

Roy started again.

'Should you have said, Lord Boscastle' (the words, the tone, sounded suspiciously like Lord Boscastle's own), 'that the Foreign Office was becoming slightly *common*?'

Lord Boscastle regarded him, and paused.

'Perhaps that would be going rather far, Calvert. All I can say is that I should never have gone in myself. And I hope my son doesn't show any signs of wanting to.'

'Oh, it must be wonderful to make treaties and go about in

secret –' cried Mrs Seymour, girlish with enthusiasm, her voice trailing off.

'Make treaties!' Lord Boscastle chuckled. 'All they do is clerk away in offices and get one out of trouble if one goes abroad. They do it like conscientious fellows, no doubt.'

'Why shouldn't you like your son to want it, Lord Boscastle?' Roy asked, his eyes very bright.

'I hope that, if he feels obliged to take up a career, he'll choose something slightly more out of the ordinary.'

'It isn't because you don't want him to get into low company?'

Lord Boscastle wore a fixed smile. Roy looked more than ever demure.

'Of course,' said Roy, 'he might pick up an unfortunate accent from one of those people. One needs to be careful. Do you think,' he asked earnestly, 'that is the reason why some of them are so anxious to learn foreign languages? Do you think they hope it will cover up their own?'

'Mr Calvert!' Lady Boscastle's voice sounded high and gentle. Roy met the gaze behind the lorgnette.

'Mr Calvert, have you been inside an embassy?'

'Only once, Lady Boscastle.'

'I think I must take you to some more. You'll find they're quite nice people. And really not unelegant. They talk quite nicely too. I'm just a little surprised you didn't know that already, Mr Calvert.'

Roy burst into a happy, unguarded laugh: a blush mounted his cheeks. I had not seen him blush before. It was not often people played him at his own game. Usually they did not know what to make of him, they felt befogged, they left him still inquiring, straight-faced, bright-eyed.

The whole table was laughing – suddenly I noticed Joan's face quite transformed. She had given way completely to her laughter, the sullenness was dissolved; it was the richest of laughs, and hearing it one knew that some day she would love with all her heart.

Lord Boscastle himself was smiling. He was not a slow-witted man, he had known he was being teased. I got the impression that he was grateful for his wife's support. But his response to being teased was to stick more obstinately to his own line. So now he said, as though summing up: 'It's a pity about Tom Seymour's girl. She ought to have fished something better for herself.'

'You'll all come round to him,' said Mrs Seymour. 'I know he'll do."

'It's a pity,' said Lord Boscastle with finality, 'that one doesn't know who he is.'

Joan, melted by her laughter, still half-laughing and half-furious, broke out:

'Uncle, you mean that you don't know who his grandfather is.'

'Joan!' Lady Muriel boomed, but, with an indulgent nod, Lord Boscastle went on to discuss in what circumstances Tom's girl had a claim to be invited to the family house. Boscastle was a great mansion: 'my house' as Lord Boscastle called it with an air of grand seigneur, 'our house' said Lady Muriel with splendour: but the splendour and the air of grand seigneur disappeared at moments, for they both had a knack of calling the house 'Bossy'. Lady Boscastle never did: but to her husband and his sister there seemed nothing incongruous in the nickname.

After port, as soon as I got inside the drawing-room, Lady Boscastle called out: 'Mr Eliot! I want you to talk to me, please.' I sat with her in a corner by the fire, and she examined me about my hopes and prospects; she was very shrewd, used to having her own way, accustomed to find pleasure in men's confidences. We should have gone on, if it had not been that Lord Boscastle, on the largest sofa a few feet away, was asking Roy to describe his work. It was a perfectly serious question, and Roy treated it so. He explained how he had to begin unravelling a language which was two-thirds unknown. Then he passed on to manuscripts in that language – manuscripts battered, often with half the page missing, so faded that much could not be read at all, sometimes copied by incompetent and careless hands. Out of all this medley he was trying to restore the text.

'Tell me, how long will it take you?' said Lord Boscastle.

'Eight years,' said Roy at once.

Lord Boscastle reflected.

'I can imagine starting it,' he said. 'I can see it must be rather fun. But I really can't imagine myself having the patience to go through with it.'

'I think you might,' said Roy simply. 'I think you might have enjoyed having something definite to do.'

'Do you think I could have managed it?'

'I'm sure,' said Roy.

'Perhaps I might,' said Lord Boscastle with a trace of regret.

The drawing-room was left with no one speaking. Then Lady Muriel firmly suggested that her brother ought to see Roy's manuscripts. It was arranged (Lady Muriel pushing from behind) that the Boscastles should lunch with Roy next day.

A few minutes later, though it was only half past ten, Roy made his apologies to Lady Muriel and left. She watched him walk the length of the room: then we heard his feet running down the stairs.

'He was a little naughty with you at dinner, Hugh,' she said to her brother, 'but you must admit that he has real style.'

'Young men ought to get up to monkey tricks,' said Lord Boscastle. 'One grows old soon enough. Yes, he's an agreeable young fellow.'

He paused, drank some whisky, inquired as though compelled to: 'Who is his father?'

'A man called Calvert,' said the Master.

'I know that,' said Lord Boscastle irritably.

'He's distinctly rich and lives in the midlands.'

'I'm afraid I've never heard of him.'

'No, you wouldn't have, Hugh,' said the Master, with a fresh smile.

'But I must say,' Lord Boscastle went on, 'that if I'd met Calvert anywhere I should really have expected to know who he was.'

This implied, I thought, a curious back-handed social acceptance. But it was not necessary, for the Master said:

'He's got everything in front of him. He's going to be one of the great Orientalists of the day. Between ourselves, I believe that's putting it mildly.'

'I can believe you,' said Lord Boscastle. 'I hope he enjoys himself. We must keep an eye on him.'

That meant definite acceptance. It was not, I thought, that Roy had 'real style', had been to Lord Boscastle's school, could pass as a gentleman through any tests except Lord Boscastle's own; it was not only that Roy had struck a human want in him, by making him think of how he might have spent his life. He might have received Roy even if he had liked him less: for Lord Boscastle had a genuine, respectful, straightforward tenderness for learning and the arts. His snobbery was a passion, more devouring as he got older, more triumphant as he found reasons for proving that almost no one came inside his own preserve, could truly be regarded as a gentleman; nevertheless, he continued to have a special entrance which let in his brother-in-law, which let in Roy, which let in some of the rest of us; and he welcomed us more as his snobbery outside grew more colossal and baroque.

Lady Boscastle was trying to resume our conversation, but the others were still talking of Roy. Mrs Seymour was rapt with vague enthusiasm.

'He's so handsome,' she said.

'Interesting-looking, I think I should say,' commented Lady Boscastle, a shade impatiently.

'He's not handsome at all,' said Joan. 'His nose is much too long.'

'Don't you like him?' cried Mrs Seymour.

'I can never get him to talk seriously,' the girl replied.

'He's very lucky.' Mrs Seymour's enthusiasm grew. 'It must be wonderful to be A1 at everything.'

No one could be freer from irony than Mrs Seymour; and yet, even on that night, those words rang through me with a harsh ironic note.

The Master was saying:

'One thing is certain. We must elect the young man to a fellowship here before long.'

'I should have thought you would jump at him,' said Lord Boscastle.

'No society of men is very fond of brilliance, Hugh,' said the Master. 'We needs must choose the dullest when we see it. However, I hope this time my colleagues will agree with me without undue pressure.'

He smiled confidentially at me.

'Between ourselves, Eliot,' he went on, 'when I reflect on the modest accomplishments of some of our colleagues, I think perhaps even undue pressure might not be out of place.'

CHAPTER 3

Two Resolves

I WOKE because of a soft voice above my bed – 'beg pardon, sir, beg pardon, sir, beg pardon, sir'. In the half-light I could see Bidwell's face, round, ruddy, simultaneously deferential and good fellow-like, wide open and cunning.

'I don't know whether I'm doing right, sir. I know I oughtn't to disturb you, and' – he inclined his head in the direction of the college clock – 'that's got twenty minutes to go to nine o'clock. But it's a young lady. I think it's a young lady of Mr Calvert's, sir. She seemed what you might call anxious to see you.'

I let him pull up the blind, and the narrow cell-like room seemed bleaker than ever in the bright cold morning sunlight. I had drunk enough at the Lodge the night before to prefer to get up slowly. As I washed in warmish water from a jug, I was too moiled and irritated to wonder much who this visitor might be.

I recognized her, though, as soon as I saw her sitting in an armchair by my sitting-room fire. I had met her once or twice before; she was a young woman of Roy's own age, and her name was Rosalind Wykes. She came across the room to meet me, and looked up contritely with clear brown eyes.

'I'm frightfully sorry to disturb you,' she said. 'I know it's very wicked of me. But I thought you might be going out to give a lecture. Sit down and I'll get your breakfast for you.'

Breakfast was strewn about the hearth, in plates with metal covers on top. Rosalind took off the covers, dusted the rim of the plates, dusted a cup, poured out my tea.

'I must say they don't look after you too well,' she said. 'Get on with your breakfast. You won't feel so much like wringing my neck then, will you?'

She was nervous; there was a dying fall in her voice which sometimes made her seem pathetic. She had an oval face, a longish nose, a big humorous mouth with down just visible on her upper lip. She was dressed in the mode, and it showed how slender she was, though she was wider across the hips than one observed at a first glance. She was often nervous: sometimes she seemed restless and reckless: yet underneath one felt she was tough and healthy and made for a happy physical life. Her hair was dark, and she had done it up from the back, which was unusual at that time: with her oval face, brown eyes, small head, that tier of hair made her seem like a portrait of the First Empire – and in fact to me she frequently brought a flavour of that period, modish, parvenu, proper outside and raffish within, material-istic and yet touching.

I drank two cups of tea. 'Better,' I said.

'You look a bit morning-afterish, I must say,' said Rosalind. At that time she was very prim in speech, much more so than most of the people among whom she moved: yet she had a singular gift for in-vesting the most harmless remark with an amorous aura. My state that breakfast-time was due, of course, to nothing more disreputable than a number of glasses of claret at dinner and some whiskies afterwards with the Master and Lord Boscastle; but, when Rosalind mentioned it, it might have been incurred through an exhausting night of love.

I began eating some breakfast, and said:

'Well, I shall revive soon. What did you get me out of bed for, Rosalind?'

She shook her head. 'Nothing very special. I only arrived yesterday and I'm going back tonight, and I shouldn't have liked to miss you altogether.'

I looked at her. The clear eyes were guileless. She glanced round the room.

'I wish you'd let me do this place up for you,' she said. 'It would look lovely with just a bit of care. I could make you so comfortable you wouldn't credit it, you know.'

I was prepared to believe that she was right. The bedroom was a monk's cell, but this sitting-room was a large and splendid medieval chamber. I knew that, given a week and a cheque-book, she would transform it. She was kind and active, she took pleasure from making one comfortable. But I did not think that she had come that morning to tell me so.

While I went on eating, she stood by the wall and examined the panelling. She asked how old it was, and I told her sixteenth century. Then, over her shoulder, she said:

'Did you notice that Roy left the dinner party early last night?'
I said yes.

'Did you know what for?'
I said no.

Still over her shoulder, in a tone with a dying fall, she said:
'I'm afraid it was to come and see me.'

It was prim, it was suggestive, shameless, and boasting. I burst into laughter, and she turned and looked at me with a lurking, satisfied, triumphant smile.

In a moment Bidwell came in, quiet-footed, to clear up. When he had left again, she said:

'Your servant has got a very sweet face, hasn't he?'

'I'm rather fond of him.'

'I'm sure you are.' Her eyes were shrewd. 'I must say, I wish you and Roy didn't leave so much to him. I hope you don't let him do your ordering.'

I did not mind Bidwell taking a percentage, I said, if it avoided fuss. She frowned, she did not want to let it pass: but there was still something on her mind. It was not only to confess or boast that she had come to see me.

'Did you know,' she said, 'that Roy is having Lord and Lady Boscastle to lunch?'

'I heard him invite them.'

'I'm making him have me too. I'm terrified. Are they dreadfully frightening?'

'What did Roy say about that?'

'He said Lord Boscastle's bark was worse than his bite. And that Lady Boscastle was the stronger of the two.'

'I think that's true,' I said.

'But what am I going to say to them?' she said. She was genuinely nervous. 'I've never met people like this before. I haven't any idea what to say.'

'Don't worry. And make love to Lord B. as lavishly as you like,' I said.

It was sound advice, for Lord Boscastle's social standards were drastically reduced in the presence of attractive young women who seemed to enjoy his company.

She smiled absently for a second, then cried again:

'I don't know anything about people like this. I don't even know what to call an earl. Lewis, what do I call them?'

I told her. I believed that was a reason for her visit. She would rather ask that question of me than of Roy.

'I'm glad I remembered to ask you,' she said disingenuously, her eyes open and clear. 'That's a relief. But I am terrified,' she added.

'Why did you work it then?' I said.

'I was dreadfully silly,' she said. 'I thought I should like to see a bit of high life.'

That may have been true, but I was sure there was a wise intuitive purpose behind it. With her recklessness, with the earthy realism that lived behind the prudish speech, she could live as though each day were sufficient to itself: so she had thrown herself at Roy, took what she could get, put up with what she called his 'moods', went to bed with him when she could, schemed no more than a month or two ahead.

But, deep in her fibres, there was another realism, another wisdom, another purpose. Her whole nature was set on marrying him. It did not need thought or calculation, it just took all of herself – though on the way to her end she would think and calculate with every scrap of wits she had. She was nervous, kind, sensitive in her fashion, tender with the good nature of one who is happy with instinctive life: she was also hard, ruthless, determined, singleminded, and unscrupulous: or rather she could act as though scruples did not exist. She meant to marry him.

So she knew that she must get on with the Boscastles. Roy was not a snob, no man was less so: but he gave himself to everyone who took his fancy, whether they came from the ill-fated and lost, or from the lucky. Usually they were the world's derelicts, for I often grumbled that he treated badly any acquaintance who might be of practical use: but if by chance he liked someone eminent, then he was theirs as deeply as though they were humble. He felt no barriers except what his affections told him. Rosalind knew this, and knew that she must acquire the same ease. Hence she had driven herself, despite her diffidence, into this luncheon party.

Hence too, I was nearly certain, she decided she must know me well. So far as anyone had influence over Roy, I had. She must make me into an ally if she could. She must charm me, she must see that I was friendly, she must take a part in my life, even if it only meant decorating my rooms. She had come that morning to ask me how to address an earl: but she would have found another reason, if that had not existed. I strongly suspected that she had bribed Bidwell to wake me up before my time.

Roy brought Rosalind back to my rooms after lunch.

'I hear you met this morning,' said Roy.

'Can you bear the sight of me again?' Rosalind said.

'He'll pretend to,' said Roy. 'He's famous for his self-control.'

She made a face at him, half-plaintive, half-comic, and said:

'I couldn't stay and see Roy's tables all littered with plates. I should want to do something about it.' She was talkative and elated, like someone released from strain.

'How did it go?' I said.

'I tried to find a corner to hide in. But it's not very easy when there are only four.'

'You got a small prize,' Roy said to her. 'Not the first prize. Only the second. You did very nicely.'

I guessed that she had been diffident, had not taken much part. But it was not as bad as she feared, and with her indomitable resolve she would try again. Roy was smiling at her, amused, stirred to tenderness because she made such heavy weather of what would, at any age, have been his own native air.

He said to me:

'By the way, old boy, you've made a great hit with Lady B. I'm extremely jealous.'

'She wanted to know all about you,' said Rosalind.

'I think she likes very weighty men.' Roy chuckled. 'Old Lewis is remarkably good at persuading them that he's extremely weighty.'

He went on to tease Rosalind about Lord Boscastle's compliments. I noticed that Roy and Rosalind were very easy with each other, light with the innocence that may visit a happy physical love.

The telephone bell rang: it was for Roy, and as he answered he exclaimed with enthusiasm – 'excellent', 'of course', 'I'm sure he would', 'I'll answer for him', 'come straight up'.

'You see, you've got to be civil now,' said Roy. 'It's Ralph Udal. He's just back from Italy. It's time you met him.'

Roy added, with a secret smile: 'Now, I wonder what he wants.'

Udal himself came in as Roy finished speaking. I had found out something about him since the episode of the bookshops: now I saw him in the flesh, I was surprised. I had not expected that he should have such natural and pleasant manners. For the stories I had heard were somewhat odd. He was an exact contemporary of Roy's at the college, and they had known each other well, though they were never intimate friends. Udal came from a professional family, but he was a poor man, and he and Roy moved in different circles. They had known each other as academic rivals, for Udal had had a brilliant undergraduate career. Then his life became very strange. He spent a year among the seedy figures of Soho – not to indulge himself, not to do good works, but just to 'let the wind of God blow through him'. Then he had served another year in a church settlement in Poplar. Afterwards, he had, passively so it seemed, become ordained. But he had not taken a curacy or any kind of job; he had written his little book on Heppenstall, and had gone off to Italy for six months.

He was a big man, tall, loose-framed, dark-haired, and dark-skinned. He looked older than his age; his face was mature, adult, and decided. As he greeted us, there was great warmth in his large, dark, handsome eyes. He was dressed in old flannels and a thin calico coat, but he talked to Rosalind as though he also had been to a smart lunch, and he settled down between her and me without any sign that this was a first meeting.

'How's the book going?' asked Roy.

'It's very gratifying,' said Udal. 'There doesn't seem to be a copy left in Cambridge.'

'Excellent,' said Roy, without blinking, without a quiver on his solemn face.

Udal had arrived back from Italy the day before.

'Didn't you adore Italy? Were the women lovely? What were you doing there?' asked Rosalind.

'Looking at churches,' said Udal amiably. Rosalind had just remembered that he was a clergyman. She looked uncomfortable, but Udal was prepared to talk about anything she wanted. He thought the women were beautiful in Venetia and Friulia, but not in the South. He suggested that one required a dash of nordic blood to produce anything more than youthful comeliness. He had gone about with his eyes open, and spoke without inhibition. Rosalind was discomfited.

She was discomfited again when, with the same ease, he began talking of his practical requirements.

'Roy,' he said, 'it's time I found a job.'

'Just so,' said Roy.

'You don't mind me talking about myself?' Udal said affably to Rosalind and me. 'But I wanted to see Roy about my best moves. I'm not much good at these things.'

'I've been thinking,' he said to Roy. 'A country living would suit me down to the ground. I can make do on three hundred a year. And it would mean plenty of leisure. I shouldn't get so much leisure in any other way.'

'That's true,' said Roy.

'How do I set about getting one?'

'Difficult,' said Roy. 'I don't think you can straightaway.'

They talked about tactics. Udal knew exactly what he wanted; but he was oddly unrealistic about the means. He seemed to think it would be easy to persuade the college to give him a living. Roy, on the other hand, was completely practical. He scolded Udal for indulging in make-believe, and told him what to do; he must take some other job at once, presumably a curacy; then he must 'nurse' the college livings committee, he must become popular with them, he must unobtrusively keep his existence before them. He must also cultivate any bishop either he or Roy could get to know.

Udal took it well. He was not proud; he accepted the fact that Roy was more worldly and acute.

'I'll talk to people. I'll spy out the land,' said Roy. He smiled. 'I may even make old Lewis get himself put on the livings committee.'

'Do what you can,' said Udal.

Rosalind was upset. She could not understand. She could not help asking Udal:

'Doesn't it worry you?'

'Doesn't what worry me?'

'Having – to work it all out,' she said.

'I manage to bear it. Would it worry you?'

'No, of course not. But I thought someone in your position –'

'You mean that I'm supposed to be a religious man,' said Udal. 'But religious people are still ordinary humans, you know.'

'Does it seem all right to you?'

'Oh, I don't know about that,' he said.

'I'm afraid I still think it's peculiar.' She appealed to Roy. 'Roy, don't you think so?'

'No,' he said. 'Not in the least.'

His tone was clear and final. Suddenly I realized she was making a mistake in pressing Udal. She was exposing a rift between herself and Roy. In other things she would have felt him getting farther away: but here she was obtuse.

'I'm not able to speak from the inside,' said Roy. 'But I believe religion can include anything. It can even include,' his face, which had been grave, suddenly broke into a brilliant, malicious smile, 'the fact that Ralph hasn't just called on me – for valuable advice.'

'That's not fair,' said Udal. For a moment he was put out.

'You need someone to unbelt. I'm sure you do.'

'I am short of money,' said Udal.

'Just so,' said Roy.

Roy's gibe had been intimate and piercing, but Udal had recovered his composure. He turned to Rosalind.

'You expect too much of us, you know. You expect us to be perfect – and then you think the rest of the world just go about sleeping with each other.'

Rosalind blushed. Earthy as she was, she liked a decent veil: while he had the casual matter-of-fact touch that one sometimes finds in those who have not gone into the world, or have withdrawn from it.

'You're not correct either way, if you'll forgive me,' Udal went on. 'Roy here wouldn't let me call him a religious man yet: but do you think he's done nothing so far but chase his pleasures? He's already done much odder things than that, you know. And I'm inclined to think he will again. I'm just waiting.'

He spoke lightly, but with immense confidence. Then he smiled to himself.

'This is the right life for me, anyway,' he said. 'It will give me all I want.'

'Will it?' said Rosalind sharply.

He was relaxed, strong in his passiveness.

But she opposed her own strength, that of someone who had gone into the world and could imagine no other life. It was not a strength to be despised. Udal looked at her, and his face was no more settled than hers.

Roy watched them with a glance that was penetrating, acute, and, it suddenly seemed to me, envious of each of them.

CHAPTER 4

A Nature Marked Out by Fate

FROM the afternoon when he forced me to confide, my relation with Roy became changed. Before, he had seemed a gifted and interesting young man whose temperament interested me, whom I listened to when he was despondent, whom I liked seeing when I had the time. Now he had reached out to me. He had put self aside, risked snubs, pierced all the defence I could throw in his way. He had made me accept him as an intimate on even terms. Insensibly, perhaps before I knew it, my friendship with him became the deepest of my life.

I had met him first, as I have said, when he was a boy of fifteen. It was only for an hour, but the circumstances were strange, and had stayed in my memory. For Roy had fallen in love, with an innocent and ecstatic adolescent passion, with a young man whom I knew. His innocence made him indiscreet – or perhaps, even then, he cared nothing for what people thought. At any rate, there was a commotion among a group of my acquaintances. Roy was brought in to tell his story: and I remember him, entirely composed, his face already sad when he was not smiling, although his smile was brilliantly and boyishly gay. His speech was curiously precise, and one heard the echoes of that precision years later; as an affirmative when we questioned him, he used a clear 'just so'.

The story was hushed up. Roy's father behaved with a mixture of energy, practical sense, and an obstinate refusal to believe that his son could do anything irregular or eccentric. Roy himself was not embarrassed by the incident either then or later. I sometimes thought, in fact, that it gave him an added and gentler sympathy. He was not the man to respect any conventions but his own. With his first-hand knowledge of life, he knew that any profound friendship must contain a little of the magic of love. And he was always as physically spontaneous as an Italian. He liked physical contact and endearing words. He would slip his arm into a friend's on the way to hall or as the team went out to field: if anyone had recalled that scandal of the past, he would only have met Roy's most mischievous and mocking grin.

After that single hour, I did not meet him again until he went to Cambridge. It was only by chance that his outburst had affected my circle, and, in the large town where we were both born, our paths were not likely to cross. I lived in the shabby genteel fringe of the lower middle class, while his father had made a considerable fortune and moved among such society as the town could give. His career and way of life were, as a matter of fact, fairly typical of the rich manufacturers of that day. His father, Roy's grandfather, had risen from the artisan class, and made enough money out of boots to send his son to a minor public school: then Roy's father, a man of obstinate inarticulate ability with an obsessional passion for detail, expanded the business and took his chance in the First World War. He became really rich, much richer than many of my London friends who were thought wealthy and lived in greater style: by 1934 he cannot have been worth less than £300,000. He did very little with it, except buy a local newspaper and a large house on the outskirts of the town, and take every opportunity of spending money on his only son. He idolized Roy, in a speechless, embarrassed, puzzled fashion; he sent him to the most fashionable preparatory and public schools (it was only by a personal accident that he came to the college, which was not particularly fashionable; his house master, whom Roy liked, happened to be a loyal old member); from the time Roy was twenty-one, his father allowed him £1,500 a year, and settled a substantial sum on him as well.

When I ran across him in his undergraduate days, he was more outwardly eccentric than he later seemed – not in dress, for he was always elegant, but in actions which at the time I thought were only a very young man's whims. I found him one night sleeping on a seat on the embankment. He did not explain himself, although he was, as usual, polite, easy-mannered, affectionate, and direct. He went in for bouts of hard drinking which seemed more abandoned than an undergraduate's blinds, more deliberately an attempt to escape. And he started his love affairs quite early. Yet each examination was a triumph for him, and he was the outstanding classic of his day.

After taking his degree, he was at a loss. He felt vaguely drawn to some kind of scholarly research, but he did not make any determined start. He drank more, went into more dissipated company, felt a despondency overcome him of which previously he had only known the shadow's edge. This was the first time that he was forced, without any help or protection at all, to know the burden of self.

In a few weeks that darkness left him, and he tried to forget it. The Master, whose subject was comparative religion, suggested that he should apply himself to oriental languages. To help himself forget the period of melancholy not long past, Roy threw all his attention into Syriac and Aramaic: and then, partly by sheer chance, came the offer of the research which was to occupy so much of his working life.

It was an odd story, how this ever reached him.

Of all the Christian heresies, one spread the farthest, touched imaginations most deeply, and had the richest meaning. Perhaps it should have been called a new religion. It was the heresy of Mani. It began towards the end of the third century A.D. in the pleasure city of Antioch and the decadent luxurious towns of Syria; it swept through them as a new religion might sweep through California today.

It was a new religion, but it drew its strength from something as old and deep as human feeling; for, just as the sexual impulse is ineluctably strong, so can the hate of it be; the flesh is seductive, beyond one's power to resist – and one hates the flesh as an enemy, one prays that it will leave one in peace. The religion of the Manichees tried to give men peace against the flesh. In its cosmology, the whole of creation is a battle of the light against the dark. Man's spirit is part of the light, and his flesh of the dark. The battle sways from side to side, and men are taking part in it, here and now. The religion was the most subtle and complex representation of sexual guilt.

Such a subtle and complex religion must have drawn its believers from the comfortable classes. There was none of the quick simple appeal that helped Christianity to spark from man to man among the hopeless dispossessed of the Roman slums. Manichaeism must have been chiefly the religion of those with time to think – and probably of a comfortable leisured class in a dying society, a class with little to do except pursue its sensual pleasures and be tormented by their guilt.

Anyway, through the third and fourth centuries the religion spread.

The Manichaean missionaries followed the trade routes, into Egypt, the African coastal fringe, Persia; churches were founded, psalm books and liturgies and statements of faith were translated from their original Syriac. And very soon the Manichees were being systematically and ruthlessly persecuted. For some reason, this subtle and gentle faith, or anything resembling it, like that of the Albigenses in Provence or the Bogomils in Bulgaria, always excited the savage hatred of the orthodox. Before long the Manichaean congregations had been exterminated in the Levant and round the Mediterranean; others were driven out of Persia and found a home for a while in what is now Chinese Turkestan. Then they too were finished off by the Moslems.

It is an error, of course, to think that persecution is never successful. More often than not, it has been extremely so. For hundreds of years, this religion, which once had rich churches in the most civilized towns in the world, which attracted to its membership such men as St Augustine (for whom Roy had a special and personal veneration), would not have been known to exist except for the writings of its enemies. It was as though Communism had been extirpated in Europe in the nineteen-twenties, and was only known through what is said of it in *Mein Kampf*. No words of the Manichees themselves were left to be read.

During the twentieth century, however, the technique and scale of archaeological expeditions were each developed, and there were one or two Manichaean finds. A psalm book and a hymnal, translated into a Coptic dialect, were discovered in upper Egypt; and one of the expeditions to Turkestan brought back what was recognized to be a complete liturgy. But it was written in an unknown variety of Middle Persian called Early Soghdian; and for a year the liturgy stayed unread.

The committee who had charge of it intended to ask an Oxford scholar to make an edition but, just at that time, he fell ill. Quite by accident, Sir Oulstone Lyall and Colonel Foulkes happened to be consulting the Master about other business. He mentioned Roy to them and introduced him. They thought he was intelligent, they knew that he had picked up Syriac at an astonishing speed; it was possible that Colonel Foulkes's devotion to cricket disposed him to take a favourable view of Roy's character. There was an amateur flavour about all this esoteric scholarship – anyway, they asked if he would like to have a shot.

Only a man of means could have risked it. If he did not get the language out, he had wasted critical years. Something caught in Roy's imagination, perhaps the religion itself, and he said yes.

That was over two years before, in the January of 1932. Within eighteen months he had worked out the language, so precisely that no one need touch it again. His Soghdian grammar and lexicon were just in proof, and were to be published during 1934. He had already transcribed part of the liturgy, and he was working faster than ever. It was a remarkable record, unbelievable to those who knew a little of his life, the loves, the drinking, the games, and parties. But to me, who saw more of him, the miracle disappeared like a conjuring trick which is explained. I knew how, even in the blackest melancholy, he could throw himself with clear precise attention into his work for seven or eight hours a day. I had seen him drink himself into stupor, sleep it off, recover over breakfast, and be back at work by nine o'clock.

His own attitude to his work was one of the most matter-of-fact things about him. His preoccupation was in the words themselves and what they meant; the slightest hitch in the text, and he was absorbed, with all his imagination and powers in play. He was intent on knowing precisely what the words of that liturgy meant, to the priests who translated it, to the scribe who copied it somewhere in a Central Asian town in the sixth century.

Outside the text his imagination, so active upon the words themselves, so lively in his everyday life, seemed not to be much engaged. He gave only a passing thought to the societies where this religion grew or to the people in the congregations which used his liturgy. There was something in such speculations which offended his taste – 'romantic' he called them, as a term of abuse. 'Romantic,' said Roy scornfully, who himself was often described in that one word.

Yet, right from the beginning, there were times when his work seemed nothing but a drug. He had thrown himself into it, in revulsion from his first knowledge of despair. Despair: the black night of melancholy: he had already felt the weight of inexplicable misery, the burden of self. I thought that too often his work was a charm against the dark. He did not seem to revel in success, to get any pleasure apart from a mild sense of skill. I watched him when he finished his Soghdian grammar. He knew it was a nice job – 'I am rather clever,' he said with a mocking smile. But when others praised him, he became irritated and angry, genuinely, morbidly angry, took to a fit of drinking and then worked such immoderate hours at the liturgy that I was afraid for his health, tough as he was.

At the dinner party Mrs Seymour had cried out how much he was to be envied. She was a silly woman, but she only said what everyone round him thought. Some people resented him because he had so much. Many saw the gaiety and felt that he could not have a worry in the world. None of them saw the weight that crushed him down.

Even Roy himself did not see it. In his boyhood and youth, he had been buoyed up by the animal spirits of the young. His spirits at twenty, like those of any vigorous man, were strong enough to defy fate or death; they drew their strength from the body, and for a time could drive away any affliction that was lying in wait. Now he was a little older he had passed through hours and days of utter blackness, in which his one feeling was self-hatred and his one longing to escape himself. But those hours and days passed off, and he still had the boundless hope of a young man. He hoped he could escape – perhaps in love (though he never counted much on that), perhaps in work, perhaps in a belief in which he could lose himself. He hoped he could escape at last, and come to peace and rest.

He did not know then that he had the special melancholy which belongs to some chosen natures. It did not come through suffering, though it caused him to suffer much. It came by the same fate as endowed him with his gifts – his intelligence, his attraction for women, his ability to strike a human response from anyone he met, his reckless bravery.

By the same fortune, he was inescapably under the threat of this special melancholy, this clear-sighted despair in which, more than anyone I knew, he saw the sadness of man's condition: this despair which drove him to outbursts of maniacal gaiety. He was born with this melancholy; it was a curse of fate, like a hereditary disease. It shadowed all his life. Perhaps it also deepened him under his caprices, perhaps it helped to make him the most selfless of men. I did not know. But I knew that I should have wished him more commonplace and selfish, if only he could cease to be so haunted.

Since I was close to him, I could see that little distance. But he exhilarated me with his gaiety, pierced me with his selflessness, deepened all I knew of life, gave my spirit wings: so I too did not see much that fate had done to him and I hoped that he would be happy.

CHAPTER 5

Lesson in Politics

THE Master's campaign to get Roy elected did not make much progress. All decisions in the college had to be taken by a vote of the fellows, who in 1934 numbered thirteen, including the Master himself: and most formal steps, such as electing a fellow, needed a clear majority of the society, that is seven votes.

For various reasons, the Master was not finding it easy to collect seven votes for Roy. First, one old man was ill and could not come to college meetings. Second, the Master was not such a power in the college as in the university; his intimate sarcasms had a habit of passing round, and he had made several irreconcilable enemies, chief among them the Bursar, Winslow, a bitter disappointed man, acid-tongued in a fashion of his own. Third, the Master, fairminded in most ways, could not conceal his dislike and contempt for scientists, and had recently remarked of one deserving candidate: 'What rude mechanical are we asked to consider now?' The comment had duly reached the three scientific fellows and did not dispose them in favour of the Master's protégé.

As a result, the political situation in the college was more than usually fluid. For most questions there existed – though no one spoke of it – a kind of rudimentary party system, with a government party which supported the Master and an opposition whose leader was Winslow. When I first arrived, the government party generally managed to find a small majority, by attracting the two or three floating votes. In all personal choices, particularly in elections to fellowships, the parties were not to be relied on, although there were nearly always two hostile cores: the remainder of the college dissolved into a vigorous, talkative, solemn anarchy. It was an interesting lesson in personal politics, which I sometimes thought should be studied by anyone who wanted to take a part in high affairs.

Through the last half of 1934 Winslow and his allies devoted themselves with some ingenuity to obstruction, for which the college statutes and customs gave considerable opportunity. Could the college

44

afford another fellow? If so, ought it not to discuss whether the first need was not for an official rather than a research fellowship? If a research fellowship, was not the first step to decide in which subject it should be offered? Did the college really need another fellow in an out-of-the-way subject? Could it really afford such luxuries, when it did not possess an engineer?

'Fellowships' occurred on the agenda for meeting after meeting in 1934. By the end of the year, the debate had scarcely reached Roy by name. This did not mean that gossip was not circulating against him at high table or in the combination room. But even in private, arguments were phrased in the same comfortable language: 'could the college afford . . .?' 'is it in the man's own best interests. . . .?' It was the public face, it was the way things were done.

Meanwhile, nothing decisive was showing itself in Roy's life. The months went by; the grammar was published, highly thought of by a handful of scholars; he tired himself each day at the liturgy. He saw Rosalind sometimes in Cambridge, oftener in London; she persuaded him to take her to Pallanza in September, but she had got no nearer marrying him. There were other affairs, light come, light go.

He became a greater favourite with Lady Muriel as the months passed, was more often at the Lodge, and had spent a week-end at Boscastle.

He knew this roused some rancour in the college, and I told him that it was not improving his chances of election. He grinned. Even if he had not been amused by Lady Muriel and fond of her, the thought of solemn head-shaking would have driven him into her company.

Yet he wanted to be elected. He was not anxious about it, for anxiety in the ordinary sense he scarcely knew: any excitement, anything at stake, merely gave him a heightened sense of living. At times, though, he seemed curiously excited when his fortunes in this election rose or fell. It surprised me, for he lacked his proper share of vanity. Perhaps he wanted the status, I thought, if only to gratify his father: perhaps he wanted, like other rich men, to feel that he could earn a living.

At any rate, it mattered to him, and so I was relieved when Arthur Brown took control. The first I heard of the new manoeuvres was when Brown invited me to his rooms on a January evening. It was wet and cold, and I was sitting huddled by my fire when Brown looked in.

'I suppose,' he said, 'that you don't by any chance feel like joining me in a glass of wine? I might be able to find something a bit special. I can't help feeling that it would be rather cheering on a night like this.'

I went across to his rooms, which were on the next staircase. Though he lived in domestic comfort with his wife and family, those rooms in college were always warm, always welcoming: that night a fire was blazing in the open grate, electric fires were glowing in the corners of the room, rich curtains were drawn, the armchairs were wide and deep. The fire crackled, and on the windows behind the curtains sounded the tap of rain. Brown brought out glasses and a bottle.

'I hope you like marsala on a cold night,' he said. 'I'm rather given to it myself as a change. I find it rather fortifying.'

He was a broad plump well-covered man, with a broad smooth pink face. He wore spectacles, and behind them his eyes were small, acute, dark, watchful, and very bright. He was the junior of the two tutors, a man of forty-four, though most of the college, lulled by his avuncular kindness, thought of him as older.

He was a man easy to under-estimate, and his colleagues often did so. He was hospitable, comfort-loving, modestly self-indulgent. He disliked quarrels, and was happy when he could compose one among his colleagues. But he was also a born politician. He loved getting his own way, 'running things', manipulating people, particularly if they never knew.

He was content to leave the appearance of power to others. Some of us, who had benefited through his skill, called him 'Uncle Arthur': 'the worthy Brown', said Winslow contemptuously. Brown did not mind. In his own way, deliberate, never moving a step faster than he wanted, talking blandly, comfortably, and often sententiously, he set about his aims. He was by far the ablest manager among the Master's party. He was a cunning and realistic, as well as a very warm-hearted, man. And in the long run, deep below the good fellowship, he possessed great obstinacy and fortitude.

We drank our wine, seated opposite each other across the fireplace.

'It is rather consoling, don't you think?' said Brown amiably, as he took a sip. He went on to talk about some pupils, for most of the young men I supervised came into his tutorial side.

He was watching me with his intent, shrewd eyes and quite casually, as though it were part of the previous conversation, he slipped in the question:

'You see something of our young friend Calvert, don't you? I suppose you don't feel that perhaps we ought to push ahead a bit with getting him considered?'

I said that I did.

Brown shook his head.

'It's no use trying to rush things, Eliot. You can't take these places by storm. I expect you're inclined to think that it could have been better handled. I'm not prepared to go as far as that. The Master's in a very difficult situation, running a candidate in what people regard as his own subject. No, I don't think we should be right to feel impatient.' He gave a jovial smile. 'But I think we should be perfectly justified, and we can't do any harm, if we push a little from our side.'

'I'm ready to do anything,' I said. 'But I'm so relatively new to the college, I didn't think it was wise to take much part.'

'That shows very good judgement,' said Brown approvingly. 'Put it another way: it'll be a year or two before you'll carry as much weight here as some of us would like. But I believe you can dig in an oar about Calvert, if we set about it in the right way. Mind you, we've got to feel our steps. It may be prudent to draw back before we've gone too far.'

Brown filled our glasses again.

'I'm inclined to think, Eliot,' he went on, 'that our young friend could have been elected last term if there weren't some rather unfortunate personal considerations in the background. He's done quite enough to satisfy anyone, even if they don't believe he's as good as the Master says. They'd have taken him if they wanted to, but somehow or other they don't like the idea. There's a good deal of personal animosity somehow. These things shouldn't happen, of course, but men are as God made them.'

'Some of them dislike the Master, of course,' I said.

'I'm afraid that's so,' said Brown. 'And some of them dislike what they've heard of our young friend Calvert.'

'Yes.'

'Has that come your way?' His glance was very sharp.

'A little.'

'It would probably be more likely to come to me. Why, Chrystal' – (the Dean, usually Brown's inseparable comrade in college politics) – 'isn't completely happy about what he hears. Of course,' said Brown steadily, 'Calvert doesn't make things too easy for his friends. But once again men are as God made them, and it would be a damned scandal if the college didn't take him. I'm a mild man, but I should feel inclined to speak out.'

'What do you think we should do?'

'I've been turning it over in my mind,' said Brown. 'I can't help feeling this might be an occasion to take the bull by the horns. It occurs to me that some of our friends won't be very easy about their reasons for trying to keep him out. It might be useful to force them into the open. I have known that kind of method take the edge off certain persons' opposition in a very surprising way. And I think you can be very useful there. You're not so committed to the Master's personal way of looking at things as some of us are supposed to be – and also you know Getliffe better than any of us.'

Under his stately, unhurried deliberations Brown had been getting down to detail – as he would say himself, he had been 'counting heads'.

'I suggest those might be our tactics for the time being,' said Brown. 'We can wait for a convenient night, when some of the others who don't see eye to eye with us are dining. Then we'll have a bottle of wine and see just how unreasonable they're prepared to be. We shall have to be careful about tackling them. I think it would be safer if you let me make the pace.'

Brown smiled: 'I fancy there's a decent chance we shall get the young man in, Eliot.' Then he warned me, as was his habit at the faintest sign of optimism: 'Mind you, I shan't feel justified in cheering until we hear the Master reading out the statute of admission.'

Brown studied the dining list each day, but had to wait, with imperturbable patience, some weeks before the right set of people were dining. At last the names turned up – Despard-Smith, Winslow, Getliffe, and no others. Brown put himself down to dine, and told the kitchen that I should be doing the same.

It was a Saturday night towards the end of term. As we sat in hall, nothing significant was said: from the head of the table, Despard-Smith let fall some solemn comments on the fortunes of the college boats in the Lent races. He was a clergyman of nearly seventy, but he had never left the college since he came up as an undergraduate. He had been Bursar for thirty years, Winslow's predecessor in the office. His face was mournful, harassed, and depressed, and across his bald head were trained a few grey hairs. He was limited, competent, absolutely certain of his judgement, solemn, self-important, and self-assured. He could make any platitude sound like a moral condemnation. And, when we went into the combination room after hall, he won a battle of wills upon whether we should drink claret or port that night.

Brown had been at his most emollient in hall, and had not given any hint of his intention. As soon as we arrived in the combination room, he asked permission to present a bottle, 'port or claret, according to the wishes of the company'.

Brown himself had a taste in claret, and only drank port to be clubbable. Francis Getliffe and I preferred claret, but were ready to drink port. But none of the three of us had any say.

We had sat ourselves at the end of the long, polished, oval table; glasses were already laid, sparkling in the light, reflected in the polished surface of the wood; the fire was high.

'Well, gentlemen,' said Despard-Smith solemnly, 'our c-colleague has kindly offered to present a bottle. I suppose it had better be a bottle of port.'

'Port?' said Winslow. 'Correct me if I am wrong, Mr President, but I'm not entirely certain that is the general feeling.'

His mouth had sunk in over his nutcracker jaw, and his nose came down near his upper lip. His eyes were heavy-lidded, his face was hollowed with ill-temper and strain; but his skin was healthy, his long body free and active for a man of nearly sixty. There was a sarcastic twitch to his lips as he spoke: as usual he was caustically polite, even when his rude savage humour was in charge. His manners were formal, he had his own perverse sense of style.

Most of the college disliked him, yet all felt he had a kind of personal distinction. He had done nothing, had not published a book, was not even such a good Bursar as Despard-Smith had been, though he worked long hours in his office. He was a very clever man who had wasted his gifts. Yet everyone in the college was flattered if by any chance they drew a word of praise from him, instead of a polite bitter snub.

'I've always considered,' said Despard-Smith, 'that claret is not strong enough for a dessert wine.'

'That's very remarkable,' said Winslow. 'I've always considered that port is too sweet for any purpose whatsoever.'

'You would s-seriously choose claret, Bursar?'

'If you please, Mr President. If you please.'

Despard-Smith looked round the table lugubriously.

'I suppose no one else follows the Bursar in pressing for claret. No. I think' – he said triumphantly to the butler – 'we must have a bottle of port.'

Francis Getliffe grinned at me, the pleasant grim smile which creased his sunburned face. He was two years older than I, and a friend of mine since we met in a large London house years before. It was through him that, as I explained earlier, I came to the college at all. We were not intimates, but we thought alike in most arguments and usually found ourselves at one, without any need to talk it over, over any college question. He was a physicist, with an important series of researches on the upper atmosphere already published: he was a just, thin-skinned, strong-willed, and strenuously ambitious man.

The port went round, Despard-Smith gravely proposed Brown's health; Brown himself asked one or two quiet, encouraging questions about Winslow's son – for Winslow was a devoted father, and his son, who had entered the college the previous October, roused in him extravagant hopes: hopes that seemed pathetically extravagant, when one heard his blistering disparagement of others.

Then Brown, methodically twirling his wineglass, went on to ask:

'I suppose none of you happen to have thought any more about the matter of electing R. C. E. Calvert, have you? We shall have to decide one way or the other some time. It isn't fair to the man to leave him hanging in mid-air for ever.'

Winslow looked at him under hooded eyes.

'I take it you've gathered, my dear Tutor, that the proposal isn't greeted with unqualified enthusiasm?'

'I did feel,' said Brown, 'that one or two people weren't altogether convinced. And I've been trying to imagine why. On general grounds, I should have expected you to find him a very desirable candidate. Myself, I rather fancy him.'

'I had the impression you were not altogether opposed,' said Winslow.

Brown smiled, completely good-natured, completely undisturbed. 'Winslow, I should like to take a point with you. I think you'll admit that everything we've had on paper about Calvert is in his favour. Put it another way: he's been as well spoken of as anyone can be at that age. What do you feel is the case against him?'

'A great deal of the speaking in his favour,' said Winslow, 'has been done by our respected Master. I have considerable faith in the Master as an after-dinner speaker, but distinctly less in his judgement of men. I still remember his foisting O'Brien on us –' It was thirty years since Royce supported O'Brien, and there had been two Masters in between; but O'Brien had been a continual nuisance, and colleges had long memories. I felt all Winslow's opposition to Roy lived in his antagonism to the Master. He scarcely gave a thought to Roy as a human being, he was just a counter in the game.

'Several other people have written nearly as highly of Calvert,' said Brown. 'I know that in a rather obscure subject it's difficult to amass quite as much opinion as we should all like –'

'That's just it, Brown,' said Francis Getliffe. 'He's clearly pretty good. But he's in a field which no one knows about. How can you compare him with a lad like Luke, who's competing against some of the ablest men in the world? I'm not certain we ought to take anyone in these eccentric lines unless they're really extraordinarily good.'

'I should go a long way towards agreeing with you,' said Brown. 'Before I came down in favour of Calvert, I satisfied myself that he was extraordinarily good.'

'I'm not convinced by the evidence,' said Francis Getliffe.

Despard-Smith intervened, in a tone solemn, authoritative, and damning:

'I can't be satisfied that it's in the man's own best interests to be elected here. I can't be satisfied that he's suited to collegiate life.'

'I don't quite understand, Despard,' said Brown. 'He'd be an asset to any society. He was extremely popular as an undergraduate.'

'That only makes it worse,' said Despard-Smith. 'I can't consider that our fellowships ought to be f-filled by young men of fashion. I'm by no means happy about Calvert's influence on the undergraduates, if we took the very serious risk of electing him to our society.'

'I can't possibly take that view,' said Brown. 'I believe he'd be like a breath of fresh air.'

'You can't take Despard's view, can you?' I asked Francis Getliffe across the table.

'I shouldn't mind what he was like, within reason,' said Francis, 'so long as he was good enough at his stuff.'

'But you've met him several times,' I said. 'What did you think of him?'

'Oh, he's good company. But I should like to know what he really values. Or what he really wants to do.'

I realized with a shock, what I should have seen before, that there was no understanding or contact between them. There was an impatient dismissal in Francis's tone: but suddenly, as though by a deliberate effort of fair-mindedness and responsibility, he turned to Despard-Smith.

'I ought to say,' he remarked sharply, 'that I should think it wrong to vote against him on personal grounds. If he's good enough, we ought to take him. But I want that proved.'

'I cannot think that he'd be an acquisition,' said Despard-Smith. 'When he was an undergraduate, I soon decided that he had no sense of humour. He used to come up to me and ask most extraordinary questions. Quite recently he sent me a ridiculous book by an unsatisfactory young man called Udal.'

'I expect he was just showing his respect,' said Brown.

'In that case,' said Despard-Smith, 'he should do it in a more sensible fashion. No, I think he would have a l-lamentable effect on the undergraduates. It's impossible to have a fellow who might attract undesirable notice. He still has women to visit him in his rooms. I can't think that it would be in his own interests to elect him.'

This was sheer intuitive hostility. Some obscure sense warned the old clergyman that Roy was dangerous. Nothing we could say would touch him: he would stay implacably hostile to the end. Brown, always realistic and never willing to argue without a purpose, gave him up at once.

'Well, Despard,' he said, 'we must agree to differ. But I should like to take a point or two with you others.'

'If you please, my dear Tutor,' said Winslow. 'I find it more congenial hearing it from you than from our respected Master. Even though you spend a little longer over it.'

Patiently, steadily, never ruffled, Brown went over the ground with them. Neither had shifted by the end of the evening: afterwards, Brown and I agreed that Winslow could only be moved if Roy ceased to be the Master's protégé, but that Francis Getliffe was fighting a prejudice and was not irretrievably opposed. We also agreed that it was going to be a very tight thing: we needed seven votes, we could see our way to five or six, but it was not certain where the others were coming from.

Through most of the Easter term, Arthur Brown was busy with talks, deliberate arguments, discussions on tactics, and bargains. It became clear that he could count on five votes for certain (the Master, Brown, and myself; the senior fellow, who was a very old man; and the Senior Tutor, Jago). Another elderly fellow could almost certainly be relied upon, but he would be abroad all the summer, and votes had to be given in person. In order to get a majority at all, Brown needed either his friend Chrystal or mine, Getliffe; in order to force an issue during the summer, he needed both. There were talks in all our rooms, late into summer nights. Chrystal might come in, reluctantly and ill-temperedly, as a sign of personal and party loyalty: I could not use those ties with Francis Getliffe, who prided himself on his fairness and required to be convinced.

Brown would not be hurried. 'More haste, less speed,' he said comfortably. 'If we have a misfire now, we can't bring our young friend up again for a couple of years.' He did not propose to take an official step until he could 'see his votes'. By statute, a fellowship had to be declared vacant before there could be any election. Brown could have collected a majority to vote for a vacancy: but it was not sensible to do so, until he was certain it could not be filled by anyone but Roy.

These dignified, broad-bottomed, middle-aged talks went on, seemingly enjoyed by most of those engaged. For they loved this kind of power politics, they knew it like the palm of their hands, it was rich with its own kind of solid human life. It was strange to hear them at work, and then see the subject of it all walk lightly through the college. There was a curious incongruity that he of all men should be debated on in those comfortable, traditional, respectable, guarded words: I felt it often when I looked at him, his white working coat over a handsome suit, reading a manuscript leaf at his upright desk: or watched him leave in his car, driving off to his London flat to meet Rosalind or another: or saw his smile, as I told him Arthur Brown's latest move – 'extremely statesman-like, extremely statesman-like', mimicked Roy, for it was Brown himself who liked to use the word.

As a research student and ex-scholar, Roy was invited to the college's summer feast. This took place near 1 June and was not such a great occasion as the two great feasts of the year, the audit and the commemoration of benefactors. The foundation plate was not brought out; nevertheless, on the tables in the hall silver and gold glittered in the candlelight. Well above the zone of candlelight, high towards the roof of the hall, the windows glowed with the light of the summer evening all the time we sat there and ate and drank. The vintages were not the college's finest, but they were good enough; the food was lavish; as the high windows slowly darkened and the candles flickered down, the faces round one shone out, flushed, bright-eyed, and content.

It was to this feast that the college invited a quota of old members each year, selected at random from the college lists. As junior fellow, I was sitting at the bottom of one of the two lower tables, with an old member on each hand: Roy came next to one of these old members, with a fellow of another college on his left. It seemed that he decided early that the fellow was capable of looking after himself; from the first courses he devoted himself to making the old member happy, so that I could concentrate on the one on my right. With half an ear I kept listening to Roy's success. His old member was a secondary schoolmaster of fifty, with a sensitive, unprepossessing, indrawn face. One felt that he had wanted much and got almost nothing. There was a streak of plain silliness in him, and failure had made him aggressive, opinionated, demanding. I tried, but he put me off before I could get close: in a few moments, he was giving advice to Roy, as an experienced man to a younger, and there was brilliance in the air. Roy teased him simply, directly, like a brother. It was all spontaneous. Roy had found someone who was naked to life. He laughed at his aggressiveness, stopped him when he produced too many opinions, got him back to his true feeling. Before the end of dinner Roy was promising to visit the school, and I knew he would.

The feast ended, and slowly the hall cleared as men rose and went by twos and threes into the combination room. At my table we were still sitting. Roy smiled at me. His eyes were brilliant, he was gay with wine, he looked at his happiest.

'It's a pity we need to move, old boy,' he said.

On our way out, we passed the high table on the dais, where a small group was sitting over cigars and a last glass of port. Roy was whispering to me, when Chrystal called out:

'Eliot! I want you to meet our guest.'

He noticed Roy, and added: 'You too, Calvert! I want you all to meet our guest.'

Chrystal, the Dean, was a bald, beaky, commanding man, and 'our guest' had been brought here specially that evening. He was an eminent surgeon to whom the university was giving an honorary degree in two days' time. He sat by Chrystal's side, red-complexioned, opulent, self-assured, with protruding eyes that glanced round whenever he spoke to make sure that all were listening. He nodded imperially to Roy and me, and went on talking.

'As I was saying, Dean,' he remarked loudly, 'I feel strongly that a man owes certain duties to himself.'

Roy was just sitting down, after throwing his gown over the back of a chair. I caught a glint in his eyes. That remark, the whole atmosphere of Anstruther-Barratt, was a temptation to him.

'And those are?' said Chrystal respectfully, who worshipped success in any form.

'I believe strongly,' said Anstruther-Barratt, 'that one ought to accept all the recognition that comes to one. One owes it to oneself.'

He surveyed us all.

'And yet, you wouldn't believe it,' he said resonantly, 'but I am quite nervous about Friday's performance. I don't feel I know all there is to be known about your academic things.'

'Oh, I think I should believe it,' said Roy in a clear voice. His expression was dangerously demure.

'Should you?' Anstruther-Barratt looked at him in a puzzled fashion.

'Certainly,' said Roy. 'I expect this is the first time you've tried it –'

Roy had a grave, friendly look, and spoke as though Anstruther-Barratt was taking an elementary examination.

It was just possible that he did not know that Anstruther-Barratt was receiving an honorary degree. Chrystal must have thought it possible, for, looking on in consternation, he tried to break in.

'Calvert, I suppose you know –'

'Is it the first time?' Roy fixed the bold protruding eyes with a gaze brilliant, steady, acute, from which they seemed unable to escape.

'Of course it is. One doesn't –'

'Just so. It's natural for you to be nervous,' said Roy. 'Everyone's nervous when they're trying something for the first time. But you know, you're lucky, being a medical – I hope I'm right in thinking you are a medical?'

'Yes.'

'It doesn't matter so much, does it? There's nothing so fatal about it.'

Anstruther-Barratt looked badgered and bewildered. This young man appeared to think that he was a medical student up for an examination. He burst out:

'Don't you think I look a bit old to be –'

'Oh no,' said Roy. 'It makes you much more nervous. You need to look after yourself more than you would have done twenty years ago. You oughtn't to do any work between now and Friday, you know. It's never worth while, looking at books at the last minute.'

'I wish you'd understand that I haven't looked at books for years, young man.'

'Calvert,' Chrystal began again.

'You've done much more than you think,' said Roy soothingly. 'Everyone feels as you do when it comes to the last day.'

'Nonsense. I tell you –'

'You must believe me. It's not nonsense. We've all been through it.' Roy gave him a gentle, serious smile. 'You ought to spend the day on the river tomorrow. And don't worry too much. Then go in and win on Friday. We'll look out for your name in the *Reporter*.'

CHAPTER 6

The Beginning of a Sleepless Night

ROY'S antic at the end of the feast meant more delay for Brown. He had listened to an indignant outburst from his old ally Chrystal, who was, like so many people, mystified by Roy's manner. 'I don't know,' Chrystal snapped. 'He may have thought Barratt was an old man who was trying to get qualified. In that case he's a born bloody fool. Or it may be his idea of a joke. But I don't want that sort of joke made by a fellow of this college. I tell you, Barratt was right up in the air about it. He earns £20,000 a year if he earns a penny, and he's not used to being made an exhibition of.'

It did not seem as though anything could make Chrystal vote for Roy now, and Brown had to change his tactics. 'It's an infernal nuisance,' he said. 'I should almost feel justified in washing my hands of the whole business. I wish you'd keep Calvert in order, the damned ass.'

But, though Brown was annoyed because his particular craft was being interfered with, he was secretly amused; and, like the born politician he was, he did not waste time thinking of opportunity lost. He was committed to getting Calvert in. He believed he was backing a great talent, he had a stubborn and unshakable affection for Roy (behind Brown's comfortable flesh there was a deep sympathy with the wild), and with all the firmness of his obstinate nature he started on a new plan. Wait for the absentee to return in October: then invite down to the college the only two men in England who were authorities on Roy's work. 'It's a risk,' said Brown in a minatory voice. 'Some people may feel we're using unfair influence. It's one thing to write for opinions, it's quite another to produce the old gentlemen themselves. But I'm anxious to give Getliffe something to think about. Our friends mustn't be allowed to flatter themselves that we've shot our bolt.'

So, in the first week of the Michaelmas term, one of the customary college notes went out:

'Those fellows who are interested in Mr R. C. E. Calvert's candidature may like to know that Sir Oulstone Lyall and Colonel E. St G. Foulkes, the chief authorities on Mr Calvert's subject, will be my guests in hall on Sunday night. A.B.'

The Master, after talking to Brown, thought it politic not to dine in hall that Sunday night; none of the old men came, though it was by now certain that the two seniors would vote for Roy; Despard-Smith had said, in a solemn grating voice the night before, that he had ordered cold supper for himself in his rooms. Winslow was the next in seniority, and he presided with his own cultivated rudeness.

'It's a most remarkable occasion that we should have you two distinguished visitors,' he said as soon as dinner began. 'We appear to owe this remarkable occasion to the initiative of our worthy Mr Brown.'

'Yes,' said Colonel Foulkes undiplomatically. 'We've come to talk about Calvert.'

He was in his sixties, but neither his black hair nor his thick, down-curling, ginger moustache showed any grey at all. His cheeks were rubicund, his eyes a bright and startled brown. He always answered at extreme speed, as though the questions were reflected instantaneously off the front of his head. Action came more easily than reflection, one felt as soon as one heard him – and hot-tempered explosions a good deal more easily than comfortable argument. Yet he was fond of explaining the profound difference Yoga had meant in giving him peace beyond this world, since his time in the Indian Army. India had also led him to the study of the early Persian languages, as well as to Yoga – and everyone agreed that he was a fine scholar. He held a great many cranky interests at once, and at heart was fervent, wondering, and very simple.

'Indeed,' said Winslow. 'Yes, I remember that we were promised the benefit of your judgement. I had a faint feeling, though, that we had already seen your opinion on paper about this young man. I may be stupid, I'm very ignorant about these things. But I seem to recall that the Master circulated what some of my colleagues would probably call a "dossier".'

'Does no harm to say it twice,' said Colonel Foulkes at once. 'You can't do better.'

'If you please?'

'You can't do better than Calvert. Impossible to get a better man.'

'It's most interesting,' said Winslow, 'to hear such a favourable opinion.'

'Not just my opinion,' said Colonel Foulkes. 'Everyone agrees who's competent to give one. Listen to Lyall.'

Sir Oulstone Lyall inclined his high, bald, domed head towards Winslow. He wore an impersonal, official, ambassadorial smile. He was used to being the spokesman for Central Asian history. He did it with a lofty gratification and self-esteem. It was noticeable that Foulkes deferred to him with admiration and respect.

'I must begin by covering myself under a warning, Mr President,' said Sir Oulstone in measured tones. 'We all try to keep our sense of perspective, but it's straining humanity not to exaggerate the importance of the subject to which one has devoted one's small abilities for most of one's life.'

Heads were nodded. The table was used to this kind of public approach. They could stand more pomp than most bodies of men.

'I must make that qualification,' said Sir Oulstone without any sign of hurry. 'I may have a certain partiality for the studies with which I have associated for longer than I sometimes care to think. But, if you will kindly allow for that partiality, I may be able to assist you about Mr Calvert.' He paused. 'I think I can say, with a full sense of responsibility, that among the younger workers Mr Calvert is the chief hope that our studies now possess.'

It never occurred to Sir Oulstone that the college might dispute his judgement. For a time, his confidence had a hypnotic effect on all there, and on Brown's face there grew a comfortable, appreciative smile. Even Winslow did not produce a caustic remark, and it was left for Francis Getliffe to cross-examine Sir Oulstone about his detailed knowledge of Roy's work. Francis, who was a precise and accurate man, knew that all Roy's published work was linguistic – and he was right in thinking that Sir Oulstone was a historian, not a linguist at all. But Sir Oulstone was quite unperturbed by the questions: he turned to Foulkes, with the manner of one whistling up a technical assistant, and said with unshaken confidence: 'Foulkes, I should like you to deal with that interesting point.' And Foulkes was off the mark at once.

Colonel Foulkes was off the mark even more rapidly when someone made a remark about Roy's character.

'Splendid fellow. Everything you could wish for,' said Foulkes.

'I have heard reports,' said Winslow, 'that the young man finds time for some night life. In the intervals of making his contribution to your subject, Sir Oulstone,' he added caustically, but I fancied that he was reluctant to bring in scandal. He had not done it before, and it was not his line.

'Nonsense,' said Colonel Foulkes instantaneously. 'Fine clean-living fellow. He's got his books and games, he doesn't want anything else.'

Someone said a word, and Foulkes became incensed. 'Listening to women's gossip.' He glared round with hot, brown eyes. 'Utterly unthinkable to anyone who knows Calvert as well as I do.'

Sir Oulstone intervened.

'I cannot pretend to have very intimate knowledge of Mr Calvert personally,' he said. 'Though I may say that I've formed a very favourable impression. He does not thrust himself forward in the presence of his elders. But my friend Colonel Foulkes has been in constant touch with him –'

'The army teaches you to see the seamy side,' said Foulkes, still irate but simmering down. 'Perhaps living in sheltered places makes you see things that aren't there. Afraid I can't leave this thing in its present state. I must correct this impression. Absolute nonsense. You couldn't have a finer specimen of a young man.'

Immediately after we rose from hall, Foulkes went away without going into the combination room. He would not let a minute pass before he 'corrected the impression', and he had gone off, hot-temperedly, loyally, without thinking twice, to see the Master. Sir Oulstone blandly continued his praise of Roy for an hour in the combination room: for all his blandness, for all his impenetrable pomposity, he had a real desire to see his subject grow. As we broke up, I could not decide what had been the effect of this curious evening.

Later that night, I called on Roy. He was alone, the opalescent viewing screen was still lighted at the top of his tall desk, but he was sunk into an armchair. At the little table by his side, books had been pushed out of order, so as to make room for a bottle of brandy and a glass.

'Tired?' I asked.

'Not tired enough.'

He did not smile, he scarcely looked at me, his face was drawn and fixed with sadness.

'Have a drink, Lewis.'

'No.'

'You don't mind me?' he said with a sad ironic courtesy, poured himself another glass, and took a gulp.

'There's nothing special the matter, is there?' I asked, but I knew that it was not so.

'How could there be?'

He seemed to struggle from a depth far away, as he asked:

'What have you been doing?'

'I've been in hall.'

'A good place, hall.'

'We were talking of you.'

'You should have something better to do,' he cried, half-angrily, half-wretchedly.

'It must happen just now, you know.' I tried to soothe him.

'They should forget me.'

'I told you, Oulstone Lyall was coming down –'

'He's a dreadful man.'

'He's pretty pompous,' I said. 'But he was doing you very proud –'

'He should be told to stop,' said Roy with a grimace, sombre and frowning. 'He's a dreadful man. He's stuffed. He's never doubted himself for a minute in his life.'

In any mood, Roy was provoked by the Lyalls, by the self-satisfied, protected, and content; they were the men he could not meet as brothers. But now he was inflamed.

'He never even doubted himself when he pinched Erzberger's work,' cried Roy.

Roy drank another brandy, and wildly told me of the scandal of thirty years before.

'It's true,' said Roy angrily. 'You don't believe it, but it's true.'

'Tell me the whole story some time.'

'You don't need to humour me. That dreadful man oughtn't to be talking nonsense about me. I need to stop him.'

I had never seen Roy so overwhelmed by despondency as this. I did not know what to expect, or what to fear next. I was appalled that night by the wild active gleam that kept striking out of the darkness. He did not submit to the despair, but struggled for anything that gave release.

All I could do, I thought, was try to prevent any action that might damage himself. I said that stretches of unhappiness had to be lived through; somehow one emerged from them; they were bad enough in themselves, it was worse if they left consequences when one was calm once again.

Roy listened, his eyes bright, bloodshot. He replied more gently than he had spoken that night.

'Dear old boy, you know what it is to be miserable, don't you? But you think it ought to be kept in separate compartments, don't you? You don't believe that it ought to interfere with really serious things. Such as getting fellowships.'

'It's better if it doesn't,' I said.

'I wish I were as stoical as you,' he said. 'Yet you've been hopeless, haven't you?'

'Yes.'

'Just so. I'll try, old boy, I'll try. I can't promise much.'

He was quiet for a time, and did not take another drink until Ralph Udal came in. Since I first met him, he had borrowed a considerable sum of money from Roy. He had followed Roy's advice, and had taken a London curacy. He kept coming up to see Roy, so as to plan support within the college; but I knew he was also watching for Roy to be converted. His watch was patient, effortless, almost sinister. However, he was not so patient about obtaining his country living. Despite Roy's instructions, he had been trying to hurry things that week-end. He had been calling on the Master, Despard-Smith, the Senior Tutor, Brown, in order to sound them about the next vacancy; he was being much more open than Roy thought wise.

'Wonderful!' shouted Roy as Udal entered. 'Old Lewis won't drink, but you will, won't you?'

Udal took a sip of brandy, and looked at Roy with passive good nature.

'Haven't you had enough?' he said.

'Probably,' said Roy, drinking again. 'Well, what did they say to you?'

Udal shrugged his shoulders. He seemed irritated and chagrined.

'They don't seem anxious to let me retire.'

'The devils,' said Roy.

'They think I'm too young to settle down in comfort. I've always had a faint objection,' said Udal, 'to people who find it necessary to make one do unpleasant things for the good of one's soul. Why do they take it on themselves to make life into a moral gymnasium?'

'Why do they, Lewis? You should know,' cried Roy.

I shook my head, and caught his eye. The gleam had come again; but, as he saw my look, anxious and disturbed, he still seemed enough in command to quieten himself.

'At any rate,' he added in a level tone, 'you're spared having a man like old Lyall talking nonsense about you.'

'Who is Lyall?' said Udal.

'You wouldn't like him. He's stuffed.' Again Roy told the scandal of Lyall and Erzberger's work, but this time in a sad, contemptuous voice.

'Yours must be a curious trade,' said Udal.

'It doesn't signify,' said Roy. 'All men are the same, aren't they?'

He went on drinking, though neither of us kept him company. It was getting late, and soon after midnight Udal and I both wanted to go. Roy begged us to stay a little longer. At last we got up, although he implored us not to leave him.

'You two may sleep, but I shan't. So why should you go?' There was a trace of a smile. 'Please don't go. What's the use of going to bed if you can't sleep? And if you do sleep, you only dream. Dreams are horrible.'

'You'll sleep now, if you go to bed,' I said.

'You don't know,' said Roy. 'I shan't sleep tonight. I'll do anything you like. Let's do anything. Let's play cards. Three-handed bezique. Please stay and play bezique with me. Good game, three-handed bezique. It's a wonderful game. Please stay and play. Please stay with me.'

CHAPTER 7

Walk in the Moonlight

DAY after day, Roy was left with the darkness on his mind. He read his manuscripts until he was faint, but no relief came to him. He had never been through melancholy that was as dark, that lasted so long. He could not sleep, and his nights were worse than his days.

It was heart-rending to watch, now I saw his affliction clear for the first time. At least once I was cowardly enough to make an excuse not to see him at night. It was agony, not to be able to lift his despair, not even for an hour. It was agony to know his loneliness – and so to know my own.

And I was frightened. I was lost. I had never before felt my way among this kind of darkness. I could read of experiences which here and there resembled it, but books are empty when one is helpless beside such suffering. Nothing I found to read, nothing I had learned myself, could tell me what was likely to come next. Often I was frightened over quite practical things: would he collapse? would he break out in some single irreparable act? I was never afraid that he might kill himself: from a distance, it might have seemed a danger, but in his presence I did not give it a thought. But I imagined most other kinds of disaster.

The melancholy, which fell on him the week-end that Lyall and Foulkes arrived, did not stay uniform like one pitch-black and un-changing night. Occasionally, it was broken by a wild, lurid elation that seemed like a fantastic caricature of his natural gaiety. The mischievous high spirits with which he took me round the bookshops or baited the surgeon at the feast – those spirits seemed suddenly distorted into a frenzy. I feared such moments most: they happened very seldom. I was waiting for them, but I did not know whether sympathy or love could help him then. Sometimes the melancholy lifted for a time much more gradually, for a day or a night, and he became himself at once, though sadder, more tired, and more gentle. 'I must be an awful bore, old boy,' he said. 'You'd better spend your time with Arthur Brown. You'll find it less exhausting.'

All through, in melancholy or false elation, his intelligence was as lucid as ever: in fact, I sometimes thought that he was more lucid and penetrating than I had ever known him. He was given none of the comfort of illusion. He worked with the same precision and resource; some of his best emendations came during a phase of melancholy. And once or twice, struggling away from his own thoughts, he talked to me about myself as no one else could have done.

Whenever he could lose himself in another, I thought one night, he gained a little ease. It was a night not long after Lyall's visit, and Roy and I were dining in the Lodge. The Master was in Oxford, and Lady Muriel had asked us to dine *en famille* with herself and Joan. After I had dressed, I went up to Roy's room, and found him in shirt-sleeves and black waistcoat studying his image in the mirror.

'If I keep out of the light, I may just pass.' He smiled at me ruefully. 'I don't look very bright for Lady Mu.'

Nights of insomnia had left stains under his eyes and taken the colour from his cheeks. There were shadows under his cheekbones, and his face, except when he smiled, was tired and drawn.

'I'll have to do my best for her,' he said. He gazed again at his reflection. 'It's bad to look like death. It makes them worry, doesn't it?' He turned away. 'I'm also going bald, but that's quite another thing.'

For once, Lady Muriel had not asked Mrs Seymour as the in-evitable partner for me. There were only the four of us, and I was invited just as an excuse for having Roy: for Lady Muriel intended to enjoy his presence without being distracted at all.

She sat straightbacked at the end of the table, but if one had only heard her voice one would have known that Roy was there.

'Why have I been neglected, Roy?' she said.

'That is extremely simple,' said Roy.

'What do you mean, you impertinent young man?' she cried in delight.

'I've not been asked, Lady Mu,' he said, using her nickname to her face, which no one else would have dared.

He was using the tone, feline, affectionate, gently rough, which pleased her most. He was trying to hide his wretchedness, he acted a light-hearted mood in order to draw out her crowing laugh.

He smiled as he watched her face, suddenly undignified and unformidable, wrinkled, hearty, joyous as she laughed.

She recovered herself for a moment, however, when she talked of the Christmas vacation. Lord Boscastle had taken a villa outside Monte Carlo, and the Royces were going down 'as soon as the Master' – as Lady Muriel always called him – 'has finished the scholarship examination'.

I mentioned that I was arranging to spend a fortnight in Monte Carlo myself.

'How very strange, Mr Eliot,' said Lady Muriel, with recognition rather than enthusiasm. 'How very strange indeed.'

I said that I often went to the Mediterranean.

'Indeed,' said Lady Muriel firmly. 'I hope we may see something of you there.'

'I hope so, Lady Muriel.'

'And I hope,' she looked at me fixedly, 'we may have the pleasure of seeing your wife.'

'I want to take her,' I said. 'She may not be well enough to travel, though.'

It was nearly true, but Lady Muriel gave an ominous: 'I see, Mr Eliot.'

Lady Muriel still expressed surprise that I should be going to Monte Carlo. She had all the incredulity of the rich that anyone should share their pleasures. Rather as though she expected me to answer with the name of an obscure *pension*, she asked:

'May I ask where you are staying?'

'The Hermitage,' I said.

'Really, Mr Eliot,' she said. 'Don't you think that you will find it very expensive?'

During this conversation, I had noticed that Joan's glance had remained on Roy. Her own face was intent. It was still too young to show the line of her cheekbones. Her eyes were bright blue, and her hair brown and straight. It struck me that she had small, beautiful ears. But her face was open and harassed; I could guess too easily what had fascinated her: I looked across for a second, away from Lady Muriel, and saw Roy, stricken and remote. Usually he would have hung on to each word of the exchange, and parodied it later at my expense: now he was not listening. It seemed by an unnatural effort that he spoke again. Lady Muriel was remarking, in order to reprove my extravagance: 'My brother considers it quite impossibly expensive to live in Monte itself. We find it much more practical to take this place outside.'

'How terrible it must be to be poor, Lady Mu,' broke in Roy's voice. Joan started as he spoke: it made what she had seen appear ghostly. He was smiling now, he teased Lady Muriel, just as she wanted. She had noticed nothing, and was very happy. She crowed as he made fun of the Boscastle finances – which amused him, for he was enough his father's son to have a lively interest in money. And she was delighted when he threatened not to be left out of the party at Christmas, but to join me at the hotel. She even regarded me with a kind of second-hand favour.

Her response to Roy was very simple, I thought. Life had never set her free, but underneath the armour she was healthy, vital, and coarse-fibred. She had borne three daughters, but no sons. Roy was the son she had never had. And he was an attractive young man, utterly unimpressed by her magnificence, who saw through her, laughed, and shook her now and then. She could never find a way to tell people she liked them, but that did not matter with this young man, who could hear what she was really saying behind the gruff, clumsy words.

And Roy? She was a continual pleasure to him in being exactly what she was, splendid in her unperceptive courage, her heavy-footedness, her snobbery, her stiff and monumental gusto. But there was much more. He came into immediate touch with her, as with so many people. He knew how she craved to be liked, how she could never confess her longing for affection, fun, and love. It was his nature to give it. He was moved deeply, moved to a mixture of pity and love, by the unexpectedly vulnerable, just as he was by the tormented, the failures, and the strays. The unexpectedly vulnerable, the strong who suffered under a façade – sometimes I thought they moved him most. So he could not resist being fond of Lady Muriel; and even that night, when left to himself he would have known only despair, he was forced to make sure that she enjoyed her party.

Roy and I had not long left the Lodge and were sitting in his rooms, when we heard a woman's footsteps on the stairs.

'What's this?' said Roy wearily.

It was Joan. She hesitated when she saw me, but then spoke direct to Roy.

'I'm sorry. But I had to come. At dinner you looked so – ill.'

'It's nice of you, Joan,' he said, but I felt he was put out. 'I'm pretty well.'

She looked at him with steady, intelligent, dark blue eyes.

'In all ways?'

'Oh yes.'

'I don't believe it,' said Joan.

Roy made a grimace, and leant back.

'Look,' she said, her expression fierce, warm-hearted, painfully diffident, and full of power, 'you don't think I like intruding, do you? But I want to ask something. Is it this wretched fellowship? We're bound to hear things we shouldn't, you must know that.'

'It would be extremely surprising if you didn't,' said Roy with a faint smile.

'We do,' said Joan, transformed by her rich laugh. 'Well, I've heard about this wretched business. Is it that?'

'Of course not,' said Roy impatiently.

'I should like to ask Lewis Eliot,' she said, and turned to me. 'Has that business got on his nerves?'

'I don't think so,' I said. 'It would be better if it were settled, of course.' I was actually anxious that his election should come through quickly, so as to divert his mind (Brown had been satisfied with the results of Lyall's and Foulkes's visit, so much so that he was pressing to have a vacancy declared at the next college meeting).

'Are you sure?' Joan looked stubborn and doubtful. She spoke to Roy again: 'You must see that it doesn't matter. Whatever they do, it can't really matter to you.'

'Just so,' said Roy. 'You need to tell your father that. It would please him if I got in.'

'He worries too much about these people,' said Joan, speaking of her father with scorn and love. 'You say you don't. I hope it's true.'

She gazed at him steadily.

'Yes?' he said.

'I was trying to imagine why you were looking as you did.'

'I can't suggest anything,' said Roy. He had been restless all the time she was questioning him: had he not noticed the physical nervousness which had made her tremble as she entered, the utter diffidence which lay behind her fierce direct attack? He felt invaded, and though his words were light they held a sting.

'Some of your young women at Girton might give you some tips. Or you might get an idea if you read enough novels.'

'I'm not so young as you think,' said Joan, and a blush climbed up her strong neck, reddened her cheeks, left her bright-eyed, ashamed, angry, and defenceless.

I went away from Roy's rooms as the clocks were chiming midnight, and was in the depth of sleep when softly, persistently, a hand on my shoulder pulled me half-awake.

'Do you mind very much?' Roy was speaking. 'I need to talk to you.'

'Put the light on,' I said crossly.

His face was haggard, and my ill-temper could not survive.

'It's nothing original,' he said. 'I can't sleep, that's all. It must be a very useful accomplishment, being able to sleep.'

He had not been to bed, he was still wearing a dinner jacket.

'What do you want to do?'

He shook his head. Then suddenly, almost eagerly, he said:

'I think I need to go for a walk. Will you come?' He caught, with poignant, evanescent hope, at anything which would pass the night. 'Let's go for a walk,' he said.

I got up and dressed. It was just after three when we walked through the silent courts towards the back gate of the college. The roofs gleamed like silver under the harvest moon, and the shadows were dense, black, and sharply edged.

A light shone in an attic window; we knew the room, it was a scholar working late.

'Poor fool,' Roy whispered, as I was unlocking the small back door. 'He doesn't realize where that may lead.'

'Where?'

'It might even keep him here,' said Roy with a faint smile. 'If he does too well. So that he's woken up in the middle of the night and taken out for walks.'

We walked along Regent Street and Hills Road, straight out of the town. It was all quiet under the moon. It was brilliantly quiet. The road spread wide in the moonlight, dominating the houses as on a bright day; the houses stood blank-faced. Roy walked by my side with quick, light, easy steps. He was soothed by the sheer activity, by being able to move without thought, by the beautiful night. He talked, with a trace of his good-natured malice, about some of our friends. We had a good many in common, both men and women, and we talked scandal and Roy imitated them as we made our way along the gleaming, empty road.

But when we turned left at the Strangeways and crossed the fields, he fell more silent. For a quarter of a mile along the Roman road neither of us spoke. Then Roy said, quietly and clearly:

'Old boy, I need some rest.'

'Yes,' I said. He did not mean sleep or bodily rest.

'Shall I ever get it?'

I could not answer that.

'Sometimes,' he said, 'I think I was born out of my time. I should have been happier when it was easier to believe. Wouldn't you have been happier? Wouldn't you?'

He wanted me to agree. I was tempted to fall in, to muffle my answer, to give him a little comfort. Yet he was speaking with absolute nakedness. I could not escape the moment in which we stood.

I hesitated. Then I told the truth.

'I don't think so.'

He walked on a few yards in silence, then looked me in the face.

'Lewis, have you never longed to believe in God?'

'No,' I said. I added:

'Not in any sense which has much meaning. Not in any sense which would mean anything to you.'

'You don't long to believe in God?' he insisted.

'No.'

'Yet you're not stuffed.' His smile was intimate, mischievous, sad. 'No man is less stuffed. In spite of your business manner. You even feel a good deal, don't you? Not only about love. That's the trouble with all those others' – he was dismissing some of our contemporaries – 'they can only feel about love. They're hollow, aren't they? But I can't accuse you of that. Yet you don't long to believe –'

His eyes searched me, bright, puzzled, almost humorous. He had been mystified about it since he first knew me well. So much of our sense of life we felt in common: he could not easily or willingly accept that it led me to different fulfilments, even to different despairs. Most of all, he could not accept that I could get along, with fairly even spirits, and not be driven by the desperate needs that took hold of him in their ineluctable clarity.

He was quiet again. Then he said:

'Lewis, I've prayed that I might believe in God.'

He looked away from me, down from the ridge; there was a veil of mist on the lower fields.

'I knew,' I said.

'It's no good,' he said, as though off-handedly. 'One can't make oneself believe. One can't believe to order.'

'That must be so,' I said.

'Either it comes or it doesn't. For me it doesn't. For some – it is as easy as breathing. How lucky they are,' he said softly. 'Think of the Master. He's not a very good scholar, you know, but he's an extremely clever man. But he believes exactly as he did when he was a child. After reading about all the religions in the world. He's very lucky.'

He was still looking over the fields.

'Then there's Ralph Udal.' Suddenly he gave me a glance acute and piercing. 'By the way, why do you dislike him so much?'

'I don't dislike him –'

'Come off it.' Roy smiled. 'I've not seen you do it with anyone else – but when you meet him you bristle like a cat.'

I had not wanted to recognize it, but it was true. I could not explain it.

'Anyway,' said Roy, 'he's not an empty man. You'd give him that, wouldn't you? And he believes without a moment's trouble.'

Slowly we began to walk back along the path. Roy was still thinking of those who did not need to struggle in order to believe in God. He spoke of old Martineau, whose story had caught his imagination. Martineau was a solicitor who had kept open house for me and my friends when I was a very young man. He was cultivated, lively, given to all kinds of interests, and in those days only mildly eccentric. Suddenly, at the age of fifty, he had given away his practice and all his possessions; he joined several quaint religious settlements in turn, and then became a tramp preacher; at that moment he was a pavement artist on the streets of Leeds, drawing pictures with a religious message. I had seen him fairly recently: he was very happy, and surprisingly unchanged.

'He must have been certain of God,' said Roy.

'I'm not at all sure,' I said. 'He was never able to explain what he really believed. That was always the hardest thing to understand.'

'Well, I hope he's certain now,' said Roy. 'If anyone deserves to be, he does.'

Then he spoke with intense feeling:

'I can't think what it's like to be certain. I'm afraid that it's impossible for me. There isn't a place for me.'

His voice was tense, excited, full of passion. As he went on, it became louder, louder than the voice I was used to, but still very clear:

'Listen, Lewis. I could believe in all the rest. I could believe in the Catholic Church. I could believe in miracles. I could believe in the inquisition. I could believe in eternal damnation. If only I could believe in God.'

'And yet you can't,' I said, with his cry still in my ears.

'I can't begin to,' he said, his tone quiet once more. 'I can't get as far as "help Thou mine unbelief".'

We left the ridge of the Roman road, and began to cross the shining fields.

'The nearest I've got is this,' he said. 'It has happened twice. It's completely clear – and terrible. Each time has been on a night when I couldn't sleep. I've had the absolute conviction – it's much more real than anything one can see or touch – that God and His world exist. And everyone can enter and find their rest. Except me. I'm infinitely far away for ever. I am alone and apart and infinitesimally small – and I can't come near.'

I looked at his face in the moonlight. It was pale, but less haunted, and seemed to be relaxed into a kind of exhausted peace. Soon he began to sing, very quietly, in a light, true, reedy voice. Quiet though it was, it became the only sound under the sky. There was a slight ironic smile on his face; for he was singing a child's prayer to be guarded while asleep.

CHAPTER 8

Election of a Fellow

FOR once in his life, Arthur Brown considered that he had been guilty of 'premature action'. After the visit of Lyall and Foulkes, he had considered Roy as good as elected, although as a matter of form he warned me against excessive optimism. Getliffe had told him, in his honest fashion, that he had been deeply impressed by the expert evidence. Even Winslow had remarked that, though the case for Calvert rested mainly on nepotism, there did appear to be a trace of merit there. Brown went steadily ahead, persuaded the college to create a vacancy and to perform the statutory rites so that there could be an election on the first Monday in November.

So far, so good. But it happened that young Luke, a scientist two years Roy's junior, finished a research sooner than anyone expected. Francis Getliffe came in with the news one night. The work was completely sound and definite, he said, though some loose ends needed tying up; it was an important advance in nuclear physics. Getliffe had been intending to bring Luke's name up the following year, but now he wanted him discussed at the fellowship meeting.

'That puts everything back in the melting pot,' said Arthur Brown. 'I don't wish Luke any harm, but it's a pity his confounded apparatus didn't blow up a fortnight ago. Just to give us time to squeeze our young friend in. I daresay Luke is pretty good, I know Getliffe has always thought the world of him. But there's plenty of time to give him a run next year. Well, Eliot, it's a great lesson to me never to count my chickens before they're hatched. I shan't take anything for granted next time I'm backing someone until I actually see him admitted in the Chapel. I don't mind telling you that I shall be relieved if we ever see Calvert there. Well, we've got to make as good a showing as we can. I'm rather inclined to think this is the time to dig in our heels.'

Brown's reflection did not prevent him from letting Francis Getliffe know that his 'present intention' would be to support Luke next year. I did the same. Francis Getliffe was not the man who would 'do a deal', but he was practical and sensible. He would get Luke in any-way, if he waited a few months: we made sure he knew it, before he went to extravagant lengths to fight an election now.

That was all we could do. Roy was still depressed, though not so acutely as on the night of our walk. About his election, I was far more anxious than he.

The day of the election was damp and dark, with low clouds, and a drizzle of rain. In the courts, red and copper leaves of creepers slithered underfoot; umbrellas glistened in the streets as they passed the lighted shops. The meeting was called for the traditional hour of half past four, with tea beforehand; to quieten my nerves, I spent the middle of the afternoon walking in the town, looking at bookshops, greeting acquaintances; the streets were busy, the window lights shone under the dark sky. There was the wistful smell of the Cambridge autumn, and in the tailors' shops gleamed the little handbills, blue letters on white with the names of the week's university teams.

At four o'clock I entered the college by the great gate. The bell was tolling for the meeting, the curtains of the combination room were already drawn. Through the curtains, the lights of the room glowed orange and drew my eyes from the dark court; like any lighted room on a dusky evening, it tempted me with domestic comfort, even though I was wishing that the meeting were all over or that I need not go.

As soon as I got inside, I knew so much of it by heart – the burn-ished table reflecting, not wineglasses and decanters, but inkpots and neat piles of paper in front of each of our chairs – old Gay, the senior fellow, aged seventy-nine, tucking with shameless greed and gusto into an enormous tea, and congratulating everyone on its excellence – the great silver teapots, the muffin covers, the solid fruit-cakes, the pastries – the little groups of two or three colloguing in corners, with sometimes a word, louder than the rest of their conversation, causing others to frown and wonder.

It did not vary meeting by meeting. Nor indeed did the business itself, when the half-hour struck, and the Master, brisk, polite, quick-witted, called us to our places, asked for the minutes, said his opening word about the day's proceedings. For by tradition the day's proceed-ings had to begin first with any questions of college livings and second with financial business. That afternoon there was only a report that someone was considering a call to the one vacant living ('he'll take it,' said Despard-Smith bleakly): but when the Master, so used to these affairs that his courtesy was second nature, his impatience long since dulled, asked: 'Bursar, have you any business for us?' Winslow replied: 'If you please, Master. If you please.' We listened to a long account of the difficulty of collecting rents from some of the college farms. We then heard the problem of the lease of one of the Cambridge shops, and discussed how to buy a house owned by another college, which was desirable in order to rectify an unstrategic frontier. It was routine, it was quite unselfconscious, it was what we were used to: it only happened that I could have dispensed with it that afternoon, that was all.

As usual, the financial business tailed away about half past five. The Master, completely fresh, looked round the table. It was a gift of his to seem formal, and yet natural and relaxed.

'That seems to bring us to our main business, gentlemen,' he said. 'As will be familiar to you, we have appointed today for the election of a fellow. I suggest we follow the custom that is becoming habitual – though it wasn't so when I was a junior fellow' – he smiled at some of the older men, as though there was a story to be told later – 'and have a straw vote first, to see if we can reach a majority for any candidate. After that, we will proceed to a formal vote, in which we have been known to put on a somewhat greater appearance of agreement.'

There were a few suppressed smiles.

'Well,' said the Master, 'the college is well aware of my own position. I thought it right and proper – in fact I felt obliged – to bring up the name of Mr R. C. E. Calvert for consideration. I have told the college, no doubt at excessive length, that in my own view Mr Calvert is our strongest candidate for years past. The college will be familiar with the written reports on his work, and I understand that some fellows had the opportunity of meeting Sir Oulstone Lyall and Colonel Foulkes in person, who probably expressed to them, as they have expressed to me, their opinions upon Mr Calvert.' For a second a slight smile crossed the Master's face. 'The whole case has been explored, if I may say so, with praiseworthy thoroughness. I seem to recall certain discussions in this room and elsewhere. I do not know whether the college now feels that it has heard enough to vote straight away, or whether there are some fellows who would prefer to examine the question further.'

'If you please, Master,' began Winslow. 'I am afraid that I should consider it rushing things,' said Despard-Smith, at the same moment.

'You wish for a discussion, Bursar?' said the Master, his colour a shade higher, but still courteous.

'*Seniores priores,*' Winslow said, inclining his head to Despard-Smith.

'Mr Despard-Smith?' said the Master.

'Master,' Despard-Smith gazed down the table with impressive gloom, 'I am afraid that I must impress upon the college the d-disastrous consequences of a risky election. The consequences may be worse than disastrous, they may be positively catastrophic. I must tell the college that my doubts about Mr Calvert are very far from being removed. With great respect, Master, I am compelled to say that nothing I have yet heard has even begun to remove my doubts. I need not tell the college that nothing would please me more than being able conscientiously to support Mr Calvert. But, as I am at present s-situated, I should be forsaking my duty if I did not raise my doubts at this critical juncture.'

'We should all be grateful,' said the Master formally.

'It is a thankless task,' said Despard-Smith, with sombre relish, 'but I feel it is in the man's own best interests. First of all, I am compelled to ask whether any of Mr Calvert's sponsors can reassure me on this point: if he were to be elected, would he take his share of the' – Despard-Smith stuttered, and then produced one of his descents into solemn anti-climax – 'the bread-and-butter work of the college? I cannot see Mr Calvert doing his honest share of the bread-and-butter work, and a college of this size cannot carry passengers.'

'Perhaps I might answer that, Master?' said Arthur Brown, bland, vigilant, his tone conciliatory, stubbornly prepared to argue all through the night.

The Master was glad to hear him.

'Anyone who knows Mr Calvert,' said Brown roundly, 'could feel no shadow of doubt about his willingness to undertake any duties the college put upon him. Put it another way: he would never let us down, whatever we asked him to do. But I must reply to Mr Despard-Smith that I myself, and I feel sure I am speaking for several fellows, would feel very dubious about the wisdom of our asking Mr Calvert to undertake these bread-and-butter duties. If he is as good at his research work as some of us are inclined to think, he should not be encumbered with more pedestrian activities. We can always find willing horses among ourselves to carry out the more pedestrian activities. As for Mr Calvert, I should be inclined to say that I don't expect a nightingale to crack nuts.'

Despard-Smith shook his head. He went on:

'Many of us have to sacrifice our own interests for the college. I do not see why this young man should be an exception. I am also compelled to ask a second question, to which I attach even more serious importance. Is Mr Calvert sound enough in character to measure up to his responsibilities? We demand from our fellows a high standard of character. It will be scandalous if we ever cease to. It will be the beginning of the end. Speaking from many years' judgement of men, I cannot conceal grave doubts as to whether Mr Calvert's character has developed sufficiently to come up to our high standard.'

It was as open as the conventions allowed. All his life Despard-Smith had been used to damning people at this table by the solemn unspoken doubt. And the debate stayed at that level, full of anger, misunderstandings, personal imperialisms, often echoes of echoes that biased men for or against Roy, that made it urgent for them to vote him in or out that afternoon. For an instant, through my fret and anxiety, I thought this was how all humans judged each other. Lightweight, said one. Dilettante, said another (which I said was the least true comment I could imagine). Charming and modest, said one of the old men, who liked his looks. 'At any rate, he's not prosaic,' declared Jago, the Senior Tutor, the dramatic and brilliant, the most striking figure in the college. Chrystal, out of loyalty to Brown, did not discuss the incident at the feast, but said he intended to reserve judgement. Conceited and standoffish, said someone. Brown met all the opinions imperturbably, softened them when he could, gave a picture of Roy – quiet, devoted to his work, anxious to become a don in the old style. The Master's politeness did not leave him, though it was strained as he heard some of the criticisms; he stayed quick and alert in the chair, and repressed all his sarcasms until the name of Luke came up.

But, when it came, his sarcasm was unfortunate. After the exchange of opinions about Roy's personality, it became clear that we could not lose that afternoon. There were twelve men present (one was still ill).

Election of a Fellow

Of the twelve, six had now declared themselves as immovably determined to vote for Roy in this election – the Master, Brown, Jago, myself, and the two senior fellows. There were four votes against for certain, with Chrystal and Getliffe still on the fence. At this point, Winslow, who had so far only interposed a few rude comments, took over the opposition from Despard-Smith. He talked of the needs of the college, gibed at the Master by speaking contemptuously of the 'somewhat exotic appeal of esoteric subjects', and finished by saying that he would like Getliffe to 'ventilate' the question of Luke. Brown greeted them both with the blandest of encouragement: it was always his tactic to be most reasonable and amiable when things were going well.

In his taut crisp fashion Getliffe described Luke's career in research. He was the son of a dockyard riveter – had won a scholarship from his secondary school, taken high firsts in his triposes ('there's no difference between him and Calvert there,' said Francis), begun research in the Cavendish two years before. 'He's just finished that first bit of work,' said Francis Getliffe. 'He's said the last word on the subject.'

'Isn't that just the trouble with some of your scientific colleagues, Mr Getliffe?' said the Master in a cheerful whisper. 'They're always saying the last word, but they never seem to say the first.'

There was laughter, but not from the scientists. Francis flushed. He was thin-skinned despite his strong will, and he was never self-forgetful on public occasions.

I was violently angry, on edge, distressed. It was innocent, it carried no meaning except that the Master liked to feel the witticism on his tongue: it was incredible that after all his years of intimate affairs he could not resist a moment's score. Francis would not forgive him.

But Arthur Brown was on watch.

'I think I should like it known, Master,' he said in his rich, deliberate, fat man's voice, 'that I for one, and I rather fancy several others, are very much interested in Mr Luke's candidature. If it weren't for what are our judgement the absolutely overwhelming claims of Mr Calvert, it would seem to me very difficult not to vote for the other young man today. He hasn't had the advantages that most of our undergraduates have, and I consider his performance is perfectly

79

splendid. Unfortunately I do feel myself obliged to vote for Mr Calvert this evening, but if Mr Getliffe brings up the other name next term, I rather fancy we can promise him a very sympathetic hearing.'

Brown gave Francis Getliffe, all down the length of the table, his broadest and most affable smile. After a moment, Francis's cheeks creased with a good-natured grin. Brown was matching him with eyes that, behind the broad smile, did not miss the shadow of an expression: as soon as he saw Francis's face relax, he spoke, still richly but very quick to get in first.

'I don't know,' said Brown, 'how far Mr Getliffe intends to press us about Luke this afternoon – in all the circumstances and considering what has just been said?'

Francis hesitated, and then said:

'No, I won't go any farther. I take the strongest exception, Master, to any suggestion that Luke's work is not original. It's as original as any work can be. And I shall propose him at the first opportunity next year. I hope the college doesn't let him slip. He's quite first class. But I'm satisfied that Calvert has done distinguished work, and looks like going on with it. I'm ready to vote for him this afternoon.'

There was a hum, a rustle, a shuffle of papers. I glanced at Winslow: he pulled in his mouth in a grimace that was twisted, self-depreciating, not unpleasant. Arthur Brown was writing with great care on a quarter sheet of paper, and did not look up: the Master gave Francis a fresh, intimate, lively smile, and said:

'I withdraw completely. Don't take it amiss.'

Brown folded up his note, and wrote a name on it. It was passed round to me. Inside it read, simply: WE MIGHT HAVE LOST.

The straw vote followed soon after. There were seven votes for Roy, four against. Chrystal did not vote.

Before we made the statutory promises and gave our formal votes in writing, Despard-Smith got in a bleak speech in which he regretted that he could not vote for Calvert even for the sake of a gesture of unanimity. Winslow said that, for his part, he was prepared to give anyone the satisfaction of meaningless concord. At last, Roy was formally elected by ten votes to two, Despard-Smith and another sticking it out to the last.

The Master smiled. It was nearly seven o'clock, he was no more stale than when we began.

'I should like to congratulate everyone,' he said with his brisk courtesy, 'on having done a good day's work for the college.'

I went out of the room to send the butler in search of Roy. When I returned, the college was indefatigably considering the decoration of the hall, a subject which came on each list of agenda, roused the sharpest animosities, and was never settled. The old fellows took a more dominant part than in the election. Some of them had been arguing over college aesthetics for over fifty years, and they still disagreed with much acerbity. They were vigorously at it when the butler opened the door and announced that Mr Calvert was waiting. According to custom, the Master at once adjourned the meeting, and eyes turned towards the door.

Roy came in, lightfooted, his head high. Under his gown, he was wearing a new dark grey suit. Everyone watched him. His face was pale and grave. No one's eyes could leave him, neither his friends' nor those who had been decrying him half an hour before. As they saw his face, did he seem, I thought, like someone strange, alien, from another species?

He stood at the table, on the opposite side to the Master. The Master himself stood up, and said:

'Mr Calvert, it is my pleasant duty to tell you that you have this day been elected into our society.'

Roy inclined his head.

'If it is agreeable to you,' the Master went on briskly, 'I propose to admit you at once.'

'Yes, Master.' They were Roy's first words.

'Then we will go into chapel this moment,' said the Master. 'Those fellows who are free will perhaps follow us.'

The Master and Roy walked together, both slender and upright, out of the combination room into the first court, dark in the November night. We followed them, two by two, along the wet shining path. We carried some wisps of fog in with us, as we passed through the chapel door, and a haze hung over the painted panels. We crowded into the fellows' stalls, where few of us now attended, except for formal duties such as this – that night Winslow and Francis Getliffe, the doctrinaire unbelievers, did not come.

Roy knelt in the Master's stall, his palms together, the Master's hands pressing his. The clear light voice could be heard all over the chapel, as he took the oath. The Master said the final words, and began shaking Roy's hand. As we moved forward to congratulate him, Brown nudged me and whispered:

'Now I really do believe that fate can't touch us.'

CHAPTER 9

Birthday Celebration

LADY MURIEL gave an intimate dinner party in the Lodge: Arthur Brown presented three bottles on the night of the election, and some more in the week that followed: the Master went round, excelling himself in cheerful, familiar whispers: Bidwell greeted Roy with his sly, open, peasant smile, and said: 'We're all very glad about that, sir. Of course we knew something was going on. We like to keep our eye on things in our own way. I'm very glad myself, if you don't mind me saying so.'

With all of them Roy pretended to be light-hearted: their pleasure would be spoilt unless he were himself delighted. He could not take joy away from those he liked. He even simulated cheerfulness with me, for he knew that I was pleased. But it was no good. The melancholy would not let him go. It was heavier than it had ever been.

He thrashed round like an animal in a cage. He increased his hours of work. Bottles of brandy kept coming into his room, and he began drinking whenever he had to leave his manuscripts. There were evenings when he worked with a tumbler of spirits beside him on the upright desk.

One night I found him in an overall, with pots of paint scattered on the floor.

'What are you doing?' I asked.

'Brightening things up,' he said. His mockery did not leave him for long, even in this state. 'I need things bright round me. Otherwise I might get depressed.'

For days he painted the room from the ceiling to the floor. In the end, the walls gleamed in pink, green, and terra cotta. The desks, once a shining white, he painted also, the platforms pink and the legs green. It picked out their strange shapes. From then on, the whole room was bright with colour, was covered with the vivid desks in their bizarre lines. It took visitors aback, when they called to inspect his manuscripts.

I felt helpless and utterly useless, though he seemed to like having

83

me with him. I feared, with a growing dread, the lightning flashes of elation. I told myself that perhaps this state would pass, and meanwhile tried to prevent him dining in hall or being seen much in the college. I did not want him to do himself harm there – and also I had the selfish and practical reason that I did not want him to do harm to myself or Arthur Brown. I dined with him in the town, we went to see friends in their colleges and houses, I persuaded him to spend several nights in his London flat. Rosalind, who had written to me often during the past eighteen months and who kept sending me presents, only needed a word by telephone: she followed him there and for the first day or two gave him release – temporary, perhaps, thoughtless, certainly, not the release he himself looked for, but still release.

It was, of course, noticed by the college that he had not dined often in hall since his election. But they concluded that he was indulging in a wild round of celebration. They minded very little; by the custom of their class, and of this particular academic society, they did not take much notice of drinking. They nodded in a matter-of-fact and cheerful way. The Master met him once in the court when his eyes were bright with drink, and said to me next day:

'Roy Calvert seems to be going about with vineleaves in his hair. I suppose it's only natural.'

I wished it were as natural as that.

I paid very little attention when Roy asked me to the meeting in honour of Lyall. It was on one of my usual evenings in London, during Roy's stay. I had gone round from my house in Chelsea to his flat in Connaught Street, just behind the Bayswater Road. Rosalind let me in. She was busy trying the effect of some new boxes with bright, painted, porcelain lids.

Roy had taken the flat while he was an undergraduate, but Rosalind was the only woman who had left her stamp on it. Soon after she first stayed there, she set about making it into something more ornate, lush, comfortable, and mondain.

'How do you like them?' she said, viewing the boxes.

'A bit boudoir-ish,' I said.

'Oh dear.' Superficially she was easy to discourage. She and I got on very well in an unexacting fashion.

'How is Roy?'

'The old thing's dressing. I don't think there's much the matter with him.'

'Is he cheerful?'

'He's as cheerful as you bright people usually manage to be. I don't take too much notice of his moods, Lewis. I've been keeping him in bed. There's plenty of life in the old thing still,' she said with a dying fall. One of her uses to him, I thought suddenly, was that she treated him as though he were a perfectly ordinary man. She loved what to her meant romance, the pink lamp-shades in the restaurant car, the Italian sky, great restaurants, all the world of chic and style: at a distance Roy was romantic because he gave her those: in the flesh, though she loved him dearly, he was a man like other men, who had better be pampered though 'there was not much wrong with him'.

Roy entered in a dressing-gown, shaved and fresh.

'You here?' he said to me in mock surprise. And to Rosalind: 'What may you be doing, dear?'

'Flirting with Lewis,' she said immediately.

He smacked her lightly, and they discussed where they should go for dinner, so that he might know what clothes to wear. 'We're not taking you, old boy,' said Roy over her shoulder: he gave her just the choice that made her eyes rounder, Claridge's, the Carlton, Monseigneur's. He seemed far less depressed than when I last saw him, and I was nothing but amused when he asked me to the Lyall celebration.

'We shan't take you tonight,' he said. 'I'm simply jealous of you with Rosalind. But I'll take you somewhere else on Thursday. You need to come and hear us honour old Lyall.'

'Oulstone Lyall?'

'Just so. I need you to come. You'll find it funny. He'll be remarkably stuffed.'

I soon had reason to try to remember that invitation exactly, for I was compelled to learn this state of his right through; but I was almost certain that there was nothing dionysiac about him at all that evening, no lightning flash of unnatural gaiety. It was probable that his ease and pleasure with Rosalind made his spirits appear higher than they were. In reality, he was still borne down, though he could appear carefree as he entertained Rosalind or laughed at me.

Sir Oulstone Lyall was seventy years of age that autumn, and scholars in all the oriental subjects had arranged this meeting as a compliment. It was arranged for the Thursday afternoon in the rooms of the British Academy. There were to be accounts of the contemporary position in various fields of scholarship – with the intention of bringing out, in a discreet and gentlemanly way, the effect and influence of Lyall's own work. It was a custom borrowed from German scholars, and the old-fashioned did not like it. Nevertheless, most of the Orientalists in the country came to the meeting.

The Master travelled up from Cambridge that morning and lunched with Roy and me. Away from the Lodge, he was in his most lively form, and it was he who first made a light remark about Sir Oulstone.

'Between ourselves,' said the Master, 'it's a vulgar error to suppose that distinguished scholars are modest souls who shrink from the glory. Knighthoods and addresses on vellum – that's the way to please distinguished scholars. I advise you to study the modesty of our venerable friend this afternoon.'

Roy laughed very loudly. There was something wild in the sound; at once I was worried. I wished I could get him alone.

'And if you want to observe human nature in the raw,' said the Master, jumping into his favourite topic, 'it's a very interesting point whether you ought to go out and find a pogrom or just watch some of our scientific colleagues competing for honours.'

'How did Lyall get there?' said Roy, in a piercing insistent tone.

'Between ourselves,' the Master replied, 'I've always felt that he was rather an old humbug.'

'I've heard a story about Erzberger. Master, do you remember anything?' said Roy, with abnormal concentration.

The Master did remember. He was himself modest and humble, his professional life was blameless. But he was always ready to indulge in a detached, abstract, and cheerful cynicism. He did not notice that Roy's glance was preternaturally attentive and acute – or perhaps he was stimulated by it.

For the rest of our lunch until it was time to walk up to Piccadilly, he told Roy what he knew of Lyall and Erzberger. The Master had actually met Erzberger when they were both young men.

'He was an astonishingly ugly Jew. I thought he was rather pushful and aggressive. He once asked me – "What does an outsider like me have to do to get a fellowship?" ' But, so we gathered from the

Master, he was brilliantly clever, and had a rarer gift than cleverness, a profound sense of reality. He went to work with Lyall, and they published several papers together on the medieval trade-routes in Central Asia. 'It was generally thought that the real views were Erzberger's.' Then there was an interval of several years, in which Erzberger told a good many people that he was preparing a major work. 'He never believed in underrating himself.' He had never been healthy, and he died in his thirties of consumption. No unfinished work was ever published, but two years after his death Lyall produced his own magnum opus, the foundation of his fame, on the subject on which they had worked together. In the preface he acknowledged his gratitude to his lamented friend Erzberger for some fruitful suggestions, and regretted his untimely death.

'Just so,' said Roy. 'Just so.'

It was a dark, foggy afternoon as we walked up Piccadilly. Cars' headlights were making swathes in the mist, and Roy's voice sounded more than ever clear as he talked to the Master all the way to Burlington House. He was intensely, brilliantly excited. A laugh kept ringing out. On the Master's other side, I walked silent and apprehensive in the murk. Could I give him calm, could anyone? Was it sensible or wise to try now? I was tied by doubt and ignorance. I knew he was suffering, but I did not know how justified my apprehensions were.

As we took off our coats, and the Master left us for a moment, I made one attempt.

'Are you desperately anxious to attend this pantomime?' I said.

'Why do you ask?' said Roy sharply.

'There are other things which might amuse us –'

'Oh no,' said Roy. 'I need to be here.' Then he smiled at me. 'Don't you stay. It was stupid of me to drag you here. You're certain to be bored. Let's meet later.'

I hesitated, and said:

'No. I may as well come in.'

The Academy room was quite small and cosy; the lights were thrown back from the fog-darkened windows. There were half a dozen men on the dais, among them Lyall and Colonel Foulkes. The Master was placed among minor dignitaries in the front row beneath. Perhaps sixty or seventy men were sitting in the room, and it struck me that nearly all of them were old. Bald heads shone, white hair gleamed, under the lights. As the world grew more precarious, rich young men did not take to these eccentric subjects with such confidence: amateurs flourished most, as those old men had flourished, in a tranquil and secure age.

Roy found me a chair, and then suddenly went off by himself to sit under the window. My concern flared up: but in a moment the meeting began.

The chairman made a short speech, explaining that we had come to mark Sir Oulstone's seventieth birthday and express our gratitude for his work. As the speech went on, Sir Oulstone's head inclined slowly weightily, with dignity and satisfaction, at each mention of his own name.

Then came three accounts of Central Asian studies. The first, given by an Oxford professor with a high, fluting voice, struck me as straightforward old-fashioned history – the various conquering races that had swept across the plateau, the rise and fall of dynasties, and so on. The second, by Foulkes, dealt with the deciphering of the linguistic records. Foulkes was a rapid, hopping, almost unintelligible speaker, and much of the content was technical and would have been, even if I could have heard what he said, unintelligible to me: yet one could feel that he was a master of his subject. He paid a gabbling, incoherent, and enthusiastic compliment to Roy's work on Soghdian.

The third account I found quite fascinating. It was delivered in broken English by a refugee, and it described how the history of Central Asia between 500 B.C. and A.D. 1000 had been studied by applying the methods of archaeology and not relying so much on documentary evidence – by measuring areas of towns at different periods, studying the tools men used and their industrial techniques. It was the history of common men in their workaday lives, and it made sense of some of the glittering, burbling, dynastic records. The pioneer work had been done over forty years before, said the speaker vigorously, in the original articles of Lyall and Erzberger: then the real great step forward had been taken by Lyall himself, in his famous and classic book.

There was steady clapping. Sir Oulstone inclined his head very slowly. The speaker bowed to him, and Sir Oulstone inclined his head again.

The speech came to an end. It had been a masterpiece of exposition, and the room stirred with applause. There followed a few perfunctory questions, more congratulations to Sir Oulstone from elderly scholars in the front row, one or two more questions. The meeting was warm with congratulation and self-congratulation, feet were just beginning to get restless, it was nearly time to go.

Then I heard Roy's voice, very clear.

'Mr Chairman, may I ask a question?'

He was standing by the window, with vacant chairs round him. Light fell directly on his face, so that it looked smooth and young. He was smiling, his eyes were brilliant, shining with exaltation.

'Of course, Mr –'

'Calvert,' said Roy.

'Ah yes, Mr Calvert,' said the chairman. Sir Oulstone smiled and bowed.

'We've listened to this conspectus of Asian social history,' said Roy precisely. 'I should like to ask – how much credit for the present position should be given to the late Dr Erzberger?'

No one seemed to feel danger. The chairman smiled at the lecturer, who replied that Erzberger deserved every credit for his share in the original publications.

'Thank you,' said Roy. 'But it does not quite meet my point. This subject has made great progress. Is it possible for no one to say how much we need to thank Dr Erzberger for?'

The chairman looked puzzled. There was a tension growing in the room. But Sir Oulstone felt nothing of it as he rose heavily and said:

'Perhaps I can help Mr Calvert, sir.'

'Thank you,' said the chairman.

'Thank you, Sir Oulstone,' came Roy's voice, clear, resounding with sheer elation.

'I am grateful to my young friend, Mr Calvert,' said Sir Oulstone, suspecting nothing, 'for bringing up the name of my old and respected collaborator. It is altogether appropriate that on this occasion when you are praising me beyond my deserts, my old helper should not be forgotten. Some of you will remember, though it was well before Mr Calvert's time,' Sir Oulstone smiled, 'that poor Erzberger, after helping me in my first efforts, was cut off in his prime. That was a tragedy for our subject. It can be said of him, as Newton said of Cotes, that if he had lived we should have learned something.'

'Just so,' said Roy. 'So he published nothing except the articles with you, Sir Oulstone?'

'I am afraid that is the fact.'

Roy said, quietly, with extreme sharpness:

'Could you tell us what he was working on before he died?'

By now many in the room had remembered the old scandal. Faces were frowning, intent, distressed, curious. But Sir Oulstone was still impervious, self-satisfied, opaque. He still looked at Roy as though he were a young disciple. Sir Oulstone acted as though he had never heard of the scandal: if there were no basis for it, if he were quite innocent, that could have been true.

As Roy waited for the answer, his glance rested on me. For a second I looked into his flashing, triumphant eyes, begging him to stop. Fiercely, impatiently, he shook his head. He was utterly possessed.

'Alas,' said Sir Oulstone, 'we have no trace of his last years of work.'

'Did he not work – on the subject of your own book?'

'There was no trace, I say.' Suddenly Sir Oulstone's voice was cracked and angry.

'Did no one publish his manuscripts?'

'We could find no manuscripts when he died.'

'You could find no result of years of work?' cried Roy in acute passionate incredulity.

'He left nothing behind him.'

'*Remarkable.*' The single word dropped into the hushed room. It plucked all nerves with its violence, scorn, and extreme abandon.

Sir Oulstone had turned bitterly angry.

'I do not consider this is very profitable. Perhaps, as Mr Calvert is a newcomer to our subject, I had better refer to my obituaries of Erz-berger in the two journals. I regard these questions as most unnecessary, sir.'

He sat down. Roy was still on his feet.

'Thank you, Mr Chairman,' he said in his normal tone, quiet, composed, and polite. 'I am so sorry to have taken the time of the meeting.'

He bowed to the chair, and went out alone.

CHAPTER 10

A Moment of Grace

THE meeting broke up, and the Master took me off to tea at the Athenaeum. On the way down St James's Street, the windows of the clubs glowing comfortably warm through the deepening fog, the Master said:

'Roy Calvert seems a little upset, Eliot. I suppose it's a phase we all go through.'

'Yes.'

'He's been overstrained, of course. Between you and me, our judicious colleagues have something to answer for. It was imbecile to make him wait so long for his fellowship.'

For once the Master was in a thoroughly bad temper. Over the toasted teacakes in the long club morning room, he broke out:

'It's nothing to worry about, Eliot. I did silly things when I was a young man. I suppose he hasn't got his feet on the earth quite as firmly as I had, but he's not so different as all that. We must just make sure that all turns out well.'

In his irritation, he let me see something of what he felt for Roy. The Master believed that Roy was far more gifted than himself; he knew that Roy was capable of the scholarly success he could never have managed – for Roy had the devotion, the almost obsessed devotion, which a scholar needs, as well as the touch of supreme confidence. The Master, who found it easier to go about from meeting to meeting using his quick wits, who in his heart felt diffident and uncreative, admired those gifts which he had never had. But also he felt an attraction of like for like. Roy's elegance and style – with those the Master could compete. Often among his colleagues he had the illusion that he was just playing at being an ordinary man. At times, in daydreams, he had seen himself like Roy.

I noticed too that, as though by instinct, he pretended that nothing much was wrong. Often it seemed to him wiser to soften the truth. The worst did not always happen. Before I left, he said, almost in his cheerful whisper:

'I don't think our colleagues need to be worried by any news of this afternoon's entertainment, do you, Eliot? We know how easily worried they are, and I shouldn't like to feel that the Bursar was losing sleep because one of the younger fellows has been overworking.'

The club was filling with men who had been present at the meeting, and the Master went across to them, pleasant-mannered, fresh-faced, not over-troubled.

I went to see Roy, but found Rosalind alone in the flat. She said he had gone out to buy some wine; they were to dine at home that night.

'It will be very nice, having the old thing to myself for once,' she said, and I could not help smiling, though this was not the most suitable time for her brand of realism.

She had seen him since the meeting. 'He's nice and relaxed,' she said. 'He's sweet when there's nothing on his mind. I wish he weren't so elusive sometimes.' She added: 'I don't know what's taken the weight off his mind. He did say that he'd made a frightful ass of himself somewhere.'

The phrase meant nothing to her, but it was a private joke of his and mine, borrowed from an elderly friend.

I saw Roy for an instant just before I went away. One glance reassured me. He was himself, composed, gentle, at ease.

'How are you?' I asked.

'Very much all right,' he said.

As I walked into the foggy street, I heard his voice call cheerfully from the window:

'Shan't be in Cambridge till next week. Come back before then. Need to talk to you.'

In college I was watching for any sign of the story coming through: I was ready to laugh it off, to explain Roy's action in terms designed to make it seem matter-of-fact, uninteresting, a mixture of a joke and an academic controversy. It was only to Arthur Brown that I confided there had been a scene; and even with him, stout-hearted, utterly dependable, capable of accepting anything in his friends, I was not quite frank – for by that time in my life I was already broken in to keeping secrets, often more so than was good for me or others. I paled down both Roy's despondency and his outburst. Arthur Brown said: 'We shall have to be very careful about our young friend.'

Then, the politician never far away, he wondered what effect the news would have upon the college, and how we could conceal it.

Curiously enough, very little news arrived, and that we were able to smother. Colonel Foulkes came to Cambridge for a meeting of electors, and I discovered that he thought nothing specially unusual had happened. Whether this was because Roy could do no wrong in his eyes, or because he really did not like Lyall, or because he was abnormally blank to human atmosphere, I could not decide. He said: 'Very interesting point, Calvert's. Perhaps not the best time to bring it up. These scholars aren't men of the world, you know. They don't learn tact. Don't have the corners rubbed off as you do in the army.'

He was so simple that I was completely at a loss, but I took him into hall, and he talked casually about the Lyall celebratory meeting and enthusiastically about Roy. The most subtle acting would not have been so effective. Some rumour about Roy had reached Despard-Smith, and he began to produce it, with solemn gratification, the next night: but Winslow, fresh from hearing Foulkes, endowed with nothing like the persistence in rancour that vitalized the old clergyman, said: 'If you please, Despard. Shall we wait until the young man starts throwing knives about in hall? In point of fact, he seems to have pleasant table manners, which I must say is more than one is accustomed to expect.'

Within three days of the meeting, the Master was able to forget his first impression and to treat the whole affair as though it had been a mischievous, high-spirited trick, like teasing the doctor after the feast. I seemed the only person who could not domesticate it so.

Even Roy, when I saw him at his flat the following week, was free from any cloud, full of fun.

'What have you been doing these days in Cambridge?' he asked.

'Nothing much.'

'Covering up tracks?'

'A little.'

He gave me a curiously protective smile.

'When you took me on, old boy,' he said, 'you took all this on yourself.'

'How are you now?' I said, but there was no need for me to ask. He was entirely tranquil.

'Better than I've been for weeks and months,' he said, with ringing joy.

He added:

'How are you? You're looking worse than I did. Too much worry. Too much drink. Above all,' his eyes flashed with the purest mischief, 'above all, not enough sleep.'

I grinned. It was hard to resist his spirits, it was hard to retain my fears.

'We'll get you better at "Monty".' Roy, precise in his speech, isolated the word to remind me of Lady Muriel; for she and Lord Boscastle, after calling the family mansion 'Bossy', took to nicknames of places with the utmost naturalness.

'Meanwhile,' said Roy, 'I need to give you some fresh air. I need to take you a walk in the park.'

We left the flat empty, for Rosalind had returned home: Roy was going to Cambridge next day. We entered the park by the Albion gate. A gusty wind was blowing from the west, the trees soughed, the last leaves were spinning under the lamps in the street. The clouds were low, it was dark early; through the trees one could see the lights of the tall houses in Bayswater Road. The wind blew in our faces as we walked down to the Serpentine. It was fresh as a night by the sea.

'It's wonderful not to be wretched,' cried Roy. 'It's all gone! It's wonderful to be free!'

He looked at me in the twilight.

'You're glum, Lewis. You've been pitying me for being wretched, haven't you? You can pity me for the gloom. That was frightful. Don't pity me for the time when I broke out. It was very exciting. For a few minutes I was let out of prison. Everything was rosy-edged.'

'It might be a slightly expensive excitement,' I said.

He smiled.

'It won't do me any good with Oulstone, will it?'

There was a trace of satisfaction in his tone. 'Oh, never mind. I wasn't cut out to be stuffed. I'll go on doing my work. But I don't want anything in return that those people can give me. I need them to leave me alone, that's all. I'll go on with the work. It's become a habit. But it isn't going to settle me, old boy. Once I hoped it might. Now I know it can't. I need to search elsewhere. I shall get there in the end.'

The wind blew, his voice was clear and happy. He said earnestly:

'Pity me for the gloom. But it made me see things – that otherwise I never could have seen. Don't think that all I told you was nonsense. Don't think I've forgotten what I saw.'

'I believe that,' I said.

He stopped suddenly, and held my arm.

'Lewis, why are you so sombre? What is hurting you?'

I did not reply.

'Are you thinking that this will happen to me *again*?'

'It may,' I said, half-miserably, half-intoxicated by his hope. 'Anyway, you ought to be ready. You won't always be so happy, will you?'

'It may,' Roy repeated. 'It may. I need to take it if it comes.' He had spoken evenly, then his voice rose: 'It's something to know the worst.' He was smiling in the dark, with no cover and no reserve: it seemed as though for a second he were deliberately challenging fate.

The next time he spoke, it was very quietly and intimately. We were getting near the water, as he said:

'I shall be all right if I can only find somewhere to rest.'

He added, gently:

'I shall find my way there. Dear old boy, it may not be the way you'd choose for me. But that doesn't matter so much to you, does it?'

We walked along the bank, the gale grew louder, the little waves lapped at our feet. He passed from his hopes to mine, selflessly mischievous, selflessly protective. For a while, in the magic of his spirits and the winter night, I could almost believe as he believed, hope as he hoped, and be as happy.

Yet my heart was rent. Never in my life had I so passionately longed to forget all that life had taught me. I wanted the magic to endure, I wanted to believe that he would find rest.

I could not. All I might do was try not to shorten by a minute this calm and beautiful state. If he must learn, let it not be through me. He was the clearest-sighted of men: for once his eyes were dulled: let them stay dulled, rather than see what I saw. Much of my life I had been in search of truth, of the truth about personalities, about the natures of those round me; I would have rather thrown it all away, lose such insight as I might have, sacrifice what I knew, than that I should be seeing the truth now. And if, and if I were seeing the truth, then I prayed that Roy never would.

For I believed that he would not find peace on this earth. He hoped so calmly that night, with such a calm and beautiful hope, that he could escape the burden of self, struggle from under the weight of life, and so leave melancholy and despair behind for ever; he knew they threatened him, but he could conquer them once he broke loose from the chains of self. He tasted, for the illusory moments that we all know, what it was like to be free – to be free of the confines of one's personality, through another person, through the enchantments of the many forms of love, through the ecstasy of the flesh (for Roy was freer, less clamped in his own mould, because of the odd secret nights he spent with women he would never see again). He had tasted what it was like to long to believe in God. And that night, while we walked in the winter gale, the Augustinian phrase kept ringing through his mind – 'Thou has created us for Thyself and our hearts can never rest until they rest in Thee.'

It sounded not as a threat, but as a promise. Perhaps that was the way he would find rest. That night he felt almost certain that it was the way. But yet, he was so confident and liquid in his hope, if not that way he would find another. There was a state of grace: perhaps it would come to him through God, perhaps in some other fashion. But he would find it, and be safe from the night of despair.

If it could be so, I thought in pain. If it could be so. Yet now I had seen him go through a bout of melancholy to the end, through the desperate sadness to the fantastic release. I believed it was part of his nature to feel that suffering, to undergo that clear-eyed misery, as much a part of him as his mischief, his kindness, his physical elegance, his bone and flesh. It was so deep that nothing could change it. He might think he had escaped, but the melancholy would crush him down once more. It was a curse that no one could take away until he died.

He was teasing me, his laugh was blown away on the wind. I would have given all the future for that moment to stay still. I did not dare to see the future. This was a moment of grace.

If I were right, there must come a time when he would know his nature. Some day his clear eyes would see. When would he know?

PART TWO

THE GLIMMER OF HOPE

CHAPTER II

Serene Night by the Sea

ROY returned to college for the rest of the Michaelmas term. His reading-lamp was alight all day; his window in the turret gleamed above the court through the dark afternoons and the December evenings. He dined regularly at high table; and no one meeting him there, polite, cheerful, teasing with a solemn face, could have guessed what he had just passed through. Though I had seen it, I often forgot. His step on my stairs at night now meant ease, and well-being. He was quite unstrained, as though he had only to wait for good things to happen.

After he had talked to them at dinner, some of his opponents felt he had been misjudged. He sat by Winslow's side for several nights running. He had a respect for the cross-grained, formidable, unsuccessful man, and he happened to know his son. It was generally thought that Dick Winslow was nothing but a stupid waster, but Roy both liked him and felt his father's vulnerable, unassuageable love. So they talked about Dick – Winslow pretending to be ironic, realistic, detached. Roy was very gentle, both at the time, and afterwards, when he said to me: 'It must be dreadful, never being able to give yourself away. He needs to stop keeping his lips so tight, doesn't he?'

Roy did not, however, make the slightest progress towards melting Despard-Smith. He began by making a genuine attempt, for Ralph Udal's sake: Despard-Smith was the most influential member of the livings committee, and, if Udal were to have a chance of a college living, the old man had to be placated. But Roy met with a signal failure. He suppressed the glint in his eye that usually visited him in the presence of the self-satisfied and self-important, those who seemed to him invulnerable and whom he called 'the stuffed'. Deferentially he discussed the Church of England, college finance, and early heresies. Despard-Smith replied bleakly and with certainty, looking at Roy with uncompromising suspicion. Roy led up to the question of a living for Udal. 'I can't speak for my colleagues, Calvert,' said Despard-Smith, meaning that he could. 'But I should personally regard it as nothing short of scandalous to let a man of Udal's age eat the bread of idleness. It certainly would not be in the man's own best interests. When he has got down to the c-collar for twenty or thirty years, then perhaps he might come up for consideration.'

'He wants peace to think,' said Roy.

'The time to get peace, as some of us know,' said Despard-Smith, 'is when one has borne the heat and burden of the day.'

Roy knew it was no good. But his next question was innocent enough. He asked who would get the vacant living, which was the second best in the college's gift.

'I've told you, I can't speak for my colleagues,' said Despard-Smith reprovingly. 'But I should personally regard Anderson as a very suitable choice. He was slightly junior to me here, so he is no longer in his first youth. But he is a very worthy man.'

'Should you say he was witty?' said Roy, no longer able to repress himself, or deciding it was not worth while.

'I don't know what you mean, Calvert.'

'Worthy people are not witty,' said Roy. 'That's how we can tell they're worthy.'

He looked at Despard-Smith with steady, serious eyes.

'Isn't that so, Despard?'

Despard-Smith looked back with mystification, anger, and disapproval.

From that time on, Roy selected Despard-Smith for his most demure and preposterous questions – partly because the old man incited him, and partly because, knowing of Despard-Smith's speeches over the election, Roy had a frail and unsaintly desire for revenge. Whenever he could catch Despard-Smith in the court or the combination room, Roy advanced on him with a shimmering net of solemn requests for information. Despard-Smith became badgered, increasingly hostile, and yet mystified. He was never sure whether

Roy might not be in earnest, at least part of the time. 'What an extraordinary young man Calvert is,' he used to grumble in a creaking, angry voice. 'He's just made a most extraordinary remark to me –'

The Boscastles had gone down to the villa at Roquebrune late in November, and the Master and his family followed them a few days before Christmas. Roy spent Christmas with his family, and I with my wife in Chelsea. She asked me to stay a little longer, and so I arrived at Monte Carlo the day after Roy.

I had lain awake all night in the train, and went to bed in the afternoon. When I woke it was early evening, and from my window I could see lights springing out along the coast. Roy was not in his room, was not in the hotel. He had already told me that we were dining that night out at the Boscastles'. It was not time to dress, and I took a walk away from the sea, through the hilly streets at the back of the town.

I was thinking of nothing, it was pleasant to smell the wood smoke and garlic in the narrow streets: then I heard two voices taking an amorous farewell. A woman's said something in Italian, was saying good-bye: then another, light, reedy, very clear in the crisp, cold air. '*Ciao*,' he called back to her, and I saw in the light from a window a girl disappearing into the house. '*Ciao*,' she called, when I could no longer see her: her voice was rough but young. '*Ciao*,' Roy replied again, softly, and then he saw me.

He was disconcerted, and I extremely amused. I knew as well as he about his minor escapades: some woman would catch his fancy, in a shop, in a theatre, behind the desk in an hotel, and he would pursue her with infinite concentration for a day. He sometimes told me of his rebuffs, but never of his conquests; and he did not like being caught at the end of one.

'Remarkable Italian they speak here,' he said with a somewhat precarious dignity, as we descended into the clean, bright, shop-lined streets. He gave me a pedantic lecture on the Italian of Liguria contrasted with Provençal; it was no doubt correct, his linguistic skill was beyond question, but I was grinning.

We came to the square; the flowers stood out brilliantly under the lights; as though unwillingly, Roy grinned too.

'It's just my luck,' he said. 'Why need you come that way?'

A motor-car drove in to take us to the Villa Prabaous.

'The Boscastles have hired three cars for all the time they're here,' said Roy. 'Plus two which they need occasionally for visitors. There's nothing like economy. They sweep in and out all day.'

On our way, along the edge of the calm sea, he was speculating with interest, with amusement, over the Boscastle fortune. 'Poor as church mice', 'they haven't two sixpences to rub together', 'it's really heroic of them to keep up the house' – we had both heard those descriptions from Lady Muriel and her friends. Yet, with occasional economies, such as taking a villa at Roquebrune, the Boscastles lived more grandly than any of the rich people we knew. The problem was complicated by the fact that the estate had, as a device through which they paid less taxes, been made into a company. The long necklace of lights twinkled through the pines on Cap Martin: Roy had just satisfied himself that, if Lord Boscastle died next day, his will would not be proved at less than £200,000.

The Villa Prabaous was rambling, large, very ugly, and, like many houses on the north side of the Mediterranean, seemed designed for a climate much hotter than where it found itself. That night an enormous log fire sputtered and smoked in the big dining-room, and we were all cold, except Lady Muriel. For Lady Muriel it provided an excellent opportunity to compare the degree of discomfort with that of several mansions she had visited in her childhood, and to advise her sister-in-law how, if one's experience were great enough, these privations could be overcome. Lady Muriel was not a passive guest.

It was exactly the same party as when Roy was first presented to the Boscastles. Mrs Seymour was staying at the villa; I had escaped her for some time past, but now found myself sitting next to her at dinner.

'It must be wonderful to see heaps and heaps of counters being pushed towards you,' she said.

'It must,' I said.

'Yes, Doris?' said Lady Muriel loudly. 'Have you been playing today?'

Mrs Seymour giggled, and was coy. I was surprised and irritated (uncharitably, but she annoyed me more than was reasonable) to meet her there. One reason, I thought, was that Lord Boscastle should never miss his evening bridge; Mrs Seymour, like Lady Muriel and Joan, was a player of good class.

Sure of his game that night, out of which I had managed to disentangle myself, Lord Boscastle wished to spend dinner talking of Saint-Simon's memoirs, which he had just been reading. I would willingly have listened, but Roy distracted him by asking his opinion of various fashionable persons staying in Monte Carlo and the villas near. Lord Boscastle, as I now knew for certain, took a perverse pleasure in acting in character. He was always ready, in fact, to caricature himself. And so, as Roy produced name after name with a flicker in his eye, Lord Boscastle was prompt with his comment. 'I don't know him, of course, but I shouldn't have thought he was anything out of the ordinary, should you have thought so?' 'I don't know whether any of you have met her, but I shouldn't have expected her to be specially distinguished.'

The Master chuckled. It was hard to guess precisely what he thought of his brother-in-law's turns; but it was patent that he was delighted to see Roy so manifestly happy and composed. The Master smiled at me with camaraderie, but rather as though I had always exaggerated the fuss. Yet I was sure that he had not shared our knowledge with anyone in the villa that night, certainly not with his wife.

Lady Muriel herself, not perceiving any secrets round her, had been led to mention acquaintances of hers who were wintering in the town. She finished by saying:

'Doris tells me the Houston Eggars have arrived. No doubt for a very short holiday. They are not staying at your hotel, I think?'

'No,' said Roy.

'Doris! Where are they staying?'

Mrs Seymour opened her eyes vaguely, then gave the name of an hotel slightly more modest than the Hermitage.

'I'm glad to hear it.' Lady Muriel looked at me accusingly. 'I should think it is very suitable to their income.'

After dinner, just before the bridge four broke away, I saw Joan take Roy aside. She was wearing a blue dress, and I thought how much prettier she was becoming. She asked him straight out:

'Why do you lead my uncle on? Why don't you make him talk about something worth while?'

'Too stupid,' said Roy.

'He's not too stupid.'

'Of course he's not. I am.'

'You're impossible.' She had begun to laugh, as she could not help doing whenever the demure and solemn expression came over him. Then she turned fierce again, stayed by him, and went on quarrelling as Lord Boscastle led off Lady Muriel, Mrs Seymour, and the Master for their bridge. Meanwhile Lady Boscastle was commanding: 'Lewis, bring your chair here, please. I am going to scold you a little.'

She glanced at me sarcastically, affectionately, charmingly, through her lorgnette.

'Yes,' she said, as I came beside her, arranged her table, filled her glass, 'I think I must scold you a little.'

'What have I done now?' I said.

'I notice that you are wearing a soft shirt tonight. It looks quite a nice shirt, my dear Lewis, but this is not quite the right time. What have you to say for yourself?'

'I loathe stiff shirts,' I said. 'This is very much more comfortable.'

'My dear boy, I should call that excuse rather – untravelled.' It was her final word of blame. 'The chief aim of civilized society is not comfort, as you know very well. Otherwise you would not be sitting in a draughty room listening to an old woman –'

She was an invalid, her temples were sunk in, her skin minutely wrinkled; yet she could make me feel that she was twenty years younger, she could still draw out the protests of admiration. And, when I made them, she could still hear them with pleasure.

'Quite nicely said.' She smiled as she spoke. 'Perhaps you would always have found some compensations in civilized society. Though we did our best to make you obey the rules.'

She flicked her lorgnette, and then went on:

'But it's not only soft shirts, my dear Lewis. Will you listen to your old friend?'

'To anything you like to tell me.'

'I want you to be a success. You have qualities that can take you anywhere you choose to go.'

'What are they?'

'Come! I've heard you called the least vain of men.'

'Not if you're going to praise me,' I said.

She smiled again.

'I needn't tell you that you're intelligent,' she said. 'You're also very obstinate. And for a man of – what is it, my dear?'

'Thirty.'

'For a man of thirty, you know something of the human heart.' She went on quickly:

'Believe me about those things. I have spent my life among successful men. You can compete with them. But they conformed more than you do, Lewis. I want you to conform a little more.'

'I don't parade my opinions –'

'We shouldn't mind if you did. I have seen that you are a radical. No one minds what a man of distinction thinks. But there are other things. Sometimes I wish you would take some lessons from your friend Roy. He couldn't do anything untravelled if he tried. I wish you would go to his tailor. I think you should certainly go to his barber. Your English accent will pass. Your French is deplorable. You need some different hats.'

I laughed.

'But these things are important,' said Lady Boscastle. 'You can't imagine your friend Roy not attending to them.'

'He's a good-looking and elegant man,' I said.

'That's no reason for your being too humble. You can do many things that he can't. Believe me, Lewis. If you took care, you could look quite impressive.'

Then she focused her lorgnette on me. Her porcelain eyes were glittering with indulgence and satire. 'Perhaps Roy is really much more humble than you are. I think you are very arrogant at heart. You just don't care. You have the sort of carelessness, my dear boy, that I have heard people call "aristocratic". I do not remember knowing any aristocrats who possessed it.'

Just as the car drew up outside to take Roy and me back to Monte Carlo, the Boscastles' son returned from a dinner party. He was only eighteen and still at school; he had been born to them when Lady Boscastle was nearly forty and they had given up hope of a child. I had not met him before, and caught just a glimpse before we left. He was slender, asthenic, with a wild, feminine face.

It was after midnight when our car dropped us at the hotel, and, like other pairs of friends in sight of the casino, we had a disagreement. One of us was addicted to gambling, and the other hated it. Some might have expected Roy to play lavishly the night through: but the facts were otherwise. It was I who spent the next two hours at baccarat; it was Roy who stood behind me, smoking cigarette after cigarette, who walked irritably round the square, who entered again hoping that I should have finished.

'Excellent,' he said, when at last I had had enough.

'Why didn't you come in?' I said, as we took a walk in the casino gardens.

'I've something better to do with my money,' said Roy, as though he were the guardian of all the prudent virtues.

I had won forty pounds, but that did not placate him.

'It'll only lead you on,' he said. 'I wish you'd lost.'

'It will pay for my holiday,' I said.

'You'll lose it all tomorrow. And a lot more.'

It was a brilliant frosty night, utterly calm on the sea. The two lights of the harbour shone, one green, one red, and their reflection lay still upon the water. The stars were bright in the moonless sky, and below the lights of the coast road blazed out.

'Extremely serene,' said Roy. 'Now I shall go and sleep.'

We were tired and contented. A few moments later, the porter at the hotel said that there was a telegram for Mr Calvert. As he read it, Roy made a grimace.

'Not quite so serene,' he said, and gave it to me. It was from Rosalind, the English words curiously distorted on the way. It must have been written as something like:

ARRIVE IN CANNES TOMORROW TWENTYNINTH PROPOSE STAY
MONTE CARLO UNLESS INCONVENIENT FOR YOU SHALL APPEAR
THIRTYFIRST UNLESS YOU SEND MESSAGE TO AMBASSADEURS
SAYING NO.

CHAPTER 12

Some Women

WE discovered that, several days before, Rosalind had reserved a room, not at the Hermitage but at the Hôtel de Paris. Whether this was to save Roy's face or simply to show off, no one could be sure. Rosalind's origins were similar to mine, though less poverty-stricken: she still lived in our native town, where she earned a large income for a young woman: she had a flair for bold dramatic design and, applying her usual blend of childish plaintiveness and business-like determination, took £600 a year from an advertising company. She lived simply at home and spent her money on extravagant presents and holidays at the most expensive hotels, which she examined with shrewd business-like eyes and basked in with a hearty provincial gusto.

When he realized that she was coming not on a sudden caprice but by plan, Roy was amused, irritated, pleased, hunted, and somewhat at a loss. He knew he could not keep her unobserved while the Boscastle party spent its days in Monte Carlo; he knew that Rosalind would see that did not happen. But he was too fond of her, too clear-sightedly, intimately, physically fond of her, to forbid her to come.

He decided that he must brazen it out. Lady Muriel and Joan lunched with us at the hotel, and half-way through Roy said, less unselfconsciously than usual:

'By the way, Lady Mu, a friend of mine is coming down on Thursday.'

'Who may that be, Roy?'

'A girl called Rosalind Wykes. I brought her in for tea one day, do you remember? I only knew she was coming this morning.'

'Indeed.' Lady Muriel looked at him. 'Roy, is this young woman staying here *alone*?'

'I should think so.'

'Indeed.'

Lady Muriel said no more. But when I arrived at the Café de Paris for tea, I found the four women of the Boscastle party engrossed in a meeting of disapproval and indignation. There were shades of difference about their disapproval, but even Lady Boscastle, the fastidious and detached, agreed on the two main issues: Roy was to be pitied, and Rosalind was not fit for human company.

'Good afternoon, Mr Eliot. I am glad you were able to join us,' said Lady Muriel, and got back to the topic in hand. 'I cannot understand how any woman has the shamelessness to throw herself at a man's head.'

'I can't help admiring her courage,' said Joan. 'But –'

'Joan! I will not listen to anything you say in her favour. She is a mercenary and designing woman.'

'I've said already,' said Joan, fierce, sulky, angry with both her mother and Rosalind, 'that I think she's absolutely unsuitable for him. And if she thinks this is the way to get him, she's even stupider than I thought. Of course, she's appallingly stupid.'

'I should have called her rather – uninformed,' said Lady Boscastle. 'I think our mothers would have thought her a little forward.'

'I don't know how any man ever allows himself to get married,' said Mrs Seymour, 'the way some women behave.'

'She's a Clytemnestra,' said Lady Muriel surprisingly. We all looked puzzled, until Lady Boscastle observed gently: 'I think you mean Messalina, Muriel.'

'She's a Messalina,' said Lady Muriel with passion and violence. 'Of course, she's not a lady. She's not even gently bred. No lady could do what this woman is doing.'

Lady Boscastle raised her lorgnette.

'I'm not quite sure, Muriel. I think this girl's behaviour is rather unbecoming – but haven't you and I known cases –?'

'It was not the same,' said Lady Muriel grandly. 'If a lady did it, she would do it in a different way.'

Soon afterwards Roy came in. When he apologized for being late, Lady Muriel was banteringly, clumsily affectionate, as though she wanted to say that he was still in favour. Then Lady Boscastle began to talk about her party on New Year's Eve.

'I have at last succeeded in persuading my husband to enter the Sporting Club. It has taken some time,' she said with her delicate, sarcastic smile. 'We are dining at ten o'clock. I am counting on you two to make up the party. Will you come, Lewis?'

I said that I should love to.

Roy hesitated.

'I don't know whether Lady Muriel has told you, Lady Boscastle,' he said, 'but a friend of mine is arriving that day.'

'I had heard,' said Lady Boscastle.

'I think I need to look after her.'

His tone was light but firm. He looked at Lady Boscastle. For a second her eyes wavered to Lady Muriel, and then came back to him. In a few moments, I knew that she would not invite Rosalind, and that he would not give way.

'I'm so sorry,' said Roy, as though there had been no challenge. 'It's a shame to miss you all on New Year's Eve. I should have enjoyed it so much.'

I was shocked that Lady Boscastle could be rude in this fashion. She was acting, so it seemed to me that afternoon, not as herself but as part of the clan. These were not her manners, but the manners of the whole Boscastle circle. Which were often, under their formal politeness, not designed to give pleasure. For instance, it was not politeness of the heart when Lady Muriel, seeing Roy and me constantly together, called him by his Christian name and me 'Mr Eliot', year in, year out, without softening or change. She was intensely fond of him, of course, and neutral to me, but some codes of manners would have concealed those feelings.

On the afternoon of the thirty-first, I was told that Rosalind had come, but I did not see her. Roy and she were together, I assumed, but they avoided the normal meeting-places of the Boscastle party. So I had tea with the Master and Lady Muriel, dressed early, and put in some hours at the tables before dinner. Mrs Seymour, who was becoming an insatiable gambler, was also in the casino, but I managed to pass her undetected. That was too good to last; and at dinner at the Sporting Club her place was inevitably on my right. Full of excitement, she described to me how she had been invited to a French house at five o'clock that afternoon and offered an apéritif.

'I don't like *wine* for *tea*,' said Mrs Seymour. For once her vagueness, even her enthusiasm vanished, and she felt like the voice of England.

Lord Boscastle's table was in an alcove which commanded the whole room. Lights shone, shoulders gleamed, jewellery flashed, expensive dresses rustled, expensive perfume touched the air: champagne buckets were being carried everywhere: there were at least a dozen people in the room whom I recognized from photographs. Lord Boscastle viewed the spectacle with disfavour.

'I don't know any of these people,' he said. He looked at his sister who, despite his approval of scholarly pursuits, he sometimes affected to think moved in a different circle of existence.

'Muriel!' he called out. 'I suppose you know who these people are?'

'Certainly I do not,' said Lady Muriel indignantly.

To her profound annoyance, an elderly man bowed to her.

'Who is that fellow?' asked Lord Boscastle.

'Lord Craycombe,' said Mrs Seymour.

'That family are nothing but nineteenth-century arrivistes,' said Lord Boscastle. 'Not a very distinguished acquaintance, my dear Muriel, I should have thought –?'

He was on the rampage. This was his revenge for being dragged into society.

'Talking of arrivistes,' he said, 'I noticed one or two over-luxurious yachts in the harbour. I didn't think they were in specially good taste. But it's obvious that people whom one simply wouldn't have known some time ago have managed to do remarkably well for themselves.'

Which noble families was he disposing of now? I wished that Roy had been there.

The party contained eight people. Houston Eggar had been asked to fill Roy's place; his wife ('Tom Seymour's girl') had already left for Rome, where they had been posted for a year past. Lord Boscastle proceeded to interrogate Eggar upon the Abyssinian war. The Boscastles had lived years in Italy; he had a passion for the country; though he called himself a whig, the squabble about a colonial war seemed to him hypocritical nonsense. Eggar tried hard to be both familiar and discreet, but I got the impression that in his heart he agreed. With one criticism of Lord Boscastle's he did not agree, however; and I could not help feeling that this particular criticism would have seemed unfamiliar to my left-wing friends. For Lord Boscastle appeared to regard the mishandling of British policy towards Italy as due to the increasingly middle-class constitution of the Foreign Office.

Joan argued stormily with her uncle. She thought he was clever but misguided, and never gave up hope of converting him. Eggar she dismissed as set in his ways. Actually, Eggar put on a tough assertive manner, as though he were anxious to talk to Lord Boscastle as man to man. Underneath the assertiveness he was deferential and eager to please. He was determined never to say anything foolish, never to let slip a confidence, never to be indiscreet. He was powerfully built, dark, young-looking for a man in early middle age; he was kindly, vulgar, inordinately ambitious, and not at all subtle.

It was eleven, and the room was full. Suddenly Joan said: 'There's Roy.'

Our table fell into silence as we watched. Across the floor, up an aisle between the tables, Roy walked, quite slowly, with Rosalind on his arm. They attracted many glances. Roy looked more than ever spruce, with a white gardenia in his buttonhole; but Rosalind took attention away from him. She was not a beauty, in the sense that several women in this room were beauties; she had none of the remoteness that beauty needs. But her face was mobile, pathetic, humorous, and living, and she had dressed to make sure that she would not be overlooked.

The aisle ran only one row of tables away from ours. As they came near, Rosalind, who was on the far side, kept talking to Roy; but he turned half-round and gave us a brilliant smile. It did not look a smile of defiance or triumph; it was fresh, cheerful, alight with high spirits.

I caught Lady Boscastle's eye. She must have seen a glint of satisfaction in mine, for she shrugged her shoulders and her mouth twitched. She had too much honour, too much sense of style, not to be amused. Yet she was stubborn in the arguments which followed.

'She's a very personable young woman,' said Lord Boscastle, approvingly. 'We'd better have them over here, Helen.'

'I don't think that would be at all suitable,' said Lady Muriel.

'Why not? I remember meeting her. Young Calvert's got an eye for a pretty woman.'

'She is rather untravelled perhaps for tonight, my dear Hugh,' said Lady Boscastle.

'Have you just discovered that? I got on perfectly well with her,' said Lord Boscastle. He was annoyed. 'And I regard Calvert as someone I know.'

Lady Boscastle, with heavy support from Lady Muriel, maintained her opposition. Lord Boscastle became nettled. One could feel the crystalline strength of Lady Boscastle's will. In that marriage, I thought, she had had the upper hand all the way through. He had been jealous, she had gone her own way, she had never sacrificed that unscratchable diamond-hard will. Yet Lord Boscastle was accustomed to being the social arbiter. In the long run, even Lady Muriel deferred to his judgement on what could and could not be done. That night he was unusually persistent. Mainly because he did not mean to be deprived of a pretty girl's company – but also he had a masculine sympathy with Roy's enjoyments.

In the end, they agreed on a compromise rather in his favour. Roy and Rosalind were to be left to have dinner alone, but were to be invited to visit our table afterwards. Lady Boscastle wrote a note: it was like her that it should be delicately phrased. 'My dear Roy, It is so nice, and such a pleasant surprise, to see you here tonight. Will you give us the pleasure of bringing your friend Miss Wykes to this table when you have finished your dinner? We are all anxious to wish you a happy new year.'

They came. Rosalind was overawed until she was monopolized for half an hour by Lord Boscastle. Afterwards I heard her talking clothes with Mrs Seymour. As the night went on, her eyes became brighter, more victorious, more resolved. She talked to everyone but Lady Muriel. She did not want the glorious night to end.

Roy did not show, perhaps he did not feel, a glimmer of triumph. He exerted himself to be his most gentle, teasing, and affectionate with the other women, particularly with Lady Muriel.

Within a few hours of the party, I heard the rumour that Roy and Rosalind were engaged. It came first from Mrs Seymour, who had been driven in alone and marked me down across the square.

'I think it's perfectly certain,' she said.

'Why do you think so?'

'I seem to remember something,' she said vaguely. 'I seem to remember that young woman giving me to understand –'

Joan came in with her father later that morning, and asked me pointblank if I knew anything.

'Nothing at all,' I said.

'Are you being honest?' she said. She was suspicious, and yet as soon as I answered her face was lightened with relief.

'Yes.'

'Do you think it's likely?'

'I should have thought not.'

She looked at me with a troubled and hopeful smile.

Another member of the New Year's party found it necessary to talk to me that morning, but on quite a different subject. Houston Eggar took me for a walk in the gardens, and there in the bright sunlight told me of an embarrassment about that day's honours list. 'You won't have seen it yet, of course,' he said. 'But they happen to have given me a little recognition. If these things come, they come.' But what had come, he felt, needed some knowledgeable explanation. Before he was appointed to Rome, he had been seconded for two years to another ministry. He considered, as an aside, that this had temporarily slowed down his promotion in the Foreign Office, but he assured me that it ought to pay in the long run. As a reward for this work, he was now being given a C.B.E.: whereas anyone of his seniority in the Foreign Office would expect, in the ordinary course of things, to be getting near a C.M.G. – 'which has more cachet, needless to say,' said Houston Eggar. 'You see, Eliot,' he went on earnestly, 'to anyone who doesn't know the background, this C of mine might seem like a slap in the face. Instead of being a nice little compliment. I'd be very much obliged if you'd explain the situation to the Boscastles. Don't go out of your way, but if you get a chance you might just remove any misconceptions. I'll do the same for you some day.'

Several more rumours about the engagement reached me during the next twenty-four hours, and I knew that Roy had heard what was bubbling round him. But I scarcely saw him; he did not eat a meal in our hotel; it was from someone else I learned that Rosalind had been invited out to the villa on 3 January – but only for tea, apparently as another compromise between Lord and Lady Boscastle.

It was the day before, 2 January, when Lady Muriel announced that she would make 'tactful inquiries' of Roy himself. 'I shall not embarrass him,' she said. 'I shall merely use a little finesse.'

Lady Boscastle raised her lorgnette, but said nothing. We had met for tea at our usual place in the window of the Café de Paris; we were a little early, and Roy was expected. *The Times* of the day before had been delivered after lunch; Lady Muriel had studied it and made comments on the honours list, which Mrs Seymour was now reading through.

'Muriel,' she cried excitedly, 'did you see that Houston has got a C.B.E.?'

'No, Doris,' said Lady Muriel with finality. 'I never read as low in the list as that.'

Roy joined us and made a hearty tea.

'I must say, Roy,' said Lady Muriel in due course, with heavy-footed casualness, 'that you're looking very well.'

It happened to be true. Roy smiled at her.

'So are you, Lady Mu,' he said demurely.

'Am I?' Lady Muriel was thrown out of her stride.

'I have never seen you look better,' Roy assured her. 'Coming back to the scene of your conquests, isn't it?'

'You're a very naughty young man.' Lady Muriel gave her crowing laugh. Then she remembered her duty, and stiffened. 'You're looking very well, Roy,' she began again. 'Have you by chance had any good news?'

'Any good news, Lady Mu?'

'Anything really exciting?'

Roy reflected.

'One of my investments has gone up three points since Christmas,' he said. 'I wonder if it could be that?'

Lady Muriel plunged desperately.

'I suppose none of our friends are getting engaged just now, are they?'

'I expect they are,' said Roy. 'But I haven't seen *The Times*. There's always a batch on New Year's Day, isn't there? I wonder why? Could I borrow *The Times*, Mrs Seymour?'

Under Lady Muriel's baffled eyes, Roy worked down a column and a half of engagements. He took his time over it. There were nearly fifty couples in the paper; and the party at tea knew at least a third of them by name, and half a dozen personally.

'There you are, Lady Mu,' said Roy at last. 'I've put a cross against two or three. Those are the ones you need to write to.'

Lady Muriel gave up.

'By the way,' Roy asked, 'is anyone going to the ballet tonight?' We all said no.

'I think we will go,' said Roy. 'I think I should take Rosalind.'

CHAPTER 13

A Complaint of Elusiveness

ROY did not, however, find it pleasant to fend off the Master. Lady Muriel made her 'tactful inquiries' on the Saturday afternoon; next morning, the Master, Roy, and I went for a walk along the hill road. The Master used no finesse; he asked no questions with a double meaning: he walked briskly between us, upright and active as a young man, breathing confidential whispers about Cambridge acquaintances, but he let it be seen that he felt Roy's silence was a denial of affection.

Roy was in a difficult position. For he was not cherishing a secret. He had not proposed to Rosalind. Yet it was awkward to contradict the rumour. For he guessed, as I had, that Rosalind had set it going herself.

He was not willing to put her to shame. He was too fond of women to romanticize them. He knew she was determined to marry him, and would, if she thought it useful, lie and cheat and steal until she brought it off. He did not think the worse of her. Nor did he think the worse of Lady Muriel because, if she could lie in ambush in the dark and cease to be a great lady, she would with relish have pulled Rosalind's hair out by the roots. He was fond of them all. But for Rosalind he felt the special animal tenderness that comes from physical delight, and he would not consent to see her humiliated among those who hated her.

So there was nothing for it but to take her round Monte Carlo, dine with her each night, ignore all hints and questions, and go on as though the rumour did not exist.

But I did not believe for a minute that Rosalind would win: she had miscalculated completely if she thought those were the best tactics. Probably she knew that, whatever happened, he would not give her away before the Royces and the Boscastles. Down to a certain level, she understood him well. But before that, I thought, she must be living with a stranger, if she imagined that she could take him by storm.

113

We turned back down the hill. In the distance, down below the white patches of houses, the sea shone like a polished shield. I made an excuse and stayed behind, taking off a shoe, so that they could have a word together. I watched their faces turn to each other, their profiles sharp against the cloudless sky. The Master was talking, Roy listening, they were near together, their faces were softened by seriousness and intimacy. In profile Roy's nose ran too long for beauty: the Master looked more regularly handsome, with trim clear lines of forehead, chin, and mouth; his skin had been tinged a little by the January sun, and he seemed as healthy as Roy, and almost as young.

After we had seen his car drive away in the direction of Roquebrune, I said to Roy:

'What did he ask you?'

'He didn't ask me anything. But he told me something.' Roy was smiling, a little sadly.

'What?'

'He told me that, if ever I thought of getting married, I was to consider nothing but my own feelings. It was the only occasion in life when one needed to be absolutely selfish in one's choice. Otherwise one brings misery to others as well as to oneself.'

Roy looked at me.

'It cost him an effort to say that,' he said. 'It was brave of him.'

He added, as though off-handedly:

'You know, old boy, if he had let himself go he could have had a high old time with the women. It's almost not too late for him to start.'

Roy spoke with the deep and playful ease of a profound personal affection. For his relation with the Master had nothing of the strain that comes between a protégé and his patron – where all emotion is ambivalent, unless both parties are magnanimous beyond the human limits: if they are ordinary humans, there is the demand for gratitude on one side, resentment on the other, and those forces must drive them farther apart. Roy's feeling was different in kind. It was deep, it had nothing to do with their positions. It was more like a successful younger brother's for an elder who has had a bad time. And underneath there was a strong current of loving envy; for, whatever had happened to the Master, his essential self had been untouched. He might regret that he had done little, he might be painfully lonely, but in his heart there was repose. Roy envied him, even that morning, when he was himself free of any shadow; in the dark nights Roy envied him passionately, above all for his simple, childish faith in God. He was cynical in his speech, sceptical in his human reflections, observant, and disinterested: how had he kept that faith?

The Boscastle cars were busy that day, carrying out guests for lunch, bringing them back; and one called in the afternoon for Roy, Rosalind, and me. Rosalind was spectacular in black and white.

'I've worn ten different outfits in four days,' she said. 'Do you think this will get by?'

She was excited, full of zest, apprehensive but not too much so to enjoy herself. She exclaimed rapturously as we drove round the beautiful stretch of coast. It did not matter to her that it had been praised before. She thought it was romantically beautiful; she said so, and gasped with pleasure.

Both the dress and Rosalind 'got by' with Lord Boscastle. Lady Boscastle was delicately polite, Lady Muriel gave what she regarded as a civil greeting; but Lord Boscastle was an obstinate man, and here was a decorative young woman asking only to sit at his feet and be impressed. He was happy to oblige. Her taste in dress might be bold, but she was incomparably better turned out than any of the women of his party, except his own wife. And each time he met her, he felt her admiration lapping round him like warm milk. He felt, as other men felt in her presence, a size larger than life.

He placed her in the chair next to his. Tea was brought in.

'I'm afraid I'm not much good at tea,' said Lord Boscastle to Rosalind, as though it were a very difficult game. 'But I expect you are, aren't you?' He pressed her to take some strawberry jam. 'From my house,' he said. 'We grow a few little things at my house, you know.'

Roy, sitting between Lady Muriel and Joan, was watching with the purest glee. It did not need his prompting that afternoon to send Lord Boscastle through his hoops.

'We have always grown a few things at my house,' said Lord Boscastle.

'Have you, Lord Boscastle?' said Rosalind.

They discussed the horticultural triumphs of the house for the past two hundred years, Lord Boscastle taking all the credit, Rosalind giving him all the applause.

Then he remembered a displeasing fact. 'The trouble is,' he said to her, 'that one never knows who is coming to live near one's house nowadays. I heard from my steward only today that someone is going to squat himself down ten miles away. His name appears to be' – Lord Boscastle reached for a letter and held it at arm's length – 'Woolston. A certain Sir Arthur Woolston.'

He pronounced the name with such painful emphasis that Lady Muriel and the rest of us waited for his next words.

'I'm afraid I don't know the fellow,' he said. 'I think,' he added, in a tone of tired dismissal, 'I think he must be some baronet or other.'

He stared across at his sister, and said:

'I suppose you probably know him, Muriel.'

'I have never heard of him,' Lady Muriel replied in dudgeon. Then, using the same technique, she turned on her sister-in-law: 'Or is he some sort of lawyer? Would your father have known him, Helen?'

'I scarcely think so,' said Lady Boscastle.

'Don't I remember one of your father's cases having something to do with the name of Woolston?'

'Perhaps you do, Muriel,' said Lady Boscastle, smiling with charm and sarcasm. 'In that case you remember more than I.'

A moment later, Lady Boscastle said to me:

'It is such a beautiful sunset, Lewis. I should like to take a little walk in the garden. Will you come with me, my dear?'

She rang for her maid, who brought her coat and wraps and dressed her. She took my arm, leaned on me, and her stick tapped slowly along the terrace. It was a magnificent evening. The sun had already set behind the hills, but the sky above was a startling luminous green, which darkened to velvet blue and indigo, so dense that it seemed tangible, as one looked over the sea towards Italy. The lights of Mentone sparkled across the water, and the first stars had come out.

'Had I told you that my father was a barrister, Lewis?' said Lady Boscastle.

'No, never,' I said.

'It may have made me more interested in you, my dear boy,' she said.

She told me his name; he had been an eminent chancery lawyer, some of whose cases I had studied for my Bar examinations. It came as a complete surprise to me. Rather oddly – so it seemed to me later – I had never inquired about her history. Somehow I had just assumed that she was born in the Boscastle circle. She had acclimatized herself so completely, she was so much more fine-grained than they, so much more cultivated, so much more sophisticated. No one could be more exquisite and 'travelled'; she told me of the sweetness of life which she and her friends had known, and, far more than Lord Boscastle or Lady Muriel, made me feel its graces; she had been famous in Edwardian society, she had been loved in the last days of the old world.

But she had not been born in that society. She had been born in a comfortable place, but not there. When I knew, I could understand how she and Lady Muriel scored off each other. For Lady Boscastle, detached as she was, was enough child of her world not to be able to dismiss Lady Muriel's one advantage; she knew she was far cleverer than Lady Muriel, more attractive to men, more certain of herself; but still she remembered, with a slight sarcastic grimace, that Lady Muriel was a great aristocrat and she was born middle class.

It might also explain, I thought, why sometimes she was more rigid than her husband. When, for example, it was a question of inviting Rosalind, and she spoke for the entire Boscastle clan, did the accident of her own birth make her less able to be lax?

We retraced our steps along the terrace, her stick tapping. The curtains had not been drawn, and we could see the whole party in the bright drawing-room. Rosalind was listening to Lord Boscastle with an expression of pathetic, worshipping wonder.

'That young woman,' said Lady Boscastle, 'is having a *succès fou*. Lewis, have you a penchant for extremely stupid women?'

'I am not overfond of intellectual women,' I said. 'But I like them to be intelligent.'

'That is very sensible,' Lady Boscastle approved.

'By the way,' I said, 'Rosalind is far from stupid.'

'Perhaps you are right,' she said indifferently. 'She is a little effusive for my taste. Perhaps I am not fair.' She added, with a hint of sarcastic pleasure: 'I shall be surprised if she catches your friend Roy. In spite of the bush telegraph.'

'So shall I.'

She glanced into the drawing-room. She did not need her lorgnette, her long-sighted blue eyes could see a clear tableau of Roy, Joan, and

Lady Muriel: Lady Muriel had turned away, as if to hide a smile, Joan was beginning her lusty, delightful laugh, Roy was sitting solemn-faced between them.

'I shall also be surprised,' said Lady Boscastle, 'if my niece Joan ever succeeds in catching him.'

'She's very young,' I said.

'Do you think she realizes that she is getting excessively fond of him?' Lady Boscastle asked. 'Which is why she quarrels with him at sight. Young women with advanced ideas and strong characters often seem quite remarkably obtuse.'

'Under it all,' I said, 'she's got great capacity for love.'

I felt Lady Boscastle shrug her shoulders as we slowly made our way.

'She will never capture anyone like your friend Roy,' she said coolly. 'Our dear Joan is rather – unadorned.'

She began to laugh, and turned up her face in the brilliant twilight. She looked puckish, monkey-like, satirical, enchanting.

'I am sure that her mother will never notice that Joan is getting fond of him,' said Lady Boscastle. 'Muriel has never been known to notice anything of the kind in her life. It was sometimes convenient that she didn't, my dear Lewis. Perhaps it was as well.'

In the small hours of the next morning, I was having my usual game of baccarat. I heard Rosalind's dying fall behind me.

'I thought I should find you here. Shall I join in?'

But she did not know the rules. Sooner than explain them, it was easier for me to take her across to a roulette table.

'Don't tell Roy that I've been here,' she said. 'Or else I shall get into trouble.'

She gambled with the utmost method. She had decided to invest exactly ten pounds. If she made it twenty, she would stop: if she lost it, she would also stop. She sat there, looking modish, plaintive, and open-eyed: in fact, I thought, if it came to a deal she was more than a match for the violet-powdered, predatory faces round her. That night the numbers ran against her, and in half an hour she had lost her quota.

'That's that,' said Rosalind. 'Please can I have a drink?'

She liked money, but she threw away sums which to her were not negligible. In presents, in loans, in inventing and paying for treats, she was the most generous of women. The ten pounds had gone, and she did not give it a thought.

We sat in two of the big armchairs by the bar.

'Where's Roy?' I asked.

'In bed, of course. And fast asleep. He sleeps like a child, bless him.'

'Always?'

'Oh, I've known him have a bout of insomnia. You knew that, did you? It was rather a bad one. But as a rule he just goes to sleep as soon as his head touches the pillow.' She smiled. 'He's rather a dear old thing.'

She looked with clear open eyes into mine. 'Lewis,' she said, 'is there any reason why I shouldn't do?'

'What do you mean?'

'You know what I mean. Does he want more from a woman than I manage to give him? He seems to like me when we're alone –' she gave her secret, prudish, reminiscent, amorous smile. 'Is there anything more he wants?'

'You ought to know.'

'I don't know,' she said, almost ill-temperedly. 'I haven't the faintest idea. I give him all the chances to speak I can think of, but he never takes them. He says nice things at the proper time, of course' – again she gave a smile – 'but that is neither here nor there. He never tells me his plans. I never know where I am with him. He's frightfully elusive. Sometimes I think I don't matter to him a scrap.'

'You do, of course.'

'Do I? Are you sure?'

'You've given him some peace.'

'That's not enough,' she said sharply. 'I want something to take hold of. I want to be certain I mean something to him.'

She added:

'Do you think he wants to marry me?'

'I don't know.'

'Do you think he ought to marry me?'

I hesitated, for a fraction of time. Very quickly Rosalind cried, no plaintively but with all her force:

'Why shouldn't I make him a passable wife?'

CHAPTER 14

One Way to Knowledge

AFTER that talk with Rosalind, I thought again that she was living with a stranger. She knew him with her hands and lips: she knew more than most young women about men in their dressing-gowns; yet she did not know, any more than his dinner partners that January in Monte Carlo, two things about him.

First, he was sometimes removed from her, removed from any human company, by an acute and paralysing fear. It was the fear that, unless he found his rest in time, he might be overcome by melancholy again. In the moment of grace when we walked by the Serpentine, that fear was far away – and so it was during most of the joyful holiday. But once or twice, as he talked, made love, and invented mischievous jokes, he felt what to another man would have been only an hour's sadness or fatigue. Roy was at once gripped, forced to watch his own mood.

It was like someone who has had an attack of a disease; he feels what may be a first symptom, which another would not notice or would laugh away: he cannot ignore it, he can attend to nothing else, he can only think '*is it beginning again?*'

Sometimes Rosalind thought he was elusive: he was distant from her because he had to attend to something else – is it beginning again? Those occasions were very rare in the winter after his outburst. The period of near-grace, of almost perfect safety, lasted right through the weeks on the Mediterranean, the months of the Cambridge spring. Rosalind came often to Cambridge, and spent week-ends in the flat in Connaught Street. She was pressing, persuading, bullying him into marrying her – with tears, pathos, storms, scenes of all kinds. But she did not know of those moments of fear.

She did not know also of his brilliant, insatiable hopes. Those he tried to tell her of; she listened indulgently, they were part of the meaningless discontent with which so many men fretted themselves. If she had been as lucky as Roy, if she had what he had, she would have been ineffably happy. God? If she had been born in a religious time, she would have enjoyed the ceremonies, she would have assumed that she believed in God. As it was, she disbelieved just as cheerfully. There was no gap in her life; it was full and it would always have been full; she was made for the bright and pagan world, and in her heart she would always have found it.

So she dismissed, tenderly, half-contemptuously, half-admiringly, all that she heard of Roy's hopes. She thus failed to understand the second reason why he was 'elusive'. For her, love was an engrossing occupation. She had not been chaste when she met Roy, she was physically tolerant, she could have loved many men with happiness; but, loving Roy, she could make do without any other human relation, either in love or outside it. She liked her friends in a good-natured casual way, she had a worldly-wise gossipy interest in those around her, she liked to talk clothes and scandal to her women confidantes, she liked to show off her knowledge of books and art to men – but, if Roy had suddenly taken her to the Pacific, she would have missed nothing that she left behind.

She could not begin to realize how profoundly different it was with him. He lived in others more than any man I knew. It was through others that he drew much of his passionate knowledge of life. It was through others, such as the Master and Ralph Udal, that he tried to find one way to belief in God. Into anything human he could project himself and learn and feel. In the stories people told him, he found not only kinship with them, but magic and a sense of the unseen.

By contrast, he often seemed curiously uninterested and insensitive about non-human things. Places meant little to him except for the human beings they contained, and nature almost nothing at all. It was like him to talk of the Boscastle finances as we drove that night along the beautiful coast. He had very little feeling for traditional Cambridge, though no one had as many friends in the living town. He was amused by my interest in the past of the college: 'romantic', he called it scornfully: even when I produced sharp, clear facts about people in the past, he was only faintly stirred; they were not real beside the people that he knew.

Because he lived so much in others, his affections had some of the warmth, strength, glamour, and imagination of love. His friendship with me did not become important to either of us until we were both grown men, but the quality he brought to it transformed it: it was different from any other of my friendships, more brilliant than anything I expected when I was no longer very young. He made others feel the same. They were the strangest variety, those to whom he brought this radiance: Lady Muriel – the 'little dancer' (who was a consumptive woman in Berlin) – Winslow, who soon looked for Roy to sit next to him in hall – Mrs Seymour – the Master. There were many others, in all sorts of places from Boscastle to the tenements of Berlin, and the number grew each year.

In nearly all those affections he gave himself without thinking twice, though his parodic interest went along with his love. He had no scrap of desire to alter or 'improve' those he loved. He was delighted by Lady Boscastle's determination to reform me, but he was himself quite devoid of any trace of reforming zeal.

There were only one or two in all his human relations where there seemed the friction and strain of self. He was fond of Ralph Udal, but he was never so utterly untroubled and unselfconscious with Udal as with ten or twenty people who mattered to him less, as with, say, Mrs Seymour or Lord Boscastle. It puzzled me for a long time – until I saw that with Udal Roy for once wanted something for himself. He wanted to know how to find the peace of God.

There were others too, besides Udal, whom Roy marked down as having spiritual knowledge denied to him. He felt they could be of use to him; he tracked them down, got to know them; he had a sharp eye for anyone who could be of this special use, as sharp an eye as a man develops who is out to borrow money or on the make. They were always youngish men, as though he felt no old man's experience could help him (he was deeply fond of the Master, he envied his religious faith, but it neither drew them closer nor came between them). Yet he was never easy with them. He gave each of them up, as soon as he felt sure they had not known his own experience. Udal was the only one for whom he had a strong personal feeling. Rosalind did not realize that, through Udal, through some of those others, Roy was living an intent and desperate search. She did realize, as she had shown with the Boscastles and with me, that Roy's friends captured his imagination and that she must know them. That was all she could see; it was a move in her plan to marry him. His hopes, his sense of life through others, his search – they would go, he would cease to be elusive, once she had him safely in the marriage bed.

It was in the early summer that he told her he could not marry her.

Rosalind let herself go. She had been crying, reproaching him, imploring him, for some days when I first heard what had happened. I went round to Connaught Street one night, and found Roy lying on the sofa, his face pale and tired. Rosalind was sitting in an armchair; the skin under her eyes was heavily powdered, but even so one could see that she had not long since been in tears.

They were in silence when I entered.

'Hallo, old boy,' said Roy. He was relieved to see me.

'I'd better tell Lewis,' said Rosalind.

'You needn't,' said Roy. 'It would be better if you didn't.'

'You'll only tell him yourself the minute you've got rid of me,' she said, angrily, pathetically.

Roy turned his face away. She faced me with open, brimming eyes.

'He's got tired of me,' she said.

'Not true,' said Roy, without turning round.

'He won't marry me. He's told me that he won't marry me.' She spoke to Roy. 'You can't deny that you've told me that, can you?'

Roy did not reply.

'I'm no good to him,' said Rosalind. She took out a crumpled handkerchief and began to cry, very quietly.

In time she said to me:

'What do you think of it, Lewis? I expect you think it's right.'

'I'm very sorry: that's all one can ever say.'

'You think he'll be better off without me, don't you?' she cried.

I shook my head. 'It's for you two only,' I said.

She made a pretence of smiling.

'You're a nice old thing, Lewis. If you don't think he will be better off without me, everyone else will. All the people who think I'm a little bitch – they'll all feel I've got what I deserve. Oh, what do I care what they all think? They don't matter, now he's turning me out.'

'I'm not turning you out.'

Roy's voice was flat and exhausted, and Rosalind found it easier to talk to him through me. She looked at his back and said:

'I've told him that I've got to get married some time. I can't wait for ever. And someone quite nice is rather anxious to marry me.'

Whether it was an invention or not, I could not guess. In any case, she had used it in order to force Roy's hand. She had thrust it in front of him: he could not be elusive any more, she thought. She had first mentioned it, hopefully, plaintively, three days before, and since then she had been blackmailing and begging. She had not reckoned that he would be so firm.

At this point Roy broke in:

'I can only say it again. If you need to marry, you should marry him.'

It was very harsh. But it was harsh through a cause I had not expected. He was jealous. As a rule he was the least jealous of men. He was resolved not to marry her, yet he was jealous that she should marry another.

'I don't know whether I could bear it.'

'I expect he will make you happier than I ever could.'

'You're horrible,' said Rosalind, and sobbed again.

She did not move him, either then or later. He stayed firm, though he became more gentle when the first shock wore off. He wanted to go on living with her, but he would not marry her. Rosalind still kept coming to see him, though more fitfully. I heard nothing more about her engagement to the other man.

The scene left Roy quiet and saddened. For some days I dreaded that he was being overcome by another wave of depression. But it fell away. It was good to see him light-hearted with relief. Yet I thought, as the summer passed, that he was never as carefree after the scene with Rosalind; even at his gayest, he never reached the irresponsible, timeless content of Monte Carlo. He became more active, impatient, eager, more set on his own search. He spent much more time with Ralph Udal in Lewisham. He persuaded me to try to trace old Martineau for him: but Martineau had moved from the Leeds pavement, no one knew where.

One afternoon in August I saw something which surprised me and set me thinking. I was being driven over the Vauxhall Bridge, when through the car window I saw Rosalind and Ralph Udal walking together. Neither was speaking, and they were walking slowly to the north side of the river. What was she doing now, I thought? Did she think that he had become the most powerful influence on Roy? Was she playing the same game that she had once played with me?

The first part of the liturgy was published in the summer. In due course, often after months of delay, there followed respectful reviews in three or four scholarly periodicals. Colonel Foulkes, as usual putting in his word without a pause, got in first with his review in the *Journal of Theological Studies*; he wrote that the complete edition of the liturgy looked like being the most authoritative piece of Oriental scholarship for a generation. But apart from him English scholars did not go out of their way to express enthusiasm. The reviews were good enough, but there was none of the under-current of gossipy personal praise. I had no doubt that, if Roy had kept quiet at the December meeting, he would have had different luck, his reputation would have been as good as made; Sir Oulstone would have paid a state visit to the college, all Sir Oulstone's friends would have been saying that Roy had once for all 'arrived'. But none of those things happened. Sir Oulstone and his school were cold and silent.

The Master was painfully disappointed. Arthur Brown said to me with sturdy resignation: 'I want to tell them, Eliot, that our young friend is the best scholar this college has had since the war. But it looks as though I shall have to wait for a few years.' He warned me comfortably: 'It's never wise to claim more than we can put on the table. People remember that you've inflated the currency, and they hold it against you next time.'

We were downcast and angry. Roy's own response was peculiar. He was amused, he treated it as a good joke at his own expense – and also at ours, who wanted him to be famous. 'It's a flop, old boy,' he said mischievously in his room one afternoon. He developed the habit of referring to his work as though he were a popular writer. 'It's a flop. I shan't be able to live on the royalties. I'm really very worried about the sales.'

I wanted him to make his peace with Lyall, but he smiled.

'Too late. Too late. Unsuccessful author, that's what I shall be. I shall need to work harder to make ends meet.' He jumped to his feet, and went towards the upright reading-desk. He was busy with a particularly difficult psalm. 'Can't stay talking,' he said. 'That won't buy Auntie a new frock.'

He was gaining a perverse satisfaction. I realized at last that he did not want the fame we wanted for him. He would do the work – that was a need, a drug, an attempt at escape – but if he could choose he would prefer to be left obscure.

Most men, I thought, are content to stay clamped within the bonds of their conscious personality. They may break out a little – in their daydreams, their play, sometimes in their prayers and their thoughts of love. But in their work they stay safely in the main stream of living. They want success on the ordinary terms, they scheme for recognition, titles, position, the esteem of solid men. They want to go up step by step within their own framework. Among such men one finds the steadily and persistently ambitious – the Lyalls and the Houston Eggars.

Roy always shied from them. He thought of them as 'stuffed'. It had been obtuse of us to imagine he would seek a career as they might seek it. Arthur Brown and I were more ordinary men than he was. We were trying to impose on him the desires we should have had, if we had been as gifted. But one could not separate his gifts from the man he was.

No one was less willing, less able, to stay clamped within the bonds of self. Often he wished that he could: he cried out in envy of the comfortable. But he was driven. He was driven to his work by the same kind of compulsion that drives an artist. It gave him the obsessed, the morbid concentration that none of the ordinary healthy ambitious scholars could achieve; it did not give him the peace he hoped, although he knew he would be lost without it; above all it did not give him the matter-of-fact ambition that everyone round him took for granted. In his place, they would all have longed to be distinguished savants, men of weight, Fellows of the British Academy, recipients of honorary degrees – and in time they would have got there. Yet, at the prospect Roy felt caught, maimed, chained to the self he was trying to leave behind. At the prospect he was driven once more, driven to fly into obscurity.

Perhaps it had been wrong of Arthur Brown and me to see that he became a fellow. He seemed to want it – but perhaps even then we were reading our desires into him. Was his outburst a shriek of protests against being caught? Was it a wild flight as he saw a new door closing?

Yet I had my own minor amusement. Roy's enemies in the college had heard the Master prophesy an overwhelming triumph; the book came out, and with gratification Despard-Smith and others slowly sensed that there was an absence of acclaim.

Despard-Smith said one night:

'I have always been compelled to doubt whether Calvert's work will s-stand the test of time. I wish I could believe otherwise. But it will be a scandal for the college if his work turns out to be a flash in the pan.'

Roy was not dining, but I told him afterwards. He was no more consistent than other men, and he became extremely angry.

'What does he know about it?' said Roy furiously, while I laughed at him. 'He's never written a line in his life, except asking some wretched farmer to pay the rent. Why should some tenth-rate mathematician be allowed to speak about my work? I need to talk to him.'

Roy spoke to Despard-Smith the next night.

'I hear that you've become an Oriental scholar, Despard?'

'I don't know what you mean, Calvert.'

'I hear that you doubt the soundness of my edition. I suppose that you needed to study it first?'

Roy was still angry, and his subtle, mystifying, hypnotic approach had deserted him. Despard-Smith felt at home, and a gleam of triumph shone in his eye.

'No, Calvert, that wasn't necessary. I relied on my judgement from what I picked up round me. Exactly as one has to do – in electing a fellow. One has to rely on one's judgement. I don't pretend to be clever, Calvert, but I do congratulate myself on my judgement. I might tell you that some people never acquire it.'

Roy had no reply. I was very much amused, but it was a joke that he did not see.

It was not long before the Master and Arthur Brown were able to score a success for Roy within the college. Roy's reputation had been high with German scholars since he brought out his grammar, and the liturgy was praised at once, more immediately and vociferously than in England. The Professor of Oriental Religions at Berlin and a colleague came to London for a conference in October, and wrote to the Master asking if he could present them to Roy. They stayed in the Lodge for a week-end and met Roy at dinner. The Professor was a stocky round-faced roguish-looking man called Ammatter. When Roy was introduced to him, he clowned and pretended not to believe it.

The Master translated his remark with lively, victorious zest. 'Professor Ammatter says,' the Master addressed himself to

Despard-Smith, 'that it is impossible anyone so young should have done such work. He says that we must be foisting an impostor upon them.'

Despard-Smith made a creaking acknowledgement, and sat as far down the table as he could. The Master and Roy each spoke excellent German; Ammatter was tricky, fluid, entertaining, comic, and ecstatic; the wine went round fast in the combination room, the Master drinking glass for glass with Ammatter and Roy. Old Despard-Smith glowered as they laughed at jokes he did not understand. The Master, cheerful, familiar, dignified though a little drunk, broke off their conversation several times in order to translate; he chose each occasion when they were paying a compliment to Roy. The Master spoke a little more loudly than usual, so that the compliments carried all over the room. It was one of his happiest evenings, and before the end Roy had arranged to spend the next three months in Berlin.

CHAPTER 15

Tea in the Drawing-Room

I RECEIVED some high-spirited letters from Germany, in which there were references to acquaintances all over Berlin, from high party officials to the outcasts and those in danger; but I did not see Roy again until early January, after we had heard bad news.

The Master had been taken ill just before Christmas; he had not been in his briskest form all through the autumn, but in his spare, unpampered fashion he thought little of it. He got worse over Christmas, vomited often and could not eat. In the first week of January he was taken to hospital and examined. They gave him a gastroscopy, and sent him back to the Lodge the same night. They had found the answer. He had an inoperable cancer. There was no hope at all. He would die within a few months.

The day after the examination, all the college knew, but the doctors and Lady Muriel agreed that the Master should not be told. They assured him that nothing was seriously the matter, only a trivial duodenal ulcer. He was to lie still, and would recover in a few weeks. I was allowed to see him very soon after they had talked to him; I knew the truth, and heard him talk cheerfully of what he would do in two years' time, of how he was looking forward to Roy's complete edition. He looked almost as fresh, young, and smooth-faced as the year before in the hills above Monte Carlo. He was cordial, sharp-tongued, and indiscreet. His anxiety had been taken away, and so powerful was the psychological effect that he felt well. He spoke of Roy with intimacy and affection.

'He always did insist on behaving like a gilded dilettante. I wonder if he'll ever get over it. Why will he insist on going about with vine-leaves in his hair?'

He looked up at the ceiling of the great bedroom, and said quietly:

'I think I know the answer to that question.'

'What do you think?'

'I think you know it too. He's not a trifler.' He paused. He did not know that he was exhausted.

He said simply: 'No, he's searching for God.'

I was too much distressed to find what he knew of Roy's search. Did he really understand, or was it just a phrase?

Most people in the college thought it was a mistake to lie to the Master. Round the table in the combination room there were arguments whether he should or should not have been told the truth. The day I went to the Lodge, I heard Joan disagree violently with her mother.

But Lady Muriel, even if all thought her wrong, had taken her decision and stood her ground. When he was demonstrably worse, when he could no longer think he would get better, he would have to be told. Meanwhile he would get a few weeks of hope and peace. It would be the last comfort he would enjoy while he was alive. Whatever they said, she would give it to him. Her daughter passionately protested. If he could choose, cried Joan, there was no doubt what he would say.

'I am positive that we are doing right,' said Lady Muriel. Her voice was firm and unyielding. There was grandeur in her bold eyes, her erect head, her stiff back.

Roy returned from Berlin a couple of days later. He had heard the news before he ran up my stairs, but he was looking well and composed. It was too late to see the Master that night, but he arranged to visit him the next afternoon, and for us both to have tea with Lady Muriel.

So next day I went over to the Lodge alone, and was shown into the empty drawing-room. I stood by the window. Snow had lain on the court for days, and, though it was thawing, the ground still gleamed white against the sombre dusk. The sky was heavy with dense grey clouds. The court was empty, it was still the depth of the vacation, no lights shone from the windows. In the drawing-room there was no light yet except the roaring fire.

Roy joined me there. His face was stricken. 'This is dreadful,' he said.

'What did he talk about?'

'The little book on the heresies which we're to work at in a year or two. After my liturgy is safely out.'

'I know,' I said.

'There was a time,' said Roy, 'when I should have jumped at any excuse for getting out of that little book.'

'You invented several good reasons.'

'Just so. Now I shall do it in memory of him.'

I doubted whether I should ever be able to dissuade him. He would do it very well, but not superbly; it would not suit him; as a scholar his gifts were, as the mathematicians say, deep, sharp, and narrow; this kind of broad commentary was not at all in his line. People would suspect that he was losing his scholar's judgement.

'I'd expected a good deal,' said Roy. 'But it is dreadful. Much worse than anyone could guess.'

Lady Muriel threw open the door and switched on the lights.

'Good afternoon, Roy,' she said. 'I'm very glad you've come to see us. It's so long since you were here. Good afternoon, Mr Eliot.'

Roy went to her, took her hand in his. 'I've been talking to the Master, you know,' he said. 'It's dreadful to have to pretend, isn't it? I wish you'd been spared that decision, Lady Mu. No one could have known what to do.'

He alone could have spoken to her so. He alone would take it for granted that she was puzzled and dismayed.

'It was not easy, but –'

'No one could help you. And you'd have liked help, wouldn't you? Everyone would.'

Her eyes filled with tears.

She was embarrassed, flustered, choked like one unused to crying: soon Roy got her sitting beside him on the sofa, and helped her to tea. She smiled at him, her bold eyes misted and bloodshot.

'I should be filling your cup. In my own drawing-room.'

Roy smiled. 'You may, the next time I come.'

She gripped hold of her drawing-room manner – for my benefit, perhaps. Her neck straightened, she made a brave attempt to talk of Roy's journey from Berlin. He told her that he had had to sleep sitting up in a crowded carriage.

'How could you?' cried Lady Muriel. 'I couldn't bear the thought of being watched when I was asleep.'

'Why not, Lady Mu?'

'One wouldn't know how one was looking before strangers. One couldn't control oneself.'

He glanced at her: in a second, her face broke, and she smiled back.

Soon afterwards Joan came into the room. She walked in with her determined, gawky stride: then she saw Roy, and her whole bearing changed. She seemed to shiver. For an instant she went stiff. She came towards him, and he jumped up and welcomed her. He said a word about her father; she looked at him steadily, shook her head, deliberately put it aside, and went on to argue with him over living in Germany.

'Don't you feel pressed down? You must feel that it's a relief to get to the frontier. I felt it very strongly –'

'The Dutch porters have no necks,' said Roy. He disliked arguments, particularly among intellectual persons.

'Seriously –'

'Seriously –' he mimicked her exactly. She flushed, and then gave her unexpected charming laugh.

'You can't get away with it by parlour tricks,' she said. 'In a police state you're bound to feel a constant friction, anyone is. And –'

'In any sort of state,' he said, 'most lives of most people are much the same.'

'I deny that,' said Joan.

'They've got their married lives, they've got their children, they've got their hobbies. They've got their work.'

'*Your* work wouldn't be affected.' She seized the chance to talk about Roy himself. 'But you're an unusual man. Your work could go on just the same – in the moon. Imagine that you were a writer, or a Civil Servant, or a parson, or a lawyer, in Berlin now. Do you deny that the police state would make a difference? You must agree.'

'Just so,' said Roy, giving in to evade the argument. 'Just so.'

Both women smiled at him tenderly. They were always amused by the odd affirmative, which seemed so out of keeping. Joan's tenderness was full of a love deep and clear-eyed for so young a woman.

Roy returned to bantering with Lady Muriel. He was out to give them some relief, but he was happy with them, and it was all light and unpretending. He told her of some Junker acquaintances in Berlin, the von Heims. 'They reminded me of you so much, Lady Mu.'

'Why ever was that?'

'The Gräfin spent most of her time reading Gotha,' said Roy, sparkling with mischief, malice, fondness. 'Just like you, Lady Mu, idly turning over the pages of Debrett.'

She gave her loud crowing laugh, and slapped his hand. Then she said seriously:

'Of course, no one has ever called me snobbish.'

She laughed again at Roy. Joan, who knew her mother well and also knew that no one could treat her as Roy did, was melted in a smile of envy, incredulity, and love.

It was a dark rainy night when Roy and I walked out of the Lodge. On the grass in the court there were left a few patches of melting snow, dim in the gloom. The rain pelted down. Roy wanted to go shopping, and soon the rain had soaked his hair and was running down beside his ears.

I said something about Joan being in love with him, but he would not talk of her. It was rare for him to want to talk of love, rarer still of the love he himself received. He was less willing than any man to hint at a new conquest.

That night he was sad over the Master, but otherwise serene. He had come back with his spirits even and tranquil. Despite the shock of the afternoon, he was enjoying our walk in the rain.

He asked me for the latest gossip, he asked gently after my concerns. The rain swirled and gurgled in the gutters, came down like a screen between us and the bright shop windows. Roy took me from shop to shop, water dripping from us on to the floors, in order to buy a set of presents. On the way he told me whom he wanted them for – the strange collection of the shady, the shabbily respectable, the misfits, who lived in the same house in the Knesebeckstrasse. Roy would go back there, though his flat was uncomfortable, whenever he went to Berlin; for the rest, the 'little dancer' and the others, had already come to be lost without him. Some thought he was an unworldly professor, a rich simple Englishman, easy to fleece.

'Poor goops.' Roy gave his most mischievous smile. 'If I were going to make a living as a shark, I should do it well, shouldn't you? We should make a pretty dangerous pair, old boy. I must try to instruct them some time.'

Nevertheless, he took the greatest pains about their presents.

CHAPTER 16

'I Hate the Stars'

ON those winter nights the light in the Master's bedroom dominated the college. The weeks passed: he had still not been told; we paid our visits, came away with shamefaced relief. We came away into a different, busy, bustling, intriguing life; for, as soon as it was known that the Master must die, the college was set struggling as to who should be his successor. That struggle was exciting and full of human passion, but it need not be described here. It engrossed Arthur Brown completely, me in part, and Roy a little. We were all on the same side, and Winslow on the other. It was the sharpest and most protracted personal conflict that the college went through in my time.

Meanwhile, Roy spent more time in the Lodge than the rest of us put together. He sat for whole afternoons with the Master, planning their book on the heresies, and he became Lady Muriel's only support. In the Lodge he forgot himself entirely. He devoted himself, everything he was, to each of the three of them. But he knew that he was in danger of paying a bitter price. Outside he remembered what he was watching there. It filled him with dread. At times he waited for the first sign of melancholy to take hold of him. I was waiting too. I watched him turn to his work with savage absorption: and there came nights when he drank for relief.

It was harrowing for anyone to watch, even for those far tougher-skinned than Roy. We saw the Master getting a little more tired each time we visited him; and each time he was more surprised that his appetite and strength were not coming back. For a few days after he had been told that all was well, the decline seemed to stop. He even ate with relish. Then slowly, imperceptibly to himself, the false recovery left him. By February he was so much thinner that one could see the smooth cheeks beginning to sag. He no longer protested about not being allowed up. The deterioration was so visible that we wondered when he would suspect, or whether he had already done so. Yet there was not a sign of it. He complained once or twice that 'this wretched ulcer is taking a lot of getting rid of', but his spirits stayed high and he confided his sarcastic indiscretions with the utmost vivacity. It was astonishing to see, as he grew worse under our eyes, what faith and hope could do.

Everyone knew that he would have to be told soon. The disease appeared to be progressing very fast, and Lady Muriel told Roy that he must be given time to settle his affairs. She was dreading her duty, dreading it perhaps more than an imaginative person would have done; we knew that she would not shirk it for an hour once she decided that the time had come.

One February afternoon, I met Joan in the court. I asked first about her mother. She looked at me with her direct, candid gaze: then her face, which had been heavy with sadness, lost it all as she laughed.

'That's just like Roy,' she said.

'What do you mean?'

'Asking the unexpected question. Particularly when it's right. Of course, she's going through more than he is at present. She will, until she's told him. After that, I don't know, Lewis. I haven't seen enough of death to be sure. It may still be worse for her.' She spoke gravely, with a strange authority, as though she were certain of her reserves of emotional power. Then she smiled, but looked at me like an enemy. She said:

'Has Roy learned some of his tricks from you?'

'I have learned them from him,' I said. She did not believe it. She resented me, I knew. She resented the times he agreed with me; she thought I over-persuaded him. She envied the casual intimacy between us which I took for granted, for which she would have given so much. She would have given so much to have, as I did, the liberty of his rooms. Think of seeing him whenever she wanted! She loved him from the depth of her warm and powerful nature. Her love was already romantic, sacrificial, dedicated. Yet she longed too for the dear prosaic domestic nearnesses of everyday.

It was a Sunday when I spoke to Joan; the Wednesday after Roy's name was on the dining list for hall, but he did not come. Late at night, long after the porter's last round at ten o'clock, he entered my room without knocking and stood on the hearth-rug looking down at me. His face was drawn and set.

'Where have you been?' I said.

'In the lodge. Looking after Lady Mu.'

'She told him this afternoon,' he added, in a flat, exhausted voice. 'She needed someone to look after her. She wouldn't have been able to cope.'

'Joan?'

'Joan was extremely cool. She's very strong.'

He paused, and said quietly:

'I'll tell you later, old boy. I need to do something now. Let's go out. I'd like to drive over to –' the town where we had both lived – 'and have a blind with old George. I can't. They may want me tomorrow. Let's go to King's. There's bound to be a party in King's. I need to get out of the college.'

We found a party in King's, or at least some friends to talk and drink with. Roy drank very little, but was the gayest person there. I was watching for the particular glitter of which I was afraid, the flash in which his gaiety turned sinister and frantic. But it did not come. He quietened down, and young men clustered round to ask him to next week's parties. He was gentle to the shy ones, and by the time we set off home was resigned, quiet, and composed.

We let ourselves into college by the side-door, and walked through the court. When we came in sight of the Lodge windows, one light was still shining.

'I wonder,' said Roy, 'if he can sleep tonight.'

It was a fine clear night, not very cold. We stood together gazing at the lighted window.

Roy said quietly:

'I've never seen such human misery and loneliness as I did today.'

I glanced up at the stars, innumerable, brilliant, inhumanly calm. Roy's eyes followed mine, and he spoke with desolating sadness.

'I hate the stars,' he said.

We went to his rooms in silence, and he made tea. He began to talk, in a subdued and matter-of-fact tone, about the Master and Lady Muriel. They had never got on. It had not been a happy marriage. They had never known each other. Both Roy and I had guessed that for a long time past, and Joan knew it. I had once heard Joan talk of it to Roy. And he, who knew so much of sexual love, accepted the judgement of this girl, who was technically 'innocent'. 'I don't believe,' said Joan, direct and uncompromising, 'that they ever hit it off physically.'

Yet, as Roy said that night, they had lived together for twenty-five years. They had had children. They had had some kind of life together. They had not been happy, but each was the other's only intimate. Perhaps they felt more intimate in the supreme crisis just because of the unhappiness they had known in each other. It was not always those who were flesh of each other's flesh who were most tied together.

So, with that life behind them, she had to tell him. She screwed up her resolve, 'and if I know Lady Mu at all, poor dear,' said Roy, 'she rushed in and blurted it out. She hated it too much to be able to tell him gently. Poor dear, how much she would have liked to be tender.'

He did not reproach her for not having told him before, he did not hate her, he scarcely seemed aware of her presence. He just said: 'This alters things. There's no future then. It's hard to think without a future.'

He had had no suspicion, but he did not mind being fooled. He did not say a word about it. He was thinking of his death.

She could not reach him to comfort him. No one could reach him. She might as well not be there.

That was what hurt her most, said Roy, and he added, with a sad and bitter protest, 'we're all egotists and self-regarding to the last, aren't we? She didn't like not mattering. And yet when she left him, it was intolerable to see a human being as unhappy as she was. I told you before, I've never seen such misery and loneliness. How could I comfort her? I tried, but whatever could I do? She's not been much good to him. She feels that more than anyone thinks. Now, at the end, all she can do is to tell him this news. And he didn't seem to mind what she said.'

Roy was speaking very quietly. He was speaking from the depth of his dark sense of life.

Silently, we sat by the dying fire. At last Roy said:

'We're all alone, aren't we? Each one of us. Quite alone.' He asked: 'Old boy – how does one reach another human being?'

'Sometimes one thinks one can in love.'

'Just so,' he said. After a time, he added:

'Yet, sometimes after I've made love, I've lain with someone in my arms and felt lonelier than ever in my life.'

He broke out:

'If she was miserable and lonely today, what was it like to be him? Can anyone imagine what it's like to know your death is *fixed*?'

After she left him, Lady Muriel had gone to his room once again, to inquire about his meals. Joan had visited him for a few minutes. He had asked to be left alone for the evening. That was all Roy knew of his state.

'Can you imagine what he's gone through tonight? Is he lying awake now? Do you think his dreams are cheating him?'

Roy added:

'I don't believe he's escaped the thought of death tonight. It must be dreadful to face your death. I wonder how ours will come.'

CHAPTER 17

Struggle through Summer Nights

WHEN he knew the truth, it was a long time before the Master asked to see any of his friends. He told Roy, who alone was allowed to visit him, that he wished to 'get used to the idea'.

He talked to Roy almost every day. Throughout those weeks, he saw no one else, except his family and his doctor. He no longer mentioned the book on the heresies. He said much less than he used to. He was often absent-minded, as though he were trying to become familiar with his fate.

Then there came a time, Roy told me, as his own spirits darkened, when the Master seemed to have thought enough of his condition. He seemed to have got bored – it was Roy's phrase, and it was not said lightly – with the prospect of death. He had faced it so far as he could. For a time he wanted to forget. And he became extraordinarily considerate.

That was at the end of term, and he invited us to call on him one by one – not for his sake, but for ours. In his detached and extreme consideration, he knew that each of us wanted to feel of some help to him. He felt, with a touch of his old sarcasm, that he could give us that last comfort.

Everyone who talked to him was impressed and moved by his disinterested kindness. Yet I was appalled to receive so much consideration from him, to be asked about my affairs with wise detached curiosity – and then face the eyes of a dying man. His cheeks were hollow and yellow, and his skin had a waxy texture; his clothes hung on him in folds, on him who had been the best preserved of men, and as well groomed as Roy. And there was one macabre feature of his appearance, which I learned afterwards had upset him for a time. He had always been slender, he was now emaciated – but under his waistcoat swelled the round pseudo-paunch of his disease.

He had never been so kind, and I went out of the room with dread. It struck me with more distress than anyone, even Roy. For Roy, each hour in the Master's bedroom had been an agony; he had seen too much of suffering, too much of the inescapable human loneliness; yet this state of detached sub-ironic sympathy, to which the Master had now come, seemed to Roy a triumph of the spirit as the body died. He was moved to admiration and love; I was moved too, in the same way; but I also felt a personality dissolving in front of my eyes, a human being already passing into the eternal dark and cold.

At the beginning of the summer, the disease seemed to slow down. The doctors had guessed that he would be at the point of death by May or June: they admitted now that they had calculated wrong. He sat up a little each day in his bedroom above the sunny court. He was slightly more exhausted, still disinterestedly kind, still curious about each of us. It was clear that he might live for several months yet.

This lengthening of the Master's life had several effects upon those round him. The tension in the college about the next Master had been growing; everyone had reckoned that the election would be settled by the summer. Now the uncertainty was going to be indefinitely prolonged – and the news did not relax the tension, but increased it. The hostility between the two main parties, the talks at night, the attempts to cajole the three or four wavering votes – they all grew more urgent. And so did the campaign of propaganda and scandal. There were all kinds of currents of emotion in that election – men were moved, not only by personal feelings in the intimate sense, but also by their prejudices in subjects, in social origins, in political belief. At least two men were much influenced by the candidates' attitude to the Spanish war, the critical test in external politics. And there was a great deal of rancour set free. On the side which Winslow led, there was a determined attempt to label us others as rackety and disreputable. Winslow himself did not take part, although he was too much committed to the struggle to control his own party. He was set on getting his candidate in. Old Despard-Smith did some sombre calumny, and one or two others became virulent.

It was inevitable that much of this virulence should direct itself at Roy. He was unusual, brilliant, disturbing; some of the men who had opposed his election, though not Winslow, envied and hated him still. And by now they knew more about him. They had had him under their eyes for nearly two years. They knew a little, they suspected much more. In such an intimate society, small hints passed into circulation; often the facts were wildly askew but the total picture preserved a sort of libellous verisimilitude. With a self-righteous satisfaction, Roy's enemies acquired a sense, groping but not everywhere false, of a wild and dissipated life. They knew something of drunken parties, of young women, of a separate existence in London. They knew something of Joan's love for him.

The slander became more venomous, as though in a last desperate campaign. One heard Roy attacked night after night in hall and the combination room and in private gossip. Very often women's names were mentioned: as the summer term went on, Joan's was the most frequent of all.

It was a curious technique, attacking our candidate through his friends and supporters. But it was not altogether ineffective. It cost us a good deal of anxiety. We tried hard to conceal these particular slanders from Roy himself, but in the end they reached him.

If he had been untroubled, he would have laughed them away. No one cared less for what others thought. He might have amused himself in executing some outrageous reprisal. But in fact he had no resilience left. He did not laugh when he heard he was being maligned. He took it darkly. It was a weight upon him. He went from the Master's bedroom to face his own thoughts through interminable sleepless nights, and harsh, jeering voices came to him as he lay lucidly and despairingly awake. For what he had been waiting for had happened. The melancholy had gripped him again. He made less fight this time. He was both more frightened and more resigned.

It did not stop him spending all his spare time at the Lodge. He worked as hard as ever, he was drinking alone at night; but, whenever they wanted him, he was there. Perhaps it was because of them that he did not make his old frantic attempts to escape from his affliction. He did not see Udal at all, he scarcely left Cambridge for a day, he had not spent a night with Rosalind for months. He was living more chastely than at any time since I knew him. He did not talk to me about his wretchedness or hopes; he seemed resigned to being alone, lost, terrified.

I knew, though he said nothing, that thoughts pressed in on him with merciless clarity as he lay staring into the long bright summer dawns. In the Lodge he had seen the approach of death, the extreme of loneliness, faith, despair, the helpless cries of human beings as they try to give each other help. He had seen it, and now saw himself in this torment of his own melancholy. I believed later that in those nights he learned about despair.

He was looking harrowed and ill. Depriving himself of his minor pleasures, he played no cricket that summer; he was mewed up all the day time with his manuscripts, or inside the Lodge, and for the first time one saw his face with no sunburn at all. There was no colour in his face, except for the skin under his eyes.

I had to submit myself again to watch him suffer so. Much of the time I lived in apprehension. Some things I feared less than the first time, some more. I knew roughly now the course of these attacks. They differed a little among themselves; this was quieter, more despondent, more rooted in human grief; but even so I had already seen the occasional darts of fantastic elation. I had not to worry so much about the unknown. I expected that, after the melancholy had deranged and played with him, in another outburst it would end. All I could do was take such precautions as I could that this outburst would not hurt him or his friends.

But I feared something much more terrible, which last time I had not feared at all. I wanted to turn my mind away from what he must bear – not because of his present misery, but because it had overcome him *again*. He must have faced it often, in his loneliness on those summer nights. He must have seen it, in different lights and shades of recognition. And all were intolerable. Sometimes – *this was a doom he was born with. He was as much condemned as the Master. There was no more he could do.* He would be swept like this all through his life; at times, as now, he would be driven without will; he would not have the appearance of will which gives life dignity, meaning, and self-respect.

The Master still had will, facing his death. *He was more condemned.* He must be ready to suffer aimlessly, for no reason, whenever this affliction came. He would always be helpless.

Sometimes – *he could still escape. But why were the doors closed?* If he could escape, why was it so preposterously harder than for others? He had to struggle, to push back the sense of doom, and still the doors would not open, and misery came upon him again. He should have escaped before this attack, and yet he was caught. It was worse to feel that he could escape, and yet be caught. It was harder to endure, if there was a way out which he could not find.

I remembered that winter evening by the Serpentine, and I was wrung by pain and by acute fear. There were nights when I too lay awake.

It was during May that Joan first told Roy that she loved him. The reprieve to her father seemed to act as a trigger to her love. It had begun long since, in the days when as an awkward girl she used to decry Roy in company and quarrel with him whenever she could make the opportunity. It had accumulated through those harsh winter days in the Lodge, when they all rested on him. Now it was set loose and pouring out.

I knew it, because she talked to me about his unhappiness. Unlike Rosalind, she could not take it as a matter of course. She was forced to discover what had stricken him. She was the proudest of young women, and yet she humbled herself to ask me – even though she thought I was her enemy, even though she felt she alone should possess his secrets. Whatever it cost her, she must learn him through and through. I was touched both by her humility and her pride. So she watched him in those weeks of affliction with eyes that were anxious, distressed, loving, hungry to understand. But she was spared the climax.

I was nervous about him almost to the end of Arthur Brown's claret party. Brown gave this party to his wine-drinking colleagues each year at the beginning of June.

That summer he arranged it for the second night of May week. As a rule this would have been the night of the college ball, but, though the Master asked that all should continue normally, it was not being held this year. The undergraduates took their young women to balls at other colleges: Roy had danced with Joan at Trinity the previous night. Now he turned up at Brown's party, heavy-eyed for lack of sleep, and deceived all the others into believing that his sparkle was the true sparkle of a joyous week.

All through the evening, I could not keep my eyes away from him for long. Time after time, I was compelled to look at him, to confirm what I dreaded. For this was the sparkle I had seen before. I wished I could take him out of danger.

Six of us sat in Brown's rooms on that warm June night, and the decanters stood in a shapely row in the evening light. Brown was giving us the best clarets of 1920 and 1924.

'I must say, Tutor,' said Winslow, 'that you're doing us remarkably proud.'

'I thought,' said Brown comfortably, 'that it was rather an opportunity for a little comparative research.'

Although it was late evening, the sun had scarcely set, and over the roofs opposite the sky glowed brilliantly. From the court there drifted the scent of acacia, sweet and piercing. We settled down to some luxurious drinking.

Roy had begun the evening with some of his malicious imitations, precise, unsparing, and realistic, which rubbed away the first stiffness of the party. Winslow, who had once more come to see him in the glare of propaganda, was soon melted.

Since then Roy had been drinking faster than any of us. The mood was on him.

He talked with acute intensity. Somehow – to the others it sounded harmless enough – he brought in the phrase 'psychological insight'. One of the party said that he had never considered that kind of insight to be a special gift.

'It's time you did, you know,' said Roy.

'I don't believe in it. It's mumbo-jumbo,' said Winslow.

'You think it's white man's magic?' Roy teased him, but the wild glint had come into his eyes.

'My dear young man, I've been watching people since long before you were born,' said Winslow, with his hubristic and caustic air. 'And I know there's only one conclusion. It's impossible for a man to see into anyone else's mind.'

Roy began again, the glint brighter than ever.

Suddenly I broke in, with a phrase he recognized, with a question about Winslow's son.

Roy smiled at me. He was half-drunk, he was almost overcome by desperate elation – but he could still control it that night when he heard my signal. Instead of the frantic taunt I had been waiting for, he said:

'You'll see, Winslow. The kind of insight that old Lewis here possesses. It may be white man's magic, but it's quite real. Too real.'

He fell quiet as Winslow talked, for the second time that evening, about his son. Soon after he entered, Brown asked about his son's examination, which had just finished. Winslow had been rude in his own style, professing ignorance of how the boy was likely to have got on. Now, in the middle of the party, he gave a different answer.

'My dear Brown,' he said, 'I don't know what kind of a fool of himself the stupid child has really made. He thinks he has done reasonably well. But his judgement is entirely worthless. I shall be relieved if the examiners let him through.'

'Oh, they'll let him through,' said Brown amiably.

'I don't know what will happen to him if they don't,' said Winslow. 'He's a stupid child. But I believe there's something in him. He's a very nice person. If they give him a chance now, I honestly believe he may surprise you all in ten years' time.'

I had never heard Winslow speak with so little guard. He gazed at Brown from under his heavy lids, and recovered his caustic tone:

'My dear Tutor, you've had the singular misfortune to teach the foolish creature. I drink to you in commiseration.'

'I drink to his success,' said Brown.

After the party, Roy and I walked in the garden. It was a warm and balmy night, with a full moon lemon-yellow in the velvet sky. The smell of acacia was very strong. On the great trees the leaves lay absolutely still.

'I shall sleep tonight,' said Roy, after we had walked round once in silence. His face was pale, his eyes filmed and bloodshot, but the dionysiac look had gone. 'I shall sleep tonight,' he said, with tired relief.

He had not been to bed for forty-eight hours, he was more than a little drunk, yet he needed to reassure himself that he would sleep.

The smell of acacia hung over us.

'I think I'll go to bed, old boy,' he said. 'I shall be able to sleep tonight. You know, I've been getting out of practice.'

CHAPTER 18

Outburst

THE last college meeting of the academic year took place a fortnight after Brown's claret party. By tradition, it was called for a Saturday morning, to distinguish it from all other meetings of the year. For this was the one at which examination results were considered; the last of the results were published that morning, and Brown and I studied them together, a couple of hours before the bell was due to ring. There were several things to interest us – but the chief was that we could not find Dick Winslow's name. Brown thought it might be a clerical mistake, and rang up the examiners to make sure. There was no mistake. He had done worse than one could have believed.

The meeting began at half past eleven. As the room filled up, whispers about young Winslow were passing round the table; Winslow himself had not yet come. In the whispers one could hear excitement, sometimes pity, sometimes pleasure, sometimes pity and pleasure mixed. At last Winslow entered and strode to his place, looking at no one there.

An old man, who had not picked up the news, said a cheerful good morning.

'Good morning to you,' said Winslow in a flat leaden desolate voice. He was remote, absent-minded in his misery.

There were some minor courtesies before the meeting. Winslow was asked a question. He sat mute. He could not rouse himself to a tart reply. His head had sunk down, bent towards the table.

Despard-Smith, who had taken the chair since the Master fell ill, at last opened the business. The sacramental order was followed, even at this special examination meeting. There was only one trivial matter connected with livings: then came the financial items, when as a rule Winslow did most of the talking and entertained us in his own style. He could usually be relied on to keep us for at least half an hour – just as he had done at Roy's election. That morning, when Despard-Smith asked:

'Bursar, will you take us through your business?'

Winslow replied in defeat and dejection:

'I don't think it's necessary. It explains itself.'

He said nothing more. He sat there, the object of curious pitying, triumphant glances. There were some who remembered his arrogance, his cutting words. An opponent made several financial proposals: Winslow had not the strength even to object.

Then the Senior Tutor (who had been an enemy of Winslow's for years past) went through the examination results name by name. There were startling successes: there was a man who had a great academic future; there were failures of the hardworking and dense, there were failures among the gilded youth. There was one failure owing to a singular personal story. The Senior Tutor went through from subject to subject, until at last he came to history, which young Winslow had studied. The table was very quiet. I looked at Roy, and his expression filled me with alarm. Roy's eyes were fixed on Winslow, eyes full of angry pity, sad and wild. Since the claret party he had been unendurably depressed, and much of the time he had shut himself up alone. Now his face was haunted.

The Senior Tutor congratulated Brown on the performance of one pupil. He exuded enthusiasm over another. Then he looked at his list and paused. He said: 'I think there's nothing else to report,' and hurried on to the next subject.

It had been meant as sympathy, I believed. How Winslow felt it, no one could know. He sat silent, eyes fixed on the table, as though he had not heard.

We had not quite finished the business by one o'clock, but broke off for lunch. Lunch was laid in an inner room; it was cold, but on the same profuse scale as the tea before the usual meetings. There were piles of sandwiches, pâtés, jellies, meringues, pastries, savouries, jugs of beer, decanters of hock, claret, burgundy: the sight of the meal drew approving cries from some of the old men.

Most of the society ate their lunch with zest. Winslow stood apart, staring out of the window, taking one single sandwich. Roy watched him; he looked at no one but Winslow, he said nothing, his eyes sharpened. I noticed him push the wine away, and I was temporarily relieved. Someone spoke to him, and received a sharp uncivil answer, unlike Roy even at his darkest.

There were only a few speeches after lunch, and then the meeting closed. Men filed out, and I waited for Roy. Then I noticed Winslow still sitting at the table, the bursarial documents, order-book and files in front of him: he stayed in his place, too lost and dejected to move. Roy's eyes were on him. The three of us were left alone in the room. Without glancing at me or speaking, Roy sat down by Winslow's side.

'I am dreadfully sorry about Dick,' he said.

'That's nice of you.'

'And I am dreadfully sorry you've had to sit here today. When one's unhappy, it's intolerable to have people talking about one. It's intolerable to be watched.'

He was speaking with extreme and morbid fervour, and Winslow looked up from the table.

'You don't care what they say,' Roy cried, his eyes alight, 'but you want them to leave you alone. But none of us are capable of that much decency. I haven't much use for human beings. Have you, Winslow, have you? You know what people are feeling now, don't you? They're feeling that you've been taken down a peg or two. They're thinking of the times you've snubbed them. They're saying complacently how arrogant and rude you've been. But they don't matter. None of us matter.'

His tone was not loud but very clear, throbbing with an anguished and passionate elation.

Winslow stared at him, his eyes startled, bewildered, wretched.

'There is something in what they say, young man,' he said with resignation.

'Of course there is. There's something in most things they say about anyone.' Roy laughed. It was a terrible, heart-rending sound. 'They say I'm a waster and seduce women. There's something in that too.'

I moved round the table, and put a hand on his shoulder. Frantically he shook it off.

'Would you like to know how much there is in it?' he cried. 'We're both miserable. It may relieve you just a bit. Would you like to know how many loving invitations I've coaxed for myself – out of women connected with this college?'

Winslow was roused out of his wretchedness.

'Don't trouble yourself, Calvert. It's no concern of mine.'

'That's why I shall do it.' Roy took a sheet of blank paper, began to write fast in his fluent scholar's hand. I seized his arm, and his pen made a line across the paper.

He swore with frenzied glee. 'Go away, Lewis,' he said. His face was wild with a pure, unmixed, uncontrollable elation. At that moment the elation had reached its height. 'Go away. You're no use. This is only for Winslow and me. I need to finish it now.'

He wrote a few more words, dashed off his signature, gave the sheet to Winslow. 'This has been a frightful day for you,' Roy cried. 'Keep this to remind you that people don't matter. None of us matter.'

He smiled, said good afternoon, went with quick strides out of the room.

There was a silence.

'This is distressing,' said Winslow.

'He'll calm down soon.' I was alert, ready to explain, ready to guard secrets once more.

'I never had any idea that Calvert was capable of making an exhibition of himself. Is this the first time it has happened?'

I evaded and lied. I had never seen Roy lose control until this afternoon, I said. It was a shock to me, as it was to Winslow. Of course, Roy was sensitive, highly-strung, easily affected by the sorrows of his friends. He was profoundly upset over the Master, and it was wearing his nerves to see so much suffering. I tried to keep as near the truth as I safely could. In addition, I said, taking a risk, Roy was very fond of Winslow's son.

Winslow was recalled to his own wretchedness. He looked away from me, absently, and it was some time before he asked, in a flat tone:

'I'm very ignorant of these matters. Should you say that Calvert was seriously unstable?'

I did not tell Winslow any of the truth. He was a very clever man, but devoid of insight; and I gave him the sort of explanation which most people find more palatable than the strokes of fate. I said that Roy was physically not at his best. His blood pressure was low, which helped to make him despondent. I explained how he had been overworking for years, how his long solitary researches had affected his health and depressed his spirits.

'He's a considerable scholar, from all they say,' said Winslow indifferently. 'I had my doubts about him once, but I've found him an engaging young man.'

'There's nothing whatever to worry about.'

'You know him well,' said Winslow. 'I expect you're right. I think you should persuade him to take a good long holiday.'

Winslow looked down at the sheet of paper. It was some time before he spoke. Then he said:

'So there is something in the stories that have been going round?'

'I don't know what he has written there,' I said. 'I've no doubt that the stories are more highly painted than the facts. Remember they've been told you by people who envy him.'

'Maybe,' said Winslow. 'Maybe. If those people have this communication,' he tapped the paper, 'I don't see how Master Calvert is going to continue in this college. The place will be too hot to hold him.'

'Do you want to see that happen?' I was keyed up to throw my resolve against his. Winslow was thinking of his enemies in the college, how a scandal about Roy would confute them, how he could use it in the present struggle. He stared at me, and told me so without any adornment.

'You can't do it,' I said, with all the power I could call on.

'Why not?'

'You can't do it. You know some of the reasons that brought Calvert to the state he was in this afternoon. They're enough to stop you absolutely, by themselves.'

'If you'd bring it to a point –'

'I'll bring it to a point. We both know that Calvert lost control of himself. He got into a state pretty near despair. And he wouldn't have got into that state unless he'd seen that you were unhappy and others were pleased at your expense. Who else had any feeling for you?'

'It doesn't matter to me one way or the other,' said Winslow.

Then I asked:

'Who else had any feeling for your son Dick? You know that Calvert was upset about him. Who else had any feeling for your son?'

Winslow looked lost, bewildered, utterly without arrogance or strength. He looked sadly away from me. He did not speak for some moments. At last, in a tired, dejected, completely uninterested tone, he said, the words coming out slowly:

'What shall I do with this?' He pointed to the sheet of paper.

'I don't mind,' I said, knowing that it was safe.

'Perhaps you'd better have it.'

Winslow pushed it towards me, but did not give another glance as I walked to the fireplace, and put a match to it over the empty grate.

CHAPTER 19

The Cost of Knowledge

I WENT up to Roy's room. He was lying on his sofa, stretched out and relaxed. He jumped up and greeted me with a smile contrite and remorseful.

'Have I dished everything?' he said.

He was quite equable now, affectionate, and happy because the shadow had passed over.

'Have I dished everything?' he said.

'I think I've settled it,' I said, in tiredness and strain. I could let myself go at last. I felt overwhelmed by responsibility, I knew that I was ageing before my time. 'But you'll do something one day that I can't settle.'

'I'm frightened of that too,' said Roy.

'I shan't always be there to pick up the pieces,' I said.

'You look pretty worn. I need to order you some strawberries for tea,' he said with tender, mocking concern. He went into his bedroom to telephone, and talked to the kitchens in the voice of the senior fellow, ludicrously like the life. I could not help but smile, despite fatigue and worry and unreasonable anger. He came back and stood looking down at me.

'It's very hard on you, dear old boy,' he said, suddenly but very quietly. 'Having me to look after as well as poor Sheila. There's nothing I can say, is there? You know as much about it as I do. Or at least, if you don't now, you never will, you know.'

'Never mind,' I said.

'Of course,' said Roy, with a joyous smile, 'just at this minute I feel that I shall never be depressed again.'

In the next few days he spent much of his time with me. He was inventive and entertaining, as though to show me that I need not worry. He was quite composed and even-spirited, but not as carefree as after the first outburst. The innocence, the rapture, the hope, did not flood him and uplift him. He put on his fireworks for my benefit, but underneath he was working something out. What it was I could not guess. I caught him looking at me several times with a strange expression – protective, concerned, uneasy. There was something left unsaid.

On a night early in July, he invited me out to dinner in the town. It was strange for us to dine together in a restaurant in Cambridge: we had not done so since he became a fellow. It was stranger still for Roy to be forcing the conversation, to be unspontaneous, anxious to make a confidence and yet held back. He was specially anxious to look after me; he had brought a bottle of my favourite wine, and had chosen the dinner in advance out of dishes that I liked. He told me some gleeful anecdotes of people round us. But we came to the end of the meal and left the restaurant: he had still not managed to speak.

It was a fine and glowing evening, and I suggested that we should walk through one of the colleges down to the river. Roy shook his head.

'We're bound to meet someone if we do,' he said. 'They'll catch us. Some devils will catch us.' He was smiling, mocking himself. 'I don't want to be caught. I need to say something to you. It's not easy.'

So we walked to Garret Hostel Bridge. There was no one standing there, though some young men and girls on bicycles came riding over. Roy looked down into the water. It was burnished in the bright evening light, and the willows and bridges seemed to be painted beneath the surface, leaf by leaf and line by line: it was the time, just as the sun was dying, when all colours gained a moment of enhancement, and the reflections of the trees were brilliant.

'Well?' I said.

'I suppose I need to talk,' said Roy.

In a moment he said:

'I know what you think. About my nature. About the way I'm made.'

'Then you know more than I do,' I said, trying to distract him, but he turned on me in a flash with a sad, teasing, acute smile.

'That's what you say when you want someone to think you're nice and kind and a bit of an old buffer. I've heard you do it too often. It's quite untrue. You mustn't do it now.'

He looked into the water again.

'I know enough to be going on with,' he said. 'I know you reasonably well, old boy. I have seen what you believe about me.'

I did not answer. It was no use pretending.

'You believe I've got my sentence, don't you? I may get time off for good conduct – but you don't believe that I can get out altogether. A bit of luck can make a difference on the surface. And I need to struggle, because that can make a little difference too. But really, whatever happens to me, I can never change. I'm always sentenced to be myself. Isn't that what you believe? Please tell me.'

I did not reply for a moment. Then I said:

'I can't alter what you say – enough to matter.'

'Just so,' he said.

He cried:

'It's too stark for me. I can't believe it.'

He said quietly:

'I can't believe as you do, Lewis. It would make life pointless. My life isn't all that important, but I know it better than anyone else's. And I know that I've been through misery that I wouldn't inflict on a living soul. No one could deserve it. I couldn't deserve it, whatever I've done or whatever I shall do. You know that –'

'Yes, I know that,' I said, with anguished pity.

'If you're right, I've gone through that quite pointlessly. And I shall again. I can't leave it behind. If you're right, it could happen to others. There must be others who go through the same. Without reason, according to you. Just as a pointless joke.'

'It must happen to a few,' I said. 'To a few unusual men.'

'I can't accept a joke like that,' he said. 'It would be like living in a prison governed by an imbecile.'

He was speaking with passion and with a resentment I had never heard. Now I could feel what the terrible nights had done to him. Yet they had not left him broken, limp, or resigned. He was still choosing the active way. His whole body, as he leaned over the bridge, was vigorous with determination and purpose.

Neither of us spoke for some time. I too looked down. The brilliant colours had left the sky and water, and the reflections of the willows were dark by now.

'There's something else,' said Roy. His tone was sad and gentle.

He added, after a pause:

'I don't know how I'm going to say it. I've needed to say it all night. I don't know how I can.'

He was still gazing down into the water.

'Dear old boy,' he said, 'you believe something that I'm not strong enough to believe. There might come a time – there might come a time when I was held back – because of what you believe.'

I muttered.

'I've got a chance,' he said. 'But it will be a near thing. I need to have nothing hold me back. You can see that, can't you?'

'I can see that,' I said.

'You believe in predestination, Lewis,' he said. 'It doesn't prevent you battling on. It would prevent me, you know. You're much more robust than I am. If I believed as you believe, I couldn't go on.'

He went on:

'I think you're wrong. I need to act as though you're wrong. It may weaken me if I know what you're thinking. There may be times when I shall not want to be understood. I can't risk being weakened, Lewis. Sooner than be weakened, I should have to lose everything else. Even you.'

A punt passed under the bridge and broke the reflections. The water had ceased swirling before he spoke again.

'I shan't lose you,' he said. 'I don't think I could. You won't get rid of me. I've never felt what intimacy means, except with you. And you –'

'It is the same with me.'

'Just so,' said Roy.

He added very quietly:

'I wouldn't alter anything if I could help it. But there may come a time when I get out of your sight. There may come a time when I need to keep things from you.'

'Has that time come?' I asked.

He did not speak for a long time.

'Yes,' he said.

He was relieved to have it over. As soon as it was done, he wanted to assure me that nearly everything would be unchanged. On the way back to the college, he arranged to see me in London with an anxiety, a punctiliousness, that he never used to show. Our meetings had always been casual, accidental, comradely: now he was telling me that they would go on unchanged, our comradeship would not be touched; the only difference was that some of his inner life might be concealed.

It was the only rift that had come between us. During the time we had known each other, his life had been wild and mine disordered, but our relation had been profoundly smooth, beyond anything in my experience. We had never had a quarrel, scarcely an irritable word.

It made his rejection of intimacy hard for me to bear. I was hurt, sharply, sickly, and bitterly hurt. I had the same sense of deprivation as if I had been much younger. Perhaps the sense of deprivation was stronger now; for, while as a younger man my vanity would have been wounded, on the other hand I should still have looked forward to intimacies more transfiguring even than this of ours; now I had seen enough to know that such an intimacy was rare, and that it was unlikely I should ever take part in one again.

Yet he could do no other than draw apart from me. If he were to keep his remnant of hope, he could do nothing else. For I could not hope on his terms: he had seen into me, and that was all.

It had been bitter to watch him suffer and know I could not help. That was a bitterness we all taste, one of the first facts we learn of the human condition. It was far more bitter to know that my own presence might keep him from peace of mind. It was the harshest of ironies: for he was he, and I was I, as Montaigne said, and so we knew each other: just because of that mutual knowledge, I stood in his way.

I had thought I was a realistic man – and yet I took it with dismay and cursed that we are as we are. But I tried not to make the change harder for him. As I told Joan in the spring, I had learned more from Roy than he from me. I had watched the absolute self-forgetfulness with which he spent himself on another, the self-forgetfulness he had so often given to me. I was not capable of his acts of selflessness, I was not made like him. But I could try to imitate him in practice. There was no question what I must do. I had to preserve our comradeship in the shape he wished, without loss of spirits and without demur. I had to be there, without trouble or pride, if he should want me.

CHAPTER 20

A Young Woman in Love

ROY and Joan became lovers during that summer. I wondered who had taken the initiative – but it was a question without meaning. Roy was ardent, fond of women, inclined to let them see that he desired them, and then wait for the next move: in his self-accusation to Winslow, he said that he 'coaxed invitations' from women, and that was no more than the truth. At the same time, Joan was a warm-blooded young woman, direct and canalized in all she felt and did. She was not easily attracted to men; she was fastidious, diffident, desperately afraid that she would lack physical charm to those she loved. But she had been attracted to Roy right back in the days when she thought he was frivolous and criticized his long nose. She had not known quite what it meant, but gradually he came to be surrounded by a haze of enchantment; of all men he was the first she longed to touch. She stayed at her window to watch him walk through the court. She thought of excuses to take a message to his rooms.

She told herself that this was her first knowledge of lust. She had a taste for the coarse and brutal words, the most direct and uncompromising picture of the facts. This was lust, she thought, and longed for him. She saw him with Rosalind and others, women who were elegant, smart, alluring, and she envied them ferociously, contemptuously, and with self-abasement. She thought they were fools; she thought none of them could understand him as she could; and she could not believe that he would ever look at her twice.

She found, incredulously, that he liked her. She heard him make playful love to her, and she repeated the words, like a charm, before she went to sleep at night. At once her longing for him grew into dedicated love, love undeviating, whole-hearted, romantic, and passionate. And that love became deeper, richer, pervaded all her thoughts, during the months her father lay dying and Roy sat with them in the Lodge.

For she was not blinded by the pulse of her blood. Some things about him she did not see, for no girl of twenty could. But others she saw more vividly, with more strength of fellow-feeling, even with more compassion, than any woman he had known. She could throw aside his caprices and whims, for she had seen him comfort her mother with patience, simplicity, and strength. She had seen him suffer with them. She had heard him speak from the depth of feeling, not about her, but about her father's state and human loneliness: after his voice, she thought, all others would seem dull, orotund, and complacent. She had watched his face stricken, or, as she put it, 'possessed by devils' that she did not understand. She wanted to spend her life in comforting him.

So her love filled her and drove her on. I thought it would be like her if, despite her shrinking diffidence, she finally asked to become his mistress. It was too easy to imagine her, with no confidence at all, talking to him as though fiercely and choosing the forthright words. But that did not really mean that she had taken the initiative. Their natures played on each other. Somehow it would have happened. There was no other end.

From the beginning, Roy felt a deeper concern for her than for anyone he loved. She was, like her mother, strong and defenceless. Stronger and abler than her mother, and even less certain of love. Roy was often irresponsible in love, with women who took it as lightly as he did. But Joan was dependent on him from the first time he kissed her. He could not pretend otherwise. Perhaps he did not wish it otherwise, for he was profoundly fond of her. He was amused by her sulkiness and fierceness, he liked to be able to wipe them away. He had gone through them to the welling depths of emotion, where she was warm, tempestuous, violent, and tender. He found her rich beyond compare.

Like her, he too had been affected by their vigil in the Lodge. It had surrounded her, and all that passed between them, with its own kind of radiance – the radiance of grief, suffering, intense feeling, and ineluctable death. In that radiance, they had talked of other things than love. He had told her more than he had told any woman of his despair, his search, his hope. He was moved to admiration by her strength, which never turned cold, never wilted, stayed steady through the harsh months in the Lodge. There were times when he rested on that strength himself. He came to look upon her as an ally, as someone who might take his hand and lead him out of the dark.

It was not that she had any obvious escape to offer him. She was not a happy young woman, except when she caught light from his presence. She had left her father's faith, and in her beliefs and disbeliefs she was typical of her time. Like me, she was radical in politics and sceptical in religion. But Roy felt with her, as he had done with me, that deep down he could find a common language. She was unusually clever, but it was not her intellect that he valued. He had spent too much time with clever men; of all of us, he was the most indifferent to the intellect; he was often contemptuous of it. It was not Joan's intellect he valued, but her warm heart and her sense of life. He thought she might help him, and he turned to her with hope.

Meanwhile, the Master's state seemed to change very little. Over the months Joan told us that she could see the slow decline. Gradually he ate less, was sick more often, spent more of his time in bed; he had had little pain throughout the illness, and was free of it now; the curve dipped very slowly, and it was often hard for her and her mother to realize that he was dying. Sometimes they felt that he had reached a permanent state, weak, tired, but full of detached kindness. He was so mellow and understanding that it humbled everyone round him, and they spoke of him with wonder and magnified affection. They spoke of him in quiet tones, full of something like hero worship. Lady Muriel, so Joan said, was gentler than anyone had ever known her.

I thought of that comment when I next saw her. Throughout the year, at the Master's request, she had stoically continued some of her ordinary entertaining, and the official Lodge lunches had gone on without check. She had, however, asked no guests at night. It was Joan's idea that Roy and I should call in after dinner one night in July, and treat her to a four at bridge. Like Lord Boscastle, Lady Muriel liked a game of bridge more than most things in the world; she had deprived herself of the indulgence since the Master fell ill.

Roy and I entered the drawing-room that night as though we had been invited by Joan, and Lady Muriel was still enough herself to treat me so.

'I am always glad for my daughter to have her friends in the house, Mr Eliot,' she said. 'I am only sorry that I have not been able to see as much of the fellows recently as I used to set myself.'

She sat in her armchair, stiff, formal, uncompromising. She looked a little older; her eyelids had become heavier, and her cheeks were pinched. But, as she spoke to me, her back was as poker-like as ever, and her voice just as unyielding. She said:

'How is your wife, Mr Eliot? I do not remember seeing her for a considerable time.'

'She's rather better, Lady Muriel.'

'I am very glad to hear it. I am still hoping that you will find a suitable house in Cambridge, so that you will not be separated so often. I believe there are suitable houses in Grantchester Meadows.'

She looked at me suspiciously, and then at her daughter, as though she were signalling my married state. It seemed incredible that she should think me a danger when she could see Joan in Roy's presence. For Joan was one of those women who are physically transmuted by the nearness of their lover, as it seemed by the bodily memory of the act of love. Her face was softer for hours together, the muscles relaxed, the lines of her mouth altered as she looked at him. Even her strong coltish gawky gait became loosened, when he was there.

Roy had been deputed to propose bridge. Lady Muriel was gratified, but at once objected:

'I couldn't, Roy. I have not touched a card for months.'

'We need you to,' said Roy. 'Do play with us.'

'I think it would be better if I left you three to yourselves,' she said.

'You don't think you ought, do you, Lady Mu?' Roy asked quietly.

She looked confused.

'Perhaps it isn't the most appropriate time –'

'Need you go without the little things?' said Roy. 'I'm sure the Master would tell you not to.'

'Perhaps he would,' said Lady Muriel, suddenly weak, unassertive, broken down.

We played some bizarre rubbers. Roy arranged for stakes of sixpence a hundred, explaining, out of pure devilry, that 'poor old Lewis can't afford more. If he's going to save up for a suitable house.' (Lady Muriel's idea of a 'suitable house' for me was something like the house of a superior college servant: and Roy had listened with delight.) Even at those stakes, Lady Muriel took several pounds from both Roy and me. It gave her great pleasure, for she had an appetite for money as well as for victory. The night passed, Lady Muriel's winnings mounted; Joan was flushed and joyful with Roy at the same table; Lady Muriel dealt with her square, masterful hands and played with gusto and confidence. Yet she was very quiet. Once the room would have rung with her indignant rebukes – 'I am surprised you had such diamonds, Mr Eliot'. But now, though she was pleased to be playing, though she enjoyed her own skill, she had not the heart to dominate the table. After Roy's word about the Master, she was subdued.

It was a long time before she seemed to notice the heterogeneous play. For it was the oddest four. Lady Muriel herself was an excellent player, quick, dashing, with a fine card memory. Joan was very good. I was distinctly poor, and Roy hopelessly bad; I might have been adequate with practice, but he could never have been. He was quite uninterested, had no card sense, disliked gambling, and had little idea of the nature of odds. It was curious to see him frowning over his hand, thinking three times as long as anyone at the table: then he would slap down the one card for which there was no conceivable justification. It was hard to guess what could be going on in his mind.

Joan was smiling lovingly. For he had entered into it out of good nature, but she knew that he was irritated. He chose to do things expertly, or not at all.

At last Lady Muriel said:

'Do you like playing bridge, Roy?'

He smiled.

'I like playing with you, Lady Mu.'

She was just ready to deal, but held the pack in her hand.

'Do you like the game?'

'Of course I do.'

'Do you really like the game, Roy?' Her tone was not her usual firm one, but insistent. Roy looked at her, and gave her an affectionate smile.

'No, not very much, Lady Mu,' he said.

'It's good of you to give up your evening,' she said. She added, in a low, almost inaudible murmur: 'I wonder if the Master ever liked the game. I don't remember asking him. I'm afraid he may have felt the same as you.'

She still did not deal. Suddenly we saw the reason. A tear rolled down her face.

She had been subjugated by the Master's disinterested kindness. She felt ashamed, she tried to imagine now things which had not troubled her for thirty years. It was almost incredible, as Roy said to me late that night in the garden, that she could have played with him night after night and never have known if he enjoyed the game. She was broken down by his heightened understanding, as he came near to death. Her imagination was quickened; she wanted to make up for all her obtuseness had cost him; she could not rest with her old content, formidable and foursquare inside herself. She felt unworthy. If his illness had made him more selfish, had worn her out with trouble, she would have undergone less pain.

I was asked myself to call on the Master towards the end of August. Roy had been obliged to return to Berlin in order to give a course of lectures, and it was Joan who gave me the message. She had heard from Roy the day before, and could not help telling me so. 'He doesn't keep me waiting for letters,' she said, happily and humbly. 'I never expected he'd write so often.' She longed to confess how much she loved him, she longed to throw away her self-respect.

By this time the Master did not often leave his bed, and I looked at him as he lay there. His face had become that of a very old man; it was difficult to remember him in the days when he seemed so well-preserved. The skin was dried up, waxy-yellow, lined and pouched. His eyes had sunk deeply in their orbits, and the lids were very dark. Yet he managed to keep his voice enough like its former self not to upset those who listened to him.

He spoke to me with the same kind, detached curiosity that had become his habit. He asked after my affairs as though nothing else interested him. Suddenly he saw that he was distressing me.

'Tell me, Eliot,' he said gently, 'would it embarrass you less if I talk of what it's like to be in this condition?'

'Much less,' I said.

'I believe you mean that,' he said. 'You're a strange man.

'Well,' he went on, 'stop me if I ramble. I've got something I particularly want to say to you, before you go. I can think quite clearly. Sometimes I fancy I think more clearly than I ever did in my life. But then the ideas start running away with me, and I get tired. Remember, this disease is something like being slowly starved.'

He was choosing the tone which would distress me least. He went on to discuss the election of his successor; he asked about the parties and intrigues, and talked with his old sarcastic humour, with extraordinary detachment, as though he were an observer from another world – watching the human scene with irony, and the kind of pity which hides on the other side of cynicism. He made one or two good jokes. Then he asked whether the college had expected to get the election over before now. I said yes. He smiled.

'It can't be long,' he said quietly. 'There are days even with this disease when you feel a little better. And you *hope*. It's ridiculous, but you hope. It seems impossible that your will should count for nothing. Then you realize that it's *certain* that you must die in six months. And you think it is too horrifying to bear. People will tell you, Eliot, that uncertainty is the worst thing. Don't believe them. Certainty is the worst thing.'

He was very tired, and closed his eyes. I thought how he was facing death with stoicism, with detachment, and with faith. Yet even he would have prayed: take this from me at least. Do not let me be certain of the time of my death. His faith assured him that he would pass into another existence. But that was a comfort far away from the animal fact. Just like the other comfort that I should one day have to use myself: they tell me that, when I am dead, I shall not know. Those consolations of faith or intellect could not take away the fear of the animal fact.

He began to talk again, but now he seemed light-headed, his words flew like the associations of a dream. I had to remind him:

'You said you had something important to tell me, before I go.'

He made an effort to concentrate. The ideas set off in flight again, but he frowned and gathered up his will. He found a clue, and said:

'What is happening about Roy Calvert?'

'He's in Berlin. The proofs of the new part of the liturgy are just coming in.'

'Berlin . . . I heard some talk about him. Didn't he take my daughter to a ball?'

'Yes.'

He was quiet. I wondered what he was thinking.

Again he frowned with concentration.

'Eliot,' he said. 'I want you to do me a favour. Look after Roy Calvert. He's the great man of the future in my field. I like to think that he won't forget all about my work. Look after him. He'll need it. People like him don't come twice in a generation. I want you to do me a favour. Look after Roy Calvert.'

That cry came partly from the sublime kindness in which he was ending his life. I was moved and shaken as I gave him my promise.

But it was not only self-forgetting kindness that brought out that cry; it was also a flicker of his own life; it was a last assertion of his desire not to be forgotten. He had not been a distinguished scholar, and he was a modest man who ranked himself lower than he deserved. But he still did not like to leave this mortal company without something to mark his place. For him, as for others I had sat by in their old age, it was abhorrent to imagine the world in which he had lived going on as though he had never been. It was a support, bare but not illusive, to know that he would leave a great scholar behind him, whom he could trust to say: 'You will find that point in one of old Royce's books. He made it completely clear.' A shadow of himself would linger as Roy became illustrious. His name would be repeated among his own kind. It was his defiance of the dark.

I thought by his bedside, and again a few minutes later when I met Joan, how tough the core of our selves can be. The Master's vanities had been burned away, he was detached and unselfish as he came towards his death, and yet the desire to be remembered was intact. And Joan was waiting for me in the drawing-room, and her first question was:

'What did he say about Roy?'

She knew that the Master had wished to tell me something. It was necessary for her to know any fact which affected Roy.

I told her that the Master had asked me to do what I could for Roy.

'Is that all?'

'Yes.'

'There was nothing else?'

I repeated one or two of the Master's observations, looking at us from a long way off.

'I mean, there was nothing else about Roy?'

She was deeply attached to her father, she had suffered by his side, she had been touched beyond expression as his self-forgetful kindness grew upon him in the last months of his life – but it counted for nothing beside her love for Roy. She was tough in her need for him. All her power was concentrated into feeling about him. Human beings in the grip of passion are more isolated than ever, I thought. She was alone with her love. Perhaps, in order to be as healthy and strong as she was, one had to be as tough.

The Master had asked me to look after Roy. As I listened to that girl, I felt that she would take on the task, even if she knew as much as I did. She would welcome the dangers that she did not know. She cross-examined me with single-minded attention. She made me hope.

CHAPTER 21

Towards the Funeral

ROY came back from Berlin in October, and I watched contrasts in
Joan as sharp as I had seen them in any woman. Often she was a girl,
fascinated by a lover whom she found enchanting, seeing him hazily,
adoringly, through the calm and glorious Indian summer. The college
shimmered in the tranquil air, and Joan wanted to boast of him, to
show off the necklace he had brought her. She loved being teased,
having her sulkiness devastated, feeling mesmerized in front of his
peculiar mischief. She was too much a girl not to let his extravagant
presents be seen by accident; she liked her contemporaries to think
she was an abandoned woman, pursued by a wicked, distinguished,
desirable, and extremely lavish lover. Once or twice, in incredulous
delight, she had to betray her own secret.

She confided it to Francis Getliffe and his wife, and Francis talked
anxiously to me. He liked and understood her, and he could not believe that Roy would bring her anything but unhappiness. Francis had
never believed that Roy was a serious character; now he believed it
less than ever, for Roy had come back from Berlin, apparently cheerful and composed, but ambiguous in his political attitude. Francis, like
many scientists of his age, was a straightforward, impatient, positive
Socialist, with technical backing behind his opinions and no nonsense
or frills. He was angered by Roy's new suggestions, which were
subtle, complex, and seemed to Francis utterly irresponsible. He was
angered almost as much by Roy's inconsistency; for Roy, despite his
friends in high places in the Third Reich, had just smuggled into England a Jewish writer and his wife. It was said that Roy had taken some
risks to do it; I knew for certain that he was spending a third of his
income on them. Francis heard this news with grudging approval,
and was then maddened when Roy approached him with a solemn
face and asked whether, in order to ease relations with Germany, the
university could not decree that Jewish scholars were 'Welsh by
statute'.

'He'll be no good to her,' said Francis.

'She's very happy now.'

'She's happy because he's good at making love,' said Francis curtly. 'It won't last. She wants someone who'll marry her and make her a decent husband. Do you think he will?'

Francis was right about Joan. She needed marriage more than most women, because she had so often felt diffident and unlike others. It was more essential to her than to someone like Rosalind, who had never tormented herself with thoughts of whether men would pass her by. Joan recognized that it was essential to her, if ever she were to become whole. She thought now, like any other girl, of marrying Roy, sometimes hoped, sometimes feared: but she was much too proud to give him a sign. She was so proud that she told herself they had gone into this love affair as equals; she had done it with her eyes open, and she must not let herself forget it.

So she behaved like a girl in love, sometimes like a proud and unusual girl, sometimes like anyone who has just known what rapture is. But I saw her when she was no longer rapturous, no longer proud, no longer exalted by the wonder of her own feelings, but instead compassionate, troubled, puzzled by what was wrong with him, set upon helping him. For she had seen him haunted in the summer, and she would not let herself rest.

She was diffident about attracting him: but she had her own kind of arrogance, and she believed that she alone could understand him. And she was too healthy a woman, too optimistic in her flesh and bone, not to feel certain that there was a solution; she did not believe in defeat; he was young, gifted, and high-spirited, and he could certainly be healed.

It was not made easy for her – for, though he wanted her help, he did not tell her all the truth. He shut out parts of his nature from her: shut them out, because he did not want to recognize them himself. She knew that he was visited by desperate melancholy, but he told her as though it came from a definite cause: if only he could find peace of mind he would be safe. She knew he was frightened at any premonition that he was going to be attacked again: she believed, as he wanted to, that they could find a charm which kept him in the light.

The Master lay overlooking the court through that lovely, tranquil autumn. Joan tried to learn what faith would mean to Roy.

She found it unfamiliar, foreign to her preconceptions of him, foreign to her own temperament. One thing did not put her off, as it did Francis Getliffe and so many others; since she loved him, she was not deceived by his mischievous jokes; she could see through them to the gravity of his thought. But the thought itself she found strange, and often forbidding.

He was searching for God. Like me, she had heard her father's phrase. But she discovered that the search was not as she imagined. She had expected that he was longing to be at one with the unseen, to know the immediate presence of God. Instead, he seemed to be seeking the authority of God. He seemed to want to surrender his will, to be annihilated as a person. He wanted to lose himself eternally in God's being.

Joan knew well enough the joy of submission to her lover; but she was puzzled, almost dismayed, that this should be his vision of faith. She loved him for his wildness, his recklessness, his devil-may-care; he took anyone alive as his equal; why should he think that faith meant that he must throw himself away? 'Will is a burden. Men are freest when they get rid of will.' She rebelled at his paradox, with all her sturdy Protestant nature. She hated it when he told her that men might be happiest under the authority of the state – 'apart from counter-suggestible people like you, Joan'. But she hated most his vision, narrow and intense, of the authority of God.

In his search of religion, he did not give a thought to doing good. She knew that many people thought of him as 'good', she often did herself – and yet any suggestion that one should interfere with another's actions offended him. 'Pecksniffery', he called it. He was for once really angry with her when she told him that he was good himself. 'Good people don't do good,' he said later, perversely. In fact, the religious people he admired were nearly all of them contemplative. Ralph Udal sponged on him shamelessly, wanted to avoid any work he did not like, prodded Roy year in, year out to get him a comfortable living, and was, very surprisingly, as tolerant of others as of himself. None of this detracted from Roy's envy of his knowledge of God. And old Martineau, since he took to the religious life, had been quite useless. To Roy it was self-evident that Martineau knew more of God than all the virtuous, active, and morally useful men.

Joan could not value them so, and she argued with him. But she did not argue about the experience which lay at the root of Roy's craving for faith. He told her, as he told me that night we walked on the Roman road, about his hallucination that he was lost, thrown out of God's world, condemned to opposition while all others were at rest. That sense had visited him once again, for the third time, during the blackness of the summer.

Joan had never met anything like it, but she knew it was a passionate experience; everything else dropped away, and her heart bled for him. For she could feel that it came from the depth of his nature; it was a portent that nothing could exorcise or soften. While the remembrance haunted him, he could not believe.

She called on all she knew to save him from that experience. She pressed love upon him, surrounded him with love (too much, I sometimes thought, for she did not understand the claustrophobia of being loved). She examined her own heart to find some particle of his despair. If she could know it herself, only a vestige, only for a moment, perhaps she could help him more. She asked others about the torments of doubt and faith – loyally, sturdily, and unconvincingly keeping out Roy's name. She talked to me: it cost her an effort, for, though she had with difficulty come to believe that I admired her and wished her well, she was never at ease with me as Rosalind was. Rosalind had confided in me when she was wildly unhappy over Roy – but it had been second nature to her to flatter me, to make me feel that in happier days she might not have been indifferent to me. With Joan, there was not a ray of flirtatiousness, not the faintest aura of love to spare. Except as a source of information, I did not exist. Each heartbeat served him, and him alone.

She came to a decision which took her right outside herself. Wise or unwise, it showed how she was spending her imagination in his life. Herself, she stayed in her solid twentieth-century radical unbelief: but him she tried to persuade to act as though he had found faith, in the hope that faith would come.

It was bold and devoted of her. And there were a few weeks, unknown at the time to anyone but themselves, when he took her guidance. He acted to her as though his search was over. He went through the gestures of belief, not in ritual but in his own mind. He struggled to hypnotize himself.

He could not keep it up. Sadness attacked him, and he was afraid that the melancholy was returning. Even so, he knew that his acts of faith were false; he felt ashamed, hollow, contemptible, and gave them up. Inexplicably, his spirits rose. The attempt was at an end.

Joan did not know what to do next. The failure left its mark on her. She was seized with an increased, an unrestrainable passion to marry him. Even her pride could not hold down a sign.

It became obvious as one saw them together in the late autumn. Often she was happy, flushing at his teasing, breaking out into her charming laugh, which was richer now that she had been loved. But more than once I saw them in a party, when she thought herself unobserved: she looked at him with a glance that was heavy, brooding, possessive, consumed with her need to be sure of him.

I was anxious for her, for about that time I got the impression that something had broken. She did not seem to know, except that she was becoming more hungry for marriage; but I felt sure that for him the light had gone out. Why, I could not tell or even guess. It did not show itself in any word he spoke to her, for he was loving, attentive, insistent on giving her some respite from the Lodge, always ready to sit with her there in the last weeks of her father's life.

He was good at dissimulating, though he did it seldom; yet I was certain that I was right. For lack of ease in a love affair is one of the hardest things to conceal – and this was particularly true for Roy, who in love or intimacy moved as freely as through the evening air.

I was anxious and puzzled. One night in late November I heard him make a remark which sounded entirely strange, coming from him. It was said in fun, but I felt that it was forced out, endowed with an emotion he could not control. The occasion was quite trivial. The three of us had been to a theatre, and Roy had mislaid the tickets for our coats. It took us some time, and a little explanation, to redeem them. Joan scolded him as we walked to the college along the narrow street.

'I didn't do it on purpose,' he said.

'You're quite absurd,' said Joan. 'It was very careless.'

Then Roy said:

'Think as well of me as you can.' He was smiling, and so was she, but his voice rang out clear. 'Think as well of me as you can.'

I had never before heard him, either in play or earnest, show that kind of concern. He was the least self-conscious of men. It was a playful cry, and she hugged his arm and laughed. Yet it came back to my ears, clear and thrilling, long after outbursts of open feeling had gone dead.

Through November the Master became weaker and more drowsy. He was eating very little, he was always near the borderline of sleep. Joan said that she thought he was now dying. The end came suddenly. On 2 December the doctor told Lady Muriel and Joan that he had pneumonia, and that it would soon be over. Two days later, just as we were going into hall for dinner, the news came that the Master had died.

After hall, I went to see Roy, who had not been dining. I found him alone in his rooms, sitting at a low desk with a page of proofs. He had already heard the news.

He spoke, sadly and gently, of Joan and her mother. He said that he would complete the 'little book' on heresies as soon as he was clear of the liturgy. He would bring it out as a joint publication by Royce and himself. 'Would that have pleased him?' said Roy. 'Perhaps it would please them a little.'

A woman's footsteps sounded on the stairs, and Joan came in. She looked at me, upset to see me there. Without a word, Roy took her in his arms and kissed her. For a moment she rested with her head against his shoulder, but she heard me get up to go.

'Don't bother, Lewis,' she said. She was quite dry-eyed. 'I've come to take Roy away, if he will. Won't you come to mother?' she asked him, her eyes candid with love. 'You're the only person who can be any use to her tonight.'

'I was coming anyway,' said Roy.

'You're very tired yourself,' I said to Joan. 'Hadn't you better take a rest?'

'Let me do what's got to be done before I think about it,' she said.

She was staunch right through. Roy went to eat and sleep in the Lodge until after the funeral. Joan made no claims on him; she asked him to look after her mother, who needed him more.

Lady Muriel was inarticulately glad of his presence. She could not say that she was grateful, she could not speak of loss or grief or any regret. She could not even cry. She sat up until dawn each night before the funeral, with Roy beside her. And each night, as she went at last to bed, she visited the room where lay her husband's body.

At the funeral service in the chapel, she and Joan sat in the stalls nearest the altar. Their faces were white but tearless, their backs rigid, their heads erect.

And, after we had returned from the cemetery to the college, word came that Lady Muriel wished to see all the fellows in the Lodge. The blinds of the drawing-room were drawn back now; we filed in and stood about while Lady Muriel shook hands with us one by one. Her neck was still unbent, her eyes pitiably bold. She spoke to each of us in her firm, unyielding voice, and her formula varied little. She said to me: 'I should like to thank you for joining us on this sad occasion. I appreciate your sign of respect to my husband's memory. I am personally grateful for your kindness during his illness. My daughter and I are going to my brother, and our present intention is to stay there in our house. We may be paying a visit to Cambridge next year, and I hope you will be able to visit us.'

Roy and I walked away together.

'Poor thing,' he said gently.

He went back to the Lodge to see them through another night. At last Lady Muriel broke down. 'I shall never see him again,' she cried. 'I shall never see him again.' In the drawing-room, where she had bidden us good-bye so formally, that wild, animal cry burst out; and then she wept passionately in Roy's arms, until she was worn out.

For hours Joan left them together. Her own fortitude still kept her from being another drag on Roy. She remained staunch, trying to help him with her mother. Yet that night words were trembling on her lips; she came to the edge of begging him to love her for ever, of telling him how she hungered for him to marry her. She did not speak.

CHAPTER 22

Strain in a Great House

ROY was working all through the spring in the Vatican Library, and then moved on to Berlin. I only saw him for a few hours on his way through London, but I heard that he was meeting Joan. He had not mentioned her in his letters to me, which were shorter and more stylized than they used to be, though often lit up by stories of his acquaintances in Rome. When I met him, he was affectionate, but neither high-spirited nor revealing. I did not see him again until he returned to England for the summer: as soon as he got back, we were both asked down to Boscastle.

I had twice visited Boscastle by myself, though not since Lady Muriel and Joan had gone to live there. Lady Boscastle had invited me so that she could indulge in two pleasures – tell stories of love affairs, and nag me subtly into being successful as quickly as might be. She had an adamantine will for success, and among the Boscastles she had found no chance to use it. So I came in for it all. She was resolved that I should not leave it too late. She approved the scope of my ambitions, but thought I was taking too many risks. She counted on me to carve out something realizable within the next three years. She was sarcastic, flattering, insidious, and shrewd. She even invited eminent lawyers, whom she had known through her father, down to Boscastle so that I could talk to them.

Since the Royces arrived at the house, I had had no word from her or them. It was June when she wrote to say that Roy was going straight there: she added, the claws just perceptible beneath the velvet, 'I hope this will be acceptable to our dear Joan. It is pleasant to think that it will be almost a family party.'

I arrived in Camelford on a hot midsummer afternoon. A Boscastle car met me, and we drove down the valley. From the lower road, as it came round by the sea, one got a dramatic view of the house, 'our house', 'Bossy' itself.

It stood on the hill, a great pilastered classical front, with stepped terraces leading up from the lawns. When I first went, I was a little surprised that not a stone had been put there earlier than the eighteenth century: but the story explained it all.

Like good whig aristocrats with an eye to the main chance, the Boscastles had taken a step up after 1688. They had been barons for the last two centuries: now they managed to become earls. At the same time – it may not have been a coincidence – they captured a great heiress by marriage. Suitably equipped with an earldom and with money, it was time to think about the house. And so they indulged in the eighteenth-century passion for palatial building.

The previous house, the Tudor Boscastle, had lurked in the valley. The domestic engineers could now supply them with water if they built on the hill. With a firm eighteenth-century confidence that what was modern was best, they tore the Tudor house down to its foundations. They had not the slightest feeling for the past – like most people in a vigorous, expanding age. They were determined to have the latest thing. And they did it in the most extravagant manner, like a good many other Georgian grandees. They built a palace, big enough for the head of one of the small European states. They furnished it in the high eighteenth-century manner. They had ceilings painted by Kent. They had the whole scheme, inside and out, vetted by Lord Burlington, the arbiter of architectural taste.

They impoverished the family for generations: but they had a certain reward. It was a grand and handsome house, far finer than the Tudor one they had destroyed. It impressed one still as being on the loftiest scale. It also impressed one, I thought as I went from my bedroom to a bathroom after tea, as being grandiosely uncomfortable. There were thirty yards of corridors before I got to my bathroom: and the bathroom itself, which had been installed in the nineteenth century, was of preposterous size and struck cold as a vault. There were also great stretches of corridor between the kitchens and the dining-rooms, and no dish ever arrived quite warm.

I discovered one piece of news before I had been in the house an hour. Lord Boscastle had in his gift several of the livings round the countryside; one of these had recently fallen vacant, and Roy had persuaded him to give it to Ralph Udal. So far as I could gather, Roy had sent letter after letter to Lord Boscastle, offered to return from Berlin to describe Udal, invoked both Joan and her mother to speak for him. He was always importunate when begging a favour for someone else.

Lord Boscastle had given way, saying that these fellows were much of a muchness, and Udal was now vicar of a small parish, which included the house of Boscastle itself. His church and vicarage were a mile or two along the coast.

I walked there before dinner, thinking that I might find Roy; but Udal was alone in the vicarage, although Roy had called that morning. Udal brought me a glass of sherry on to the lawn. It was a long time since we had last met, but he greeted me with cordiality and with his easy, unprickly, almost impersonal good nature. He had altered very little in appearance; the hair was turning grey over his ears, but since he was twenty-five he had looked a man in a tranquil and indefinite middle age. He was in shirtsleeves, and looked powerful, sunburnt, and healthy. He drank his sherry, and smiled at me, with his eyes narrowed by interest and content.

'How do you think Roy is?' he said easily, going back to my question about Roy's visit.

'How do you?'

'You see much more of him than I do,' said Udal, also stonewalling.

'Not since he's been abroad,' I said.

'Well,' said Udal, after a pause, 'I don't think he is to be envied.' He looked at me with his lazy kindness. 'To tell you the truth, Eliot, I didn't think he was to be envied the first time I set eyes on him. It was the scholarship examination. I saw him outside the hall. I said to myself "that lad will be too good for you. But he's going to have a rough time."'

He smiled, and added: 'It seems to me that I wasn't far wrong.'

He asked me about Roy's professional future. I said that everything must come to him; the university could not help creating a special readership or chair for him within three or four years.

Udal nodded his head.

'He's very talented,' he said. 'Yet you know, Eliot, sometimes I think it would have been better – if he had chosen a different life.'

'Such as?'

'He might have done better to join my trade. He might have found things easier if he'd become a priest.' Suddenly Udal smiled at me. 'You've always disliked my hanging round, in case he was going to surrender, haven't you? I thought it was the least I could do for him, just to wait in the slips, so to speak.'

I asked him how much Roy had talked to him about faith. He said, with calm honesty, very little: was there really much to say? Roy had not been looking for an argument. Whichever side he emerged, he had to live his ways towards it.

Udal went on:

'Sometimes I wonder whether he would have found it easier – if he'd actually lived a different life. I mean with women.'

'It would have been harder without them,' I said.

'I wonder,' said Udal. 'There's much nonsense talked on these matters, you know. I'm trying to be guided by what I've seen. And some of the calmest and happiest people I've seen, Eliot, have led completely "frustrated" lives. And some of the people I've seen who always seem sexually starved – they're people who spend their whole time hopping in and out of bed. Life is very odd.'

We talked about some acquaintances, then about Roy again. Udal said:

'Well, we shall never know.' Then he smiled. 'But I can give him one bit of relief, anyhow. Now I've got this job, I don't see any particular reason why I should have to borrow any more money from him. It will save him quite a bit.'

I laughed, but I was put off. I tried to examine why. From anyone else, I should have found that shameless candour endearing. Like Roy, I did not mind his sliding out of duties he did not like. I did not mind, in fact I admired, his confidence in his own first-hand experience. I did not mind his pleasure, quite obvious although he was so settled, in an hour of scabrous gossip. They were all parts of an unusual man, who had gone a different way from most of our acquaintances.

Yet I was on edge in his company. Roy had once accused me of disliking him. As we talked that afternoon, I felt that was not precisely true. I did not dislike him, I found him interesting and warm – but I should be glad to leave him, I found his presence a strain. I could not define it further. Was it that he took everything that happened to him too much as his by right? He had slid through life comfortably, without pain, without much self-questioning: did I feel he ought to be more thankful for his luck? Did he accept his own nature too acquiescently? His idleness, his lack of conscience, his amiable borrowing – he took them realistically, without protest, with what seemed to me an over-indulgent pleasure. He looked at himself, was not dissatisfied, and never kicked against the pricks.

It was strange. Though I was not comfortable with him, he seemed perfectly so with me. He told me of how he proposed to adjust his life, now that at last he had arrived at a decent stopping place.

He intended to devote Sunday and one other day a week to his parish: three days a week to his own brand of biographical scholarship: one day to sheer physical relaxation, mowing his lawn, ambling round the hills, sitting by the sea: which would leave one day 'for serious purposes'. I was curious about the 'serious purposes', and Udal smiled. But he was neither diffident nor coy. He meant to spend this one day a week in preparing himself for the mystical contemplation. One day a week for spiritual knowledge: it sounded fantastically business-like. I said as much, and Udal smiled indifferently.

'I told Roy about it,' he said. 'It's the only time I've ever shocked him.'

It struck me as so odd that I spoke to Roy when we met in the inner drawing-room before dinner. I said that I had heard Udal's time-table.

'It's dreadful,' said Roy. 'It makes everything nice and hygienic, doesn't it?' He was speaking with a dash of mockery, with hurt and bitter feeling. He shrugged his shoulders, and said:

'Oh, he may as well be left to it.'

Just then Lady Muriel entered and caught the phrase. She gave me a formal, perfunctory greeting: then she turned to Roy and demanded to know whom he was discussing. Her solid arms were folded over her black dress, as I had seen them in the Lodge: my last glimpse of her after the funeral, when she kept erect only by courage and training, was swept aside: she was formidable and active again. Yet I felt she depended more on Roy than ever.

Roy put his preoccupations behind him, and talked lightly of Udal. 'You must remember him, Lady Mu. You'll like him.' He added: 'You'll approve of him too. He doesn't stay at expensive hotels.'

Lady Muriel did not take the reference, but she continued to talk of Udal as we sat at dinner in the 'painted room'. The table was a vast circle, under the painted Italianate ceiling, and there were only six of us spread round it, the Boscastles, Lady Muriel and Joan, Roy and I.

Lady Muriel's boom seemed the natural way to speak across such spaces.

'I consider,' she told her brother, 'that you should support the new vicar.'

Lord Boscastle was drinking his soup. The butler was experimenting with some device for reheating it in the actual dining-room, but it was still rather cold.

'What are you trying to get me to do now, Muriel?' he said crossly.

'I consider that you should attend service occasionally.' She looked accusingly at her sister-in-law. 'I have always regarded going to service as one of the responsibilities of our position. I am sorry to see that it has not been kept up.'

'I refuse to be jockeyed into doing anything of the kind,' said Lord Boscastle with irritation. I guessed that, as Lady Muriel recovered her energies, he was not being left undisturbed. 'I did not object to putting this fellow in to oblige Roy. But I strongly object if Muriel uses the fellow to jockey me with. I don't propose to attend ceremonies with which I haven't the slightest sympathy. I don't see what good it does me or anyone else.'

'It was different for you in college, Muriel,' said Lady Boscastle gently. 'You had to consider other people's opinions, didn't you?'

'I regarded it as the proper thing to do,' said Lady Muriel, her neck stiff with fury. She could think of no retort punishing enough for her sister-in-law, and so pounded on at Lord Boscastle. 'I should like to remind you, Hugh, that the Budes have never missed a Sunday service since they came into the title.'

The Budes were the nearest aristocratic neighbours, whom even Lord Boscastle could not pretend were social inferiors. But that night, pleased by his wife's counter-attack, he reverted to his manner of judicial consideration, elaborate, apparently tentative and tired, in reality full of triumphant contempt.

'Ah yes, the Budes. I forgot you knew them, Muriel. I suppose you must have done before you went off to your various new circles. Yes, the Budes.' His voice trailed tiredly away. 'I should have thought they were somewhat rustic, shouldn't you have thought?'

Revived, Lord Boscastle proceeded to dispose of Udal.

'I wish someone would tell him,' he said in his dismissive tone, 'not to give the appearance of blessing me from such an enormous height.'

'He's a very big man,' said Roy, defending Udal out of habit.

'I'm a rather short one,' said Lord Boscastle promptly. 'And I strongly object to being condescended to from an enormous height.'

But, despite the familiar repartees, there was tension through the party that night.

One source was Joan: for she sat, speaking very little, sometimes, when the rest of us were talking, letting her gaze rest broodingly on Roy. There was violence, reproach, a secret between them. Roy was subdued, as the Boscastles had never seen him, although he put in a word when Lady Muriel was causing too much friction.

Even if Roy and Joan had been in harmony, however, there would still have been frayed nerves that night. For the other source of tension was political. At Boscastle, when I first stayed there, people differed about political things without much heat. There was no danger of a rift if a political argument sprang up. But it was now the summer of 1938, and on both sides we were feeling with the force of a personal emotion. The divisions were sharp: the half-tones were vanishing: in college it was 8–6 for Chamberlain and appeasement; here it was 3–3. On the Chamberlain side were Lord Boscastle, Lady Muriel, and Roy. On the other side (which in college were called 'warmongers', 'Churchill men', or 'Bolsheviks') were Lady Boscastle, Joan, and I.

Roy's long ambivalence had ended, and he and I were in opposite camps.

Bitterness flared up in a second. Lady Muriel favoured a temporary censorship of the Press. I disagreed with her. In those days I did not find it easy to hold my tongue.

'Really, Mr Eliot,' she said, 'I am only anxious to remove the causes of war.'

'I'm anxious,' I said, 'not to lose every friend we have in the world. And then stagger into a war which we shall duly lose.'

'I'm afraid I think that's a dangerous attitude,' said Lord Boscastle.

'It's an attitude which appears to be prevalent among professional people. Mr Eliot's attitude is fairly common among professional people, isn't it, Helen?' Lady Muriel was half-angry, half-exultant at having taken her revenge.

'I should think it very likely,' said Lady Boscastle. 'I think I should expect it to be fairly common among thinking people.' She raised her lorgnette. 'But it's easy to exaggerate the influence of thinking people, shouldn't you agree, Hugh?'

Lord Boscastle did not rise. He was out of humour, I was less welcome than I used to be, but he was never confident in arguing with his wife. And Roy broke in:

'Do you like thinking people, Lady Boscastle?'

He was making peace, but they often struck sparks from each other, and Lady Boscastle replied in her high sarcastic voice:

'My dear Roy, I am too old to acquire this modern passion for dumb oxen.'

'They're sometimes very wise,' said Roy.

'I remember dancing with a number of brainless young men with cauliflower ears,' said Lady Boscastle. 'I found them rather unenlightening. A modicum of brains really does add to a man's charm, you know. Hasn't that occurred to you?'

She was a match for him. When he was at his liveliest, she studied him through her lorgnette and capped his mischief with her ivory sarcasm. Of all the women we knew, he found her the hardest to get round. That night, with Joan silent at the table, he could not persevere; he gave Lady Boscastle the game.

But the rift was covered over, and Lady Muriel began asking energetically what we should do the following day. We were still at dinner, time hung over the great dining-room. No one had any ideas: it seemed as though Lady Muriel asked that question each night, and each night there was a waste of empty time ahead.

'I consider,' said Lady Muriel firmly, 'that we should have a picnic.'

'Why should we have a picnic?' said Lord Boscastle wearily.

'We always used to,' said Lady Muriel.

'I don't remember enjoying one,' he said.

'I always did,' said Lady Muriel with finality.

Lord Boscastle looked to his wife for aid, but she gave a slight smile.

'I can't see any compelling reason why we shouldn't have a picnic, Hugh,' she said, as though she also did not see any compelling reason why we should. 'Apparently you must have had a regular technique. Perhaps Muriel –'

'Certainly,' said Lady Muriel, and shouted loudly to the butler, who was a few feet away. 'You remember the picnics we used to have, don't you, Jonah?' The butler's name was Jones. He had a refined but lugubrious face. 'Yes, my lady,' he said, and I thought I caught a note of resignation. Lady Muriel made a series of executive decisions, like a staff major moving a battalion. Hope sounded in the butler's voice only when he suggested that it might rain.

Lord Boscastle was having a bad evening. We did not stay long over port, for Roy only took one glass and was so quiet that it left all the work to me. When we went into the biggest of the drawing-rooms (called simply the 'sitting-room'; it was a hundred feet long) Lord Boscastle received another blow. His wife never played bridge, and he was relying on Joan to give him his rubber. He asked whether she was ready for a game, with an eager expectant air: at last he was in sight of a little fun.

'I'm sorry, Uncle. I can't,' said Joan. 'I've promised to go for a walk with Roy.'

She said it flatly, unhappily, and with finality.

Lord Boscastle sulked: there was no other word for it. He stayed in the room for a few minutes, complaining that it did not seem much to ask, a game of cards after dinner. People were willing to arrange picnics, which he detested, but no one ever exerted themselves to produce a four at bridge. He supposed that he would be reduced to inviting the doctor next.

That was the limit of degradation he imagined that night. In a few minutes, he took a volume from his collection of eighteenth-century memoirs and went off sulkily to bed.

Roy and Joan went out immediately afterwards, and Lady Boscastle, Lady Muriel, and I were left alone in the 'sitting-room'. It was clear that Lady Boscastle wanted to talk to me. She made it crystal clear: but Lady Muriel did not notice. Instead, she brought out a series of improvements which Lady Boscastle should adopt in her régime for the house.

Lady Boscastle could not move up to her own suite, for that meant calling her maid to help her. In all this gigantic mansion, she could not speak a word to me in private. It seemed very comic.

At last she insinuated some doubts about the orders for the next day's picnic. Lady Muriel rebuffed them, but was shaken enough to agree that she should confer with the butler. 'In your study, my dear,' said Lady Boscastle gently, and very firmly. 'You see, you will have plenty of paper there.'

Lady Muriel walked out, business-like and erect.

'Our dear Muriel's stamina used to be perfectly inexhaustible.' Lady Boscastle's eyes were very bright behind her lorgnette. 'She has changed remarkably little.'

She went on:

'Lewis, my dear boy, I wanted to talk to you a little about Humphrey. I think I should like your advice.'

Humphrey was the Boscastles' son, whom I had met at Monte Carlo; he was a wild effeminate lad, clever, violent-tempered, restlessly looking for gifted people to respect.

'All his friends,' said Lady Boscastle, 'seem to be singularly precious. I'm not specially concerned about that. I've known plenty of precious young men who became extremely satisfactory afterwards.' She smiled. 'But I should be relieved if he showed any sign of a vocation.'

She talked with cool detachment about her son. It was better for him to do something: he would dissipate himself away, if he just settled down to succeed his father. Their days were over. Lord Boscastle was not willing to accept it, preferred that his son should wait about as he himself had done; but Lord Boscastle's response to any change was to become more obstinate. Instead of taking a hand in business, he plunged himself into his gorgeous and proliferating snobbery. There was imagination and self-expression in his arrogance. It was his art – but his son would never be able to copy him.

Lady Boscastle asked me to take up Humphrey.

'He will do the talking if you sit about,' she said. 'That is one of your qualities, my dear boy. Do what you can, won't you? I shouldn't like him to go off the rails too far. He would always have his own distinction, you know, whatever he did. But it would distress his father so much. There are very strong bonds between them. These Bevill men are really very unrestrained.'

Lady Boscastle gave a delicate and malicious smile. She had an indulgent amused contempt for men whose emotions enslaved them.

There was a cat-like solitariness about her, which meant she could disinterest herself from those who adored her. That night, while everyone else in the party was bored or strained, she was bright-eyed, mocking, cynically enjoying herself. Her concern about her son did not depress her. She waved it away, and talked instead of Roy and Joan; for now, in her invalid years, observing love affairs was what gave her most delight.

She had, of course no doubt of their relation. Her eyes were too experienced to miss anything so patent. In fact, she was offended because Joan made it too patent. Lady Boscastle had a fastidious sense of proper reserve. 'Of course, my dear boy, it is a great pleasure to brandish a lover, isn't it? Particularly when one has been rather uncompeted for.' Otherwise it seemed to her only what one would expect. She was not used to passing judgements, except on points of etiquette and taste. And she conceded that Roy 'would pass'. She had never herself found him profoundly '*sympathique*'. I thought that night that I could see the reason. She was suspicious that much of his emotional life had nothing to do with love. She divined that, if she had been young, he would have smiled and made love – but there were depths she could not have touched. She would have resented it then, and she resented it now. She wanted men whose whole emotional resources, all of whose power and imagination, could be thrown into gallantry, and the challenge and interplay of love.

She would have kept him at a distance: but she admitted that other women would have chased him. Her niece was showing reasonable taste. As for her niece, Lady Boscastle had a pitying affection.

She speculated on what was happening that night. 'There's thunder in the air,' she said. She looked at me inquiringly.

'I know nothing,' I said.

'Of course, he's breaking away,' said Lady Boscastle. 'That jumps to the eye. And it's making her more infatuated every minute. No doubt she feels obliged to put all her cards on the table. Poor Joan, she would do that. She's rather unoblique.'

Lady Boscastle went on:

'And he feels insanely irritable, naturally. It's very odd, my dear Lewis, how being loved brings out the worst in comparatively amiable people. One sees these worthy creatures lying at one's feet and protesting their supreme devotion. And it's a great strain to treat them with even moderate civility. I doubt whether anyone is nice enough to receive absolutely defenceless love.

'Love affairs,' said Lady Boscastle, 'are not intriguing unless both of you have a second string. Never go love-making, my dear boy, unless you have someone to fall back upon in case of accidents. I remember – ah! I've told you already.' She smiled with a reminiscence, affectionate, sub-acid, and amused. 'But our dear Joan would never equip herself with a reserve. She'll never be *rusée*. She's rather undevious for this pastime.'

'It's a pity,' I said.

'Poor Joan.' There was contempt, pity, triumph in Lady Boscastle's tone. 'Of course it's she who's taken him out tonight. It's she who wants to get things straight. You saw that, of course. She has insisted on meeting him after dinner tonight. I suppose she's making a scene at this minute. She couldn't wait another day before having it out. I expect that is how she welcomed Master Roy this morning. Poor Joan. She ought to know it's fatal. If a love affair has come to the point when one needs to get things straight, then' – she smiled at me – 'it's time to think a little about the next.'

CHAPTER 23

A Cry in the Evening

THE next day was fine, and the rooms of Boscastle stood lofty and deserted in the sunshine. I had breakfast alone, in the parlour, which was the image of the 'painted room' but on the south side of the house, away from the sea. The Boscastles breakfasted in their rooms, and there was no sign of Joan or Roy. Lady Muriel had been up two hours before, and was – so I gathered from whispered messages which a footman kept bringing to the butler – issuing her final orders for the picnic.

The papers had not yet arrived, and I drank my tea watching the motes dance in a beam of sunshine. It was a warm, hushed, shimmering morning.

The butler came and spoke to me. His tone was hushed, but not at all sleepy. He looked harassed and overburdened.

'Her ladyship sends her compliments, sir, and asks you to make your own way to the picnic site during the morning.'

'I haven't any idea where the site is,' I said.

'I think I can show you, sir, from the front entrance. It is just inside the grounds, where the wall goes nearest to the sea.'

'Inside the grounds? We're having this picnic inside the grounds?'

'Yes, sir. Her ladyship's picnics have always been inside the grounds. It makes it impossible for the party to be observed.'

I walked into the village to buy some cigarettes. At the shop I overheard some gossip about the new vicar. Apparently a young lady had arrived the night before at one of the hotels. She had gone to the vicarage that morning. They were wondering suspiciously whether he intended to get married.

On my way to the site I wondered casually to myself who it might be. The thought of Rosalind crossed my mind, and then I dismissed it. I went into the grounds, through the side gates which opened on to the cliff road, down through the valley by the brook. It was not hard to find the site, for it was marked by a large flag. Lady Muriel, who was already sitting beside it on a shooting stick, looked as isolated as

Amundsen at the South Pole. The ground beside her was arrayed with plates, glasses, dishes, siphons, bottles of wine. She called out to me with unexpected geniality.

'Good morning. You're the first. I'm glad to see someone put in an appearance. We couldn't have been luckier in the weather, could we?'

From the site there was no view, except for the brook and trees and wall, unless one looked north: there one got a magnificent sight of the house of Boscastle: the classical front, about a mile away, took in the whole foreground. It was a crowning stroke, I thought, to have chosen a site with that particular view.

But Lady Muriel was on holiday.

'I consider that all the arrangements are in hand,' she said. 'Perhaps you would like me to show you some things?'

She led me up some steps in the wall, which brought us to a small plateau. From the plateau we clambered down across the road over to a headland. Below the headland the sea was slumberously rolling against the cliffs. There was a milky spume fringing the dark rocks: and farther out the water lay a translucent green in the warm, misty morning.

'We used to have picnics here in the old days,' said Lady Muriel. 'Before I decided it was unnecessary to go outside our grounds.'

She looked towards the mansion on its hill. It moved her to see it reposing there, the lawns bright, the house with the sun behind it. She was as inarticulate as ever.

'We're lucky to have such an excellent day.' Then she did manage to say: 'I have always been fond of our house.'

She tried to trace the coast-line for me, but it was hidden in the mist.

'Well,' she said briskly, in a moment, 'we must be getting back to our picnic. All the arrangements are in order, of course. I have never found it difficult to make arrangements. I did not find them irksome in the Lodge. I have found it strange not to have to make them – since my husband's death.'

She missed them, of course, and she was happy that morning.

We had begun to leave the headland, with Lady Muriel telling me of how she used to climb the rocks when she was a girl. Then, in the distance along the road, I saw a woman walking. I thought I recognized the walk. It was not stately, it was not poised, it was hurried, quick-footed, and loose. As she came nearer, I saw that I was right. It was Rosalind. She was wearing a very smart tweed suit, much too smart by the Boscastles' standards. And she was twirling a stick.

I hoped that she might not notice us. But she looked up, started, broke into a smile open-eyed, ill-used, pathetic, and brazen. She gave a cheerful, defiant wave. I waved back. Lady Muriel did not stir a muscle.

When we saw Rosalind's back, Lady Muriel inquired, in an ominous tone:

'Is that the young woman who used to throw her cap so abominably at Roy?'

'Yes,' I said.

'What is she doing here?'

'She is a friend of Ralph Udal's,' I said. 'She must be visiting him.' To myself I could think of no other explanation. So far as I knew, she had given up the pursuit of Roy. In any case, she could not have known that he was staying at Boscastle that week. It was a singular coincidence.

'Really,' said Lady Muriel. Her indignation mounted. She was no longer genial to me. 'So now she sees herself as a clergyman's wife, does she? Mr Eliot, I understand that the lower classes are very lax with their children. If that young woman had been my daughter, she would have been thrashed.'

She continued to fume as we made our way back to the site. It was too far from the house for Lady Boscastle to walk; she had been driven as far as the path would take a car, and supported the rest of the way by her maid. Lord Boscastle was sitting there disconsolately, and complaining to Roy. Roy listened politely, his face grave. It was the first time I had seen him that day, and I knew no more than the night before.

Lady Muriel could not contain her disgust. She gave a virulent description of Rosalind's latest outrage.

'You didn't know she was coming, Roy, I assume?'

'No. She hasn't written to me for a year,' said Roy.

'I'm very glad to hear it,' said Lady Muriel, and burst out into fury at the picture of Rosalind walking 'insolently' past the walls of Boscastle.

Roy said nothing. I fancied there was a glint – was it admiration? – in his eye.

'I hope this fellow Udal isn't going to be a nuisance,' said Lord Boscastle. 'There's a great deal to be said for the celibacy of the clergy. But I don't see why the young woman shouldn't look him up. I always felt you were hard on her, Muriel.'

'Hard on her?' cried Lady Muriel. 'Why, she's nothing more nor less than a trollop.'

Soon after, Joan came walking by the brook. Her dress was white and flowered, and glimmered in the sunshine. As she called out to us, in an even voice, I was watching her closely. She was very pale. She had schooled herself not to do more than glance at Roy. She made conversation with her uncle. She was carrying herself with a hard control. She had all her mother's inflexible sense of decorum. In public, one must go on as though nothing had happened. How brave she was, I thought.

A file of servants came down from the house with hampers, looking like the porters on de Saussure's ascent of Mont Blanc. Cold chickens were brought out, tongues, patties: Lady Muriel jollied us vigorously to get to our lunch. Meanwhile Lady Boscastle's lorgnette was directed for a moment at Joan, and then at Roy.

'I don't for the life of me see,' said Lord Boscastle, gazing wistfully at the house, 'why I should be dragged out here. When I might be eating in perfect comfort in my house.'

It sounded a reasonable lament. It sounded more reasonable than it was. For in the house we should in fact have been eating a tepid and indifferent lunch, instead of this delectable cold one. Lady Muriel had bludgeoned the kitchen into efficiency, which Lady Boscastle did not exert herself to do. It was the best meal I remembered at Boscastle.

We ended with strawberries and moselle. Lady Boscastle, who was eating less each month, got through her portion.

'It's a fine taste, my dear Muriel,' she said. 'I recall vividly the first time someone gave it me –'

I recognized that tone by now. It meant that she was thinking of some admirer in the past. I did not know how much Joan was listening to her aunt: but she made herself put a decent face on it.

After lunch, Lady Muriel was not ready to let us rest.

'Archery,' she said inexorably. Another file of servants came down with targets, quivers, cases of bows. The targets were set up and we shot through the sleepy afternoon. Lord Boscastle was fairly practised, and it was the kind of game to which Roy and I applied ourselves. I noticed Lady Boscastle watching the play of muscle underneath Roy's shirt. She kept an interest in masculine grace. I thought she was surprised to see how strong he was.

Joan shot with us for a time. She and Roy spoke to each other only about the game, though once, when he misfired, she said, with a flash of innocence, intimacy, forgetfulness: 'It must have bounced off that joint. Didn't you feel it?' She was speaking of the first finger of his left hand; the top joint had grown askew. She was not looking at his hand. She knew it by heart.

Lady Boscastle was assisted to the car before tea. For the rest of us, tea was brought down from the house, though Lady Muriel maintained the al fresco spirit by boiling our own water over a spirit stove. Lord Boscastle said, as though aggrieved: 'You ought to know by now, Muriel, that I'm no good at tea.' He drank a cup, and felt that he had served his sentence for the day. So he too went towards the house, having taken the precaution of booking Joan for bridge that night.

Some time after, the four of us started to follow him. Lady Muriel had uprooted the flag, and was carrying it home; all the paraphernalia of the meals was left for the servants. The site looked overcrowded with crockery: we had left it behind when Roy suddenly challenged me to a last round with the bow.

'Just two more shots, Lady Mu,' he said. 'We'll catch you up.'

Joan hesitated, as if she were pulled back to watch. Then she walked away with her mother.

Roy and I shot our arrows. As we went towards the targets to retrieve them, Roy said:

'It's over with Joan and me.'

'I was afraid so.'

'If she comes to you, try and help. She may not come. She's dreadfully proud. But if she does, please try and help.' His face was angry, dark, and strained. 'She has so little confidence. Try everything you know.'

I said that I would.

'Tell her I'm useless,' he said. 'Tell her I can't stand anyone for long unless they're as useless as I am. Tell her I'm mad.'

He plucked an arrow from the target, and spoke quietly and clearly:

'There's one thing she mustn't believe. She mustn't think she's not attractive. It matters to her – intolerably. Tell her anything you like about me – so long as she doesn't think that.'

He was torn and overcome. He was unusually reticent about his love affairs: even in our greatest intimacy, he had told me little. But that afternoon, as we walked up the valley, he spoke with a bitter abandon. Physical passion meant much to Joan, more than to any woman he had known. Unless she found it again, she could not stop herself becoming harsh and twisted. We were getting close behind Joan and her mother, and he could not say more. But before we caught them up, he said: 'Old boy, there's not much left.'

It was some days before I spoke to Joan. She was not a woman on whom one could intrude sympathy. The party stretched on through empty days. Roy took long walks with Lady Muriel, and I spent much time by Lady Boscastle's chair. She had diagnosed the state of her niece's affair, and had lost interest in it. 'My dear boy, the grand climaxes of all love affairs are too much the same. Now the overtures have a little more variety.' At dinner the political quarrels became rougher: we tried to shut them out, but the news would not let us. There was only one improvement as the days dragged by: Roy and I became steadily more accurate with the long bow.

One night towards the end of the week I went for a walk alone after dinner. I climbed out of the grounds and up to the headland, so as to watch the sun set over the sea. It was a cloudless night: the western sky was blazing and the horizon clear as a knife-edge.

As I stood there, I heard steps on the grass. Joan had also come alone. She gazed at me, her expression heavy and yet open in the bright light.

'Lewis,' she said. So much feeling welled up in the one word that I took a chance.

'Joan,' I said, 'I've wanted to say something to you. Twelve months ago Roy told me I made things harder for him. You ought to know the reason. It was because I understood a little about him.'

'Why are you telling me this?' she cried.

'It is the same with you.'

'Are you trying to comfort me?'

She burst out:

'I wonder if it's true. I don't know. I don't know anything now. I've given up trying to understand.'

I put my arm round her, and at the touch she began to speak with intense emotion.

'I can't give him up,' she said. 'Sometimes I think I only exist so far as I exist in his mind. If he doesn't think of me, then I fall to pieces. There's nothing of me any more.'

'Would it be better,' I said, 'if he went away?'

'No,' she cried, in an access of fear. 'You're to tell him nothing. You're not to tell him to go. He must stay here. My mother needs him. You know how much she needs him.'

It was true, but it was a pretext by which Joan saved her pride. For still she could not bear to let him out of her sight.

Perhaps she knew that she had given herself away, for suddenly her tone changed. She became angry with a violence that I could feel shaking her body.

'He'll stay because she needs him,' she said with ferocity. 'He'll consider anything she wants. He's nice and considerate with her. So he is with everyone – except me. He's treated me abominably. He's behaved like a cad. He's treated me worse than anyone I could have picked up off the streets. He's wonderful with everyone – and he's treated me like a cad.'

She was trembling, and her voice shook.

'I don't know how I stood it,' she cried. 'I asked less than anyone in the world would have asked. And all I get is this.'

Then she caught my hand. The anger left her as quickly as it had risen. She had flared from hunger into ferocity, and now both fell away from her, and her tone was deep, tender, and strong.

'You know, Lewis,' she said, 'I can't think of him like that. It's perfectly true, he's treated me abominably, yet I can't help thinking that he's really good. I see him with other people, and I think I am right to love him. I know he's done wicked things. I know he's done wicked things to me. But they seem someone else's fault.'

The sun had dipped now to the edge of the sea. Her eyes glistened in the radiance; for the first time that night, they were filmed with tears. Her voice was even.

'I wish I could believe,' she said, 'that he'll be better off without me. I might be able to console myself if I believed it. But I don't. How does he expect to manage? I'm sure he's unhappier than any human soul. I can look after him. How does he expect to manage, if he throws it away?'

She cried out:

'I don't think he knows what will become of him.'

PART THREE

THE LAST ATTEMPT

CHAPTER 24

Two Dismissals

AFTER Boscastle I saw little of Roy for months. He altered his plans, and returned to Germany for the summer and autumn; I heard rumours that he was behaving more wildly than ever in his life, but the difference between us was at its deepest. We met one day in September, when he flew back at the time of Munich. It was a strange and painful afternoon. We knew each other so well; at a glance we knew what the other was feeling; though we were on opposite sides, we were incomparably closer than with an ally. Yet our words were limp, and once or twice a harsh note sounded.

I talked about myself, on the chance of drawing a confidence from him. But he was mute. He was mute by intention, I knew. He was keeping from me some inner resolve and a vestige of hope. He was secretive, hard, and restless.

I thought for the first time that the years were touching him. His smile was still brilliant, and made him look very young. But the dark nights had at last begun to leave their mark. The skin under his eyes was prematurely rough and stained, and the corners of his mouth were tight. His face was lined less than most men's at twenty-eight – but it showed the wear of sadness. If one met him now as a stranger, one would have guessed that he had been unhappy. The mould was shaped for the rest of his life.

There was another change which, as I noticed with amusement, sometimes ruffled him. It ruffled him the morning of our discoveries about Bidwell.

Roy had come back to the college in November and was working in Cambridge until the new year. One December morning, Bidwell woke me in the grey twilight with his invariable phrase: 'That's nine o'clock, sir.' He pattered soft-footed about my bedroom and said, in his quiet soothing bedside voice: 'Mr Calvert sends his compliments, sir. And he wonders if you would be kind enough to step up after breakfast. He says he has something to show you, sir.'

The message brought back more joyous days, when Roy 'sent his compliments' two or three mornings a week – usually with some invitation or piece of advice attached, which Bidwell delivered, as honest-faced, as solemn, as sly-eyed, as a French mayor presiding over a wedding.

I went up to Roy's rooms immediately after breakfast. His sitting-room was empty: the desks glinted pink and green and terra cotta in the crepuscular morning light. Roy called from his bedroom:

'Bidwell is a devil. We need to stop him.'

He was standing in front of his mirror, brushing his hair. It was then I noticed that he was taking some care about it. His hair was going back quickly at the temples, more quickly than I had realized, since he managed to disguise it.

'Still vain,' I jeered. 'Aren't you getting too old for vanity?' I was oddly comforted to see him at it. The face in the mirror was sad and grave; yet somehow it brought him to earth, took the edge from my forebodings, to watch him seriously preoccupied about going bald.

'Nothing will stop it,' said Roy. 'The women will soon be saying – "Roy, you're bald." And I shall have to point a bit lower down and tell them – "Yes, but don't you realize that I've got nice intelligent eyes?"'

Then he turned round.

'But it's Bidwell we need to talk about. He's a devil.'

Roy had now been back in his rooms for a fortnight. During that time, he had made a list of objects which, so far as he remembered, had disappeared during his months abroad. The list was long and variegated. It included two gowns, several bottles of spirits, a pair of silver candlesticks, most of his handkerchiefs, and several of his smartest ties.

I was amused. Our relations with Bidwell had been curious for a long while past. We had known that he was mildly dishonest. There was a narrow line between what a college servant could regard by tradition as his perquisites and what his fingers should not touch. We had known for years that Bidwell crossed that line. Any food left over from parties, half-empty bottles – those were legitimate 'perks'. But Bidwell did not content himself with them. He took a kind of tithe on most of the food and drink we ordered. Neither of us had minded much. I shut my eyes to it, through sheer negligence and disinclination to be bothered: Roy was nothing like so careless, and had made one sharp protest. But we were neither of us made to persist in continuous nagging.

We happened to be very fond of Bidwell. He was a character, sly, peasant-wise, aphoristic. He had a vivid picture of himself as a confidential gentlemen's servant, and acted up to it with us. He loved putting on his dress suit and waiting at our big dinner parties. He loved waking us up with extreme care after he had found the glasses of a heavy night. He loved being discreet and concealing our movements. 'I hope I haven't done wrong, sir,' he used to say with a knowing look. We did not mind his being lazy, we were prepared to put up with some mild dishonesty: we felt he liked us too much to go beyond a decent friendly limit.

Roy worked him harder than I did, but we were both indulgent and tipped him lavishly. Each of us had a suppressed belief that he was Bidwell's favourite. Our guests at dinner parties, seeing that wise, rubicund, officiating face, told us how much they envied our luck in Bidwell. All in all, we thought ourselves that we were lucky.

I was half-shocked, half-amused, to hear of his depredations at Roy's expense. I was still confident that he would not treat me anything like as badly: we had always been on specially amiable terms.

'You haven't much for him to pinch,' said Roy. 'He doesn't seem to like books.'

Then suddenly a thought occurred to Roy.

'Do you look at your buttery bills?' he said.

'I just cast an eye over them,' I said guiltily.

'Untrue,' said Roy. 'I bet you don't. I once caught the old scoundrel monkeying with a bill. Lewis, I want to look at yours.'

I had not kept any, but Roy found copies in the steward's office. Soon he glanced at me.

'You drink too much,' he said. 'Alone, I suppose. I never knew.'

He made me study the bills. I used to order in writing one bottle of whisky a fortnight; on my account, time after time, I was put down for four bottles. I asked for the latest order, which, like the rest, had been taken to the office by Bidwell. The figure 1 had been neatly changed into a 4. As I looked at other items, I saw some other unpleasant facts. I felt peculiarly silly, angry, and ill-used.

'He must have cost you quite a bit,' said Roy, who was doing sums on a piece of paper. 'Haven't you let him "bring things away" from your tailor's?'

'I'll bring it away from the shop' was a favourite phrase of Bidwell's.

'Yes,' I said helplessly.

'You're dished, old boy,' said Roy. 'We're both dished, but you're absolutely done.' He added: 'I think we need to speak to Bidwell.'

Neither of us wanted to, but Roy took the lead. He sent another servant to find Bidwell, and we waited for him in Roy's room.

Bidwell came in and stood just inside the door, his face benign and attentive.

'They said you were asking for me, sir?'

'Yes, Bidwell,' said Roy. 'Too many things have gone from these rooms.'

'I'm very sorry to hear that, sir.'

'Where have they gone?'

'What might the old things be, sir?' Bidwell was wary, deferential, impassive. In the past he had diverted Roy by his use of the word 'old', but now Roy had fixed him with a hard and piercing glance. He did not wilt, his manner was perfectly possessed.

Roy ran through the list.

'That's a terrible lot to lose, I must say.' Bidwell frowned. 'If you don't mind me saying so, sir, I never did like the steward using this as a guest room when you were away. We had men up for examinations' – Bidwell shook his head – 'and I know I'm doing wrong in speaking, sir, but it's the class of men we have here nowadays. It's the class of men we get here today. Things aren't what they used to be.'

Bidwell was not an ordinary man in any company, but he ran true to his trade in being a snob, open, nostalgic, and unashamed.

Roy looked at me. I said:

'I've been going through my buttery bills, Bidwell.'

'Yes, sir?'

'I've never ordered four bottles of whisky at a go since I came here.'

'Of course not, sir. You've never been one for whisky, have you? I spotted that as soon as you came on my staircase. It was different with an old gentleman I used to have before your time, sir. When I had you instead of him, it made a big old difference to my life.'

'I gave you an order for one bottle last week. The buttery say that when you handed it in, that order was for four bottles.'

Bidwell's face darkened, and instantaneously cleared.

'I meant to tell you about that, sir. I may have done wrong. You must tell me if I have. But I heard the stock was running low, and I took it on myself to bring away what you might call a reserve –'

'Come off it, Bidwell,' said Roy clearly. 'We know you've been cheating us. And you know we know.'

'I don't like to hear you saying that, sir –'

'Look here,' said Roy, 'we like you. We hope you like us. Do you want to spoil it all?'

Bidwell ceased to be impassive.

'It would break my heart, Mr Calvert, if either of you went away.'

'Why have you done this?'

'I'm glad you've both spoken to me,' said Bidwell. 'It's been hurting me – here.' He pressed his hand to his heart. 'I know I oughtn't to have done what I have done. But I've got short of cash now and again. I don't mind telling this to you two gentlemen – I've always said that everyone has a right to his fancy. But it's made me do things I shouldn't have done. I haven't treated you right, I know I haven't.'

His mouth was twitching, his eyes were tearful, we were all raw and distressed.

'Just so,' said Roy quietly. 'Well, Bidwell, I'm ready to forget it. So is Mr Eliot. On one –'

'You've always been every inch a gentleman, sir. Both of you.'

'On one condition,' said Roy. 'Listen. I mean this. If anything else goes from these rooms, I go straight to the steward. And you'll be sacked out of hand.'

'It won't happen again, sir.'

'Wait a minute. Listen again. I shall go through Mr Eliot's bill myself each week. You can trust me to do it, can't you?'

'Yes, sir. Mr Eliot can never be bothered with his old bills, sir.'

'I can,' said Roy. 'You've got it clear? If you take another penny from either of us, I shan't stop to ask Mr Eliot. I shall get you sacked.'

'Yes, sir. I'm very much obliged to both of you gentlemen.'

Bidwell went out, his face once more rubicund, open, benign, and composed. Both Roy and I were puzzled. His emotion was genuine: yet he had pulled it out with his intuitive cunning. How had he played on that particular note, which was certain to affect us both? Was there a touch of triumph about his exit? Like Arthur Brown, Bidwell's was a nature that became deeper and tougher when once one was past the affable fat man's façade.

Roy teased me because I – 'the great realist', as he called me – was upset at Bidwell's duplicity. He told me that I bore major treacheries better than domestic ones. For my part, I was thinking how final his own manner had become. In giving his ultimatum to Bidwell, his voice was keen, as though it were a relief to take this action, to take any kind of action. He was restless, he was driven to do things once for all.

I heard him speak with finality again before that term ended.

The college chaplain had just resigned, as some friendly bishop had given him preferment. As soon as he heard the news, Arthur Brown set unhurriedly to work: the chaplaincy did not carry a fellowship, it had no political importance in the college, but Brown's instinct for patronage was too strong for him: he was obliged to keep his hand in. So he went round 'getting the feeling of a few people', as he explained to Roy and me. The upshot was that, before he spoke to us, he had invited Udal to spend a night in college. 'I'm not committing anyone, naturally,' said Arthur Brown. 'But I thought it might be profitable to explore the ground a little. I'm afraid I've rather taken it for granted that you wouldn't object to the idea, Calvert, if we get as far as mentioning his name. I remember that you backed him strongly at several meetings.'

Roy gave a slight smile – I wondered if it was at his own expense.

'I don't know how you'd feel about it, Eliot? I'm inclined to think myself that Udal would be rather an addition to the combination room.'

'If you all want him,' I said, 'I'm ready to fall in.' I looked at Roy: he smiled again, but the mention of Udal had disturbed him.

Udal arrived in time for dinner, and Arthur Brown brought him into hall. It was one of the few occasions that I had seen him wearing a dog-collar. He towered above the rest of us in the combination room, polite, cheerful, perfectly at ease. If he wanted the job, I thought in hall, he was doing pretty well. Perhaps he was a little too casual; most societies liked a touch of nervousness when a man was under inspection – not too much, but just a fitting touch. Udal would have been slightly too natural in any company or any interview.

After we had drunk port in the combination room, we moved on to Brown's rooms – Brown and Udal, Roy and I. The room was warm, the fire bright as usual: and as usual Brown went straight to unlock his cupboard.

'I don't know what the company would say to a sip of brandy,' he remarked. 'Myself, I find it rather gratifying at this time of night.'

We sat round the fire with our glasses in our hands, and Brown began to speak with luxurious caution.

'Well, Udal,' he said, 'we were a bit rushed before dinner, but I tried to give you the lie of the land. We mustn't promise more than we can perform. The chaplain is elected by the college, and the college is capable of doing some very curious things. Put it another way: I never feel certain that we've got a man in until I see it written down in black and white in the order book. I shouldn't be treating you fairly if I gave you the impression that we could offer you the chaplaincy tonight. But I don't think I'm going farther than I should if I say this – let me see' – Brown chose his words deliberately – 'if you see your way to letting your name go forward, I regard it as distinctly possible that we should be able to pull it off. I can go as far as that. I've spoken to one or two people, and I'm fairly satisfied that I'm not being over-optimistic.'

This meant that Arthur Brown had a majority assured for Udal, if he decided to stand. There would be bitter opposition from Despard-Smith, but the old man was losing his power, even on clerical matters. Step by step, Arthur Brown had become the most influential person in the college.

'It's very nice of you to think of me,' said Udal. 'In many ways there's nothing I should like better. Of course, there's a good deal to weigh up. There's quite a lot to be thought of for and against.'

'Of course there must be,' said Arthur Brown, who had a horror of premature decisions. 'I should have thought you ought to sleep on it, before you even give us an indication of which way you're going to come down. I don't mean to suggest' – Brown added – 'that you can possibly give us an answer tomorrow. But you might be able to produce one or two first impressions.'

I was certain that Udal would not take the job, and so was Roy. I did not know about Brown. He was so shrewd and observant that he must have caught the intonation of refusal: but it was part of his habit to proceed with negotiations for a decent customary period, even when it was clear that the other had made up his mind. Brown's intuitions were quick, but he disliked appearing to act on them. He preferred all the panoply of reasonable discussion. He knew as well as any man that most decisions are made on the spot and without thought; but it was proper and wise to behave as though men were as rational and deliberate as they pretended to be. So, with every appearance of interest and enjoyment, he answered Udal's questions about the chaplaincy, the duties, stipend, possibilities of a fellowship: he met objections, raised some of his own, compared prospects, examined the details of Udal's living. He even said:

'If, as I very much hope, we finally manage to get you here, Udal, there is just one slightly delicate matter I might take this opportunity of raising. I take it that you wouldn't find it absolutely necessary to introduce observances that some of us might think were rather too high?'

'I think I could promise that,' said Udal with a cheerful smile.

'I'm rather relieved to hear you say so,' Brown replied. 'I shouldn't like to interfere between any man and his religion. Some of the Catholics we've had here are as good chaps as you're ever likely to meet. But I do take the view rather strongly that the public services of the college ought to keep a steady middle course. I shouldn't like to see them moving too near the Holy Joes.'

'Someone once said,' Roy put in, 'that the truth lies at both extremes. But never in the middle. You don't believe that, Brown, do you?'

'I do not,' said Brown comfortably. 'I should consider it was a very cranky and absurd remark.'

At last Udal said that he thought he could soon give a reply. Brown stopped him short.

'I'm not prepared to listen to a word tonight,' he said. 'I'm not prepared to listen until you've slept on it. I've always regretted the occasions when I've spoken too soon. I don't presume to offer advice to people like Eliot and Calvert here, but I've even sometimes suggested to them that they ought to sleep on it.'

Brown departed for his home in the town, and the rest of us went from his room to mine. It was dark, bare, inhospitable after Brown's; we drew the armchairs round the fire.

Roy said to Udal:

'You're not taking this job, are you?'

'No,' said Udal. 'I don't think I shall.'

'Less money. Much more work.'

'It's not quite as simple as that,' said Udal, slightly nettled.

'No?' Roy's smile was bright.

'No,' said Udal. 'I don't specialize in bogus reasons, as you know. But there are genuine ones why I should like to come. It would be pleasant' – he said with easy affection – 'to be near you.'

'What for?' said Roy sharply.

'It doesn't need much explanation.'

'It may,' said Roy. 'You used to hope that you'd catch me for your faith. Isn't that true?'

'I did hope so,' said Udal.

'If you were here, you think it might be more likely. Isn't that true as well?'

'It had crossed my mind,' said Udal.

'You can forget it,' said Roy. 'It will never happen now. It's too late.'

'It's not too late,' said Udal impassively.

'Listen, Ralph. I know now. I've known for some time.' Roy was speaking with absolute finality. I was reminded of that scene with Bidwell. It was as though he were driven restlessly on, cutting ties which had once been precious. Bidwell's was a minor one; now he was marking the end of something from which he had hoped so much. He was excited, sad but excited. He had to make this dismissal to go on. He said clearly:

'I shall not come your way now. I shall not believe. It's not for me.'

Udal could not mistake the tone. He did not dissent. He said, with compassion and warmth:

'I'm more sorry than I can say.'

For the first time, I saw Udal uncertain of himself, guilty, hesitating. He added:

'I can't help feeling some of this is my fault. I feel that I've failed you.'

Roy did not speak.

'Have I failed you?' said Udal.

Roy's eyes, acutely bright, pierced him. Roy could have answered yes. For a second, I thought he was going to. It was at Boscastle that Roy knew without the slightest particle of doubt that Udal was no use to him – when he heard him plan his days, allow one day's exercises for the integral knowledge of God. It was a little thing, but to Roy it meant much. It turned him away without hope from Udal's experience, that seemed now so revoltingly 'hygienic', so facile and easy. He had once thought that Udal, never mind his frailties, had discovered how to throw away the chains of self. Now it seemed to Roy that he was unbelievably self-absorbed, content to be self-absorbed.

Roy answered gently:

'No one could have made any difference. I should never have found it.'

'I hope you're speaking the truth,' said Udal simply.

'I think I am,' said Roy.

'I haven't failed you,' said Udal, 'because of Rosalind?'

'Of course not.' Roy was utterly surprised: had she been on Udal's mind all the time?

'You see,' Udal went on, 'I'm thinking of marrying her.'

'Good luck to you,' said Roy. He was taken aback, he gave a bewildered smile, full of amusement, memory, chagrin, and shock. 'Give her my love.'

'It isn't certain,' said Udal.

Udal was lying back in his chair, and I watched his face, heavy-featured and tranquil. It was a complete surprise to me. I wondered if he could be as confident as he seemed. I wondered about Rosalind, and why she had done it.

Then Roy leaned forward, so that his eyes gleamed in the firelight. He did not speak again about Rosalind. Instead, he said, very quietly:

'Could there be a world, Ralph, in which God existed – but with some people in it who were never allowed to believe?'

'It would be a tragic world,' said Udal.

'Why shouldn't it be tragic?' Roy cried. 'Why shouldn't there be some who are rejected by God from the beginning?'

'It isn't my picture of the world,' said Udal.

Suddenly Roy's face, which had been sombre, set, and haunted, lit up in his most lively and impish smile.

'No,' he said, 'yours is really a very nice domestic place, isn't it? Tragic things don't happen, do they? You're an optimistic old creature in the long run, aren't you?'

Udal could not cope with that lightning change of mood. Roy baited him, as though everything that night had passed in fun. It was in the same light, teasing tone that Roy said a last word to Udal before we went to bed.

'I expect you think I ought to have tried harder to believe, don't you? If one tries hard enough, things happen, if you're an optimistic old creature, don't they? I did try a bit, Ralph. I even pretended to myself that I did believe. It didn't come off, you know. I could have gone on pretending, of course. I could have pretended well enough to take you in. I've done that before now. I could even have taken old Lewis in. I could have taken everyone in – except myself and God. And there wouldn't have been much point in that, would there?'

We walked with Udal through the courts towards the guest-room. On the way back, I stumbled over a grass verge: there was no moon, the lamps in the court had been put out at midnight, and I could not see in the thick darkness. Roy took my arm, so that he could steer me.

'I shouldn't like to lose you just yet,' he said.

I knew that he was smiling. I also knew that he was within an inch of confiding. There had been horror behind what he had said a few minutes before – and yet there was still hope. It was not easy just at that moment to reject our intimacy.

The moment passed. He took me to the foot of my staircase.

'Good night, old boy. Sleep well.'

'Shall you?' I said.

There I could see him smile.

'I might,' he said. 'You never know. I did, last Tuesday.'

CHAPTER 25

A Nest of People

ROY went back to Berlin just after Christmas. I did not hear from him, but one morning in February I received a letter with the Boscastle crest. It was from Joan, saying that she urgently wanted to talk to me about Roy – 'don't misunderstand me', she wrote with her bleak and painful honesty. 'There is nothing to say about him and me. I want your advice on something much more important, which concerns him alone.'

She suggested that she should give me dinner at her London club. I nearly let her, for I was far less considerate than Roy in the way I behaved to my women friends. Part of this was due to my taste for the company of beautiful women – for beautiful women needed, of course, much less attention, could be entertained much more casually, since one's bad manners did not touch their self-respect. It was this taste of mine which drew me to Lady Boscastle; I should no doubt have fallen in love with her, if we had been born in the same generation. Roy did not share at all the taste for beauty, and some people found the difference between us the opposite of what they had expected.

But I had learned much from him, and I took Joan to the Berkeley. She had dressed herself up, and, though her mission was an anxious one, she was glad to be there. As she sat on the other side of the table, I thought her face was becoming better looking as she grew older; she had lost the radiance of happy love, but the handsome structure of her cheekbones was beginning to give her distinction; it was a face in which character was showing through the flesh.

She went straight to it.

'I'm very worried about Roy,' she said, and told me her news. Houston Eggar had recently got a promotion, after steady and resolute pushing; he had left Rome and been sent to Berlin as an extra counsellor. Late in January, he had written out of the blue to Lord Boscastle about Roy. He said that he was presuming upon his wife's relationship to Lord Boscastle's family; he knew that Roy was a friend of theirs, and the whole matter needed to be approached with the utmost discretion. I thought as I listened that Eggar was in part doing his duty, in part showing his natural human kindness, and in part – and probably a very large part – seizing an opportunity of getting into Lord Boscastle's good books. If he exerted himself, he could be valuable to Eggar's career. But thoughts of Eggar soon vanished as Joan described his report. It sounded factual, and we both believed it.

Roy, so Eggar said, was being a great social success in Berlin. He was being too great a social success. He was repeatedly invited to official and party functions. He was friendly with several of the younger party leaders. With some of them he had more influence than any Englishman in Berlin. 'I wish I could be satisfied,' ran Eggar's letter, which Joan gave to me, 'that he was using his influence in a manner calculated to help us through this difficult period. It is very important that Englishmen with contacts in the right quarters should give the authorities here the impression that they are behind the policy of H.M.G. Calvert has gone too far in the direction of encouraging the German authorities that they have the sympathy and understanding of Englishmen like himself. I can give you chapter and verse of several unfortunate remarks.'

Eggar had done so. They had the tone of Roy. Some of them might have been jokes, uttered with his mystifying solemnity. One or two had the touch, light, first-hand, and grave, which Joan and I had heard him use when he was most in earnest. And Eggar also quoted a remark in 'very embarrassing circumstances' about the Jewish policy: at an august official dinner, Roy had recklessly denounced it. 'You're a wonderful people. You're brave. You're gifted. You might begin a new civilization. I wish you would. I'm speaking as a friend, you see. But don't you think you're slightly mad? Your treatment of the Jews – why need you do it? It's unnecessary. It gets you nowhere. It's insane. Sometimes I think that, whatever else you do, it will be enough to condemn you.'

It had been said in German, and I did not recognize the phrases as typically Roy's. But the occasion was exactly in his style. It had given offence to 'important persons', and Eggar seemed as concerned about that as about the other 'indiscretions'. All his reporting seemed objective, and Joan and I were frightened.

We were not simply perturbed, as Eggar was, that he might commit a gaffe at an awkward time. Eggar obviously thought that he was a frivolous and irresponsible young man who was flirting with a new creed. Eggar was used to Englishmen in society who for a few months thought they had discovered in Rome or Berlin a new way of life, and in the process made things even more difficult for a hard-working professional like himself. To him, Roy was just such another.

Across the table, Joan and I stared at each other, and wished that it were so. But we knew him too well. We were each harrowed because of him and for him.

Because of him – since we were living in a time of crisis, and it was bitter to find an opponent in someone we loved. Both Joan and I believed that it hung upon the toss of a coin whether or not the world would be tolerable to live in. And Roy was now wishing that we should lose. It was a wound of life. We had taken our stand, we each knew we should not change: but this positive news of Roy weakened our will. For we should be the last people to dispose of him as frivolous. Our doctrinaire friends would no doubt feel convinced that he was nothing but a rich man out to preserve his money: to us, that was a crassness that broke the heart. No one alive knew his vagaries as deeply as we did. We could not pretend to disregard anything he truly believed. We thought his judgement was dead wrong; but anything he felt, came from the depth of his sense of life: anything he said, we should have to listen to.

We were harrowed for him. We could only guess what he was going through, and where this would lead him. But he was without fear, he was without elementary caution. He had none of the cushions of self-preservation which guard most men; he did not want success, he cared nothing for others' opinion, he had no respect for any society, he was alone. There was nothing to keep him safe, if the mood came on him.

'Ought I to go and see him?' said Joan.

I hesitated. She was distracted for him, with a devotion that was unselfish and compassionate – and also she wanted any excuse to meet him again, in case the miracle might happen. Her love was tenacious, it was stronger than pride, she could not let him go.

'He might still listen to me,' Joan insisted. 'It will be difficult, but I feel I've got to try.'

Nothing would put her off. That was the advice she had come to get. Whether she got it or not, she was determined to go in search of him.

I heard another, and a very different, account of Roy a few days later. It came from Colonel Foulkes, whom I ran into by chance when I was lunching as a guest at the Athenaeum. Oulstone Lyall had died suddenly at the end of 1938 (I was interested to see in one of the obituaries a hint of the Erzberger scandal: it seemed now that the truth would never be known) and Foulkes had become the senior figure in Asian studies.

'Splendid accounts of Calvert,' he said without any preliminaries, as we washed our hands side by side. The Oriental faculty at Berlin University had decided, Foulkes went on, that Roy was the finest foreign scholar who had worked there since the First World War. 'They're thinking of doing something for him,' Foulkes rapped out. 'Only right. Only right. Subject's cluttered up with old has-beens. Such as me. Get rid of us. Get rid of us. That's what they ought to do.'

He had also heard that Roy was sympathetic to the régime, but it did not cause him the slightest concern. 'Great deal to be said for it, I expect,' said Foulkes, briskly towelling his hands. 'Great deal to be said for most things. People ought to be receptive to new ideas. Only way to keep young. Glad to see Calvert is.'

He had himself, it then appeared, just become absorbed in theosophy. It had its advantages, I thought, being able to over-trump any eccentricity. He remained curiously simple, positive, and unimaginative, and he took it for granted that Roy was the same.

I had a letter from Roy himself early in March. He invited me to spend a week or two of the vacation with him in Berlin. He seemed acutely desirous that I should go, but the letter was not an intimate one. It was stylized, almost awkward, almost remote – usually he wrote with liquid ease, but this invitation was stiff. I suspected a purpose that he wished to hold back. There was nothing for it but to go.

I arrived at the Zoo station in Berlin on a snowy afternoon in March. I looked for Roy up and down the platform, but did not see him. I was cold, a little apprehensive; I spoke very little German, and I stood there with my bags, in a fit of indecision.

Then a young woman spoke to me:

'You are Mr Eliot, please?'

She was spectacularly thin. Beneath her fur coat, her legs were like stalks. But she had bright clever grey eyes, and as I said yes she suddenly and disconcertingly burst into laughter.

'What is the joke?' I asked.

'Please. I did not quite understand you.' She spoke English slowly, but her ear was accurate and her intonation good.

'Why do you laugh?'

'I am sorry.' She could not straighten her face. 'Mr Calvert has said that you will look more like a professor than he. But he said you are really less like.'

She added:

'He has also said that you will have something wrong with your clothes. Such as shoelace undone. Or other things.' She was shaken with laughter as she pointed to the collar of my overcoat, which I had put up against the cold and which had somehow got twisted. She thought it was an extraordinarily good joke. 'It is so. It is so.'

It was one way of being recognized, I thought. I asked why Roy was not there.

'He is ill,' she said. 'Not much. He works too hard and does not think of himself. He must stay in bed today.'

As we got into a taxi, she told me that her name was Mecke, Ursula Mecke. I had already identified her as the 'little dancer': and she told me: 'I am *Tänzerin*.' I liked her at sight. She was ill, hysterical, and highly-strung; but she was also warm-hearted, good-natured, and had much insight. She was quick and business-like with the taxi driver, but when she talked about her earnings on the stage, I felt sure she was hopelessly impractical in running her life. I did not think she had been a love of Roy's. She spoke of him with a mixture of comradeship and touching veneration. 'He is so good,' she said. 'It is not only money, Mr Eliot. That is easy. But Mr Calvert thinks for us. That is not easy.' She told me how that winter her mother had fallen ill in Aachen. The little dancer could not afford to go; she was always in debt, and her salary, after she had paid taxes and the party contributions, came to about thirty shillings a week. But within a few hours she found in her room a return ticket, a hamper of food for the journey, an advance on her salary, and a bottle of Lanvin scent. 'He denies it, naturally,' said Ursula Mecke. 'He says that he has not given me these things. He says that I have an admirer. Who else has given me them, Mr Eliot?' Her grammar then got confused in her excitement:

but she meant who else, in those circumstances, would have remembered that she would enjoy some scent.

The Knesebeckstrasse lay in the heart of the west end, between the Kurfürstendamm and the Kantstrasse. No. 32 was near the Kantstrasse end of the street; like all the other houses, it was six-storeyed, grey-faced, and had once been fashionable. Now it was sub-let like a complex honeycomb. Roy had the whole suite of five rooms on the ground floor, but the storeys above were divided into flats of three rooms or two or one: the *Tänzerin* had a single attic right at the top.

All Roy's rooms were high, dark, and panelled in pine which had been painted a deep chocolate brown; they were much more sparsely furnished and stark than anywhere else he had lived, although he had added to them sofas, armchairs, and his inevitable assortment of desks. The family of von Haltsdorff must have lived there in dark, dignified, austere poverty; now that Roy had leased the flat from them they had gone to live in austere poverty on their estate on the Baltic. They had permitted themselves one decoration in the dining-room; on the barn-like expanse of wall, there stood out a large painted chart on which their eyes could rest. It was the family genealogy. It began well before the Great Elector. It came down through a succession of von Haltsdorffs, all of whom had been officers in the Prussian Army. They had intermarried with other Prussian families. None had apparently had much success. The chart ended with the present head, who was a retired colonel.

We had to pass through the dining-room on the way to Roy. I glanced at the chart, and wondered what Lord Boscastle would have said.

Roy's bed was placed in the middle of another high, spacious room: the bed itself had four high wooden posts. Roy was lying underneath a great pillow-like German eiderdown.

'How are you?' I said.

'Slightly dead,' said Roy.

But he did not look or sound really ill. He was pale, unshaven, and somewhat bedraggled. I gathered that he had had a mild influenza; his friends in the house, Ursula Mecke and the rest, had rushed round fetching him a doctor, nursing him, expressing great distress when he wanted to get up. He could not laugh it off without hurting them.

That night I sat at his bedside while he held a kind of levee. A dozen people looked in to inquire after him as soon as they arrived home from work (they did not get home so early as their equivalents in England). Several of them stayed talking, went away for their supper, and returned after Roy had eaten his own meal. There was a clerk, a school-teacher, a telephone girl, a cashier from a big shop, a librarian, a barber's assistant, a draughtsman.

Some of them were nervous of me, but they were used to calling on Roy, and he talked to them like a brother. It mystified them just as much. His German sounded as fluent as theirs, and after supper, when I was alone with Ursula, I asked how good it was. She said that she might not have known he was a foreigner, but she would have wondered which part of Germany he came from. It was not surprising he was so good; he was a professional linguist, had been in and out of Germany for years, and was a natural mimic. But I envied him, when I found the fog of language cutting me off from his friends. Both he and I picked up so much from words and from the feeling behind words. He could tell from the form of a sentence, from the hesitation over a word, some new event in the librarian's life, just as piercingly as though it were Despard-Smith saying 'in his own best interests'. I wanted to know these people, but I could not begin to. I saw an interesting face, Roy told me a scrap of a story, and that was all. It was a frustration.

Faces told one something, though. The lined forehead of the librarian, with the opaque pallor one often sees in anxious people: he had a kind, gentle, terrified expression, frightened of something he might have left undone. The hare eyes and bulbous nose of the elderly women school-teacher, who had strong opinions on everything, not much sense of reality, and an unquenchable longing for adventure: at the age of fifty-eight, she had nearly saved up enough money for a holiday abroad. The diagonal profile of the draughtsman; he was musical, farouche, and shy. The hot glare, swelling neck, and smooth unlined cheeks of the clerk, who was a man of forty: he had got religion and sex inextricably mixed up. It was he who was keeping the barber's assistant, Willy Romantowski; though some of the rooms in the house were very cheap, like Ursula's, none of them would have come within that boy's means.

They were interesting people, and I wished I could talk to them as Roy did. Of them all, I found the little dancer the most sympathetic.

A Nest of People

I did not much like young Romantowski, but he was the oddest and perhaps the ablest of them. He had the kind of bony features one sometimes meets in effeminate men: so that really his face, and his whole physique, were strong and masculine, and his mincing smile and postures seemed more than ever bizarre. His manner was strident, he insisted on getting our attention, he was petulant, vain, selfish, and extremely shrewd. He was not going to be content with a two-room flat in the Knesebeckstrasse for long. He was about twenty-two, very fair and pale: Roy called him the 'white avised', by contrast with his patron, who was the 'black avised' and who doted on him.

When they had all gone, I asked Roy their stories; he lay smoking a cigarette, and we speculated together about their lives. What would happen to the little dancer? Was there any way of getting her into a sanatorium? She must have been a delightful girl ten years before: she had wasted herself in hopeless devotions for married men: why had it happened so? Might she find a husband now? How long would Romantowski stay with his patron? Would the school-teacher be disappointed in her holiday, if ever she achieved it?

Roy was fond of them in his own characteristic fashion – unsentimental, half-malicious, on the look-out in everyone for some treat he could give without their knowing, attentive to those secret kindnesses which appeared like elaborate practical jokes.

Perhaps he had a special tenderness for some of them, for they were riff-raff and outcasts: and often it was among such that he felt most at home.

But I had a curious feeling as we talked about those friends of his. He was interested, scurrilous, tender – but he was cross that I had seen them. He was impatient that I had become caught up, just as it might have been in Pimlico, in a tangle of human lives. Whatever he had invited me for, it was not for that.

CHAPTER 26

Loss of a Temper

ALTHOUGH Roy got up the day after I arrived, it was too cold for him to leave the house. Through the afternoon and evening, we sat in the great uncomfortable drawing-room, and for a long time we were left alone.

All the time, I knew that Roy did not want us to be left alone. He was listening for steps in the hall, a knock on the door – not for any particular person, just anyone who would disturb us.

I was distressed, apprehensive, at a loss. He was affectionate, for that was his first nature. He was even amusing, as he made the minutes pass by mimicking some of our colleagues: but he would have done the same to an acquaintance in the combination room. I felt he was desperately sad, but he did not utter a word about it: once he had been spontaneous in his sadness, but not now. He seemed to be suppressing sadness, suppressing any relief, suppressing any desire to let me know. It was as though he had fixed his eyes on something apart from us both.

There was one interruption, when for a few minutes he behaved as in the old days. By the afternoon post he received a letter with a German stamp on; I saw him study the postmark and the handwriting with a frown. As he read the note, which was on a single piece of paper, the frown became fixed and guilty.

'She's run me down,' he said. Joan had arrived in Berlin, and was staying with the Eggars. Roy looked at me, as he used to when he was out-manoeuvred by a woman from whom he was trying to escape. For Joan he had a special feeling; he thought of her more gravely than of any woman, and with incomparably more remorse; yet there were times when she seemed just another mistress, and when he felt he was going through the accustomed moves.

He was confused. Clean breaks did not come easy to him. He would have liked to spend that night with Joan. If it had been someone who minded less, like Rosalind, he would have rung her up on the spot. But he could not behave carelessly with Joan. He had done so once, and it was a burden he could not shift.

So he sat, irresolute, rueful, badgered. There was something extremely comic about the winning end of a love affair, I thought. It needed Lady Boscastle's touch. For she never had much sympathy with the agony of the loser, the one who loved the more, the one who ate out her heart for a lover who was becoming more indifferent. Lady Boscastle had not suffered much in that fashion. She had been the winner in too many love affairs – and so she was superlatively acid about the comic dilemmas of love.

At last Roy decided. There was no help for it: he must meet Joan; it was better to meet her in public. He started to arrange a party, before he spoke to her. From his first call, it was clear the party would be an eccentric one. For he rang up Schäder, his most influential friend in the German government. From Roy's end of the conversation, I gathered that Schäder was free for a very late dinner the following night and that he insisted on being the host. When Roy had put down the telephone, he looked at me with acute, defiant eyes.

'Excellent. I needed you to meet him. He is an interesting man.'

I asked what exactly his job was. Roy said that he was the equivalent of a Minister in England, the kind of Minister who is just on the fringe of the cabinet.

'He's extremely young,' said Roy. 'About your age. You must forget your preconceived ideas. He's not a bit stuffed.'

They had arranged that Roy should invite the party. He found one German friend already booked, but got hold of Ammatter, the Orientalist whom I had met in Cambridge. Then he rang up Joan. She was demanding to see him at once, that afternoon, that night: Roy nearly weakened, but held firm. At last she acquiesced. I could imagine the fierce, sullen, miserable resignation with which she turned away. She was to bring Eggar 'if he does not think it will set him back a peg or two'. Roy also invited Eggar's wife, but she was expecting a child in the next fortnight. 'It looks like being Joan and five men,' he said. He was smiling fondly and mockingly, as he must have done when they were in love.

'That's her idea of a social evening. A well-balanced little party. She likes feeling frivolous, you know. Because it's not her line.' He sighed. 'Oh – there's no one like her, is there?'

The next morning, he was well enough to take me for a walk through the Berlin streets. It was still freezingly cold, and the sky was steely. The weather had not changed since the German army marched into Prague, a few days before I set out. Outside Roy's house, the pavement rang with our footsteps in the cold: the street was empty under the bitter sky. Roy was wearing earcaps, as though he were just going to plunge into a scrum.

He took me on a tour under the great grey buildings; lights twinkled behind the office windows; the shops and cafés were full, people jostled us on the pavements, the air was frosty and electric; an aeroplane zoomed invisibly overhead, above the even pall of cloud. We walked past the offices of the Friedrichstrasse and the Wilhelm-strasse; the rooms were a blaze of light. Roy was only speaking to tell me what the places were. He showed me Schäder's ministry, a heavy nineteenth-century mansion. Official motor-cars went hurtling by, their horns playing an excited tune.

We came to the Linden. The trees were bare, but the road was alive with cars and the pavements crammed with men and women hurrying past. Roy stopped for a moment and looked down the great street. He broke his silence.

'It has great power,' he said. 'Don't you feel that it has great power?'

He spoke with extreme force. As he spoke, I knew for sure what I had already suspected: he had brought me to Berlin to convert me.

For the rest of that morning we argued, walking under the steely sky through the harsh, busy streets. We had never had an argument before – now it was painful, passionate, often bitter. We knew each other's language, each of us knew all the experience the other could command, it was incomparably more piercing than arguing with a stranger.

When once we began, we could not leave it all day; on and off we came back to the difference between us. Most of the passion and bitterness was on my side. I was not reasonable that day, either as we walked the streets or sat in his high cold rooms. I kept breaking out with incredulity and rancour. We were still talking violently, when it was ten o'clock and time to leave for the Adlon.

He seemed to be using his gifts, his imagination, his penetrating insight, his clear eyes, for a purpose that I detested. He had not wanted me to become absorbed in the rag tag and bobtail of the Knesebeck-strasse. He loved them, but it was not that part of Germany he wanted me to see. They did not talk politics, except to grumble passively at laws and taxes which impinged on them; the only political remarks on the night I arrived were a few diatribes against the régime by the school-teacher, who was as usual opinionated, hot-heated, and some-what half-baked. Roy warned her to be careful outside the house. There was an asinine endearingness about her.

Roy wanted me to see the revolution. That day he made his case for it, in a temper that was better than mine, though even his was some-times sharp; sometimes he put in mischievous digs, as though anxious to lighten my mood. He had set out to convince me that the Nazis had history on their side.

The future would be in German hands. There would be great suffering on the way, they might end in a society as dreadful as the worst of this present one: but there was a chance – perhaps a better chance than any other – that in time, perhaps in our life time, they would create a brilliant civilization.

'If they succeed,' said Roy, 'everyone will forget the black spots. In history success is the only virtue.'

He knew how to use the assumptions that all our political friends made at that period. He had not lived in the climate of 'fellow travellers' for nothing. Francis Getliffe, like many other scientists, had moved near to the Communist line: we had all been affected by that climate of thought. Men needed to plan on a superhuman scale, said Roy, with a hint of the devil quoting scripture; Europe must be one, so that men could plan wide and deep enough; soon the world must be one. How could it become one except by force? Who had both the force and the will? No price was too high to pay, to see the world made one. 'It won't be made one by reason. Men never give up jobs and power unless they must.'

Only the Germans or Russians could do it. They had both got energy set free, through a new set of men seizing power. 'They've got the energy of a revolution. It comes from very deep.' They had both done dreadful things with it, for men in power always did dreadful things. But the Promethean force might do something wonderful. 'Either of them might. I've told you before, the truth lies at both ex-tremes,' said Roy. 'But I'll back these people. They're slightly crazy, of course. All revolutionaries are slightly crazy. That's why they are revolutionaries. A good solid well-adjusted man like Arthur Brown just couldn't be one. I'm not sure that you could. But I could, Lewis. If I'd been born here, I should have been.'

Not many people had the nature to be revolutionaries, said Roy. And those who had, felt dished when they had won their revolution and then could not keep their own jobs. Like the old Bolsheviks. Like Röhm. The Nazis had collected an astonishing crowd of bosses – some horrible, some intensely able, some wild with all the turbulent depth of the German heart. 'That's why something may come of them,' said Roy. 'They may be crazy, but they're not commonplace men. You won't believe it, but one or two of them are good. *Good*, I tell you.'

It was that fantastic human mixture that had taken hold of him. They were men of flesh and bone. They were human. He said one needed to choose between them and the Russians. He had made his choice. Communism was the most dry and sterile of human creeds – 'no illustrations, no capital letters. Life is more mixed than that. Life is richer than that. It's darker than the Communists think. They're optimistic children. Life is darker than they think, but it's also richer. You know it is. Think of their books. They're the most sterile and thinnest you've ever seen.' Roy talked of our Communist friends. 'They're shallow. They can't feel anything except moral indignation. They're not human. Lewis, I can't get on with them any more.'

Inflamed by anxiety and anger, I accused him of being perverse and self-destructive: of being intoxicated by the Wagnerian passion for death; of losing all his sense through meeting, for the first time, men surgent with a common purpose: of being seduced by his liking for Germany, by the ordinary human liking for people one has lived among for long.

'This isn't the time to fool yourself,' I cried. 'If ever there was a time to keep your head –'

'Are you keeping yours?' said Roy quietly. He pointed to the mirror behind us. His face was sombre, mine was white with anger. I had lost my temper altogether. I accused him of being overwhelmed by his success in Berlin, by the flattery and attentions.

'Not fair,' said Roy. 'You've forgotten that you used to know me. Haven't you?'

Out of doors, as we walked to the Adlon, the night was sullen. The mercury-vapour lamps shone livid on the streets and on the lowering clouds. We made our way beneath them, and I recovered myself a little. Partly from policy: it was not good to let a man like Schäder see us shaken. But much more because of that remark of Roy's: 'You used to know me.' He had said it without a trace of reproach. Deeper than any quarrel, we knew each other. Walking in the frosty night, I felt a pang of intolerable sorrow.

At the hotel, we were shown into a private room, warm, glowing, soft-carpeted, the table glittering with linen, silver, and glass. Houston Eggar had decided that the party would not harm his prospects; he gave us his tough, cheerful greeting, and talked to us and Joan in a manner that was masculine, assertive, anxious to make an impression, both on the niece of Lord Boscastle and on a comely woman. He had also noted me down as potentially useful – not useful enough to make him fix a lunch during my remaining days in Berlin, but quite worth his trouble to say with matey heartiness that we must 'get together soon'. I had a soft spot for Eggar. There was something very simple and humble about his constant, untiring, matter-of-fact ambitiousness. Incidentally, he was only a counsellor at forty-five: he had still to make up for lost time.

Joan said to Roy:

'Are you better? You look very tired.'

'Just so,' said Roy. 'Through listening to Lewis. He gets more eloquent.'

'You shouldn't have got up. It's stupid of you.'

'He could talk to me in bed.'

Joan laughed. His solemn expression had always melted her. For the moment, she was happy to be near him, on any terms.

Servants flung open the door, and Schäder and Ammatter came in. Roy introduced each of us: Schäder spoke good English, though his accent was strange: in an efficient, workman-like, and courteous fashion, he discovered exactly how much German we each possessed.

'We shall speak English then,' said Schäder. 'Perhaps we find difficulties. Then Roy shall translate and help us.'

This left Ammatter out of the conversation for most of the dinner. But he accepted the position in a flood of what appeared to be voluble and deferential compliments. It was interesting to notice his excessive deference to Schäder. Ammatter was, as I had seen in Cambridge, a tricky, round-faced, cunning, fluid-natured man, very much on the make. But I was familiar with academic persons on the make, and I thought that, even allowing for his temperament, his obsequiousness before official power marked a real difference in tradition. At the college, Roy and I were used to eminent politicians and Civil Servants coming down for the week-end; the connexion in England between colleges such as ours and the official world was very close; perhaps because it was so close, the visitors did not receive elaborate respect, but instead were liable to be snubbed caustically by old Winslow.

Ammatter made up unashamedly to Schäder, who took very little notice of him. Schäder said that it was late, asked us whether, as soon as we had finished a first drink, we would not like to begin dinner. He took Joan to the table, and I watched him stoop over her chair: he had come into more power than the rest of us had ever dreamed of. I might not meet again anyone who possessed such power.

He was, as Roy had said, in the early thirties. His face was lined and mature, but he still looked young. His forehead was square, furrowed, and massive, and there was nearly a straight line from temple to chin, so that the whole of his unusual, strong, intelligent face made up a triangle. His hair was curly, untidy in a youthful fashion; he seemed tough and muscular. It was the kind of physical make-up one does not often find in 'intellectual' people, though I knew one or two businessmen who gave the same impression of vigour, alertness, and activity.

As he presided over the dinner, his manners were pleasant, sometimes rather over-elaborate. He was the son of a bank clerk and in his rush to power he had, as it were, invented a form of manners for himself. And he showed one aching cavity of a man who had worked unremittingly hard, who had attained great responsibility early, who had never had time to play. He was getting married in a month, and he talked about it with the naïve exaggerated trenchancy of a very young man. He was a little afraid.

I thought that he knew nothing of women. It flashed out once that he envied Roy his loves. As a rule, his attitude to Roy was comradely, half-contemptuous, half-admiring. He had a kind of amused wonder that Roy showed no taste for place or glory. With pressing friendliness, he wanted Roy to cut a figure in the limelight. If nowhere else, then he should get all the academic honours – and Schäder asked Ammatter sharply when the university would do something for Roy.

Dinner went on. Schäder passed some elaborate compliments to Joan: he was interested, hotly interested like a young man, in her feeling for Roy. Then he called himself back to duty, and addressed me:

'Roy has told me, Mr Eliot, that you are what we call a social democrat?'

'Yes.'

Schäder was regarding me intently with large eyes in which there showed abnormally little white: they were eyes dominating, pertinacious, astute. He grinned.

'We found here that the social democrats gave us little trouble. We thought they were nice harmless people.'

'Yes,' I said. 'We noticed that.'

Roy spoke to Schäder.

'Don't think that Eliot is always orthodox and harmless. His politics are the only *bürgerlich* thing about him. I can never understand why he should be such an old burger about politics. Safe in the middle of the road.'

'I am sure,' said Schäder with firm politeness, 'that I shall find much in common with Mr Eliot.'

It was clear that I had to do the talking. Eggar was too cautious to enter the contest; he made an attempt to steer us away to placid subjects, such as the Davis Cup. Roy gave him a smile of extreme *diablerie*, as though whispering the letters 'C.M.G.'. It was left to me to stand against Schäder, and in fact I was glad to. It was a relief after the day with Roy. I was completely in control of my temper now. Joan was an ally, backing me up staunchly at each turn of the conflict. I had never felt her approve of me before.

First Schäder tried me out by reflecting on the machinery of government. What did I think about the way governments must develop – not morally, that should not enter between us, said Schäder, but technically? Did I realize the difference that organized science must mean? Two hundred years ago determined citizens with muskets were almost as good as the King's armies. Now the apparatus is so much more complex. A central government which can rely on its armed forces is able to stay in power for ever. 'So far as I can see, Mr Eliot, revolution is impossible from now on – unless it starts among those who hold the power. Will you tell me if I am wrong?'

I thought he was right, appallingly right: it was one of the sinister facts of the twentieth-century scene. He went on to tell me his views about what the central government could and must control, and how it must operate. He knew it inside out; there was no more sign of the young man unaccustomed to society, timid with women; he was a born manager of men, and he had already had years of experience. Although he was a minister, he did much work that in England would have been done by his permanent secretary: as a matter of fact, he seemed to do a considerable amount of actual executive work, which in an English department would never have reached the higher Civil Servants, let alone the minister. It had its disadvantages, but I thought it gave him a closer feel of his job. He ran his department rather as an acquaintance of mine, a gifted English industrialist, ran his business. It was the general practice of the régime; sometimes it made for confusion, particularly (as Schäder straightforwardly admitted) when the party officials he had introduced as his own staff got across the old, regular, German Civil Service. He made another admission: they were finding it hard to collect enough men who could be trained into administrators, high or low. 'That may set a limit to the work a government can do, Mr Eliot. And we are an efficient race. If you plan your society, you will find this difficulty much greater – for you educate such a small fraction of your population. Also, forgive me, I do not think you are very efficient.'

'We're not so stupid as we look,' I said.

Schäder looked at me, and laughed. He went on questioning me, stating his experience on the technique of government – the mechanical technique, the paper-work, the files, the use of men.

He was being very patient in coming to his point. At last he knew enough about me. He said:

'Tell me, Mr Eliot, what is to cause war between your country and mine? You are not the man to give me hypocritical reasons. Do you think you will fight for the balance of power?'

I waited for a second.

'I think we should,' I said.

He narrowed his eyes.

'That is interesting. You cannot keep the balance of power for ever. Why should you trouble –'

'No one is fit to be trusted with power,' I said. I was replying to Roy, as well as to him. 'No one. I should not like to see your party in charge of Europe, Dr Schäder. I should not like to see any group of men in charge – not me or my friends or anyone else. Any man who has lived at all knows the follies and wickedness he's capable of. If he does not know it, he is not fit to govern others. And if he does know it, he knows also that neither he nor any man ought to be allowed to decide a single human fate. I am not speaking of you specially, you understand: I should say exactly the same of myself.'

Our eyes met. I was certain, as one can be certain in a duel across the table, that for the first time he took me seriously.

'You do not think highly of men, Mr Eliot.'

'I am one,' I said.

He shrugged his shoulders. He got back to his own ground, telling me that he did not suppose my countrymen shared my rather 'unusual reasons' for believing in the balance of power. I was taking up the attack now, and replied that men's instincts were often wiser than their words.

'So you think, if we become too powerful, you will go to war with us?'

I could see nothing at that table but Roy's face, grave and stricken. During this debate he had been silent. He sat there before my eyes, listening for what I was bound to say.

'I think we shall,' I said.

'You are not a united country, Mr Eliot. Many people in England would not agree with you?'

He was accurate, but I did not answer. I said:

'They hope it will not be necessary.'

'Yes,' said Roy in a passionate whisper. 'They hope that.'

Joan was staring at him with love and horror, praying that he would not say too much.

'We all hope that,' she said, in a voice that was deep with yearning for him. 'But you've not been in England much lately. Opinion is changing. I must tell you about it – perhaps on the way home?'

'You must,' said Roy with a spark of irony. But he had responded to her; for a moment she had reached him.

'Will they not do more than hope?' said Schäder.

'It depends on you,' said Joan quickly.

'Will they not do more than hope?' Schäder repeated to Roy.

'Some will,' said Roy clearly.

Joan was still staring at him, as though she were guarding him from danger.

Eggar intervened, in a cheerful companionable tone:

'There is all the good will in the world —'

'Let us suppose,' said Schäder, ignoring him, 'that it comes to war. Let us suppose that we decide it is necessary to become powerful. To become more powerful than you and your friends believe to be desirable, Mr Eliot —'

'Believe to be safe,' I said.

'Let us suppose we have to extend our frontiers, Mr Eliot. Which some of your friends appear to dislike. You go to war. Then what happens?'

'We have been to war before,' I said.

'I am not interested in history. I am interested in this year and the next and the next. You go to war. Can you fight a war?'

'We must try.'

'You will not be a united people. There will be many who do not wish for war. There will be many who like us. They see our faults, but they like us. If there is a war, they will not wish to conquer us. What will they do?'

He expected Roy to answer. So did Joan and I. But Roy sat looking at the table. Was he moved by her love? Was he considering either of us? His eyes, usually so bright, were remote.

Schäder looked at him curiously. Not getting an answer, Schäder paused, and then went on:

'How can you fight a war?'

In a few moments the conversation lagged, and Joan said, quite easily:

'I really think I ought to get Roy to his house, Dr Schäder. This is his first day out of bed, you know. He looks awfully tired.'

Roy said without protest:

'I should go, perhaps.' He gave a slight smile. 'Eliot can stay and talk about war, Reinhold. You two need to talk about war.'

Schäder said, with the comradely physical concern that one often meets in aggressive, tough, powerful men: 'Of course you must go if you are tired. You must take care, Roy. Please look after him, Miss Royce. He has many friends who wish to see him well.'

He showed them out with elaborate kindness, and then returned to Eggar and me. Eggar had realized that he must let Joan have Roy to herself, and he stayed listening while Schäder and I talked until late. I told Schäder – much more confidently than I felt at the time – that he must not exaggerate the effect of disunity in England. It was easy to alter opinions very quickly in the modern world. We had a long discussion on the effectiveness of propaganda. In the long run, said Schäder, it is utterly effective. 'If we entertained you here for a few years, Mr Eliot, you would accept things that now you find incredible. In the long run, people believe what they hear – if they hear nothing else.'

He was a formidable man, I thought, as I walked home with Houston Eggar. I was troubled by his confidence: it was not the confidence of the stupid. He was lucky in his time, for he fitted it exactly. He was born for this kind of world. Yet he was likeable in his fashion.

'Calvert is not as discreet as he ought to be,' said Eggar, as we walked down the deserted street.

'No.' All my anxiety returned.

'It does *not* make our job easier. I wish you'd tell him. I know it's just thoughtlessness.'

'I will if I get the chance,' I said.

'Between ourselves,' said Houston Eggar, 'this is a pretty thankless job, Eliot. I suppose I can't grumble. It's a good jumping-off ground. It ought to turn out useful, but sometimes one doesn't know what to do for the best. Everyone likes to have something to show for their trouble.'

I was touched. For all his thrust and bounce, he wanted some results from his work.

A clock was striking two when I let myself in at Roy's front door. I had been anxious ever since he left the dinner. Now I was shaken by a sudden, unreasonable access of anxiety, such as one sometimes feels on going home after a week away.

I tip-toed in, across the great cold rooms. Then, worried and tense, I meant to satisfy myself that he was no worse. I went to his bedroom door. I stopped outside. Through the oak I could hear voices, speaking very quietly. One was a woman's.

I lay awake, thinking of them both. Could Joan calm him, even yet? I wished I could believe it. It was much later, it must have been four o'clock, before I heard the click of a door opening. By that time I was drowsing fitfully, and at the sound I jumped up with dread. Another door clicked outside: Joan had left: I found it hard to go to sleep again.

CHAPTER 27

Under the Mercury-vapour Lamps

Roy did not refer to Joan's visit. She stayed with the Eggars a day or two longer, and then moved on to some friends of the Boscastles in Stockholm. I saw her with Roy only once. She seemed precariously hopeful, and he gentle.

For the rest of my week in Berlin, he was quiet and subdued, though he seemed to be fighting off the true melancholy. He took time from his work to entertain me; he arranged our days so that, like tourists, we could occupy ourselves by talking about the sights.

We slippered our way round Sans Souci, stood in the Garrison Church at Potsdam, sailed along the lakes in the harsh weather, walked through the Brandenburg villages. We had often travelled in Europe together, but this was the first time we had searched for things to see: it was also the first time we had said so little.

I did not meet Schäder again, nor any of his official friends. But I saw a good deal of Ammatter and the university people, in circumstances of fairly high-class farce. Months before, Ammatter had interpreted Schäder's interest in Roy to mean that the university should give him some honour. Ammatter promptly set about it. And, academic dignitaries having certain characteristics in common everywhere, his colleagues behaved much as our college would have done.

They suspected that Ammatter was trying to suck up to high authorities; they suspected he had an eye on some other job; they could not have been righter. The prospect of someone else getting a job moved them to strong moral indignation. They promptly took up positions for a stately disapproving minuet. What opinions of Roy's work besides Ammatter's had ever been offered? Ammatter diligently canvassed the Oriental faculty in Berlin, Tübingen, Stuttgart, Breslau, Marburg, Bonn: there seemed to be no doubt, the senate reluctantly admitted, that this Englishman was a scholar of extreme distinction.

That step had taken months. The next step was according to pattern. Though everyone would like to recognize his distinction (which was the positive equivalent of 'in his own best interests'), surely they were prevented by their code of procedure? It was impossible to give an honorary degree to a man of twenty-nine; it would open the door to premature proposals of all kinds; if they departed from custom for this one Orientalist, they would be flooded with demands from all the other faculties. It was even more impossible to make him a Corresponding Member of the Academy: the Orientalists were already above their quota: it would mean asking for a special dispensation: it was unthinkable to ask for a special dispensation, when one was breaking with precedent in putting forward a candidate so young.

Those delays had satisfactorily taken care of several more months. I thought that the resources of obstruction were well up to our native standard – though I would have backed Arthur Brown against any of them as an individual performer, if one wanted a stubborn, untiring, stone-wall defence.

That was the position at the time of our dinner with Schäder. Ammatter had taken Schäder's question as a rebuke and an instruction to deliver a suitable answer in quick time. So, during that week, he conferred with the Rector. If they abandoned the hope of honorary degrees and corresponding memberships, could they not introduce the American title of visiting professor? It would recognize a fine achievement: it would cost them nothing: it would do the university good. No doubt, I thought when I heard the story, there was a spirited and enjoyable exchange of sentiments about how the university could in no way whatsoever be affected by political influences. No doubt they agreed that, in a case like this which was crystal-pure upon its own merits, it would do no harm to retain a Minister's benevolent interest.

The upshot of it all was that Roy found himself invited to address a seminar at very short notice. At the seminar the Rector and several of the senate would be present: Roy was to describe his recent researches. Afterwards Ammatter planned that the Rector would make the new proposal his own; it would require 'handling', as Arthur Brown would say, to slip an unknown title into the university; it was essential that the Rector should speak from first-hand knowledge. Apparently the Rector was convinced that it would be wise to act.

I heard some of the conferences between Ammatter and Roy, without understanding much of them. It was when we were alone that Roy told me the entire history. His spirits did not often rise nowadays to their old mischievous brilliance: but he had not been able to resist giving Ammatter the impression that he needed recognition from the University of Berlin more than anything on earth. This impression had made Ammatter increasingly agitated; for he took it for granted that Roy told Schäder so, and that his, Ammatter's, fortunes hung on the event. Ammatter took to ringing up Roy late at night on the days before the seminar: another member of the senate was attending: all would come well. Roy protested extreme nervousness about his address, and Ammatter fussed over the telephone and came round early in the morning to reassure him.

I begged to be allowed to come to the seminar. With a solemn face, Roy said that he would take me. With the same solemn face, he answered Ammatter on the telephone the evening before: I could hear groans and cries from the instrument as Ammatter assured, encouraged, cajoled, reviled. Roy put down the receiver with his most earnest, mystifying expression.

'I've told him that I must put up a good show tomorrow,' he said. 'But I was obliged to tell him that too much depends on it. I may get stage fright.'

Roy dressed with exquisite care the next morning. He put on his most fashionable suit, a silk shirt, a pair of suede shoes. 'Must look well,' he said. 'Can't take any risks.' In fact, as he sat on the Rector's right hand in the Oriental lecture-room at the university, he looked as though he had strayed in by mistake. The Rector was a bald fat man with rimless spectacles and a stout pepper-coloured suit; he sat stiffly between Roy and Ammatter, down at the lecturer's desk. The theatre ran up in tiers, and there sat thirty or forty men in the three bottom rows. Most of them were homely, academic, middle-aged, dressed in sensible reach-me-downs. In front of their eyes sat Roy, wooden-faced, slight, elegant, young, like a *flâneur* at a society lunch.

It was an Oriental seminar, and so Ammatter was in the chair. He made a speech to welcome Roy; I did not understand it, but it was obviously jocular, flattering, the speech of an impresario who, after much stress, knows that he has pulled it off. Roy stood up, straight and solemn. There was some clapping. Roy began to speak *in English*. I saw Ammatter's face cloud with astonishment, used as he was to hear Roy speak German as well as a foreigner could. Other faces began to look slightly glazed, for German scholars were no better linguists than English ones, and not more than half a dozen people there could follow spoken English comfortably, even in a tone as clear as Roy's. But many more had to pretend to understand; they did not like to seem baffled; very soon heads were nodding wisely when the lecturer appeared to be establishing a point.

Actually Roy had begun with excessive formality to explain that his subject was of great intricacy, and he found it necessary to use his own language, which of course they would understand. His esteemed master and colleague, his esteemed professor Ammatter, had said that the lecture would describe recent advances in Manichaean studies. 'I think that would be *much* too broad a subject to attempt in one after-noon. It would be extremely rash to make such an attempt,' said Roy solemnly, and uncomprehending heads began to shake in sympathy. 'I should regard it as coming dangerously near *journalism* to offer my learned colleagues a kind of popular précis. So with your permission I have chosen a topic where I can be definite enough not to offend you. I hope to examine to your satisfaction five points in Soghdian lexicography.'

He lectured for an hour and twenty minutes. His face was im-perturbably solemn throughout – except that twice he made a grotesque donnish pun, and gave a shy smile. At that sign, the whole room rocked with laughter, as though he had revealed a ray of humour of the most divine subtlety. When he frowned, they shook their heads. When he sounded triumphant, they nodded in unison.

Even those who could understand his English must have been very little the wiser. For he was analysing some esoteric problems about words that he had just discovered; they were in a dialect of Soghdian which he was the only man in the world to have unravelled. To add a final touch of fantasy, he quoted long passages of Soghdian: so that much of the lecture seemed to be taking place in Soghdian itself.

He would recite from memory sentence after sentence in this lan-guage, completely incomprehensible to anyone but himself. The strange sounds finished up as though he had asked a question. Roy proceeded to answer it himself.

'Just so,' he said firmly, and then went on in Soghdian to what appeared to be the negative view. That passage came to an end, and Roy at once commented on it in a stern tone. 'Not a bit of it,' he said.

I was sitting with a handkerchief pressed to my mouth. It was the most elaborate, the most ludicrous, the most *recherché*, of all his tricks: it was pure 'old-brandy', to use a private phrase. He knew that, if one had an air of solemn certainty and a mesmerizing eye, they would never dare to say that it was too difficult for them. None of these learned men would dare to say that he had not understood a word.

An hour went by. I wondered when he was going to end. But he had set himself five words to discuss, and even when he arrived at the fifth he was not going to leave his linguistic speculations unsaid. He finished strongly in a wave of Soghdian, swelled by remarks in the later forms of the language, with illustrations from all over the Middle East. Then he said, very modestly and unassumingly:

'I expect you may think that I have been too bold and slap-dash in some of my conclusions. I have not had time to give you all the evidence, but I think I can present it. I very much hope that if any of my colleagues can show me where I have been too superficial, he will please do so now.'

Roy slid quietly into his seat. There was a little stupefied applause, which became louder and clearer. The clapping went on.

Ammatter got up and asked for contributions and questions. There was a long stupefied silence. Then someone rose. He was an eminent philologist, possibly the only person present who had profited by the lecture. He spoke in halting, correct English:

'These pieces of analysis are most deep and convincing, if I may say so. I have one thing to suggest about your word –'

He made his suggestion which was complex and technical, and sounded very ingenious. At once Roy jumped up to reply – and replied at length *in German*. In fluent, easy, racy German. Then I heard the one complaint of the afternoon. Two faces in the row in front of me turned to each other. One asked why he had not lectured in German. The other could not understand.

Roy's discussion with the philologist went on. It was not a controversy; they were agreeing over a new possibility, which Roy promised to investigate (it appeared later as a paragraph in one of his books). The Rector made a speech to thank Roy for his lecture. Ammatter supported him. There was more applause, and Roy thanked the meeting in a few demure and solemn words.

Before we departed from the lecture theatre, Ammatter went up to Roy in order to shake hands before parting for the day. He was smiling knowingly, but as he gazed at Roy I caught an expression of sheer, bemused, complete bewilderment.

Roy and I went out into the Linden. It was late afternoon.

'Well,' said Roy, 'I thought the house was a bit cold towards the middle. But I got a good hand at the end, didn't I?'

I had nothing to say. I took him to the nearest café and stood him a drink.

That afternoon brought back the past. I hoped that it might buoy him up, but soon he was quiet again and stayed so till we said good-bye at the railway station.

He was quiet even at Romantowski's party. This happened the night before I left, and many people in the house were invited, as well as friends from outside. Romantowski and his patron lived in two rooms at the top of the house, just under the little dancer's attic. It was getting late, the party was noisy, when Roy and I climbed up.

The rooms were poor, there was linoleum on the floor, the guests were drinking out of cups. Somehow Romantowski's patron had managed to buy several bottles of spirits. How he had afforded it, Roy could not guess. Presumably he was being madly extravagant in order to please the young man. Poor devil, I said to Roy. For it looked as though Romantowski had demanded the party in order to hook a different fish. There were several youngish men round him, randy and perverted.

I asked what Schäder and his colleagues would think of this sight. 'Schäder would be shocked,' said Roy. 'He's a bit of a prude. But he needn't mind. Most of these people will fight – they'll fight better than respectable men.'

That reminded him of war, and his face darkened. We were standing by the window over the street: we looked inwards to the shouting, hilarious, rackety crowd.

'If there is a war,' said Roy, 'what can I do?'

He was seared by the thought. Living in others, he was seared by his affections in England, his affections here. He said:

'There doesn't seem to be a place for me, does there?'

The little dancer joined us, lapping up her drink, cheerful, lively, bright-eyed.

'How are you, Ursula?' said Roy.

'I think I am better,' she said, with her unquenchable hope. 'Soon it will be good weather.'

'Really better?' said Roy. He had still not contrived a plan for sending her to the mountains: he did not dare talk to her direct.

'In the summer I shall be well.'

She laughed at him, she laughed at both of us, she had a bright cheeky wit. I thought again how gallant-hearted she was.

Then Romantowski came mincing up. He offered me a cigarette, but I said I did not smoke. 'Poor you!' said Willy Romantowski, using his only English phrase, picked up heaven knows how. He spoke to Roy in his brisk Berlin twang, of which I could scarcely make out a word. I noticed Roy mimic him as he replied. Romantowski gave a pert grin. Again he asked something. Roy nodded, and the young man went away.

'Roy, you should not!' cried Ursula. 'You should not give him money! He treats poor Hans' (Hans was the clerk, the 'black avised') 'so badly. He is cruel to poor Hans. He will take your money and buy clothes – so as to interest these little gentlemen.' She nodded scornfully, tolerantly, towards the knot in the middle of the room. 'It is not sensible to give him money.'

'Too old to be sensible.' Roy smiled at her. 'Ursula, if I don't give him money, he will take it from poor Hans. Poor Hans will have to find it from somewhere. He is spending too much money. I'm frightened that we shall have Hans in trouble.'

'It is so,' said Ursula.

Roy went on to say that we could not save Willy for Hans, but we might still save Hans from another disaster. Both Roy and the little dancer were afraid that he was embezzling money, to squander it on Willy. Ursula sighed.

'It is bad,' she said, 'to have to buy love.'

'It can be frightful,' said Roy.

'It is bad to have to run after love.'

'Have you seen him today?' said Roy, gently, clearly, directly.

'No. He was too busy.' 'He' was an elderly producer in a ramshackle theatre. Ursula's eyes were full of tears.

'I'm sorry, my dear.'

'Perhaps I shall see him tomorrow. Perhaps he will be free.'

She smiled, lips quivering, at Roy, and he took her hand.

'I wish I could help,' he said.

'You do help. You are so kind and gentle.' Suddenly she gazed at him. 'Roy, why are you unhappy? When you have so many who love you. Have you not all of us who love you?'

He kissed her. It was entirely innocent. Theirs was a strange tenderness. The little dancer wiped her eyes, plucked up her hope and courage, and went off to find another drink.

The air was whirling with smoke, and was growing hot. Roy flung open the window, and leaned out into the cold air. Over the houses at the bottom of the road there hung a livid greenish haze: it was light diffused from the mercury-vapour lamps of the Berlin streets.

'I like those lamps,' said Roy quietly.

He added:

'I've walked under them so often in the winter. I felt I was absolutely – anonymous. I don't think I've ever been so free. I used to put up my coat collar and walk through the streets under those lamps, and I was sure that no one knew me.'

CHAPTER 28

Self-hatred

IN Cambridge that May, the days were cold and bright. Roy played cricket for the first time since the old Master's death; I watched him one afternoon, and was surprised to see that his eye was in. His beautiful off-drive curled through the covers, he was hooking anything short with seconds to spare, he played a shot of his own, off the back foot past point; yet I knew, though he did not wake me nowadays, that his nights were haunted. He was working as he used in the blackest times; I believed he was drinking alone, and once or twice I had heard in his voice the undertone of frantic gaiety. Usually he sat grave and silent in hall, though he still bestirred himself to cheer up a visitor whom everyone else was ignoring. Several nights, he scandalized some of our friends by his remarks on Germany.

Towards the end of May, he had a letter from Rosalind, in which she said that she would soon be announcing her engagement to Ralph Udal. When he told me, I wondered for an instant whether she was playing a last card. Had she put Roy right out of her mind? Or did she allow herself a vestige of hope that he would swoop down and stop the marriage?

He smiled at the news. Yet I thought he was not quite indifferent. He had been wretched when the letter came, and he smiled with a kind of scathing, humorous fondness. But Rosalind had been able to rouse his jealousy, as no other woman could. In their time together, she had often behaved like a bitch and he like a frail and ordinary lover. Even now, in the midst of the most frightening griefs, he was sharply moved by the thought of losing her for good. He wrote to Ralph and to her. Somehow, the fact that she should have chosen Ralph added to Roy's feeling of loss and loneliness, added to an entirely unheroic pique. He said that he had told Rosalind to call on him some time. 'I expect she'll come with her husband,' said Roy with irritated sadness. 'It will be extremely awkward for everyone. I've never talked to her politely. It's absurd.'

The announcement was duly published in *The Times*. Roy read it in the combination room, and Arthur Brown asked him inquisitively:

'I see your friend Udal is getting married, Roy. I rather fancied that I remembered the name of the young woman. Isn't it someone you introduced me to in your rooms quite a while ago?'

'Just so,' said Roy.

'From what I remember of her,' said Brown, 'of course it was only a glimpse, I shouldn't have regarded her as particularly anxious to settle down as a parson's wife in a nice quiet country living.'

'No?' said Roy blankly. He did not like the sight of their names in print: he was not going to be drawn.

But, annoyed though he was at the news, he could not help chuckling with laughter at a letter from Lady Muriel. It was the only time in those dark weeks that I saw him utterly unshadowed. He had written several times to Lady Muriel about that time; for the Boscastles were visiting Cambridge in June, to mark the end of Humphrey's last term at Magdalene, and Roy had been persuading Lady Muriel to come with them. So far as I knew, he had not asked Joan – I was not certain what had happened between them, but I was afraid that it was the final, irreparable break.

Roy showed me Lady Muriel's letter. She was delighted that he was pressing her to come to Cambridge; since she left the Lodge, she had been curiously diffident about appearing in the town. Perhaps it was because, after domineering in the Lodge, she could not bear taking a dimmer place. But she was willing to accompany the Boscastles, now that Roy had invited her. She went on:

'You will have seen this extraordinary action on the part of our vicar. I am compelled to take very strong exception to it. Unfortunate is too mild a word. I know this young woman used to be a friend of yours, but that was a different matter. You may sometimes have thought I was old-fashioned, but I realize men have their temptations. That cannot however be regarded as any excuse for a *clergyman*. He is in a special position, and I have never for a single moment contemplated such an outrage from any vicar of our own church. I do not know what explanations to give to our tenants, and I find Helen no help in this, and very remiss in performing her proper duties. I have found it necessary to remind her of her obligations (though naturally I am always very careful about keeping myself in the background). I consider our vicar has put me in an impossible position. I do not see how I can receive this woman in our house. Hugh says it is your fault for bullying him into giving the living to our present vicar – but I defend you, and tell him that it takes a woman to understand women, and that I knew this woman was a designing hussy from the first moment I set eyes on her. Men are defenceless against such creatures. I have noticed it all my life, or certainly since Hugh got married. I shall be most surprised,' Lady Muriel finished in magnificent rage, 'if this woman does not turn out to be *barren*.'

'Now just why has Lady Mu decided that?' cried Roy.

It gave him an hour's respite. But the days were dragging by in black searing fears and ravaged nights, in anguish from the moment when, after he had lain awake through the white hours of the early morning, he roused himself exhaustedly to open the daily paper. The news glared at him – for his melancholy was the melancholy of his nature, but it had drawn into him the horror of war.

Most of the college were uncomfortable and strained about the prospect of war; only one or two of the very old escaped. Several men were torn, though not so deeply and tragically as Roy. They were solid conservatives, men of property, used to the traditional way of life; they were not fools, they knew a war must destroy many of their comforts and perhaps much else; they had hated Communism for twenty years, in their hearts they still hated it more than National Socialism; yet, with the obstinate patriotic sense of their class and race, they were slowly coming to feel that they might have to fight Germany. They felt it with extreme reluctance. Even now, they were chary of the prospect of letting 'that man Churchill' into the cabinet. There might still be time for a compromise. In May, that was the position which Arthur Brown took up. He was just as stubborn as he was in college politics: he was appreciably more anti-German than most of the college right. Some were much more willing to appease at almost any cost.

They had all gathered rumours about Roy's sympathies, they had heard some of his comments in hall. Ironically, his name was flaunted about, this time as an authority, by old Despard-Smith. The old man was virulently pro-Munich, bitterly in favour of any other accommodation. He kept quoting Roy: 'Calvert has just come back from

Germany and he says . . .' 'Calvert told someone yesterday . . .' Roy smiled, to find himself approved of at last in that quarter.

But Francis Getliffe did not smile at all. He was away from Cambridge many days in that summer term; we knew he was busy on Air Ministry experiments, but it was only much later that we realized he had been occupied with the first installations of radar. He came back and dined in hall one night, looking as tired as Roy – looking in fact more worn, though not so hag-ridden. It happened to be a night when most of the left were not dining. Nor was Winslow, who was an old-fashioned liberal but spoke caustically on Getliffe's side – he had quarrelled acidly with the older men over Munich.

That night Despard-Smith and others were saying that war was quite unnecessary. Francis Getliffe, short-tempered with fatigue, told them that they would soon present Hitler with the whole game. 'Calvert says,' began Despard-Smith. Getliffe interrupted him: 'Unless you all keep your nerve, the devils have got us. It's our last chance. I'm tired of this nonsense.'

The high table was truculent and quarrelsome in its own fashion, but it was not used to words so openly harsh. With some dignity, old Despard-Smith announced that he did not propose to drink port that night: 'I have been a fellow for fifty years next February, and it is too late to begin having my head bitten off in this hall.'

Arthur Brown, Roy, Francis Getliffe, and I were left in the combination room, and Brown promptly ordered a bottle of port.

'It's rather sensible to drink an occasional bottle,' said Brown, looking kindly and shrewdly at the others. 'We never know whether it will be so accessible in the near future.'

'I'm sorry, Brown,' said Francis Getliffe. 'I oughtn't to have cursed the old man.'

'It's all right, old chap,' said Arthur Brown comfortingly. 'Everyone wants to address a few well-chosen remarks to Despard on some subject or other. How are you yourself?' He smiled anxiously at Francis, for Arthur Brown, whatever his hopes of a compromise, believed in keeping his powder dry: and hence scientists wearing themselves out in military preparations had to be cherished.

'In good order,' said Francis. But it was false: he seemed as though he should be put to bed for a fortnight. He was painfully frayed, thinking of his experiments, thinking of how he could flog himself on, thinking of how many months were left. He turned to Roy:

'Calvert, you're doing harm.'

'Harm to what?'

'To our chances of winning this war.'

'The war hasn't come.'

'It will. You know as well as I do that it will.'

'I'm frightened that it will,' said Roy.

'The only thing to be frightened about,' said Francis harshly, 'is that we shall slide out of it. That's what I'm frightened of. If we get out of it this time, we're finished. The Fascists have won.'

'I suppose you mean the Germans,' said Arthur Brown, who never accepted anything which he suspected was a left-wing formula. 'I don't think I can go all the way with you, Getliffe. It might suit our book to have another breathing space.'

'No,' said Francis. 'Our morale will weaken. Theirs will get tougher.'

'Yes,' said Roy clearly, 'theirs will get tougher.'

'You like the idea, don't you?' Francis cried.

'They are remarkable people.'

'Good God.' Francis's face was flushed with passion. 'You like authority wherever it rears its head.'

'That may be so. I haven't been very clever at finding it, have I?'

Roy had spoken with the lightness that deceived, and Francis did not realize that he had struck much deeper than he knew. Neither Arthur Brown nor I could take our eyes from Roy's face.

'I don't know what you've found,' said Francis impatiently. 'I should have thought you might be content among your Fascist friends.'

'If so,' said Roy, 'I might have stayed there.'

'I don't see why not.'

'No,' said Roy, 'you wouldn't see why not.'

'You'd be less dangerous there than you are here,' shouted Francis, stung to bitter anger.

'I dare say. I'm not so concerned about that as you are.'

'Then you've got to be,' Francis said, and the quarrel became fiercer. Arthur Brown tried to steady them, offered to present another bottle of port, but they were too far gone. Brown listened with a frown of puzzlement and concern. He admired Francis Getliffe, but his whole outlook, even his idioms, were foreign to Brown. Francis took it for granted, in the way in which he and I and many of our generation had been brought up, that there were just two sides in the world, and that the battle between them was joined, and that no decent man could hesitate an instant. 'My Manichaeans had the same idea,' said Roy, which made Francis more angry.

To Francis, to all men like him and many less incisive, it all seemed starkly plain in black and white. Issues have to seem so at the fighting-points of history. It was only later, looking back, that one saw the assumptions we had made, the ignorant hopes we had indulged, the acts of faith that looked strange in the light of what was actually to come. At that moment, Francis was saying, everything must be sacrificed to win: this was the great crisis, and until it was over we could not afford free art, disinterested speculation, the pleasures of detachment, the vagaries of the lonely human soul. They were luxuries. This was no time for luxuries. Our society was dying, and we could not rest until we had the new one safe.

Roy replied, sometimes with his light grave clarity, sometimes with the kind of frivolous gibes that infuriated Francis most. 'Do you believe everything that's written in Cyrillic letters?' asked Roy. 'I must learn Russian. I'm sure you'd be upset if I translated *Pravda* to you every night.' He told Francis that Communism (or Francis's approach to it, for Francis was not a member of the party) was a 'romantic' creed, for all its dryness. 'It's realistic about the past. Entirely so. But it's wildly romantic about the future. Why, it believes it's quite easy to make men good. It's far more optimistic than Christianity. You need to read St Augustine, you know. Or Pascal. Or Hügel. But then they knew something of life.'

Once or twice Brown chuckled, but he was uneasy. He was deeply fond of Roy; much of what Roy said came far nearer to him than anything of Francis's.

But Brown was cautious and realistic. He believed Roy was completely reckless – and every word he said on Germany filled Brown with alarm. Brown was ready to anticipate that his protégés would get into trouble. Roy's folly might be the most painful of all.

As for me, I was watching for the terrible elation. His wretchedness had weighed him down for weeks; it was melancholy at its deepest, and it was beginning to break into the lightning flashes.

I was expecting an outburst, and this time I was terrified where it would end.

It was that sign I was listening for, not anything else in their quarrel. But Roy's last words that night were quite calm.

'You think I'm dangerous, don't you?' he said. 'Believe this: you and your friends are much more so. You know you're right, don't you? It has never crossed your mind that you might be wrong. And that doesn't seem to you – dreadful.'

For a few days nothing seemed to change. Roy did not often dine in hall, but I listened in dread for each rumour about him: when I saw Arthur Brown walking towards me in the court, intending to carry me off for a confidential talk, I wanted to shy away – but it was only to consider whether the time had come to 'ventilate' the question of a new fellow. Wars might be near us, but Arthur Brown took it for granted that the college government must be carried on. I asked Bidwell each morning how Mr Calvert was. 'He's not getting his sleep, sir,' said Bidwell. 'No, he's not getting his sleep. As I see it, sir – I know it's not my place to say it – but it's all on account of his old books. He's overtaxed his brain. That's how I see it, sir.'

Then, as a complete surprise, I received a note from Lady Muriel. She was staying at the University Arms: would I excuse the short notice, and go to the hotel for tea? I knew that she had arrived, I knew that Roy had given her dinner the night before: but I was astonished to be summoned. I had never been exactly a favourite of hers. I felt a vague malaise: I was becoming morbidly anxious.

Lady Muriel had taken a private sitting-room, looking out upon Parker's Piece. She greeted me as she used to in the Lodge; she seemed almost to fancy that she was still there.

'Good afternoon, Mr Eliot. I am glad that you were able to come.' Her neck was stiff, her back erect as ever; but it took more effort than it used. Trouble was telling, even on her. 'I will ring at once for tea.'

She asked about my work, my pupils, and – inexorably – my wife. It all sounded like the rubric of days past. She poured out my cup of Indian tea; it was like her, I thought, to remember that I disliked China, to disapprove of my taste and attribute it firmly to my lowly upbringing, and yet still to feel that a hostess was obliged to provide for it. She put her cup down, and regarded me with her bold innocent eyes.

'Mr Eliot, I wish to ask you a personal question.'

'Lady Muriel?'

'I do not wish to pry. But I must ask this question. Have you noticed anything wrong with Roy?'

I was taken aback.

'He's desperately overstrained,' I said.

'I considered that you might have noticed something,' said Lady Muriel. 'But I believe it is worse. I believe he has some worry on his mind.'

She stared at me.

'Do you know what this worry is, Mr Eliot?'

'He's very sad,' I began. 'But –'

'Mr Eliot,' Lady Muriel announced, 'I am a great believer in woman's intuition. Men are more gifted than we are intellectually. I should never have presumed to disagree with the Master on a purely intellectual matter. But it takes a woman to see that a man is hiding some private worry. Roy has always been so wonderfully carefree. I saw the difference at once.'

She sighed.

'Is it because of some woman?' she said suddenly.

'No.'

'Are you certain of that?'

'Absolutely.'

'We must put our finger on it,' said Lady Muriel. She was baffled, distressed, unhappy; her voice was firm and decided, but only by habit; her whole heart went out to him. 'Surely he knows we want to help him. Does he know that I would do anything to help him?'

'I am quite sure he does.'

'I am very glad to hear you say that. I should like to have told him. But there are things one always finds it impossible to say.'

She turned her head away from me. She was looking out of the window, when she said:

'I tried to get him to confide this worry last night.'

'What did you do?'

'I used a little finesse. Then I asked him straight out.'

She burst out:

'He put me off. I know men like to keep their secrets. But there are times when it is better for them to talk. If only they would see it. It is so difficult to make them. And one feels that one is only an intruder.'

She faced me again. Then I knew why she had averted her eyes. She was fighting back the tears.

She collected herself, and spoke to me with exaggerated firmness, angry that I had seen her weak.

'There is one thing I can do, Mr Eliot. I shall ring up my daughter Joan. She knows Roy better than I do. Perhaps she will be able to discover what is wrong. Then between us we could assist him.'

I used all my efforts to dissuade her. I argued, persuaded, told her that it was unwise. But the only real reason I could not give: and Lady Muriel stayed invincibly ignorant.

'Mr Eliot, you must allow me to judge when to talk to my daughter about a common friend.' She added superbly: 'My family have been brought up to face trouble.'

On the spot, she telephoned Joan, who was in London. There could be only one answer, the answer I had been scheming to avoid, the answer which Joan would want to give from the bottom of her heart. It came, of course. Joan would catch the next train and see Roy that evening.

Lady Muriel said good-bye to me.

'My daughter and I will do our best, Mr Eliot. Thank you for giving me your advice.'

I went straight from the hotel to Roy's rooms. It was necessary that he should be warned at once. His outer door was not locked, as it was most evenings now – but he himself was lying limp in an armchair. There was no bottle or glass in sight; there was no manuscript under his viewing lamp, and no book open; it was as though he had lain there, inert, for hours.

'Hullo,' he said, from a far distance.

'I think you should know,' I said. 'Joan will be here in an hour or two.'

'Who?'

I repeated my message. It was like waking him from sleep.

At last he spoke, but still darkly, wearily, from a depth no one could reach.

'I don't want to see her.'

Some time afterwards he repeated:

'I don't want to see her. I saw her in Berlin. It made things worse. I've done her enough harm.'

'Roy,' I said, pressingly, 'I'm afraid you must.'

His answer came after a long interval.

'I won't see her. It will be worse for her. It will be worse for both of us. I'm not fit to see anyone.'

'You can't just turn her away,' I said. 'She's trying to care for you. You must be good to her.'

Another long interval.

'I'm not fit to see anyone.'

'You must,' I said. 'You've meant too much to her, you know.'

Up to then I had had very little hope. In a moment I should have given up. But then I saw an astonishing thing. With a prodigious strain, as though he were calling frantically on every reserve of body and mind, Roy seemed to bring himself back into the world. He did not want to leave his stupor: there he had escaped, perhaps for hours: but somehow he forced himself. The strain lined him with grief and suffering. He returned to searing miseries, to the appalling melancholy. Yet he was himself, normal in speech, quiet, sad, able to smile, very gentle.

'I need to put a face on it,' he said. 'Poor dear. I shouldn't have brought her to this.'

He glanced at me, almost mischievously:

'Am I fit to be seen now?'

'I think so.'

'I've got to look pretty reasonable when Joan comes. It's important, Lewis. She mustn't think I'm ill.' He added, with a smile: 'She mustn't think I'm – mad.'

'It will be all right.'

'If she thinks I'm really off it,' again he smiled, 'she will want to look after me. And I might want her to. That mustn't happen, Lewis. I owe her more than the others. I can't inflict myself upon her now.'

He went on:

'She will try to persuade me. But it would do us both in. I was never free with her. And I should get worse. I don't know why it is.'

Nor did I. Of all women, she was most his equal. Yet she was the only one with whom he was not spontaneous. Somehow she had invaded him, she had not let him lose himself; by the very strength of her devotion, by her knowledge of him, by her share in his struggle, she had brought him back to the self he craved to throw away.

'Poor dear,' he said. 'I shall never find anyone like her. I must make her believe that I'm all right without her. If there's no other way, I must tell her I'm better without her. That's why I've got to look reasonable, Lewis. I've done her enough harm. She must get free of me now. It doesn't matter what she thinks of me.'

He smiled at me with sad and mischievous irony. Then he spoke in a tone that was matter-of-fact, quiet, and utterly and intolerably unguarded.

'I hate myself,' said Roy. 'I've brought unhappiness to everyone I've known. It would have been better if I'd never lived. I should be wiped out so that everyone could forget me.'

I could not go through the pretence of consoling him, I could not reply until he spoke again. He had spoken so quietly and naturally that a shiver ran down my spine. It was anguish to hear such naked, simple anguish. He said:

'You would have been much happier if I'd never lived, old boy. You can't deny it. This isn't the time to be hearty, is it?'

'Never mind about happiness,' I said. 'It can cut one off from too much. My life would have been different without you. I prefer it as it is.'

For a second, his face lit up.

'You've done all you could,' he said. 'I needed to tell you that – before it's too late. You've done more than anyone. You've done more even than she did. Now I must send her away. There will only be you whom I've ever talked to.'

He was sitting back in his chair. The limpness had gone, and his whole body was easy and relaxed. His face was smoothed by the golden evening light.

'You won't sack me just now, will you?' he said. 'Whatever I do? I shall need you yet.'

I went back to my rooms, and from the window seat watched

Joan enter the court. The undergraduates were in hall, she was alone on the path, walking with her gawky, sturdy step. She passed out of sight on her way to Roy's staircase. I sat there gazing down; I had missed dinner myself, I could not face high table that night; the court gleamed in the summer evening. The silence was broken as men came out of hall; they shouted to each other, sat on the edge of the grass; then they went away. Lights came on in some of the dark little rooms, though it was not yet sunset and bright in the court. Beside one light I could see a young man reading: the examinations were not yet finished, and the college was quiet for nine o'clock on a summer night.

I turned my thoughts away from Roy and Joan, and then they tormented me again. Would she see that he was acting? Would she feel the desperate effort of pretence? Did she know that tomorrow he would be half-deranged?

At last I saw her pass under my window again. She was alone. Her face was pallid, heavy, and set, and her feet were dragging.

CHAPTER 29

Realism at a Cricket Match

LADY MURIEL'S observations on Roy might once have amused me. I should like to have told him that, for the first occasion since we met her, she had noticed something she had not been told; and he would have laughed lovingly at her obtuseness, her clumsiness, the pent-in power of her stumbling, hobbled feelings.

In fact, that afternoon she had made me more alarmed. Roy must be visibly worse than I imagined. Living by his side day after day, I had become acclimatized to much; if one lives in the hourly presence of any kind of suffering, one grows hardened to it in time. I knew that too well, not only from him. It is those who are closest and dearest who see a fatal transformation last of all.

I reassured myself a little. Apart from Arthur Brown, no one in the college seemed to have detected anything unusual in Roy's state that summer. He dined in hall two or three nights a week, and, except for his views on Germany, passed under their eyes without evoking any special interest. For some reason he stayed preternaturally silent when he dined (I once taxed him with it, and he whispered 'lanthanine is the word for me'), but nevertheless it was curious they should observe so little. They were, of course, more used than most men to occasional displays of extreme eccentricity; most of our society, like any other college at this period, were comfortable, respectable, solid middle-aged men, but they had learned to put up with one or two who had grown grotesquely askew. It was part of the secure, confident air.

After Lady Muriel talked to me, I was preparing myself for a disaster. I tried to steady myself by facing it in the cold merciless light of early morning: this will be indescribably worse than what has happened before, this will be sheer disaster. I might have to accept any horror. What I feared and expected most was an outburst about Germany and the war – a speech in public, a letter to the Press, a public avowal of his feeling for the Reich. I feared it most for selfish reasons – at that period, such an outburst would be an excruciating ordeal for me.

After he sent Joan away, he was sunk in the abyss of depression. But he did nothing. The day that the Boscastles arrived, he even sustained with Lord Boscastle a level, realistic, and sober conversaton about the coming war.

The Boscastles had invited us to lunch, and Lady Muriel and Humphrey were there as well.

Through the beginning of the meal Lord Boscastle and Roy did all the talking. They found themselves in a strong and sudden sympathy about the prospect of war. They could see no way out, and they were full of a revulsion almost physical in its violence. Lady Muriel looked startled that men should talk so frankly about the miseries of war: but she knew that her brother had been decorated in the last war, and it would never even have occurred to her that men would not fight bravely if it was their duty.

'It will be frightful,' said Roy. Throughout he had spoken moderately and sensibly; he had said no more than many men were saying; he had remarked quietly that he did not know his own courage – it might be adequate, he could not tell.

'It will be frightful.' Lord Boscastle echoed the phrase. And I saw his eyes leave Roy and turn with clouded, passionate anxiety upon his son. Humphrey Bevill was still good-looking in his frail, girlish way; his skin was pink, smooth, and clear; he had his father's beaky nose, which somehow did not detract from his delicacy. His eyes were bright china blue, like his mother's. He had led a disreputable life in Cambridge. He had genuine artistic feeling without, so far as I could discover, a trace of talent.

Lord Boscastle stared at his son with anxiety and longing; for Lord Boscastle could not restrain his strong instinctive devotion, and for him war meant nothing more nor less than danger to his beloved son.

I watched Lady Boscastle mount her lorgnette and regard them both, with a faint, charming, contemptuous, coolly affectionate quiver on her lips.

Then Lord Boscastle took refuge in his own peculiar brand of stoicism. He asked Humphrey to show him again the photograph of that year's Athenaeum. This bore no relation to the Athenaeum where

I had tea with the old Master, the London club of successful professional men. The Cambridge Athenaeum was the ultra-fashionable élite of the most fashionable club for the gilded youth; it was limited to twenty, and on the photograph of twenty youthful, and mainly titled, faces Lord Boscastle cast a scornful and dismissive eye.

At any rate, he appeared to feel, there was still time to reject these absurd pretensions to be classed among their betters. Several of them had names much more illustrious than that of Bevill; but it took more than centuries of distinction to escape Lord Boscastle's jehovianic strictures that afternoon. 'Who is this boy, Humphrey? I'm afraid I can't for the life of me remember his name.' He was told 'Lord Arthur –' 'Oh, perhaps that accounts for it, should you have thought? They have never really quite managed to recover from their obscurity, should you think they have?' He pointed with elaborate distaste to another youth. 'Incorrigibly parvenu, I should have said. With a certain primitive cunning in financial matters. Such as they showed when they fleeced my great-grandfather.'

Lord Boscastle placed the photograph a long way off along the table, as though he might get a less displeasing view.

'Not a very distinguished collection, I'm afraid, Humphrey. I suppose it was quite necessary for you to join them? I know it's always easier to take the course of least resistance. I confess that I made concessions most of my life, but I think it's probably a mistake for us to do so, shouldn't you have thought?'

The Boscastles, Lady Muriel, and I were all dining with Roy the following night. I did not see any more of him for the rest of that day, and next morning Bidwell brought me no news. Bidwell was, however, full of the preparations for the dinner. 'Yes, sir. Yes, sir. It will be a bit like the old times. Mr Calvert is the only gentleman who makes me think back to the old times, sir, if you don't mind me saying so. It will be a pleasure to wait on you tonight, I don't mind telling you, sir.'

So far as I could tell, Roy was keeping to his rooms all day. I hesitated about intruding on him; in the end, I went down to Fenner's for a few hours' escape. It was the Free Foresters' match. Though it was pleasant to chat and sit in the sunshine, there was nothing noteworthy about the play. Two vigorous ex-blues, neither of them batsmen of real class, were clumping the ball hard to extra cover. If one knew the game, one could immerse oneself in points of detail. There could not have been a more peaceful afternoon.

Then I felt a hand on my shoulder.

'They told me I should find you here, but I didn't really think I should.' The voice had a dying fall; I looked round and saw the smile on Rosalind's face, diffident, pathetic, impudent. I apologized to my companion, and walked with Rosalind round the ground.

'I wonder if I could beg a cup of tea?' she said.

I gave her tea in the pavilion; with the hearty appetite that I remembered, she munched several of the cricketers' buns. She talked about herself and me, not yet of Roy. Her manner was still humorously plaintive, as though she were ill-used, but she had become more insistent and certain of herself. Her determination was not so far below the surface now. She had been successful in her job, and had schemed effectively for a better one. She was making a good many hundreds a year. Her eyes were not round enough, her voice not enough diminuendo, to conceal as effectively as they used that she was a shrewd and able woman. And there was another development, minor but curious. She was still prudish in her speech, still prudish when her eyes gave a shameless hint of lovemaking – but she had become remarkably profane.

She looked round the pavilion, and said:

'We can't very well talk here, can we?'

Which, since several of the Free Foresters' team were almost touching us, seemed clear. I took her to a couple of seats in the corner of the ground: on the way, Rosalind said:

'I know I oughtn't to have interrupted you, really. But it is a long time since I saw you, Lewis, isn't it? Did you realize it, I very nearly tracked you down that day at Boscastle?'

'It's a good job you didn't,' I said. 'Lady Muriel was just about ready to take a stick to you.'

Rosalind swore cheerfully and grinned.

'She's in Cambridge now, by the way,' I said.

'I knew that.'

'You'd better be careful. If you mean to marry Ralph Udal.'

'Of course I mean to marry him. Why ever do you say such horrid things?' She opened her eyes wide.

'Come off it,' I said, copying Roy's phrase. It was years since I had been her confidant, but at a stroke we had gone back to the old terms.

'No, I shall marry Ralph, really I shall. Mind you, I'm not really in love with him. I don't think I shall ever really fall in love again. I'm not sure that I want to. It's pretty bloody, being too much in love, isn't it? No, I shall settle down with Ralph all right. You just won't know me as the vicar's wife.'

'That's true,' I said, and Rosalind looked ill-used.

We had just sat down under one of the chestnut trees.

'I shall settle down so that you wouldn't believe it,' said Rosalind. 'But I'm not going to fool myself. After old Roy, other men seem just a tiny little bit dull. It stands to sense that I should want to see the old thing now and again.'

'It's dangerous,' I said.

'I'm not so bad at covering up my traces when I want to,' said Rosalind, who was only willing to think of practical dangers.

She asked, with a glow of triumph:

'Do you think I oughtn't to have come? The old thing asked me to look him up. When he wrote about me and Ralph. And he did seem rather pleased to see me last night. I really think he was a bit pleased to see me.'

She laid her hand on my arm, and said, half-guiltily, half-provocatively:

'Anyway, he asked me to go to a ball with him tonight.'

'Are you going?'

'What do you think? It's all right, I'll see that the old gorgon doesn't find out. I'm not going to have her exploding down in Boscastle. I won't have Ralph upset. After all,' she grinned at me, 'a husband in the hand is worth two in the bush.'

She and Roy had arranged to go to a ball at one of the smaller colleges, where none of us had close friends. I warned her that it was still a risk.

She pursed her lips. 'Why do you want to stop us?' she said. 'You know it might take the old thing out of himself. He's going through one of his bad patches, isn't he? It will do him good to have a night on the tiles.'

I could not prevent myself laughing. Under the chestnut, an expensive lingering scent pervaded the hot afternoon. There was a bead of moisture on her upper lip, but her hair was swept up in a new, a rakish, a startling Empire coiffure. I asked when she had had time to equip herself like the Queen of the May.

'When do you think?' said Rosalind with lurking satisfaction. 'I went up to town first thing this morning and told my hairdresser that she'd got to do her damnedest. The idiot knows me, of course, and when she'd finished she said with a soppy smile that she hoped my fiancé would like it. I nearly asked her why she thought I should care what my fiancé thinks of it. It's what my young man thinks of it that I'm interested in.'

What was going through her head, I wondered, as I walked back across Parker's Piece? She was reckless, but she was also practical. If need be, she would marry Ralph Udal without much heartbreak and without repining. But need it be? I was ready to bet that, in the last few hours, she had asked herself that question. I should be surprised if she was in a hurry to fix the date of her wedding.

As I was dressing for dinner, Roy threw open my bedroom door. His white tie was accurately tied, his hair smooth, but I was thrown into alarm at the sight of him. His eyes were lit up.

I was frightened, but in a few minutes I discovered that this had been only a minor outrage. It came as a respite. I even laughed from relief when I found how he had broken out. But I felt that he was on the edge of sheer catastrophe. It could not be far away: perhaps only a few hours. His smile was brilliant, but frantic and bitter; his voice was louder than usual, and a laugh rang out with reedy harshness. The laugh made my pulses throb in tense dismay. This fearful excitement must break soon.

Yet his actions that afternoon were like hitting out at random, and would not do much harm. They had been set off by an unexpected provocation. The little book on the heresies, by Vernon Royce and R. C. E. Calvert, had been published at last, early in the summer. Since Lyall's death, Roy's reputation had increased sharply in English academic circles, owing to the indefatigable herald-like praise by Colonel Foulkes, who was now quite unhampered. But the heresy book had been received grudgingly and bleakly; most of the academic critics seemed to relish dismissing Royce now that he was dead. That morning Roy had read a few sentences about the book in the *Journal of Theological Studies*: '. . . Mr Calvert is becoming recognized as a scholar of great power and penetration. But there is little sign of those qualities in this book's treatment of a subject which requires the most profound knowledge of the sources and origins of religious belief and its perversions. From internal evidence, it is not over-difficult to attribute most of the insufficiently thought-out chapters to the late Mr Royce, who, in all his writings on comparative religion, never revealed the necessary imagination to picture the religious experience of others nor the patient and detailed scholarship which might have given value to his work in the absence of the imaginative gifts . . .'

Roy was savagely and fantastically angry. He had sent off letters of which he showed me copies. They were in the Housmanish language of scholarly controversy, bitter, rude, and violent – one to the editor asking why he permitted a man 'ignorant, unteachable, stupid, and corrupt' to write in his journal, and one to the reviewer himself. The reviewer was a professor at Oxford, and to him Roy had written: 'I have before me your witty review. You are either too old to read: or too venal to see honestly. You attribute some chapters to my collaborator and you have the effrontery to impugn the accuracy of that work, and so malign the reputation of a better man than yourself. I wrote those chapters; I am a scholar; that you failed to see the chapters were precise is enough to unfit you for such tasks as reading proofs. If you are not yet steeped in your love of damaging others you will be so abashed that you will not write scurrilities about Royce again. You should state publicly that you were wrong, and that you stand guilty of incompetence, self-righteousness, and malice.'

Roy was maddened that they should still decry Royce. With the desperate clarity which visited him in his worst hours, he saw them gloating comfortably, solidly, stuffed with their own rectitude, feeling a warm comfortable self-important satisfaction that Royce had never come off, could not even come off after his death: he saw them saying in public what a pity it was that Royce was not more gifted, how they wanted so earnestly to praise him, how only duty and conscience obliged them so reluctantly to tell the truth. He saw the gloating on solid good-natured faces.

As we walked through the court to his dinner party, he broke out in a clear, passionate tone:

'All men are swine.'

He added, but still without acceptance, charity, or rest:

'The only wonder is, the decent things they manage to do now and then. They show a dash of something better, once or twice in their lives. I don't know how they do it – when I see what we are really like.'

CHAPTER 30

Waiting at Night

THE desks in Roy's sitting-room had been pushed round the wall, where one noticed afresh their strange shapes and colours. In the middle, the table had been laid for eight – laid with five glasses at each place and a tremendous bowl of orchids in the middle. It was not often Roy indulged in the apolaustic; he used to chuckle even at the subdued, comfortable, opulent display of Arthur Brown's claret parties; extravagant meals were not in Roy's style, they contained for him something irresistibly comic, a hint of Trimalchio. But that night he was for once giving one himself. Decanters of burgundy and claret stood chambering in a corner of the room; the cork of a champagne bottle protruded from a bucket; on a small table were spread out plates of fruit, marrons glacés, petits fours, cold savouries for apéritifs and after-tastes.

The person who enjoyed it all most was undoubtedly Bidwell. He took it upon himself to announce the guests; the first we knew of this new act was when Bidwell threw open the door, decorous and rubicund, the perfect servant, and proclaimed with quiet but ringing satisfaction:

'Lady Muriel Royce!'

And then, slightly less vigorously (for Bidwell needed a title to move him to his most sonorous):

'Mrs Seymour!'

'Mrs Houston Eggar!'

Since Lady Muriel left the Lodge, I had escaped my old dinner-long conversations with Mrs Seymour; in the midst of despondency, Roy had been able to think out that joke; it was time to see that she pestered me again. Before they came in, he had been talking to me with his fierce, frightening excitement. As he greeted her, he was enough himself to give me a glance, sidelong and mocking.

I attached myself to Mrs Eggar, whom I had only met once before. Eggar had sent her back from Berlin with her baby, and she was staying with Mrs Seymour for the summer. She was a pretty young woman with a beautiful skin and eyes easily amused, but a thin, tight, pinched-in mouth. She had considerable poise, and often seemed to be laughing to herself. I found her rather attractive, somewhat to my annoyance, for she was obstinate, self-satisfied, vain, and narrow, far less amiable than her pushing, humble, masterful husband.

Bidwell came to the door again and got our attention. Then he called out in triumph:

'The Earl and Countess of Boscastle!'

It was a moment for Bidwell to cherish.

His next call, and the last, was an anticlimax. It was simply:

'Mr Winslow!'

I was surprised; I had not known till then who was making up the party. It seemed a curious choice. Roy had not been seeing much of the old man. He was not even active in the college any longer, for he had resigned the bursarship in pride and rage over a year before. Yet in one way he was well-fitted for the party. He had been an enemy of the old Master's, Lady Muriel had never liked him – but still he had been the only fellow whom she treated as some approximation to a social equal. Winslow was fond of saying that he owed his comfortable fortune to the drapery trade, and in fact his grandfather had owned a large shop in St Paul's Churchyard; but his grandfather nevertheless had been a younger son of an old county family, a family which had remained in a curiously static position for several hundred years. They had been solid and fairly prosperous country gentlemen in the seventeenth century: in the twentieth, they were still solid country gentlemen, slightly more prosperous. Winslow referred to his ancestors with acid sarcasm, but it did not occur to Lady Muriel, nor apparently to Lord Boscastle, to inquire who they were.

With Roy in the state I knew, I was on edge for the evening to end. (I was strung up enough to suspect that he might have invited Winslow through a self-destructive impulse. Winslow had watched one outburst, and might as well have the chance to see another.) In any other condition, I should have revelled in it. To begin with, Winslow was patently very happy to be there, and there was something affecting about his pleasure. He was, as we knew, cross-grained, rude, bitter with himself and others for being such a failure; yet his pleasure at being asked to dinner was simple and fresh. I had the impression that it was years since he went into society. He did not produce any of the devastating snubs he used on guests in hall; but he was not at all overborne by Lord Boscastle, either socially or as a man. They got on pretty well. Soon they were exchanging memories of Italy (meanwhile Mrs Seymour, who was, of course, seated next to me, confided her latest enthusiasm in an ecstatic breathless whisper. It was for Hitler – which did not make it easier to be patient. 'It must be wonderful,' she said raptly, 'to know that everyone is obliged to listen to you. Imagine seeing all those faces down below. . . . And no one can tell you to stop').

The dinner was elaborate and grand. Roy had set out to beat the apolaustic at their own game. And he had contrived that each person there should take special delight in at least one course – there were oysters for Lady Muriel, whitebait for me, quails for Lady Boscastle. Most of the party, even Lady Boscastle, ate with gusto. I should have been as enthusiastic as any of them, but I was only anxious that the courses should follow more quickly, that we could see the party break up in peace. Roy was not eating and drinking much; I told myself that he had a ball to attend when this was over. But I should have been more reassured to see him drink. His eyes were brighter and fuller than normal, and his voice had changed. It was louder, and without the inflections, the variety, the shades of different tone as he turned from one person to another. Usually his voice played round one. That night it was forced out, and had a brazen hardness.

He spoke little. He attended to his guests. He mimicked one or two people for Winslow's benefit: it affected me that the imitations were nothing like as exact as usual. The courses dragged by; at last there was a chocolate mousse, to be followed by an ice. Both Lord Boscastle and Winslow, who had strongly masculine tastes, refused the sweet. Lady Muriel felt they should not be left unreproved.

'I am sorry to see that you're missing this excellent pudding, Hugh,' she said.

'You ought to know by now, Muriel,' said Lord Boscastle, defensively, tiredly, 'that I'm not much good at puddings.'

'It has always been considered a college speciality,' said Lady Muriel, clinching the argument. 'I remember telling the Master that it should become recognized as the regular sweet at the audit feast.'

'I'm very forgetful of these matters,' said Winslow, 'but I should be slightly surprised if that happened, Lady Muriel. To the best of my belief, this admirable concoction has never appeared at a feast at all.'

He could not resist the gibe: for it was not a function of the Master to prescribe the menus for feasts, much less of Lady Muriel.

'Indeed,' said Lady Muriel. 'I am astonished to hear it, Mr Winslow. I think you must be wrong. Let me see, when is the next audit?'

'November.'

'I hope you will pay particular attention.'

'If you please, Lady Muriel. If you please.'

'I think you will find I am right.'

They went on discussing feasts and college celebrations as though they were certain to happen, as though nothing could disturb them. There was a major college anniversary in 1941, two years ahead.

'I hope the college will begin its preparations in good time,' said Lady Muriel. 'Two years is not long. You must be ready in two years' time.'

Suddenly Roy laughed. They were all silent. They had heard that laugh. They did not understand it, but it was discomforting, like the sight of someone maimed. 'Two years' time,' he cried. He laughed again.

The laugh struck into the quiet air. Across the table, across the sumptuous dinner, Lady Boscastle looked at me; I was just going to try. But it was Lady Muriel who awkwardly, hesitatingly, did not shirk her duty.

'I know what you are feeling, Roy,' she said. 'We all feel exactly as you do. But it is no use anticipating. One has to go on and trust that things will get better.'

Roy smiled at her.

'Just so, Lady Mu,' he said.

Perhaps it was best that she had spoken. Her very ineptness had gone through him. He became calmer, though his eyes remained fiercely bright.

With ineffable relief, even though it meant only a postponement, I saw the port go round, the sky darken through the open windows. We heard the faint sound of music from the college ball.

Mrs Eggar had to leave early because of her child. Roy escorted her and Mrs Seymour to their taxi and then came back. He was master of himself quite enough to seem unhurried; no one would have thought that he was waiting to go to a young woman. It was between eleven and twelve. Lord Boscastle and Winslow decided to stroll together in the direction of Winslow's home; Lady Boscastle wished to stop in my rooms for a little; so Roy was free to take Lady Muriel to the hotel.

I helped Lady Boscastle into an armchair beside my fireplace.

'I haven't had the chance to tell you before, my dear boy,' she said, 'but you look almost respectable tonight.'

But she had not settled down into sarcastic badinage before Bidwell, who was on duty at the ball, tapped softly at the door and entered. 'Lord Bevill is asking whether he can see Lady Boscastle, sir.' I nodded, and Bidwell showed Humphrey Bevill into the room.

Humphrey had been acting in an undergraduate performance, and there were still traces of paint on his face. He was exhilarated and a little drunk. 'I didn't really want to see you, Lewis,' he said. 'I've been trying to discover where my mother is hiding.' He went across to Lady Boscastle. 'They've kept you from me ever since you arrived, mummy. I won't let you disappear without saying good night.'

He adored her; he would have liked to stay, to have thrown a cushion on the floor and sat at her feet.

'This is very charming of you, Humphrey.' She smiled at him with her usual cool, amused indulgence. 'I thought I had invited myself to tea in your rooms tomorrow – tête-à-tête?'

'You'll come, won't you, mummy?'

'How could I miss it?' Then she asked: 'By the way, have you seen your father tonight?'

'No.'

'He'd like to see you, you know. He has probably got back to the hotel by now.'

'Must I?'

'I really think you should. He will like it so much.'

Humphrey went obediently away. Lady Boscastle sighed.

'The young are exceptionally tedious, Lewis, my dear. They are so preposterously uninformed. They never realize it, of course. They are very shocked if one tells them that they seem rather – unrewarding.'

She smiled.

'Poor Humphrey,' she said.

'He's very young,' I said.

'Some men,' said Lady Boscastle, 'stay innocent whatever happens to them. I have known some quite well-accredited rakes who were innocent all through their lives. They never knew what this world is like.'

'That can be true of women too,' I said.

'Most women are too stupid to count,' said Lady Boscastle indifferently. 'No, Lewis, I'm afraid that Humphrey will always be innocent. He's like his father. They're quite unfit to cope with what will happen to them.'

'What will happen to them?'

'You know as well as I do. Their day is done. It will finish this time – if it didn't in 1914, which I'm sometimes inclined to think. It will take someone much stronger than they are to live as they've been bred to live. It takes a very strong man nowadays to live according to his own pleasure. Hugh tried, but he hadn't really the temperament, you see. I doubt whether he's known much happiness.'

'And you?'

'Oh, I could always manage, my dear. Didn't you once tell me that I was like a cat?'

She was scrutinizing her husband and her son with an anthropologist's detachment. And she was far more detached than the rest of them about the fate of their world. She liked it; it suited her; it had given her luxury, distinction, and renown; now it was passing for ever, and she took it without a moan. 'I thought,' she said, 'that your friend Roy was rather *égaré* tonight.'

'Yes.'

'What is the matter? Is my niece still refusing to let him go? Or am I out of date?'

She said it airily. She was not much worried or interested. If Roy had been exhibiting some new phase of a love affair, she would have been the first to observe, identify, and dissect. As it was, her perception stopped short, and she was ready to ignore it.

She leaned back against the head-rest of the chair. Under the reading-lamp, her face was monkey-like and yet oddly beautiful. The flesh was wizened, but the architecture of the bones could never be anything but exquisite. She looked tired, reflective, and amused.

'Lewis!' she asked. 'Do you feel that you are doing things for the last time?'

I was too much engrossed in trouble to have speculated much.

'I do,' said Lady Boscastle. 'Quite strongly. I suppose the chances are that we shall not dine here again. It tends to give such occasions a certain poignancy.'

She smiled.

'It didn't happen so last time, you know. It all came from a clear sky. A very clear sky, my dear boy. Have I ever told you? I think I was happier in 1914 than I ever was before or since. I had always thought people were being absurdly extravagant when they talked of being happy. Yet I had to admit it. I was ecstatically happy myself. It was almost humiliating, my dear Lewis. And distinctly unforeseen.'

I had heard something of it before. Of all her conquests, this was the one to which she returned with a hoarding, secretive, astonished pleasure. She would not tell me who he was. 'He has made his own little reputation since. I am not quite ungallant enough to boast.' I believed that it was someone I knew, either in person or by name.

The whirr and clang and chimes of midnight broke into a pause. Reluctantly Lady Boscastle felt that she must go. I was just ringing for a taxi, when she stopped me.

'No, my dear,' she said. 'I have an *envie* for you to take me back tonight.'

Very slowly, for she had become more frail since I first met her, she walked on my arm down St Andrew's Street. The sky had clouded, there was no moon or stars, but the touch of the night air was warm and solacing. Her stick stayed for an interval on the pavement at each step; I had to support her; she smiled and went on talking, as we passed Emmanuel, decked out for a ball. Fairy lights glimmered through the gate, and a tune found its way out. A party of young men and women, in tails and evening frocks and cloaks, made room for us on the pavement and went in to dance. They did not imagine, I thought, that they had just met a great beauty recalling her most cherished lover.

Lord Boscastle was waiting up for her in their sitting-room at the hotel.

'How very nice of you, Hugh,' she said lightly, much as she spoke to her son. 'I have been keeping Lewis up. Do you mind if I leave you both now? I think I will go straight to my room. Good night, Hugh, my dear. Good night, Lewis, my dear boy.'

Lord Boscastle did not seem inclined to let me go. He poured out a whisky for me and for himself, and, when I had drunk mine, filled the tumbler again. He was impelled to find out what his wife and I had been saying to each other; he could not ask directly, he shied away from any blunt question, and yet he went too far for either of us to be easy. There was a curious tone about those inquiries, so specific that I was certain I ought to recognize it – but for a time I could not. Then, vividly, it struck me. To think that he was jealous of his wife's affection for me was, of course, ridiculous. To think he was still consumed by the passionate and possessive love for her which had (as I now knew) darkened much of his manhood – that was ridiculous too. But he was behaving as though the habit of that consuming passion survived, when everything else had died. In his youth he had waited up for her; it was easy to imagine him striding up and down the opulent rooms of Edwardian hotels. In his youth he had been forced to question other men as he had just questioned me; he was forced under the compulsion of rivalry, he was driven to those intimate duels. At long last the hot and turbulent passion had died, as all passions must; but it had trained his heart to habits he could not break.

His was a nature too ardent to have come through lightly; I thought it again when he confronted me with Roy's demeanour that night.

'I was afraid the man was going to make an exhibition of himself,' he said.

I had no excuse to make.

'He'll have to learn that he mustn't embarrass his guests. We've all sat through dinners wanting to throw every scrap of crockery on to the floor. But we've had to hide it. Damn it, I shall wake up in the night wondering what's wrong with the young man.'

He added severely:

'One will have to think twice about accepting invitations – if there's a risk of being made miserable. One will just have to refuse.'

It sounded heartless. In a sense, it came from too much heart. It was the cool, like Lady Boscastle, who could bear to look at others' wretchedness. Her husband became hurt, troubled, angry – angry with the person whose wretchedness embarrassed him so much.

When I went out into the street, I stood undecided, unable to make up my mind. Should I look in at the ball where Roy was dancing – to ease my mind, to see if he was there? Sometimes any action seemed soothing: it was better than waiting passively to hear bad news. It was difficult to check myself, I began to walk to the ball. Then, quite involuntarily, the mood turned within me. I retraced my steps, I went down the empty street towards my rooms.

CHAPTER 31

Absolute Calm

I SLEPT fitfully, heard the last dance from the college hall, and then woke late. Bidwell did not wake me at nine o'clock; when he drew up the blind, he told me that he had let me sleep on after last night's party. He also told me that he had not seen Roy that morning: Roy had not been to bed nor come in to breakfast.

I got up with a veil of dread in front of the bright morning. I ate a little breakfast, read the newspaper without taking it in, read one or two letters. Then Roy himself entered. He was still wearing his dress suit: he was not smiling, but he was absolutely calm. I had never seen him so calm.

'I've been waiting about outside,' he said. 'Until you'd finished breakfast. Just like a pupil who daren't disturb you.'

'*What have you done?*' I cried.

'Nothing,' said Roy.

I did not believe him.

'You have finished now, haven't you? I didn't want to hurry you, Lewis.' He looked at me with a steady, affectionate glance. 'If you're ready – will you come into the garden?'

Without a word between us, we walked through the courts. Young men were sitting on the window sills, some of them still in evening clothes; through an open window, we heard a breakfast party teasing each other, the women's voices excited and high.

Roy unlocked the garden gate. The trees and lawns opened to us; no sight had ever seemed so peaceful. The palladian building stood tranquil under a cloudless summer sky.

'*What have you done?*' I cried again.

'Nothing,' said Roy.

His face was grave, quite without strain, absolutely calm. He said:

'I've done nothing. You expected me to break out, didn't you? No, it left me all of a sudden. I've done nothing.'

Then I believed him. I had an instant of exhausted ease. But Roy said:

'It's not so good, you know. I've done nothing. But I've seen it all. Now I know what I need to expect.'

His words were quiet, light, matter-of-fact. Suddenly they pierced me. They came from an affliction greater than any horror. No frantic act could have damaged him like this. Somehow his melancholy had vanished in an instant; during the night it had broken, not into violence, but into this clear sight. At last he had given up struggling. He had seen his fate.

'It's not easy to take,' said Roy.

He looked at me, and said:

'You've always known that I should realize it in the end.'

'I was afraid so,' I said.

'That's why I hid things from you.' He paused, and then went on:

'I don't see it as you do. But I see that I can't change myself. One must be very fond of oneself not to want to change. I can't believe that anyone would willingly stay as I am. Well, I suppose I must try to get used to the prospect.'

He did not smile. There was a humorous flick to the words, but the humour was jet-black.

'Shall I go mad?' he asked quietly.

I said: 'I don't know enough.'

'Somehow I don't think so,' said Roy with utter naturalness. 'I believe that I shall go through the old hoops. I shall have these stretches of abject misery. And I shall have fits when I feel larger than life and can't help bursting out. And the rest of the time –'

'For the rest of the time you'll get more out of life than anyone. Just as you always have done. You've got the vitality of three men.'

'Except when –'

I interrupted him again.

'That's the price you've got to pay. You've felt more deeply than any of us. You've learned far more of life. In a way, believe this, you've known more richness. For all that – you've got to pay a price.'

'Just so,' said Roy, who did not want to argue. 'But no one would choose to live such a life.'

'There is no choice,' I said.

'I've told you before, you're more robust than I am. You were made to endure.'

'So will you endure.'

He gazed at me. He did not reply for a moment. Then he said, as though casually:

'I shall always think it might have been different. I shall think it might have been different – if I could have believed in God. Or even if I could throw myself into a revolution. Even the one that you don't like. Our friends don't like it much either.'

The thought diverted him, and he said in a light tone:

'If I told them all I'd done – some of our friends would have some remarkable points to make. Fancy telling Francis Getliffe the whole story. He would look like a judge and say I must have manic-depressive tendencies.'

For the first time that morning, Roy gave a smile.

'Very wise,' he said. 'I could have told him that when I was at school. If that were all.'

He talked, concealing nothing, about how the realization had come. It had been in the middle of the night. Rosalind was dancing with an acquaintance. Roy was smoking a cigarette outside the ballroom.

'It had been breaking through for a long time. Some of my escapes were pretty – unconvincing. You would have seen that if I hadn't kept you away. Perhaps you did. But in the end it seemed to come quite sharply. It was as sharp as when I have to lash out. But it wasn't such fun. Everything became terribly lucid. It was the most lucid moment I've ever had. It was dreadful.'

'Yes,' I said.

'I shall be lucky if I forget it. It was like one of the dreams of God. But I knew that I could not get over this. I had seen how things must come.

'Lewis,' he said, 'if someone gave me a mirror in which I could see myself in ten years' time – I should not be able to look.'

We had been sitting down; now, without asking each other, we walked round the garden. The scent of syringa was overmastering in that corner of the garden, and it was only close to that one could pick up the perfume of the rose.

'It's not over,' said Roy. 'We've got some way to go, haven't we?'

His step was light and poised on the springy turf. After dancing all night, he was not tired.

'So we can be as close as we used to be,' he said. 'I hope you can bear it. You won't need to look after me now. There will be nothing to look after.'

He was speaking with extreme conviction. He took it for granted that I should understand and believe. He spoke with complete intimacy, but without any trace of mischief. He said gravely:

'I should like to be some good to you. I need to make up for lost time.'

PART FOUR

CLARITY

CHAPTER 32

A Noisy Winter Evening

I HAD thought, at the dinner party in the Adlon, how in England it was still natural for men like Roy and me to have our introductions to those in power. I thought it again, at the beginning of the war; for, within a few days, Roy had been asked for by a branch of Intelligence, Francis Getliffe had become assistant superintendent of one of the first radar establishments, I was a Civil Servant in Whitehall. And so with a good many of our Cambridge friends. It was slick, automatic, taken for granted. The links between the universities and 'government' were very strong. They happened, of course, as a residue of privilege; the official world in England was still relatively small and compact; when in difficulties it asked who was a useful man, and brought him in.

Of all our friends, I was much the luckiest. Francis Getliffe's job was more important (he broke his health in getting the warning sets ready in time for the air battle of 1940 – and then went on obstinately to improvise something for the night fighters), Roy's was more difficult, but mine was the most interesting by far. My luck in practical matters had never deserted me, and I landed on my feet, right in the middle of affairs. I was attached to a small ministry which had, on paper, no particular charge; in fact, it was used as a convenient ground for all kinds of special investigations, interdepartmental committees, secret meetings. These had to be held somewhere, and came to us simply because of the personality of our minister. It was his peculiar talent to be this kind of handy man. I became the assistant to his Permanent Secretary, and so, by sheer chance, gained an insight into government such as I had no right to hope for. In normal times it could not have come my way, since one can only live one life. It was a constant refreshment during the long dark shut-in years.

At times it was the only refreshment. For I went through much trouble at that period. My wife died in the winter of 1939. Everyone but Roy thought it must be a relief and an emancipation, but they did not know the truth. That was a private misery which can be omitted here. But there was another misery which I ought to mention for a moment. I was often distressed about the war, in two quite different ways. And so was Roy, though in his own fashion.

I will speak of myself first, for my distresses were commonplace. I often forgot them in the daytime; for it was fun to go into White-hall, attend meetings, learn new techniques, observe men pushing for power, building their empires, very much as in the college but with more hanging on the result; it was fun to go with the Minister to see a new weapon being put into production, to stay for days in factories and watch things of which I used to be quite ignorant; it was fun to watch the Minister himself, unassuming, imperturbably discreet, realistic, resilient, and eupeptically optimistic.

But away from work I could not sustain that stoical optimism. For the first three years of the war, until the autumn of 1942, I carried a weight of fear. I was simply frightened that we should lose. It was a perfectly straightforward fear, instinctive and direct. The summer of 1940 was an agony for me: I envied – and at times resented – the cheerful thoughtless invincible spirits of people round me, but I thought to myself that the betting was 5 : 1 against us. I felt that, as long as I lived, I should remember walking along Whitehall in the pitiless and taunting sun.

As long as I lived. I also knew a different fear, one of which I was more ashamed, a fear of being killed. When the bombs began to fall on London, I discovered that I was less brave than the average of men. I was humiliated to find it so. I could just put some sort of face on it, but I dreaded the evening coming, could not sleep, was glad of an excuse to spend a night out of the town. It was not always easy to accept one's nature. Somehow one expected the elementary human qualities. It was unpleasant to find them lacking. Most people were a good deal less frightened than I was – simple and humble people, like my housekeeper at Chelsea, the clerks in the office, those I met in the pubs of Pimlico. And most of my friends were brave beyond the common, which made me feel worse. Francis Getliffe was a man of cool and disciplined courage. Lady Muriel was unthinkingly gallant, and Joan as staunch in physical danger as in unhappy love. And Roy had always been extremely brave.

He noticed, of course, that I was frightened. He did not take it as seriously as I did. Like many men who possess courage, he did not value it much. Without my knowing, he took a flat for me in Dolphin Square, the great steel-and-concrete block on the embankment, about a mile from my house. He told me mischievously, sensibly, that it was important I should be able to sleep. He also told me that he had consulted Francis Getliffe upon the safest place in the safest type of building. London was emptying, and it was easy to have one's pick. He had incidentally given Francis the impression that he was inquiring for his own sake. He made it seem that he was abnormally preoccupied about his own skin. It was the kind of trick that he could not resist bringing out for Francis. Francis replied with scientific competence – 'between the third and seventh floor in a steel frame' – and thought worse of Roy than ever. Roy grinned.

For himself, Roy did not pay any attention to such dangers. He gave most acquaintances the impression that he did not care at all. They thought the war had not touched him.

He worked rather unenthusiastically in a comfortable government job. He stayed at the office late, as we all did, but he did not tire himself with the obsessed devotion that he had once spent on his manuscripts. At night he went out into the dark London streets in search of adventure. He found a lot of reckless love affairs. He gave parties in the flat in Connaught Street, he went all over the town in chase of women, and often, just as I used to find so strange when he was a younger man, he went to bed with someone for a single night and then forgot her altogether. Rosalind often came to see him, but, when the air-raids started, she tried to persuade him to meet her out of London. He would not go.

It was an existence which people blamed as irresponsible, trivial, out of keeping with the time. He attracted a mass of disapproval, heavier than in the past. Even Lady Muriel wondered how he could bear to be out of uniform. I told her that, having once been forced into this particular job, he would never get permission to leave. But she was baffled, puzzled, only partially appeased. All her young relations were fighting. Even Humphrey was being trained as an officer in motor torpedo boats. She was too loyal to condemn Roy, but she did not know what to think.

I saw more of him than I had done since my early days in Cambridge. Our intimacy had returned, more unquestioning because of the time we had been kept at a distance. We knew each other all through now, and we depended on each other more than we had ever done. For these were times when only the deepest intimacy was any comfort. Casual friends could not help; they were more a tax than strangers. We were each in distress; in our different ways we were hiding it. We had both aged; I had become guarded, middle-aged, used to the official life, patient and suspicious; he was lighter in speech than ever, not serious now even though it hurt others not to be serious, dissipated, purposeless, and without hope. He was still kind by nature, perhaps more kind than when he thought he would come through; he was often lively; but he could see no meaning in his life.

No one could know why we had changed so much, unless they knew all that had happened to us. That we had never told in full. We each had women friends to whom we confided something; Joan knew a great deal about Roy, and there were others who understood part of his story. It was the same with me. It was only in extremity that we needed to be known for what we truly were. That extremity had now come for both of us. We needed to be looked at by eyes that had seen everything, would not be fooled, were clear and pitiless, and whose knowledge was complete; we needed too the compassion of a heart which had known despair. So we turned to each other for comfort, certain that we should find knowledge, acceptance, humour, and love.

I knew that he was suffering more than I. It was not the war, though it had become tied up with that – for many states of unhappiness are like a vacuum which fills itself with whatever substance comes to hand. The vacuum would remain, if whatever was now filling it were taken away. So with Roy: the cause lay elsewhere. War or no war, he would have been tormented. If there had been no war, the vacuum would have filled itself with a different trouble. For the wound could not heal: as soon as he realized that his melancholy was an act of fate, that he could not throw off his affliction by losing himself in faith, he could see nothing to look forward to.

Brave as he was, full of life as he was, he was not stoical. Many blows he would have taken incomparably better than I; wherever his response could be active, he was better fitted to cope. But this affliction – it was easy to think so, but I believed it was true – I should have put up with more stubbornly than he. He could not endure the thought of a life preyed on meaninglessly, devastated all for nothing. For him, the realization was an acute and tragic experience. He could not mask it, cushion it, throw it aside. It took away the future with something of the finality that stunned the old Master when he was told that he was dying of cancer. Roy felt that he was being played with. He felt intensely humiliated – that he should be able to do nothing about it, that his effort and will did not begin to count! Angrily, hopelessly, frantically, he rattled the bars of his cage.

I could not forget the darkness of his face that morning in the college garden. For him it had been the starkest and bitterest of hours. He could not recover from it. Though for the next year or more he did not undergo the profoundest depression again, he never entered that calm beautiful high-spirited state in which his company made all other men seem leaden; with me he was usually subdued, affectionately anxious to help me on, controlled and sensible. His cries of distress only burst out in disguise, when he talked about the war.

He hated it. He hated that it should ever have happened. He hated any foreseeable end.

He did not simply dread, as I did, that England might be defeated. He knew what I felt; he felt my spirits fall and rise with the news, in the bad days he encouraged me. But his own dread was nothing like so simple. He shared mine up to a point; he too was chilled by the thought that his own country might lose; but he went farther. He had an intensely vivid picture of what defeat in this war must bring. He could not shut it out from his imagination. He could not stand the thought for his own country – and scarcely less for Germany. Whatever happened, it seemed to him hideous without relief. Any world in which it could come about seemed meaningless – as meaningless as a life shadowed by the caprice of fate.

So he watched me through the bright and terrible summer of 1940 with protective sympathy, with a feeling more detached and darker than mine. And, as the news got a little better in my eyes, as it became clear through the winter that the war would not end in sudden disaster, I had to accept that he could not share my pleasure and relief. For me the news might turn better; for him all news about the war was black, and brought to his mind only the desert waste to come.

It was an evening in the early spring of 1941, and already so dark that I had to pick my way from the bus stop to Dolphin Square. It had become a habit to arrive home late, in the dark, tired and claustrophobic. I had to pull my curtains and tamper with a fitting, before I could switch on the light. I lay on my sofa, trying to rouse myself to go down to the restaurant for dinner, when Roy came in. He usually called in at night, if he was not entertaining one of his young women.

Although our flats were two miles apart, he visited me as often as when we lived on neighbouring staircases. His face had changed little in the last years, but he was finding it harder to pretend that his hair still grew down to his temples. That night he seemed secretly amused.

'Just had a letter,' he said. 'I must say, a slightly remarkable letter.'

'Who from?'

'You should have said where from. Actually, it comes from Basel.'

'Whom do you know in Basel?'

'I used to be rather successful with the Swiss. They laughed when I made a joke. Very flattering,' said Roy.

'It must be some adoring girl,' I said.

'I can't think of any description which would please him less,' said Roy. 'No, I really can't. It's an old acquaintance of yours. It's Willy Romantowski.'

I said a word or two about Willy, and then exclaimed how odd it was.

'It's extremely odd,' said Roy. 'It's even odder when you see the letter. You won't be able to read it, though. You're not good at German holograph, are you? Also Willy uses very curious words. Sometimes of a slightly *slangy* nature.' Roy looked at me solemnly and began to translate.

It was a puzzling letter.

'Dear Roy,' so his translation went, 'Since you left Berlin I have not had a very good time. They made me go into the army which made me sick. So I got tired of wasting my time in the army, and decided to come here.'

'He makes it sound simple,' I interjected.

'I have arrived here,' Roy went on, 'and like it much better. But I have no money, and the Swiss people do not let me earn any. That is why I am writing you this letter, Roy. I remember how kind you were to us all at No. 32. You were always very kind to me, weren't you? So I am hoping that you will be able to help me now I am in difficult circumstances. I expect you have a Swiss publisher. Could you please ask him to give me some money? Or perhaps you could bring me some yourself? I expect you could get to Switzerland somehow. I know you will not let me starve. Your friend Romantowski (Willy).' And he had added: 'There were some changes at No. 32 after you left, but I have not heard much since I went into the army.'

The letter was written in pencil, in (so Roy said) somewhat illiterate German. He had never seen Willy's handwriting, so he had nothing to compare it with. It gave an address in a street in Basel, and the postmark was Swiss. The letter had been opened and censored in several different countries, but had only taken about a month to arrive.

We were both excited. It was a singular event. We could not decide how genuine the letter was. As stated, Willy's story sounded highly implausible. From the beginning Roy was suspicious.

'It's a plant,' he said. 'They're trying to hook me.'

'Who?'

'I don't know. Perhaps Reinhold Schäder. They think I might be useful. They're very thorough people.'

I could believe that easily enough. But I could not understand why, if Schäder or Roy's other high-placed friends were behind the move, they should use this extraordinary method. It seemed ridiculous, and I said so.

'They sometimes do queer things. They're not as rational as we are.' Then he smiled. 'Or of course they may have mistaken my tastes.'

He considered.

'That shouldn't be likely. Perhaps Willy was the only one who'd volunteer to do it. You can't imagine the little dancer trying to get hold of me for them, can you? But Willy wasn't a particularly scrupulous young man. Or do you think I'm misjudging him?'

I chuckled, and asked him what he was going to do about it.

'You're not going to reply?' I asked.

'Not safe,' said Roy. I had half-expected a different reply, but he was curiously prudent and restrained at that time. 'I need to stop them getting me into trouble. It might look shady. I'm not keen on getting into trouble. Particularly if they're trying to hook me.'

He had, in fact, already behaved with sense and judgement. The letter had arrived the day before. Roy had at once reported it to his departmental chief, and written a note to Houston Eggar, who was back at the Foreign Office handling some of the German work. Roy had told them (as Eggar already knew) that he had many friends in Berlin, and that this was a disreputable acquaintance. He added that one or two of the younger German ministers had reason to believe that he was well-disposed to them and to Germany.

He was far more cautious than he used to be, I thought. His chief and Eggar had both told him not to worry; it was obviously none of his doing; Eggar had gone on to say that the Foreign Office might want to follow the letter up, since they had so little contact with anyone who had recently been inside Germany.

Outside, the sirens ululated. They were late that night. In a few minutes, down the estuary we heard the first hollow thud of gun-fire. The rumble came louder and sharper. It was strangely warming to be sitting there, in that safe room, as the noise grew. It was like lying in front of the fire as a child, while the wind moaned and the rain thrashed against the windows. It gave just the same pulse of rich, exalted comfort.

We turned off the light and drew aside the curtains. Searchlights were weaving on the clouds: there was an incandescent star as a shell burst short, but most were exploding above the cloud shelf. There were only a few aircraft, flying high. The night was too stormy for a heavy raid. Two small fires were rising, pink, rosy, out to the east. The searchlights crossed their beams ineffectively, in a beautiful three-dimensional design.

The aircraft were unseen, undetected, untouched. We heard their engines throbbing smoothly and without a break. They flew west and then south; the gunfire became distant again, and died away.

We looked out into the dark night; one searchlight still smeared itself upon the clouds.

'They won't find it so easy soon,' I said.

'Who'll stop them? Getliffe and his gang?'

'They'll help,' I said. 'It won't be any fun to fly.'

'You're sure, old boy?' said Roy very clearly, in the dark room.

'I'm pretty sure,' I said. I had always had a minor interest in military history: since the war, with the opportunities of my job, it had become more informed. 'It was the most dangerous job in the last war. It's bound to become so again.'

'On both sides?'

'Yes.'

'What do you mean – the most dangerous job?'

I defined what I meant. I said that special élite troops on land, like commandos, might take greater risks than the average fighting airman; but that the whole fighting strength of the air force would suffer heavier casualties than any similar number of men on land or sea.

'They'll take very heavy losses,' I said, staring at the night sky.

'And we shall too?'

'Quite certainly,' I said. 'I don't know how many fighting airmen will survive the war. It won't be a very large percentage.'

'Just so.' I heard the clear voice behind me.

Two mornings later, Houston Eggar rang me up at my office. He was excessively mysterious. In him discretion was becoming both a passion and an art; both he and I had secret telephones, but he thought it safest not to speak. It would be wiser to meet, he said zestfully, revelling in his discretion. He would not give me an inkling of the reason. Would I mind going round to the Foreign Office?

I was annoyed. I did not believe that he was as busy as I was. I knew that he enjoyed all the shades of secrecy. Irritated, I went past guards, sandbags, into the dingy entrance of the Foreign Office, followed a limping messenger down corridors and up stairs.

Eggar was occupying a tiny ramshackle room, marked off by a pasteboard partition. The building was overcrowded, and, somewhat to his chagrin, he could not be accommodated according to his rank. One window had been blown out, and was not yet boarded over. It was a cold morning, and bitter draughts kept sweeping in. Eggar sat there in his black coat and striped trousers, muscular, vigorous, cheerful. He did not mind the cold. He worked like an engine, and he would be sitting in that arctic room until late at night, plodding through the day's stack of files.

He greeted me with his effusive cordiality, man-to-man, eyes looking straight into eyes.

'Between ourselves,' he said, 'I think I've got a job for you.'

'I'm pretty well booked,' I said.

'I know you're not *disponible*. I know you're getting well-thought-of round here. I hear your minister thinks the world of you.' Eggar was a generous-hearted man, and he was genuinely pleased that I should get some praise. Also he was thinking of one of his own simple, cunning, pushful moves. 'But I want you for something important. I think we may be able to extract you for a week or two.'

'I do rather doubt it,' I said. 'What do you want me for?'

'You've kept in touch with young Calvert, have you?'

The question surprised me.

'Yes.'

'Well, this is strictly in confidence – we're particularly anxious that it shouldn't get round, for reasons that I'm obliged to keep to myself. Strictly in confidence, young Calvert has received a letter from a German friend of his. I don't want to give you a wrong impression. There's nothing to blame Calvert for. He has behaved perfectly correctly.' Eggar told me the story of Romantowski's letter over again; he produced a copy of the original, and I listened to another translation.

'Very curious,' I said.

'It may be useful,' said Eggar. 'We're finding out whether this chap Romantowski is really living at that address. If so, we want to chase it up.' He explained, as he had done to Roy, that they were uncomfortably short of news from inside Germany. 'We think it might be worth the trouble of sending Calvert to talk to him.'

I nodded.

'Yes, we shall probably send Calvert out,' said Eggar.

He looked at me, and added:

'If we do, we should like you to go with him.'

'Why?'

Then Eggar took me completely aback.

'Between ourselves, Eliot, you ought to know. You ought to remember that two or three years ago Calvert was inclined to see some good points in the German set-up. I don't count it against him: a lot of people did the same. I'm not saying for a minute that today he isn't a hundred per cent behind the war. But we can't afford to take chances. I should be more comfortable if you went and helped him out in Switzerland. I expect he would be more comfortable too.'

It was informal, rough-and-ready, fixed up like an arrangement between friends. It was the way things got done. I felt a new respect for Eggar's competence.

I could not escape being persuaded. If they wanted news badly enough to send Roy, it was as well that I went with him. Eggar beamed at me triumphantly. He would not have got me ordered there against my will, but now all was clear, he said, for him to call upon my minister. It was quite unnecessary, for the minister was the least ceremonious of men; I could have explained it to him in five minutes.

But he was also a uniquely influential man, and Eggar was determined to know him. On its own merits, it was a good idea to despatch me to look after Roy; Eggar could always keep one eye on the ball. But the other eye was fixed elsewhere. From the moment he had thought of sending me, Eggar had been determined to make the most of the opportunity. It was an admirable excuse to introduce himself to the minister; he was out to create the best of impressions. He would never have a finer chance.

CHAPTER 33

Journey into the Light

'WE'LL get you there somehow,' said Houston Eggar heartily, when I asked about our route. The more I thought of it, the more my apprehensions emerged. In fact, it was so difficult to arrange the journey that it was cancelled twice. Each time I felt reprieved. But Eggar was determined that we should go, and at last he managed it.

The Foreign Office had been able to trickle a few people in since the fall of France, and Eggar used the same method for us: but even so, and getting us the highest priority, he took weeks to produce our papers complete. The delay was almost entirely caused by the French, for we needed a visa through Vichy France.

Though I viewed the journey with trepidation, I could not help being amused at the technique. For we were to fly to Lisbon in the ordinary way; there was nothing comic about that, but then the unexpected began; we were instructed to catch a German plane from Lisbon to Madrid, and another on the standard Lufthansa route from Madrid up north through Europe. We were to get off at Lyons, though the plane went on to Stuttgart. It had been done several times before by visitors on important missions, said Eggar: like them, we should carry Red Cross papers, and he expected all would be well. The French at last gave way. Eggar told us as though he had done all the difficult part, and ours was trivial; but, as a matter of fact, he was beginning to feel responsible.

He became slightly too genial, and stood us a dinner the night before we left.

We flew from Bristol on a halcyon spring afternoon. But we saw nothing of it, for the windows of the aircraft were covered over, and let in only a dim, tawny, subfusc light. The dimness made my plan for getting through the journey a little more difficult; I had to reckon on three hours' sheer fright before we landed at Lisbon, and to help myself through I read quotas of fifty pages at a go before letting myself look at my watch. I had taken the *Tale of Genji* with me. Subtle and lovely though it was, I wished it had more narrative power. I could not keep myself from listening for unpleasant sounds. Once more I cursed and was ashamed of my timidity. I very much envied Roy.

He was lively, exhilarated, much as he had been in the most joyous days. He had been exhilarated ever since he was asked to make the journey. He seemed glad that I was going, as though it had been a holiday when we were much younger; he had not shown the slightest suspicion or resentment; he had not asked a single question why I should be there. Yet I felt he was too incurious. He could not accept it as naturally as he seemed to. He was much too astute not to guess. Still, his face lit up at the news of our journey, just as it used before any travel. He had always been excited by the thought, not of anything vague like the skies of Europe, but the unexpected and exact things which he might hear and see: I remembered the postcards that used to arrive as he went from library to library: 'Palermo. The post office here has pillars fifty-six feet high, painted red, white, and blue.' 'Nice. Yesterday a Romanian poetess described her country and France as the two bulwarks of Latin civilization.' 'Berlin. The best cricketer of German nationality is called Maus. (All German cricketers appear to have very short names.) He is slightly worse than I am, slightly better than you.'

He was excited again in just that fashion, as we got into the aircraft. He was stimulated, became more brilliantly alive, through the faint tang of danger. I envied him, reading my book with forced concentration, hearing him chat to a Portuguese businessman. He knew that I should be frightened, that I should prefer to be left sullenly alone. His imagination was at least as active as mine, but it produced an utterly different result: the thought of danger made him keen, braced, active, like a first-class batsman who requires just enough of the needle, just enough tingle of the nerves, to be brought to the top of his form. Portuguese was a language Roy had never had reason to look at, but he was asking his acquaintance to pronounce some words: Roy was mimicking the squashed vowel sounds, apparently with accuracy, to judge from the admiring cries.

My first quota of pages dragged by, then in time another, then another. I had to read a good many pages again, to draw any meaning from them; not that they were obscure (they were about lords and ladies of the Japanese court in the year 1000, making an expedition to view the beauty of the autumn flowers), but I was listening too intently for noises outside. I wondered for an instant how the Genji circle would have faced times like ours. They happened to live in an interval of extreme tranquillity, though their civilization was destroyed a couple of generations later. The Victorians too – they lived in an interval of tranquillity, though they did not feel it so. How would they have got on, if they had been born, like Roy and me and our friends, into one of the most violent times? About the same as we did, I thought. Not better. They would have endured it, for human beings are so made that they struggle on. The more one saw of human beings in violence and adversity, the more astonishing it was how much they could bear.

The plane began to lose height earlier than I calculated. I was alarmed, but Roy had picked up a word, and smiled across at me affectionately, mockingly, with an eyebrow lifted:

'We're here, old boy. Lisbon.'

It was comforting to feel the bumps beneath the wheels, comforting to walk with Roy across the aerodrome.

'Five o'clock,' said Roy. 'In time for tea. You need some tea. Also some cakes.'

We were staying that night in Lisbon, and we strolled through the brilliant streets in the warm and perfumed air. For five minutes, it was a release after the darkness of England. The lights streamed from the shops and one felt free, confined no longer. But almost at once, one forgot the darkness, we were walking in lighted streets as we had done before. Roy went from shop to shop, sending off presents; except that the presents were mostly parcels of food, it might have been a night in Cambridge in days past.

We caught the German aeroplane next day. It seemed a little bizarre, but not so much as when I first heard that this was the most practical way. The lap was a short one, Lisbon to Madrid; the windows were not darkened, I looked down on the tawny plains of Estremadura and Castille; we were all polite, everything went according to plan. I had been in Madrid just before the beginning of the civil war; it was strange to sit in a café there again, to read newspapers prophesying England's imminent defeat, to remember the passions that earlier war had stirred in England. It had been the great plane of cleavage between left and right; we could recall Arthur

Brown, the most sensible and solid of Conservatives, so far ceasing to be his clubbable self as to talk about 'those thieves and murderers whom Getliffe and Eliot are so fond of'.

Roy mimicked Arthur Brown making that reproachful statement, and one saw again the rubicund but frowning face by the fire in the combination room. 'I regard a glass of port as rather encouraging on a cold night,' Roy went on mimicking. We were sometimes nostalgic for those cosy autumn nights.

The Lufthansa plane, on the run Madrid–Barcelona–Lyons–Stuttgart, was full of German officials, businessmen, and officers. They knew we were English; one or two were stiffly courteous, but most of them were civil, helpful, anxious to be kind. Roy's German was, of course, an aid: there is something disarming in a foreigner who speaks one's language within a shade of perfection and who knows one's country from the inside. I could now carry on some sort of conversation myself, and one youngish businessman pressed sandwiches on us with a naïve, clumsy, puppyish kindness.

I was not expecting to be treated with such simple, amiable consideration. I did not understand why they should have gone out of their way to be kind. They were worried about our reception at Lyons, but anxious to assure us that we should be well looked after at Basel. 'It is like a German town,' they said. 'Yes, it is a fine town. All will be well when you come to Basel.'

So, in that odd company, I had my first glimpse of the Mediterranean for three years, as we flew over the Catalan coast. Since we landed at Lisbon, I was not so timid about physical danger; but I had two other cares on my mind. I was not sure whether it was a convenience for both sides to let Englishmen travel under this deception of ours. If not, it was always possible that someone here would report our names when he got to Germany: Roy was well enough known in Berlin for it to be a finite risk. I did not believe that the German Intelligence would be taken in for a moment by our Red Cross status – and we were due to return on this same route.

For the same reason, I was nervous about the weather. If it did not let us touch down at Lyons, we should inevitably be taken on to Stuttgart. Could we possibly get away with it? Roy would have to do most of the talking: could I trust him to throw himself into whole-hearted lying? This time I was more afraid for him: of all men, he was the least fit to stand prison. I watched the clouds rolling up to the east.

Once (it was an ironical memory) we had been forced down at Lyons. Flying home from Monte Carlo after that happy holiday with the Boscastles, we had met a snowstorm. It was uncomfortable to remember now.

This time the weather did not interfere with us. We made our proper landing. Our German acquaintances inside the aeroplane wished us good luck, and I felt that now we had put the last obstacle behind us. It turned out otherwise. The French officials were not willing to let us disembark: they held the aircraft, the German officers getting first bleakly, then bitterly angry, while we were questioned. Our papers were in order; they could not find anything irregular; they remained sharp, unsatisfied, hostile, suspicious. Both Roy and I lost our tempers. Though I was too angry to note it then, I had never seen him abandoned to rage before. He thumped on the table in the control-room; he was insolently furious; he demanded that they put us in touch immediately with the protecting power; he treated them like petty officials; he loved riffraff and outcasts and those who were born to be powerless – but that afternoon, when he was crossed, he assumed that authority must be on his side.

Suddenly, with a good many shrugs and acid comments, they let us through. They had no formal case against us – but they might have persisted longer if we had kept our tempers and continued with rational and polite argument. As we walked into the town to the railway station (there was no car and they would not help us to find any sort of vehicle) it occurred to me that we were angry because of their suspicions: we were the more angry because the suspicions happened to be entirely justified. It was curious, the genuine moral outrage one felt at being accused of a sin of which one was guilty. I told Roy.

'Just so,' he said, with a smile that was a little sour.

The train was crowded up to the frontier, with people standing in each carriage. It arrived hours late at Annemas, and there we had another scene. At last we sat in a Swiss train, clean and empty.

'Now you can relax,' said Roy. He smiled at me protectively; but that smile vanished, as the excitement and thrill of the journey dropped from him. He looked out of the window, as the train moved towards Geneva; his face was pensive, troubled, and grave.

When there was no excitement to brighten his eyes, he had become by this time in his life sad without much intermission. It was not like the overmastering bouts of melancholy; he had not been invaded by irresistible melancholy since that last summer of peace. I wondered if it was creeping on him now. It was hard to tell, when so much of his time he was burdened – burdened without much up and down, as though this was a steady, final state. As he looked out of the window, I wondered if he was specially burdened now. Was he thinking of what awaited him at Basel?

He turned away from the window, and found my eyes upon him. His own gaze met mine. I noticed his eyes as though it were the first time. They were brilliant, penetrating: most people found them hard to escape: they had often helped him in his elaborate solemn dialogues, in the days when he played his tricks upon the 'stuffed'.

'Anxious?' he said.

'Yes.'

'About me?'

'Yes.'

'You needn't worry, Lewis,' he said. 'I shan't disgrace you. I shan't do anything unorthodox.'

He looked at me with a faint smile.

'There's no need to worry. I promise you.'

He spoke as he had come to speak so often – quietly, sensibly, kindly, without fancy. There was still just a vestigial trace of mischief in his tone. I accepted the reassurance implicitly. I knew I had nothing to fear at the end of this journey. It was a relief. Whatever happened now, I could cease to worry at the level of practical politics, at the level where Houston Eggar would be concerned.

Yet, in those quiet, intimate words, there was an undercurrent of something more profound. Perhaps I did not hear it at its sharpest. I was not then attuned. But could anyone, still struggling with hope, still battling on with the selfish frailty of a human brother, be so considerate, so imaginatively detached, so desperately kind?

We arrived at Basel late at night, and went at once to Willy Romantowski's address. We were met by an anticlimax. Yes, he was living there. No, he was not in. He had been staying with some friends for a night or two. He was expected back tomorrow or the next day.

'Willy must have found someone very, very nice,' said Roy with a grin, as we left the house. 'Really, I'm surprised at the Swiss. Very remarkable.'

I grinned too, though I was more frustrated than he by the delay. I wanted to get it over, return safely to England, clear off the work that was waiting for me. Roy did not mind; he was relaxed, quite ready to spend some time in this town.

He remarked that Willy was not doing himself too badly. It was midnight, and difficult to get an impression of a strange street. But it was clearly not a slum. The street seemed to be full of old middle-class houses, turned into flats – not unlike the Knesebeckstrasse, except that the houses were less gaunt, more freshly painted, and spick-and-span. Willy was living in a room under the eaves.

'His standard of living is going up,' said Roy. 'Why? Just two guesses.'

Willy did not get in touch with us the next day, and we spent the time walking round Basel; I was still very restless, and Roy set out to entertain me. At any other time, I should have basked in the Gothic charm of the streets round our hotel, for the consul had found us rooms in a quarter as medieval as Nuremberg. There were only a few of these Gothic streets, which led into rows of doctors' houses, offices, shops, as trim as the smart suburb of a midland town in England; but, if one did not walk too far, one saw only red roofs, jutting eaves, the narrow bustling old streets, the golden ball of the Spalenthor above the roofs, gleaming in the spring sunlight. It took one back immediately to childhood, like the smell of class-room paint; it was as though one had slept as a child in one of those tiny bedrooms, and been woken by the church bells.

We used an introduction to some of the people at the university. They took us out and gave us a gigantic dinner, but they regarded us with a regretful pity, as one might look at someone mortally ill. For they took it for granted that England had already lost the war. They were cross with us for making them feel such painful pity – just as Lord Boscastle sounded callous at having his heart wrung by Roy's sorrow. I found myself perversely expressing a stubborn, tough, blimpish optimism which I by no means felt. They became angry, pointing out how unrealistic I was, how like all Englishmen I had an over-developed character and very little intelligence.

Roy took no part in the argument. He was occupying himself, with the professional interest that never left him, in learning some oddities of Swiss-German.

Roy had left a note for Willy, and we called again at his lodging house. At last he came to our hotel, on our second afternoon there. His mincing mannerisms were not flaunted quite so much; he was wearing a pin-stripe suit in the English style, his cheeks were fatter, he looked healthy and well-fed. He was patently upset to find me with Roy. Roy said that he was sure Willy would be glad to see another old friend, and asked him to have some tea.

Willy would love to. He explained that he had become very fond of tea. He had also become, I thought, excessively genteel.

Roy began by asking him about the people at No. 32. Willy said that he had not seen them for eighteen months (both Roy and I thought this was untrue). But the little dancer had unexpectedly and suddenly married a schoolmaster, back in her native town; she had had a child and was said to be very happy. We were delighted to hear it. In the midst of strain, that news came fresh and calm. We sent for a bottle of wine, and drank to her. For a few moments, we were light-hearted.

Roy questioned Willy up to dinner, through the meal, through the first part of the night. Roy mentioned the clerk, Willy's old patron, the 'black avised' – Willy shrugged his shoulders: 'I do not know where he is. He was tiresome. I left him. I do not know him any more.' Roy scolded him: 'It is hard to be kind to those who love you, Willy. But you need to try. It is shameful not to try.' It was strange that he took the trouble to rebuke Willy, who had always seemed to me inescapably hard, petty, and vain. Perhaps Roy was something else. Perhaps he remembered that he himself had some-times behaved unforgivably to those who loved him.

From the black avised, he switched to Willy's own adventures. Here we became inextricably entangled for a long time: it was difficult to pick out exactly where he was lying. His first, as it were official, story was this: he had been called up in the summer of 1939, had gone with an infantry division into Poland, had spent the winter with the army of occupation, had been transferred to the Western

Front in the spring of 1940. His division had been sitting opposite Verdun, and had done no fighting; in the winter, they were moved across Europe again to the Eastern Front. It was then that Willy 'got tired of it'. He had deserted, on the way through Germany, and smuggled himself over the Swiss frontier. Since then he had been living in Basel. 'How are you keeping alive?' asked Roy. 'Thanks to friends,' said Willy, turning his eyes aside modestly – but added in a hurry: 'I am poor. Will you please help me, Roy?'

Most of those statements were lies. That was quite clear. It was also quite clear that, if he wanted to make a proposition to Roy, he would have to admit they were lies. So we examined him, tripped him up on inconsistencies, just to give him a chance to come down to the real business. Meanwhile I was hoping, in the exchange, to collect a few useful facts.

I ought to say in passing that the results were disappointing.

Willy was sharp, quick-witted, acquisitive, but he did not know enough. All he could have told us, even if he had had the will, was the day-to-day gossip of Berlin and the personal facts he had observed. Roy made some deductions from the gossip which proved more right than wrong: I missed the significance of something Willy let fall. He said that the draughtsman at No. 32 had not been able to find a job for months. I ought to have pounced on that remark, but I was just obtuse: it seemed incredible then that their administration should be fundamentally, for all its streamlined finish, less sensible, less directed, less business-like than ours.

We drank a good deal before and during dinner. We hoped to get him drunk, for we were both, of course, accustomed to wine. But he turned out to have, despite his youth, an abnormally strong head. Roy said to me in English, over dinner: 'We shall be dished, old boy – if he sees us under the table.'

However, after dinner Willy made some pointed hints that I should leave him and Roy alone. I did not budge. Willy pouted. He might be acquiring great gentility, I thought, but he still had some way to go. His patience was not lasting – all of a sudden he began commiserating with Roy on the dangers of life in England. 'You too will be destroyed. It is stupid to stay in England. Why do you not come to Germany? It can be arranged. We will have everything nice for you.'

So that was it. I glanced at Roy. It was certain now that he would get more from Willy if I went away. He nodded. I made an excuse. 'Don't be too late,' said Roy. 'He won't have gone when you come back.' Willy regarded me with an absence of warmth.

I sat at a café in the Petergraben, not far away. The night was warm enough for all the windows to be open; lusty young men and girls went by on the narrow pavement. It was all cosy, cheerful, jolly with bodily life. It was different from anything we should know for long enough.

I bought a paper, ordered a large glass of beer, and thought about this affair of Willy Romantowski. It was grotesque. I was not worrying; I had faith that Roy would behave like the rest of us. Yet it was grotesque. Who had suggested it? What lay behind it? Maybe the motives were quite commonplace. In the middle of bizarre events, it was hard to remember that they might be simply explained. Yet I doubted whether we should ever know the complete truth behind Willy's invitation.

I was sure of one minor point – that Willy himself was a singularly unheroic character. He was terrified of the war and determined to avoid it. It seemed to me distinctly possible that he had volunteered to fetch Roy in order to establish a claim on a good safe job back in Berlin. I remembered Roy's judgement on how gallant these epicene young men would be: this was a joke against him.

I returned to the Spalenbrunnen. From outside, I could see Roy and Willy still sitting at the dinner-table. When I joined them, I noticed with a shock that Willy was in tears.

'Nearly finished, Lewis,' said Roy to me. 'I've been telling Willy that I can't go back with him. I've asked him to tell my friends that I love them. And that I love Germany.'

'I only came for your good,' said Willy, full of resentment, plaintiveness, and guilt.

'You must not pretend, Willy,' said Roy gently. 'It is not so.'

Willy gulped with distress – perhaps through disappointment at not bringing off his *coup*, perhaps through a stab of feeling. He shook hands with Roy: then, though he hated me to perdition, he remembered his manners and shook hands with me. Without another word, he went out of the room.

'Very remarkable,' said Roy. He looked tired and pale.

I took him out of the smoky room, and we sauntered along the street. Roy had packed a black hat for the journey, and he pulled it down low over his forehead. The lights were uneven in the gothic lanes, and his face was shadowed, a little sinister. I laughed at him. 'Special hat,' he said. Whatever else left him, the mockery stayed. 'Suitable for spying. I chose it on purpose.'

He was now certain that the first move had come from Schäder, though Willy did not have much idea. Someone from the 'government' (no doubt an official in Schäder's ministry) had gone to the Knesebeckstrasse to discover whether anyone knew Roy. Willy had been there, and had been only too anxious to please.

That was intelligible. But why had he been despatched to Basel, long before they had the slightest indication that Roy would come? That was one of the puzzling features of the whole story. Roy brought out the theory that Willy was given other work to do in Switzerland. This was only one of his jobs. He was the kind of low-grade agent that the Germans used for their petty inquiries, and no doubt other governments as well. He had a nose for private facts, particularly when they were unpleasant. Probably he mixed pleasure with business, and put in a little blackmail on the side.

But Roy had not been able to make him confess. It was no more than a guess. About the connexion with Schäder, however (whom Willy had hardly heard of, any more than a bright cockney of the same class would have heard of a junior cabinet minister), Roy was able to convince me. For Willy had produced, parrot-like, several messages which he could not possibly have invented. The most entertaining ran thus: a few days before the war began, the university had resolved that Roy's work during his stay in Berlin 'had been of such eminence as to justify the title of visiting professor, and this title could properly be bestowed upon him, if he did similar work at a later period'. That is, the opposition had stone-walled until they got a compromise which must have irritated everybody. It was a piece of stately academic mummery, and we stood by the gold-painted fountain at the corner roaring with laughter.

Why had Schäder taken this trouble to lure Roy? It was true that Roy knew things that would be of use – but how had they discovered that? was it in any case sufficient reason? I suggested that it might be, in part, friendly concern.

'They must be absolutely confident that they've got it won,' I said. 'It must be easy to sit back and do a good turn for a friend.'

'I wonder if they are so confident,' said Roy. 'I bet they still think sometimes of defeat and death.'

He knew them so much better than I did. He went on:

'Reinhold Schäder is a bit like you, old boy. But he's very different when it comes to the point. He's a public man. He never forgets it. He might think of doing something disinterested. Such as fetching me out for the good of my health. But he wouldn't do it. Unless he could see a move ahead. No, they must think I could be some use. It's very nice of them, isn't it?'

Then there was the final puzzle. Schäder, or his subordinates, must have thought it out. Roy said that there were complete arrangements for passing him into Germany. How likely had they reckoned the chance of getting him? Did Schäder really think that Roy would go over?

Roy shook his head.

'Too difficult,' he said.

Then he said simply:

'Did you think I should go?'

I replied, just as directly:

'Not this time.'

'You came to watch over me, of course,' said Roy, not as a question, but as a matter of fact.

'Yes.'

'You needn't have done,' said Roy. His tone was casual, even, sad, as though he were speaking with great certainty from the depth of self-knowledge. It was a tone that I was used to hearing, more and more. Suddenly it was broken humour. 'If I'd wanted to go, what would you have done, old boy? What could you have done? I wish you'd tell me. It interests me, you know.'

I would not play that game. We walked silently out by the old town gate, and Roy said, again in that even tone which seemed to hold all he had learned of life:

'It wouldn't be easy to be a traitor.'

He added:

'One would need to believe in a cause – right to the end. If our country went to war with Russia – would our Communist friends find it easy to be traitors?'

I considered for a second.

'Some of them,' I said, 'would be terribly torn.'

'Just so,' said Roy. He went on:

'I may be old-fashioned. But I couldn't manage it.'

So we walked through the old streets of Basel, talking about political motives, the way our friends would act, the future so far as we could see it. Roy said that he had never quite been able to accept the Reich. It was a feeble simulacrum of his search for God. Yet he knew what it was like to believe in such a cause. 'If they had been just a little different, they would have been the last hope.' I said that was unrealistic: by the nature of things, they could not have been different. But he turned on me:

'It's as realistic as what you hope for. Even if they lose, the future isn't going the way you think. Lewis, this is where your imagination doesn't seem to work. But you'll live to see it. It will be dreadful.'

He spoke with extreme conviction, almost as though he had the gift of foresight. In all our lives together, it was the one subject on which we had deeply disagreed. Yet he spoke as though he were reading the future.

We turned back, each of us heavy with his thoughts. Then Roy said:

'I used to be sorry that I hurt you. When I tried to fall in on the opposite side.'

Between the gabled houses, the shadows were dramatic; Roy's face was pale, brilliantly lit on one cheek, the features unnaturally sharp.

'I was clutching at anything, of course,' he said.

'Yes.'

'It was my last grab.' He smiled. 'It left me with nothing, didn't it? Or with myself.'

The clocks struck from all round us. He said lightly:

'I'm keeping you up. I mustn't. High officials need to become respectable. It's time you did, you know. Part of your duties.'

CHAPTER 34

Surrender and Relief

SHORTLY after we returned from Basel, Roy's department was moved out of London, and I did not see him for some months. But I heard of him – just once, but in a whisper that one believes as soon as one hears, one seems to have known it before. I heard of him in a committee meeting: it was Houston Eggar who told me, in a moment's pause between two items on the agenda.

We used to meet in the Old Treasury, in a room which over-looked Whitehall itself, just to the north of Downing Street. It was a committee at Under-Secretary level, which was set up to share out various kinds of supplies; there were several different claimants – Greece, when she was still in the war, partisan groups which were just springing up by the end of the summer of 1941, when this meeting took place, and neutrals such as Turkey.

The committee behaved (as I often thought, with frantic irritation or human pleasure, according to the news or my own inner weather) remarkably like a college meeting. Each of the members was representing a ministry, and so was speaking to instructions. Sometimes he was at one with his instructions, and so expressed them with energy and weight; Houston Eggar, for instance, could nearly always feel as the Foreign Office felt. Sometimes a member did not like them; sometimes a strong character was etching out a line for himself, and one saw policy shaped under one's eyes by a series of small decisions. (In fact, it was rare for policy to be clearly thought out, though some romantics or worshippers of 'great men' liked to think so. Usually it built itself from a thousand small arrangements, ideas, compromises, bits of give-and-take. There was not much which was decisively changed by a human will. Just as a plan for a military campaign does not spring fully-grown from some master general; it arises from a sort of Brownian movement of colonels and majors and captains, and the most the general can do is rationalize it afterwards.) Sometimes one of the committee was over-anxious to ingratiate himself or was completely distracted by some private grief.

As in a college meeting, the reasons given were not always close to the true reasons. As in a college meeting, there was a public language – much of which was common to both. That minatory phrase 'in his own best interests' floated only too sonorously round Whitehall. The standard of competence and relevance was much higher than in a college meeting, the standard of luxurious untrammelled personality perceptibly lower. Like most visitors from outside, I had formed a marked respect for the administrative class of the Civil Service. I had lived among various kinds of able men, but I thought that, as a group, these were distinctly the ablest. And they loved their own kind of power.

Houston Eggar loved his own kind of power. He loved to think that a note signed by him affected thousands of people. He loved to speak in the name of the Foreign Office: '*my* department', said Houston Eggar with possessive gusto. It was all inseparable as flesh and blood from his passion for getting on, his appetite for success – which, as it happened, still did not look certain to be gratified. It had become a race with the end of the war. He was forty-eight in 1941, and unless the war ended in five or six years he stood no chance of becoming an ambassador. However, he was a man who got much pleasure from small prizes; his C.M.G. had come through in the last honours list, which encouraged him; he plunged into the committee that afternoon, put forward his argument with his usual earnestness and vigour, and thoroughly enjoyed himself.

He was propounding the normal Foreign Office view that, since the amount of material was not large, it was the sensible thing to distribute it in small portions, so that no one should be quite left out; we should thus lay up credit in days to come. The extreme alternative view was to see nothing but the immediate benefit to the war, get a purely military judgement, and throw all this material there without any side-glances. There was a whole spectrum of shades between the two, but on the whole Eggar tended to be isolated in that company and had to work very hard for small returns. It was so that day. But he was surprisingly effective in committee; he was not particularly clever, but he spoke with clarity, enthusiasm, pertinacity, and above all weight. Even among sophisticated men, weight counted immeasurably more than subtlety or finesse.

Accordingly he secured a little more than the Foreign Office could reasonably expect. It was a hot afternoon, and he leaned back in his chair, mopping his forehead. He always got hot in the ardour of putting his case. He beamed. He was happy to have won a concession.

I was due to speak on the next business, but the chairman was looking through his papers. I was sitting next to Eggar; he pushed an elbow along the table, and leant towards me. He said in a low voice, casual and confidential:

'So Calvert is getting his release.'

'What?'

'He has got his own way. Good luck to him. I told his chief there's no use trying to keep a man who is determined to go.'

'Where is he going?'

Eggar looked incredulous, as though I must know.

'Where is he going?' I said.

'Oh, he wants to fly, of course. It's quite natural.'

I had known nothing of it, not a word, not a hint. For a second, I felt physically giddy. A blur of faces went round me. Then it steadied. I heard the chairman's voice, a little impatient:

'Isn't this a matter for you, Eliot?'

'I'm sorry, Mr Chairman,' I said, and mechanically began to explain a new piece of government machinery. I could hear my own words, faint and toneless like words in a dream – yet they came out in a shape fluent, practised, articulate. It was too hard to break the official habit. One was clamped inside one's visor.

Eggar left before the end of the meeting, and so I could not get another word with him. I put through a call to Roy's office, but he was out. I gave a message for him: would he telephone me at my flat, without fail, after eleven that night?

I went straight from my office to have dinner with Lady Muriel and Joan. They had come to London in the first week of the war, and were living in the Boscastles' town house in Curzon Street. They were extravagantly uncomfortable. The house was not large, judged by the magnificent criterion of Boscastle (Lord Boscastle's grandfather had sold the original town mansion); but it was a good deal too large for two women, both working at full-time jobs. It was also ramshackle and perilously unsafe. Nothing would persuade Lady Muriel to forsake it. A service flat seemed in her eyes common beyond expression – as for danger, she dismissed us all as a crowd of 'jitterbugs' getting the idiom wrong. 'This disturbance is much exaggerated,' she said, and slept with a soundness that infuriated many of us and put us to shame.

Her sense of duty would not permit her to employ any servants who could possibly do other work. In fact, they had two women who had been with the family all their lives, both well over seventy and infirm. Lady Muriel did all the cooking herself when she gave a dinner party, but made them both wait at table. It was a quixotic parody of nights in the Lodge and Boscastle.

She and Joan were sitting together in the drawing-room. The pictures had been taken away for safety, and the walls were bare.

'Good evening, Mr – Lewis,' said Lady Muriel. 'It is good of you to come and see us.'

Nowadays, she used my Christian name when she remembered. The explanation was a little complicated. It did not mean for a minute that she thought the time had come to relax her social standards. As a matter of fact, the exact opposite was the case. She might officiate at a refugee centre each day and every day – which she did inexorably. She submitted to being slapped on the back by cheery women helpers: it was part of her job. But at night, in the privacy of Curzon Street, where she had lived as a girl, she became so magniloquently snobbish that her days in the Lodge came to seem like slumming. It was her defence, her retort, to those who kept saying that the day of her kind was gone for ever. Lord Boscastle responded in just the same fashion – not with accommodation, not trying to fit in, but with an exaggerated, a considered, a monumental arrogance. They were both dropping most of their old acquaintances.

No, when Lady Muriel called me by my Christian name it certainly did not imply that she accepted me in any social sense. Perhaps she liked me a little more; with her, getting used to people and liking them tended to run together. But really her softening came from quite a different cause: it was a gesture of respect towards the government and those who organized the war. She was passionately determined that her country should win; and it made her curiously respectful to anyone who seemed to be in control. She had decided that I was far more important than in fact I was; she had also decided that I knew every conceivable military secret. Nothing would remove these misconceptions; a flat denial merely strengthened her faith in my astuteness and responsibility. Then someone told her that I was doing well, and that finished it. She listened open-mouthed to every word I said about the war, like a girl student with a venerated teacher; she drew inferences when I was silent; and, with a certain effort, she brought herself after all those years to use my Christian name.

I smiled at Joan. Despite her exertions, thick and heavy as she was, Lady Muriel was well preserved at fifty-five. But Joan no longer looked a girl. She had worked in the Treasury from the first winter, and her face had changed through success as well as unhappiness. She had shown how able she was; it was just the outlet for her tough, strong nature; and it had stamped its mark on her, for on the surface she was a little more formidable, a little more decisive, ruthless, and blunt.

Though everyone praised her, though she knew that she could go high if she wanted, she recoiled. She liked it and hated it. In protest, she lived at night the gayest life she could snatch. She went out with every man who asked her. I saw her often in public houses and smart bars and restaurants. She was searching for a substitute for Roy, I knew – and yet also she longed for the glitter and the lights more than many giggling thoughtless women.

I did not want to tear open her wound, but I was driven to ask at once about Roy. I could not begin to make conversation. I had to ask: did they know anything of him?

To my consternation, Joan smiled.

'You must have heard.' She told me the same news as Eggar.

'I've heard nothing.'

'I should have thought he would have told you,' said Joan. 'He let me know.'

'It was only to be expected,' said Lady Muriel, 'that he should let us know.'

I gathered that he had written to Lady Muriel. Joan was glad that she had heard the secret, and I had not; even now her love would not let her go, searched for the slightest sign, found an instant of dazzling hope in a letter to her mother. His friend had not been told; was this letter a signal to her?

'He seems content,' said Joan. 'I hope it's right for him. I think perhaps it is.'

'It is certainly right for him,' said Lady Muriel.

'He's such a strange man,' said Joan. 'I hope it is.'

'I've always known that he's been uncomfortable since the war began. A woman feels these things,' said Lady Muriel superbly. 'I can rely on my intuition.'

'What has it told you, Mother?' said Joan, as though she had picked up a spark of mischief from Roy.

'He could not bear being kept back while others fought. I consider that he would never have been happy until he fought.'

Joan smiled at her. Now that Joan had been battered by her own experience, she was much fonder of her mother, much kinder to her, more able to see the rich nature behind the absurd, forbidding armour. She was more ready to put up with her mother's lack of perception – when Joan was a girl, before she had loved, it had merely made her aggressive and fierce. As the years passed, they were growing together.

They took the news of Roy quite differently, and yet with one point in common. For Lady Muriel, all was now clear and well. When she gave her trust, she gave it naïvely and absolutely, like a little girl; white was white, and she admired with her whole heart; and there was no one whom she admired more than Roy. She tried to get used to a war in which young men had safe jobs, did not want to leave them; but she could not manage it. She could not reconcile herself to Roy inert and indecisive. Now her trust was justified. She could worship again, in her simple, loyal, unqualified fashion. 'I always knew it would happen,' said Lady Muriel, forgetting that she had ever been troubled, forgetting it just as completely as she forgot she had once herself opposed the war.

Joan's feelings were far less simple. Although she had not spoken to him for two years, she could divine some of the reasons that had impelled him. She imagined how the war must outrage him. She knew how reckless he was and how self-destructive. Her heart went out to cherish him – and yet she had loved him partly because of that dark side. She was frail enough to rejoice that he did not find his life sweeter after he had deserted her. The news had softened her face, revived her yearning tenderness. It shone out of her: she was both *relieved* and proud.

She and her mother had one point in common. They did not give much thought to his danger. It was the first thing that had struck me: as the committee room went round, I was thinking of that only: he stood about an even chance of coming through alive. Yet Lady Muriel and Joan took it without a blench. Partly, of course, they were ignorant of the statistics, Lady Muriel entirely so; they did not realize how dangerous it was; they had not been, as I had, behind the scenes in the bitter disputes about the bombing 'master plan'. But, even if they had, it would not have made much difference. They were stout-hearted themselves, and they assumed the same courage in their men. They were bred to a tradition of courage. They were warm-hearted, but they had very strong nerves.

In fact, Lady Muriel found a certain bellicose relish in having her beloved Roy to set against Humphrey Bevill. It had been bitterly galling to her to hear first that her nephew Humphrey had shown unexpected skill in charge of a small boat – and then, that he was taking risks in the Channel skirmishes with a wild, berserk bravery. He had just been cited for a D.S.C. It might have pleased Lady Muriel to see credit come to the family name; perhaps it did a little. But much more, it brought back a grief. Lady Muriel had craved for a son, and she was taunted by having daughters. It taunted her again when her sister-in-law, after being childless so long, bore a son. It had seemed just to Lady Muriel that the boy should turn out worthless, dissipated, bohemian, effeminate. Now he was suddenly talked about as the bravest young man in their whole circle. Lady Muriel was not good at disguising her rancour. I had always known that she both envied and despised Lady Boscastle: now I saw that she detested her.

I got back to my flat before eleven, in time for the telephone call; I found Roy there himself. He was sitting in a dressing-gown, clean from a bath but heavy-eyed.

'Just going to bed,' he said. 'Night duty last night. I'm extremely tired.'

He was still working in his civilian office. He had received my message, and taken the first train to London.

'I hear the news is true,' I said.

'It's true,' said Roy.

'Why didn't you tell me?'

'It was the one thing I couldn't tell you.' He looked at me with a troubled, piercing gaze, as though I and he each knew the reason. Yet nothing came home to me; I was angry and mystified. Quickly, he went on:

'I've nothing to keep from you now. You see? I've come tonight to tell you something no one else knows. I'm going to get married.'

'Who to?'

'Rosalind, of course.'

Roy was smiling.

'You're not to speak of it,' he said. 'I haven't asked her yet. I don't know whether she'll have me. I hope she will.'

'I think she might.'

'Excellent,' said Roy, taking my sarcasm equably. 'You've always had a weakness for her yourself, old boy. Remember: I shall be a jealous husband. I need a child.'

He went on:

'I couldn't ask her, of course, until the other thing was settled. It will be nice to have everything settled.'

Then he said that he could not keep his eyes open, and must go to bed. I fetched him a book, in case he wanted to read in the morning: he was asleep before I went out of the room.

I could not think of sleep myself. I turned off the lights, pulled back the curtains, and gazed out of the window for a long time. The night was very still. There was no moon; the river glistened in the starlight; there was neither light nor sound down there, except for a moment when an engine chugged across to the southern bank. All over the sky, the stars were brilliant. 'I hate the stars.' I heard that cry again.

So he had no hope left at all. I could see no other meaning. I could understand Joan's relief. I shared it, and knew it was selfish at the root. If he must be driven so – I had felt more than once that night – then I was selfishly glad he could make this choice: I was glad he could choose a way which those round him could accept and approve. It might have been far otherwise. Somehow he had kept within society. It was a help to Joan and me, who cared for society more than he did.

Surrender and Relief

Yet that was a trivial relief, by the side of his surrender. For he had given up now. For years he had struggled with his nature. Now he was tired of it, and he had given up. Active as he was, still eager with the pulse of life, he had done it in the most active way. He was going into battle, he wanted a wife and child. But he had no hope left.

I looked at the brilliant stars. There was no comfort there.

CHAPTER 35

Consequences of a Marriage

Roy's marriage caused more stir than his other choice. The wedding took place in the autumn, three weeks before he sailed across to America for his flying training. I was held in London and could not attend it. One of the features of those years was the geographical constraint under which we had to live; a few years earlier, we had had more leisure than most people in the world; now I could not get out of my office even for the day of Roy's wedding. In fact, I had only seen him for an hour or two since that night he made the special visit to tell me his news. We were all confined, as it were in prison. Many friends I had not seen since the beginning of the war.

But sitting in London, dining now and then with the Royces, I heard enough furore about the marriage. Lady Muriel was at first incredulous; then, contrary to all expectations, she became unusually indulgent. 'I refuse to blame him,' she said. 'I've seen other men make marriages almost as impossible as this before they went to fight. When a man goes off to fight, he feels a basic need to find a – squaw. I consider this young woman is simply his squaw. As for the future,' she said in a grand, gnomic fashion, 'I prefer not to speak.'

Joan suffered afresh from all the different wounds of humiliated and unrequited love. She could feel her confidence and self-respect seeping away; she ached with the hunger of her fibres; she was lost in the depth of her heart. She had been able to adjust herself to loss before, while she could believe that he was weighted down with misery, that neither she nor any woman could reach or console him. But now he had married a stupid, scheming, ordinary woman, as though he were an ordinary domestic man!

Joan was not only hurt to the quick, but bitterly angry. And the anger was good for her. It burned away some of her self-distrust. Anything was better than that she should be frightened off love for good. She might feel that no man would ever truly love her; for her, that would be a mortal wound. But her formidable temper blazed out. I was glad to see it. I was glad to see her defiantly going from party to party on the arm of another man.

From two sources I heard that Ralph Udal had also taken it bitterly. Apparently Rosalind had not considered it necessary to break her engagement to him until she was simultaneously engaged to Roy. Had he suspected nothing? Was he so self-sufficient that he convinced himself all was well? I had not met Lady Boscastle since that final end-of-the-world week in Cambridge, but this was a subject peculiarly suited to her talents. She wrote me several feline, sub-acid letters about the 'emotional misadventures of our unfortunate vicar'.

Udal was really unhappy. He showed it by one clear sign. He could not bear to stay in Boscastle where Rosalind had so often visited him, where – as even Lady Boscastle admitted – he must have known delight. He begged Arthur Brown to find him a living, any kind of living, 'even one', Arthur Brown reported over the telephone with a rotund wily chuckle, 'even one with slightly less amenities'. Arthur Brown had exerted himself with his usual experienced kindliness; he managed to find Udal a slightly better living in Beccles.

Before Ralph Udal left the vicarage at Boscastle, Roy stayed with him for a week-end. It happened while Roy was on embarkation leave, and I did not see him afterwards. I would have given much to know what they said to each other; I was beginning to realize that Udal was a more singular man than I had at first detected. I guessed that they each felt a surge of their old friendship, unconstrained, warmer, and more spontaneous than one could credit.

During the autumn, Rosalind came to see me. It was her first visit to London since Roy married her, and she was living in state at the Dorchester. As soon as she arrived in my flat, she busied herself tidying it up.

'I must find someone to look after you. It's time you married again,' she scolded me. 'I must say, it depresses me to think of you coming back here – and nothing ready for you.'

Then she sat down with a smile, knowing, self-important, triumphant.

'I'd better be careful,' she said. 'It's a bit of a drag for the first few months, so they tell me.' It was her way of telling me that she was pregnant. 'We didn't waste much time, did we?' Again she gave her mock-modest, humorous, surreptitious grin. 'Of course, there wasn't much time to waste. We only had three weeks, and that isn't very long, is it?'

I laughed.

'It did mean we had to rush things rather,' said Rosalind. She gave an affectionate, earthy frown, and went on:

'It's all Roy's fault. I've got no patience with him. I could kick him. The bloody old fool. If only he'd had the sense to marry me years ago, when I wanted to, we should have had a wonderful time. I ought to have dragged him to church by the scruff of his neck. Why didn't he ask me then, the blasted fool? Our eldest child would be six now. That's how it ought to be. You know, Lewis, I do wish I'd worked on him.'

She was serene, blissfully happy, but matter-of-fact in her triumph. I almost reminded her that she had no cause to reproach herself: she had done her damnedest. But well as I knew her, shameless and realistic as she was, I held my tongue. Curiously, it would have hurt her. She had the kind of realism that buried schemes as soon as they were no longer necessary. She would have stopped at nothing to marry Roy; but, having brought it off, she conveniently shelved all memory of plans, lies, stratagems, tears, pride abandoned. If she were confronted with it, she would look and feel ill-used.

She basked in her well-being.

'He is a nice old thing, though, isn't he?' she said. 'Do you know, Lewis, I enjoy looking at him when he's reading. He *has* got a nice face. Don't you think it's lucky for a woman when she likes a man for something different' – she dropped her eyes – 'and then finds she enjoys just looking at his face? I've never thought he was handsome – but it is a nice face.'

As the evening went on, I was unkind enough to remind her of Ralph Udal. She showed a faint, kind, sisterly desire that he should find a wife. As for herself, she would never have done, she said, contentedly. It was much better for him that she had broken it off: 'in his own best interests', I thought to myself, and made a note to tease Roy with it some time.

Her only worry was where to have the child. Roy would not have returned before it was born. His father was ill, and she could not (and for some reason was violently disinclined to) stay in the

Calverts' house. I suspected that she had not been well received; the Calverts knew her family, since her grandfather and Roy's had started in the same factory. In any case, Rosalind was determined not to live near her home. After marrying Roy, she did not intend to spend any time at all in the provincial town. She had thrown up her job; her skill and reputation meant nothing to her, she was happy not to earn another penny. Roy would not be rich until his father died, but they were comfortably off. Rosalind meant to spread herself.

She would have liked to live in London; but though the nights were quiet then, the autumn of 1941, war-time London was not a good place to bear a child. And Rosalind said without any shame that she was a coward; she would come to London at the end of the war. Meanwhile, she hesitated. Suddenly she had her mind made up for her in an utterly unlooked-for manner. Lady Muriel took a hand.

Lady Muriel heard that Rosalind was with child; how I did not know, but I suspected that Rosalind had flaunted the news. She was kind and careless, but she liked revenge; the Royces used to snub her, Joan had taken away Roy for years, even in her triumph Rosalind was obscurely jealous of her. It was shameful to exult over her, but Rosalind was not likely to be deterred, when it was so sweet. I ought to have foreseen it, and have warned her not to gloat. But it seemed that she had had an hour of womanly triumph.

Anyway, Lady Muriel knew, and was strongly affected. Since her husband died, she had invested all the suppressed warmth of her heart in Roy. She felt responsible and possessive about anything of his. Most of all a child. His child must be cared for. Her feeling for her own babies had been outwardly gruff, in truth healthy and animal: and she was moved at the thought of one of Roy's. It must be cared for.

Lady Muriel had no doubt forgotten that she had once pronounced Rosalind barren. Here was Rosalind in the flesh, in the luxurious, triumphant, pregnant flesh. If Lady Muriel were to help with Roy's child, she had to accept that 'impossible young woman'.

Lady Muriel gave way. She was humbled by love. She did not see much of Rosalind; that was too bitter to stomach; she wrote her suggestions (which soon became orders) in letters which began 'Dear Mrs Calvert'. Sometimes, I thought to myself, she behaved remarkably as though the child were illegitimate. It had to be cherished for the father's sake – meanwhile one made as few concessions as possible to the sinful mother.

Yet it was a strange turn of the wheel. For like it or not, Lady Muriel had to become interested in Rosalind's plans. Soon she became more than interested, she became the planner. For Lady Muriel decided that the baby should be born at Boscastle.

She would not listen to arguments against. Was there not plenty of room there? Would they not be reasonably waited on – despite her sister-in-law's unworthy management? Was it not as safe, as far from the war, as anywhere in England? Did not the estate grow its own food, which was important nowadays? Could not Lady Muriel guarantee the competence of the family doctor?

But, of course, she wanted it for her own sake. It would give her a claim on the child.

Rosalind effaced herself. She was prepared to put up with insults, high-handedness, Lady Muriel's habit of disregarding her, anything that came, if only this could happen. The idea entranced her. It was like a gorgeous, unexpected present. Like most realistic people, Rosalind was not above being a snob.

A correspondence took place between Lady Muriel and Lady Boscastle – firm, hortatory, morally righteous on Lady Muriel's side, sarcastic and amused on Lady Boscastle's. At first Lady Boscastle did not take the proposal seriously. Then she saw that it was being inexorably advanced. She objected. She was not a particular friend of Roy's, she found Rosalind tiresome, she was bored by the war, she saw no reason why she should be inconvenienced; unlike Lady Muriel, she was not buoyed up by sheer vigour of the body, by the impulse of good crude health; Lady Boscastle often felt old, neglected, uninterested now, and she did not see why she should put herself out.

Lady Muriel quoted passages from her sister-in-law's letters with burning indignation. Lady Boscastle, with cynical ingenuity, raised the question of the tenants' peace of mind; they knew of Rosalind's engagement to the late vicar; what would they be likely to think now? Usually, Lady Muriel was only too preoccupied with the tenants' moral welfare; but she had not room for two concerns at once, and she brushed that point aside as though they were Tasmanian aborigines.

On paper, Lady Boscastle had the better of the argument; but, as usual when there was a difference about the family house, Lady Muriel had the greater staying-power, and harangued the others until she prevailed. Lord Boscastle appeared to turn into an ally; and in the end Lady Boscastle sent Rosalind an invitation. Lady Boscastle knew when she was beaten, and her letter was far more friendly than any Lady Muriel wrote to Rosalind (Lady Muriel still began 'Dear Mrs Calvert'): Rosalind showed it to me with delight: I thought I could detect just one malicious flick, put in for the writer's own benefit.

Rosalind accepted by return, and went to Boscastle in time for Christmas. In February, I had a letter myself from Lady Boscastle, in that fine, elegant, upright hand.

'This is really quite ridiculous,' she wrote. 'God appears to have a misplaced sense of humour, which he reserves for those who haven't taken him too seriously. There is no question, he scores in the end. Lewis, my dear boy, I once was pursued with singular pertinacity by a young gentleman of literary pretensions. He was remarkably, in fact embarrassingly faithful, and had a curious knack of turning up in unexpected places. I did not find him a particular useful young man, but he added an element of interest by indulging in throaty prophecies about my future. He used to quote "*Quand tu seras bien vieille*" in impassioned but distinctly imperfect French. He produced so many pictures of my old age that I was prepared for one of them to turn out right. (I should remark that he appeared to find them deeply moving: he was, as you would expect, a little too fervent for my taste.)

'But now I am *bien vieille* – pity me, for it is the only tragedy, as you will discover, my dear. Now I am *bien vieille*, and none of that young man's absurd prognostications were anything like so undecorated as the truth. Really I did not expect this. It is a little much. I attribute it entirely to poor Muriel's unappreciated virtue.

'Imagine me listening to the opinions, confessions, and simple aspirations of your friend Rosalind. It seems to me the most improbable occupation for my declining years. Except when I am immobilized and kept in bed (which, I have a feeling, will happen more often in the next few months), I do little else. Your friend Rosalind appears to think that I am a sympathetic listener. I have pointed out the opposite, but she laughs indulgently and feels it is just my little way.

'I have never been an admirer of my own sex. Listening to this young woman, I reflect on such interesting themes as why men are so obtuse as to be taken in. Feminine delicacy? Refinement? Frailty? Fineness of feeling? I reflect also on poor Muriel and poor Joan. I have to grant them certain estimable but slightly unlovable qualities: should one, under the eye of eternity, really prefer them to this companion of mine? To which of them does one give the prize for womanhood? I have never been a confidante of your Roy, but I admit I should like his answer to that question.

'I have met very few people, even very few women, who are as singularly unmoral as this young woman. I have known many whose interest in morality was slightly detached: but this one scarcely seems to have heard of such a subject. I must admit that I find it engaging when she assumes the same of me. It has not taken her long to regard herself and me as sisters.

'By the way, it also did not take her long to become unimpressed by the battlements and other noble accessories. Including my poor Hugh. She rapidly recognized that she could reduce him to a state of gibbering admiration. They both get a good deal of innocent pleasure from their weekly bridge with the new vicar and his wife. I suspect they are happier because my less enthusiastic eye is removed. Possibly I am becoming slightly maudlin about the ironies of time; but I do feel it is unfitting that nowadays Hugh should be reduced to this one high event each week. He fidgets intolerably each Thursday evening, as we wait for the vicar and his wife. No one could call the vicar a deep thinker, and he has large red ears.'

All through that winter and spring, I was attending committees, preparing notes for the minister, reading memoranda, talking to Francis Getliffe and his scientific friends; for decisions were being taken about the bombing campaign, and we were all ranged for or against. In fact, all the people I knew best were dead against. My minister was one of the chief opponents in the government; through Francis, I had met nearly all the younger scientists, and they were as usual positive, definite, and scathing. They had learned a good deal about the effect of bombing, from the German raids; they worked

out what would be the results, if we persisted in the plan of bombing
at night. I read the most thorough of these 'appreciations'. I could not
follow the statistical arguments, but the conclusions were given as
proved beyond reasonable doubt: we should destroy a great many
houses, but do no other serious damage; the number of German
civilians killed would be relatively small; our losses in aircrew would
be a large proportion of all engaged; in terms of material effect,
the campaign could have no military significance at all. The minister
shook his head; he had seen too many follies; he was a sensible man,
but he did not believe in the victory of sense; and he knew that too
many in power had a passionate, almost mystical faith in bombing.
They were going to bomb, come what may; and naturally human
instruments arose who could fit in. Against the scientific arguments,
the advocates of bombing fell back on morale. There was something
the scientists could not speak about nor measure. The others said, as
though with inner knowledge, that the enemy would break under the
campaign.

I went to a committee where Francis Getliffe made one of the last
attempts to put the scientific case. Like most of his colleagues, Francis
had left the invention of weapons and, as the war went on, took to
something like the politics of scientific war. He was direct, ruthless,
and master of his job; he had great military sense; he had never
found any circumstances which gave him more scope, and he became
powerful in a very short time. But now he was risking his influence
in this war. Opponents of bombing were not in fashion. Bombing
was the orthodoxy of the day. As I observed it, it occurred to me that
you can get men to accept any orthodoxy, religious, political, even
this technical one, the last and oddest of the English orthodoxies;
the men who stood outside were very rare, and would always be so.

But Francis's integrity was absolute. He was pliable enough to bend
over little things; this was a very big thing. Someone ought to oppose it
to the end; he was the obvious person; he took it on himself to do it.

He was much the same that afternoon as he used to be at college
meetings – courteous, formal, clear, unshakably firm. He was high-
strung among those solid steady official men, but his confidence had
increased, and he was more certain of his case than they were. He
was impatient of less clever men: his voice had no give in it. But he
was very skilful at using his technical mastery.

He was setting out to prove the uneconomic bargain if we threw our resources into bombing. The amount of industrial effort invested in bombers was about twice what those same bombers would destroy. Bombing crews were first-class troops, said Francis Getliffe. Their training was very long, their physical and mental standard higher than any other body of troops. For every member of an air-crew killed, we might hope to kill three or four civilians. 'That's not business,' said Getliffe. 'It's not war. It doesn't begin to make sense.' He described what was then known of the German radar defences. Most of us round that table were ignorant of technical things. He made the principles of the German ground control limpidly clear. He analysed other factors in the probable rate of loss.

It was a convincing exposition. He was putting forward a purely military case. He was passionately engrossed in the war. He was out to win at any cost. He would not have minded bombing Germans, if it helped us to win. He would not have minded losing any number of aircrews, if we gained an advantage from their loss.

For me, his words struck cold. Roy would be back in this country by August. He would be flying in operations before the new year.

I had to fend off the chill. Someone had just admitted that their defences were a 'pretty bit of work'. I listened to the fierce argument in the smoky air; I was in attendance on the minister, and could not take part myself. The minister did his best, but his own stock was going down. As was inevitable, Francis Getliffe lost: he could not even get a few equipments diverted to the submarine war.

We went away together to have a drink.

'I'm on the way out,' said Francis Getliffe grimly. 'This is the best test of judgement there's ever been. Anyone who believes in this bloody nonsense will believe anything.'

From that day, the department in which I worked had to accept the decision. We did other things: but about a fifth of our time was spent on the bombing campaign. I found it irksome.

All that spring I was imprisoned in work, living in committee rooms, under the artificial light. I saw less still of my friends. I had an occasional lunch with Joan, and letters came from Boscastle. When I dined with Lady Muriel, she pronounced that the course of the pregnancy was satisfactory.

The child was born at midsummer. It was a girl, and was christened

Muriel. That fact moved Lady Boscastle to write to me, at her most characteristic. I chuckled, but thought it wise to burn the letter.

During those months, I heard a few times from Roy. He was not being a great success on his pilot's course. He was having to struggle to be allowed through; it irritated him, who liked to do things expertly, and I could not help smiling at that touch of vanity. He thought he would have done better ten years earlier; at thirty-two one did not learn so easily. In the end, he managed to pass, and landed in England in September.

After a week with Rosalind, he spent a night in my flat. He was sunburned and healthy; in uniform, his figure was less deceptive, one could have guessed that he was strong; at last his face was carrying the first lines, but he looked very tranquil. He was so tranquil that it was delightful to be with him. His spirits were not so intoxicatingly high as in his days of exaltation, but he laughed at me, talked about our friends, mimicked them with his features plastic, so that one saw a shadow of Lord Boscastle, of Arthur Brown, of Houston Eggar. We were happy. Since he had to return next day, we sat up most of the night. He seemed no longer driven.

He did not say much of his future – except that he would now be sent to his training in heavy aircraft. There was not much for either of us to say. But he talked of his daughter with extreme pleasure.

'It's good to have a child,' he said. 'It's a shame you haven't some, old boy. You'd like it, wouldn't you?'

'Of course.'

'You must soon. It's very important.'

His pleasure was simple, natural, radiant.

'She'll be pretty,' he said happily. 'Very pretty. Excellent.'

A month later, I received an unexpected telephone call from wife. I knew she was coming to London, for Lady Muriel had announced that her godchild was staying with her for a week-end and had invited me to dine; it was only during the course of the invitation that Lady Muriel reluctantly mentioned 'Roy's wife'. Rosalind's voice always sounded faint, falling-away, on the telephone, but that morning she seemed worried and urgent. 'I must see you at lunch time. No, it can't wait till tonight. I can't tell you in front of Lady Battleship.'

I put off an appointment and met her for lunch.

'I want you to help me, Lewis,' she said. 'Roy mustn't hear a word about it.'

She was dressed in the height of style, her shoulders padded, her hat tilted over one eye; but her expression was neither gamine nor mock-decorous, but tired, strained, intent. I jumped to a conclusion.

'What is wrong with him?'

'Nothing,' said Rosalind impatiently, as though I did not understand. 'He's very well and very happy. Didn't you think I should make him happy? The old thing has never been so comfortable in his life. He's got a bit of peace.'

She stared at me with hurt brown eyes, pleading and determined.

'Lewis, I want you to help me get him out of flying.'

'Does he want it?'

'Do you think he'd ever say so? Men never dare to confess that they're frightened. God's truth, I've got no patience with you all.'

She was desperately moved. I said:

'My dear, I think it would be impossible.'

'You'd rather let things happen than try,' she flared out like a cat.

'No. Remember he left an important job. He made a nuisance of himself to get out. It would be very hard to persuade the Air Ministry to leave go now.'

'Wouldn't he be more useful on the ground? How many people in the world speak all the languages he speaks?'

'That's true,' I said.

'Then we must get to work.'

'I'm afraid,' I said, 'that they won't leave go of a single man. They've been given complete priority.'

'Why are they so keen to keep them?' she cried. 'Because they're going to lose so many?'

'Yes.'

'They won't throw him away if I can help it.' Her face was dark and twisted, as if she were in physical pain. 'Let me tell you something. The other night I got him to talk a bit. I know he doesn't talk to me as he does to you. He says you're the only person who knows everything about him. But I got him to talk. It was in the middle of the night. He hasn't been sleeping too well this last week. It's not as bad as it used to be, but I know that he's been lying awake. Somehow I can't sleep if I think he's lying there with his eyes open.'

She paused. She was crying out with the intimacy of the flesh.

'The other night I knew he was awake. I hadn't been to sleep either. In the middle of the night I asked him if anything was the matter. He said no. I asked him if he was happy with me. He said yes. Then I got into his bed and cried till he promised to talk to me. He said it was a long story and that no one understood it all but you. You know how he speaks when he's being serious, Lewis? As though he was laughing and didn't give a damn. It makes my blasted heart turn over. Anyway he said that he'd been miserable for years. It was worse than being mad, he said. He hoped he'd get out of it. He'd struggled like a rat in a trap. But he couldn't escape. So he couldn't see any point in things. He might as well be eliminated. That was why he chose to fly.'

She stared at me.

'Then he kissed me, and laughed a bit. He said that nowadays it didn't always seem such a good idea. He was caught again. But he needn't worry this time, because there was nothing to do.'

I exclaimed.

'You know, Lewis,' Rosalind went on, 'he must have got it all worked out when he decided to fly. He said that he was looking round for the easiest way to disappear. He didn't want to give too much trouble. So he found out from someone reliable what was the most dangerous thing to do.'

She cried out sharply:

'What's the matter, Lewis? Why are you looking so terrible?'

'Nothing,' I said, trying to speak in an even tone. 'I just thought of something else.'

Rosalind watched me.

'I hope you're all right,' she said. 'I want you to help me today.'

CHAPTER 36

The End of a Reproach

ROSALIND had two lines of attack ready planned. She was cunning, she had not been successful at her business for nothing; she knew it was worse than useless for a move to come from Roy's friends. The only hope was to get hold of people of influence. She wanted two different kinds of plea: first, by the leading Orientalists, to say that as a scholar he was irreplaceable; second, by officials, to say that he was needed for a special job in an office. She was cunning but she did not know her way about this world; she needed me to tell her where to try.

She had no luck that afternoon. I sent her to old Foulkes, who was back in uniform again, a brigadier at the War Office. He had worked there seven days a week since the beginning of the war. I took her to the door in the side-street, and waited on the pavement. It was an hour before she came out. She was angry and downcast. 'I don't believe the old idiot has ever seen a woman before. Oh, I suppose he's rather sweet, but it's just my luck to find someone who's not susceptible.' Foulkes had told her that her husband had a European reputation. 'Tell anyone so. Often do. Only man to keep our end up.' Rosalind parodied Foulkes ill-temperedly. But Foulkes would not say a word that would stand in the way of a man who wanted to fight. He had heard his colleagues wonder why Calvert had thrown up a safe job. 'I've told them,' Foulkes had said, with his usual vigour. 'No mystery. No mystery at all. He just wants to fight for his country. Proud of him. So ought you to be,' he had finished at great speed.

There was no other scholar in reach that day; and the officials who might be useful had all gone home for the week-end. Rosalind was frustrated, aching for something to do; but I persuaded her there was nothing, at least for the moment, and she returned to Curzon Street for tea. When I saw her next, as I arrived there for dinner that same night, I noticed at once that she was more restless. She was savage in her concern.

I was surprised to see the table laid for four. I had expected that Joan would spare herself; but she had decided with tough, masochistic endurance, to stick it out, and meet Roy's wife and child. Both Joan and Lady Muriel agreed that it was a beautiful baby. I watched Joan nurse it with an envious satisfaction, a satisfaction that to my astonishment seemed stronger than envy. Her voice, like her mother's, was warm and loving when she spoke to it.

At dinner she was far more at her ease than Rosalind, who sat silent, dark-faced, going over her plans. Joan tried to cheer her up. I was not prepared for such magnanimity. And I was not prepared to hear Rosalind suddenly tell them that she intended to go to any lengths to get Roy out.

'Behind his back?' Lady Muriel inquired.

'It's the only way,' said Rosalind.

'I should consider that quite unsuitable, Mrs Calvert,' said Lady Muriel.

'You can't, Rosalind,' cried Joan. 'You can't do such a thing.'

'I may want you to introduce me to people,' said Rosalind to Lady Muriel.

'I couldn't think of it without Roy's permission,' said Lady Muriel, outraged, shocked to the core. 'I know he would not consider giving it. It would be unforgivable to go behind his back.'

Rosalind had not expected such opposition. She had wanted Lady Muriel as an ally. Now she was dejected, angry, hostile.

'If you were his wife,' she said, 'you wouldn't be so ready to do nothing.'

Joan put in:

'I know how you feel.' Her face was heavy: she spoke with deep emotion. 'We should all feel like that. It's awful to do nothing. But you've got to think of him.'

'I'm thinking of nothing else –'

'I mean in another way. He has made his choice, Rosalind. It wasn't an easy choice, surely you must know. It came out of all he's gone through. He hasn't had an easy life. You must leave him free. You can't presume to interfere with him. There are some parts of anyone's life – however much you love them – that you have to force yourself to leave alone.'

313

She was consumed with feeling. She leaned forward and asked Rosalind, in a quiet low tone:

'Do you deny for a moment that Roy would say the same?'

'Of course he'd say the same,' said Rosalind. 'He'd have to. He's too proud to do anything else. But –'

'He's not proud,' cried Joan. 'No one could possibly be less proud. This is so much deeper, it's part of him, surely you must see.' She hesitated, and then spoke sternly, almost harshly:

'Perhaps this will make you understand. You know that I loved him?'

'Yes.'

'I would go to him now if he called me. Well, if he had been mine – I should have done what I'm telling you to do. It would have been agony – it is agony enough now, don't you see? – but I should have left him alone.'

For a moment Rosalind was overawed by the passionate force of the other woman. Then Rosalind said:

'I've got to keep him alive.'

They looked at each other with dislike and misunderstanding. They would never understand each other. They knew him quite differently, I thought. Joan knew the struggle of his spirit, his melancholy, his tragic experience, better than any woman. Rosalind did not seem to know those at all. She paid no attention to the features which distinguished him among men. She knew him where he was like all other men – she took it for granted that, like all other men, he was frail, frightened, a liar to himself and her. She took him for granted as a creature of flesh and bone; whatever he said, whatever the dark moods, he longed to live.

Was that why he had married her? Had she given him a hope of the fibres, a hope of the press of life itself, stronger than any despair?

I caught sight of Lady Muriel, stiff-necked, troubled, heavy-footedly leading the conversation away. She was horrified. Perhaps until that moment she had not let herself recognize her daughter's love for Roy. Now it had been proclaimed in public: that was the final horror. Her sense of propriety was ravaged. It plucked away the screen behind which she had been trained to live. She gazed at her daughter with dismay, indignation – and an inarticulate pity.

Rosalind left London next day, and she did not confide her plan to me again. However, she sent me a note, saying that Roy had discovered what she was up to, and had stopped her. It was probably true, I thought, that he had found out. But I very much doubted whether it would stop her: she would merely take more care about her secrecy. For of us all she was the most singleminded. When she was set on a purpose, it was with every scrap of her body, cunning, and will.

Yet she did not bring it off. I was certain that she was not deterred by Roy's order. Probably she was only stopped by a more remote, abstract obstacle: it was next door to impossible to extract a trained pilot. I talked the whole affair over with the minister. He was the most adept of men at knowing when a door would give. He shook his head, and said it was too late.

After listening to Rosalind, I had to speak to Roy alone. He had borrowed a house in Cambridge for her and the baby; he was training on an East Anglian airfield, and it was long odds that he would be stationed on one the following spring; he could get back to Cambridge often. I wrote that I must see him; I would take an evening off: could he arrange to dine in hall one night?

When I arrived at the college, it was just before dinner time. Roy was waiting for me at the porter's lodge. He was wearing one of his old elegant suits, and had a gown thrown over his shoulder.

'My dear old boy,' he said.

We walked through the court. It was half past seven on an October night, and already dark. The lights at the foot of the staircases were very dim, and one could scarcely see the lists of names. Mine was still there, the white paint very faded; when we passed Roy's old staircase, we saw a new name where his had been.

'On the shelf,' said Roy.

The bell began to clang. Roy mentioned, as we went towards the combination room, that he had not dined in college since he returned. I asked him why not; he was frequently in Cambridge and still, of course, a fellow.

'Too much changed,' said Roy.

'It's not much changed,' I said.

'Of course it's not,' said Roy. 'I have, though.'

Sherry in the combination room: dinner in hall: they happened as they used to. It was a small party. Arthur Brown had discovered that

Roy and I were dining, had put himself down at short notice, and had asked Winslow to come in. Otherwise there was only Despard-Smith, gloomily presiding.

Much of the college was unchanged. Francis Getliffe, Roy, and I were away, as well as the new Master and the two most junior fellows; the others were all in residence. There had been a few of the secular changes which everyone reckoned on, as college officers came to the end of their span; Arthur Brown, for instance, was now Senior Tutor. Some of the old men were visibly older, and one noticed the process more acutely if one saw them, as I did, at longish intervals. Winslow was not yet seventy, but he was ageing fast. His mouth had sunken deeply since I last met him the year before; his polished rudeness was going also, and he was gentler, more subdued, altogether less conspicuous. His son had inflicted another disappointment on him, though not a dramatic one. Dick Winslow had not been able to get through his officer's training course, and had been returned to his unit; he was now a corporal in the Ordnance Corps, completely safe for the rest of the war. I should have liked a crack or two of old Winslow's blistering sarcasm. It was hard to see him resigned and defeated at last.

Despard-Smith showed no effect of time at all. He was seventy-six now, still spare, solemn, completely self-confident, self-righteous, expecting to get his own way by moral right. He was actually more certain of his command than we remembered him. Partly because it was harder to get spirits, which at one time he drank heavily, alone in his dark rooms: partly because the young men had gone away, and there was a good deal of executive work about the college for anyone who volunteered, Despard-Smith had taken on some of the steward's work, which Francis Getliffe had left. It was a new lease of power. The servants were grumbling but the old man issued per-nickety instructions, went into nagging detail, just as in his prime: he was able to complain with a croaking, gloating satisfaction, that he had 'to bear the heat and burden of the day'.

He greeted Roy and me with his usual bleak courtesy. Winslow's face lit up as he shook hands with Roy: 'Good evening to you, young man. May I sit next to you?'

Not much had changed, except through the passage of time. But the conversation in hall was distinctly odd. Arthur Brown, the good-natured, kind, and clubbable, had developed a passion for military detail. In his solid conservative fashion, he was as engrossed in the war as Francis Getliffe. He believed – with a passion that surprised those who took him at his face value – in 'killing Germans'. With bellicose interest, he wanted to hear about Roy's training.

Roy was going through his first practice flights at night. He said simply that he hated it.

'Why?' said Arthur Brown.

'It's dreadful, flying at night. Dark. Cold. Lonely. And you lose your way.'

It was the last phrase which made Arthur Brown frown. He interrupted Roy. He just could not believe it. Hadn't our aeroplanes got to learn to attack individual factories? Roy replied, that up to six months ago they had done well to get to the right country. Brown was angry: what was all this he had heard about factories going up in sheets of flame? And all this about pin-pointing targets? He regarded all those reports as too well established to doubt. I joined in on Roy's side. Arthur Brown was discomfited, out of humour with both of us, still not convinced. For a man so shrewd in his own world, he was curiously credulous about official news. (I remembered Schäder's remarks on how propaganda convinced everybody in time.) Here were Roy and I, his protégés and close friends: he loved us and trusted us: he realized that we both knew the facts, Roy in the flesh, I on paper: yet he found it hard to believe us, against the official news of *The Times* and the BBC.

But he smiled again, benignly, enjoying the treat he had prepared for us, as soon as we got back into the combination room. Two decanters stood ready on the table, one of port, one of claret. In front of them was a basket of silver wicker-work, full of walnuts.

'They're a bit special,' said Arthur Brown, as he confided in a discreet whisper what the two wines were. 'I'm going to ask for the pleasure of presenting them. I thought they'd be rather bracing on a foggy night. It's splendid to have the two of you back at once.'

We filled our glasses. The crack of the nuts was a cheerful noise. It was a night in that room such as we had often known in other autumns. There were wisps of mist in the courts, and the leaves were falling from the walls. Here it was warm; the rich curtains glowed placidly, the glasses gleamed; even though one liked claret better than port, perhaps one could do no better than drink port with the nuts.

Arthur Brown smiled at Roy. Despard-Smith expressed thanks in a grating voice, cracked more nuts than any of us, rang the bell and asked why salt had not been served. He finished his first glass of port before the decanter had come round to him again.

We talked as we had talked in other autumns. The Master of another college had died suddenly, whom would they elect? We produced some names in turn. Despard-Smith rejected all of ours solemnly and disapprovingly. One: 'I have heard things against him.' Another: 'That would be catastrophic, Eliot. The man's no better than a bolshevik.' A third (whose wife had deserted him twenty years before): 'I should not think his college would be easy about his private life. They ought not to take the risk of electing someone unstable. It might bring the place down round their ears.'

Then he made his own suggestion.

'Isn't he extremely stuffed?' said Roy lightly.

Despard-Smith looked puzzled, deaf, and condemnatory.

'*Stuffed*,' Roy repeated.

'I'm afraid I don't know what you mean, Calvert. He's a very sound man. He's not a showman, but he's sacrificed himself for his college.'

Once, I thought, Roy would have followed up with mystifying questions. But he sat back, smiled, drank his wine, and played no trick. By now Despard-Smith had got into his stride. He was, in the Master's absence, acting as chairman of the livings committee. It happened that the college's best living was still vacant. The last incumbent had gone off to become an archdeacon. The committee, which for the moment meant Despard-Smith, could not make up its mind. In reality, the old man could not bear to bestow so desirable a prize. Most of the college livings were worth four or five hundred a year, since they had not risen as the value of money fell; but this one was nearly two thousand. In the nineteenth century it had meant riches, and there had been some resolute jockeying on the part of fellows to secure it in time for their marriage. It was then, and still remained, one of the richer livings of the Church of England. Even now, it would give some clergyman a comfortable middle-class life.

'It's a heavy responsibility,' said Despard-Smith. He began to run through all the old members of the college who were in orders. He disapproved of all of them, except one or two who, for different reasons, could not be offered this living. One man had the month before taken one at three hundred and fifty a year. 'It would be no kindness to him,' said Despard-Smith, 'to go so far as mention this vacancy. He is a man of conscience, and he would not want to leave a charge he has just undertaken.'

Brown pleaded this man's cause. 'It's wretched luck,' he said. 'Can't we find a way round? I should regard it as legitimate to put in someone for a decent interval, say a year or two —'

'I'm afraid that would be a scandalous dereliction of duty,' said Despard-Smith. No one ever got more relish out of moral judgements. No one was more certain of them.

Winslow drank another glass of claret, and took no part. He used, in his style as a nineteenth-century unbeliever, to make caustic interjections on 'appointments in this mysterious profession'. He used to point out vinegarishly that he had not once attended chapel. Now he had not the heart for satire.

Despard-Smith looked at Roy with gloomy satisfaction.

'I seem to remember that Udal was a friend of yours, Calvert. He was your exact contemporary, if I'm not mistaken.'

'Just so,' said Roy.

'I needn't say that we have carefully considered whether we could invite him to take Melton. He is a man of higher intellectual quality than we are accustomed to get in the Church in its present disastrous condition. We have given Udal's name the most careful consideration, Calvert. I am very sorry to say that we don't feel able to approach him. It would only do him harm to give him exceptional promotion at his age. I was very sorry, but naturally we were thinking entirely of the man himself.'

Roy was looking at him with bright, piercing, steady eyes.

'You must not say that, Despard,' said Roy, in a clear and deliberate tone. 'It is not so.'

'What do you mean, Calvert?' said Despard-Smith, with grating anger.

'I mean that you've not thought of Udal at all. You don't know him. He is a very difficult man to know. You have no idea what is best for him. And you do not care. You must not say these things.'

'I'm not prepared to listen,' Despard-Smith was choking. 'Scandalous to think that my responsibility –'

Roy's eyes were fixed on the old clergyman's, which were bleared, full, inflamed.

'You like your responsibility,' said Roy. 'You like power very much. You must not disguise things so much, Despard. You must not pretend.'

Roy had spoken throughout calmly, simply, and with extreme authority. It was exactly – I suddenly remembered – as he had spoken to Willy Romantowski; he had even used the same words. I had seen him with many kinds of human beings, in many circumstances: those two, the old clergyman and the young blackmailing spy, were the only ones I had ever heard him judge.

Arthur Brown hurriedly filled Despard-Smith's glass. I thought there was a faint appreciative twinkle under Winslow's hooded lids. The party got back to ordinary small-talk. That room was used to hard words. The convention was strong that, after a quarrel, the room made an attempt at superficial peace.

So, for a few minutes, we did now. Then we broke up, and Arthur Brown took Roy and me to his rooms. He finished off his treat for us by giving us glasses of his best brandy.

Then he settled himself down to give a warning.

'I must say,' he scolded Roy, 'that I wish you hadn't gone for old Despard. I know he's maddening. But he'll stick about in this college for a long time yet, you know, and he still might be able to put a spoke in your wheel. There's no point in making an unnecessary enemy. I wish you'd wait till you've absolutely arrived.'

'No, Arthur.' Roy smiled. 'We wait too long, you know. There isn't so much time.'

'I expect you think I'm a cautious old woman,' said Arthur Brown, 'but I'm only anxious to see you getting all the honours this place can give you. I am anxious to have that happiness before I die.'

'I know, Arthur,' said Roy. 'But I shall need to say a word now and then.'

He said it with affection and gratitude, to the man who had guarded his career with such unselfishness and so much worldly skill. But he meant more than he said. He meant that his pupilage was quite over. He was mature now. He had learned from his life.

For the rest of his time, he would know what mattered to him, whom and what to take risks for, and when to speak.

Roy took another brandy, and set Arthur Brown talking about his water colours. Roy was in no hurry to be left alone with me; he had sensed what I had come to ask, and was avoiding it. Brown liked staying with us, and it was reluctantly that he pressed our hands, said how splendid it would be when we both returned for good, promised to save 'something special' to celebrate the occasion.

Roy and I went up to my sitting-room. It struck dank through being empty for so long; there was a low smouldering fire, built up of slack.

'The old devil,' said Roy, grinning at the thought of Bidwell: since I went away, my rooms were being slowly and methodically stripped of their smaller objects.

I pulled down the old iron draught-screen to its lowest socket. Soon the flames began to roar. Roy pushed the sofa in front of the fireplace, and lay with his legs crossed, his hands behind his head.

I sat in my armchair. Those had been our habitual places in that room. I looked at him, and said:

'I want to talk a little.'

'Better leave it,' he said. 'Much better to leave it,' he repeated insistently.

'No,' I said. 'I must know.'

'Just so,' said Roy.

'I didn't say much when you chose to –'

I hesitated, and Roy said, in a light, quiet tone:

'Try to get myself killed.'

'It was too clear,' I said.

'I got tired of struggling,' he said. 'I thought it was time for me to resign.'

'I knew that,' I said. 'I hadn't the heart to speak.'

'I told you once,' he said with desperate feeling, 'you'd done all you could. Believe me. No one on earth could have done as much.'

I shook my head.

'I was no use to you in the end,' I said.

'Everyone is alone. Dreadfully alone,' said Roy. 'You've thought that often enough, haven't you? One hates it. But it's true.'

'Sometimes,' I said, in pain, 'it does not seem so true.'

'Often,' Roy repeated, 'it does not seem so true.'

Suddenly he smiled brilliantly. 'I'm not as tough as you. Sometimes it wasn't true. I've not been alone always. You may have been – but I've not.'

I could not smile back.

'I hadn't the heart to speak,' I said slowly. 'It was too clear what had happened to you. But I didn't understand one thing. Why did you make that particular choice? Why did you decide to go and fly?'

With one quick move he sat upright. His eyes met mine, but they were troubled, distraught, almost – shifty.

He was for once not ready with a word.

'Was it,' I said, 'because of that night in Dolphin Square? When you asked me what was the most dangerous thing to do?'

'Oh God,' said Roy, 'that was why I kept it from you. I was afraid you'd guess. I didn't want you to learn from other people. But if I'd told you myself what I was doing, I should have given it away. You'd have remembered that night.'

'I remember it now,' I said.

'It was only a chance,' he said violently. 'We happened to be talking. If I hadn't seen you that night, I should have asked someone else. We happened to be talking, that was all.'

'What I said – decided you?'

'Yes.'

'You might have spared me that,' I cried.

We looked at each other; quite suddenly, reproach, remorse, guilt, all died away; the moment could hold them no more. There was no room for anything but the understanding which had sustained us for so long. We had the comfort of absolute acceptance.

In a tone that was simple and natural, Roy said:

'I wasn't mad when I decided to resign, you know. I couldn't struggle any more, but I wasn't a bit mad. Did you think I should be?'

'I wasn't sure,' I said, just as easily.

'I thought you might feel that I did it when I was lashing out. As I did with poor old Winslow once. No, it wasn't so. I haven't had one of those fits for quite a long time. But I'd been depressed for years. Until I threw in my hand. I was sad enough when you saw me, wasn't I? I was much worse when you weren't there. It was dreadful, Lewis.'

'I knew,' I said.

'Of course you did. I was quite lucid, though. All the time. Just like that night in May week. When I threw in my hand, I was frightfully lucid. Perhaps if everyone were as lucid as that, they would throw in their hand too.' He smiled at me. 'I've always felt you covered your eyes at the last minute. Otherwise why should you go on?'

It was half-envious, half-ironic: it was so intimate that it lit our faces: with magic, it lit up the room.

'You'll always have a bit of idiot hope, won't you?' said Roy. 'I'm glad that you always will.'

'Sometimes I think you have,' I said. 'Deeper than any of your thoughts.'

Roy smiled.

'It's inconvenient – if I have it now.'

He went on:

'What would have happened to me, Lewis, if there hadn't been a war? I don't know. I believe it wouldn't have made much difference. I should have come to a bad end.'

He smiled again, and said:

'It makes things a bit sharper, that's all. One can't change one's mind. It holds one to it. That's all.'

The fire had flared up now, and his face was rosy in the glow. The shadows exaggerated his smile. We talked on, so attuned that each word resounded in the other's heart. And at the same moment that I felt closer to him than I had ever done, I was seized and shaken by the most passionate sense of his nature, his life, his fate. It was a sense which shook me with resentment, fear, and pity, with horror and unassuageable anxiety, with wonder, illumination, and love. I accepted his nature with absolute gratitude; but I could not accept how fate had played with him and caught him. While I delighted in our talk that night, I cried to myself with the bitterness of pity; to know him was one of the two greatest gifts of my life; and yet it was anguish to see how his life had brought him to this point.

He had once said, just before the only flaw in our intimacy, that I believed in predestination. It was not true in full, though it was true as he meant it. I believed that neither he nor any of us could alter the essence of our nature, with which we had been born. I believed that he would not have been able to escape for good from the melancholy, the depth of despondency, the uncontrollable flashes and the brilliant calm, the light and dark of his nature. That was his endowment. Despite his courage, the efforts of his will, his passionate vitality, he could not get rid of that burden. He was born to struggle, to pursue false hopes, to know despair – to know what, for one of his nature, was an intolerable despair. For, with the darkness on his mind, he could not avoid seeing himself as he was, with all hope and pretence gone.

Most men are saved from that tragic suffering. Nothing could have saved him. Knowing him – as I realized on that walk by the Serpentine years before – I was bound to watch him go through his journey, sometimes hopeful, sometimes tormented, often both together, until in the white and ruthless light of self-knowledge, he perceived himself.

So far, I believed in what he called 'predestination'. I believed that some parts of our endowment are too heavy to shift. The essence of our nature lay within us, untouchable by our own hands or any other's, by any chance of things or persons, from the cradle to the grave. But what it drove us to in action, the actual events of our lives – those were affected by a million things, by sheer chance, by the interaction of others, by the choice of our own will. So between essence and chance and will, Roy had, like the rest of us, to live his life.

It was the interplay of those three that had brought him to that moment in my room, smiling, talking of his 'bad end'. They had brought him to his present situation. I felt the delight of our intimacy – and from his situation I shrank back in anguish and appalled.

For it could have happened otherwise. In any case, perhaps, he would have known despair so black that he would have been driven to 'throw in his hand', he would have felt it was time to 'resign'. That was what he meant by a 'bad end'. If we had been born in a different time, when the outside world was not so violent, it was easy to imagine ways along which he might have gone. He might not have been driven into physical danger: he might have tried to lose himself in exile or the lower depths.

But that was not his luck. He had had to make his choice in the middle of a war. And war, as he said, 'held one to it'. It made his choice one of life and death. It was irrevocable. It gave no time for the obstinate hope of the fibres, which underlay even his dark vision of the mortal state, to collect itself, steady him, and help him to struggle on.

And I felt that hope was gathering in him now. Through his marriage, through his child, perhaps ironically through the very fact that he had 'resigned' and needed to trouble no more, he had come out of the dark. Perhaps he had married Rosalind because he did not trouble any more; it was good for him not to care. He was more content than he had been since his youth. Hope was pulsing within him, the hope which is close to the body and part of the body's life, the hope that one possesses just because one is alive.

He was going into great danger. He said that it was 'inconvenient' to hope now. The mood in which he had made his choice should have lasted. But he was not to be spared that final trick of fate. He was to go into danger: but his love of life was not so low; it was mounting with each day that passed.

He was smiling, happy that we should be enjoying this evening together by my fire. Each second, each sound, seemed extraordinarily distinct. I was happy with him – and yet I did not want to see, I wished my eyes were closed, I could not bear the brightness of the room.

CHAPTER 37

Mist in the Park

ROY began to fly on bombing raids in the January of 1943. From that time, he came to see me regularly once a fortnight; it was his device for trying to ease my mind. He could come to London to visit me more easily than I could get away. He had far more leisure, which seemed a joke at my expense. His life had become strangely free; mine was confined; I did not so much as see a bombing aerodrome through the whole length of the war.

When we met, Roy kept nothing from me. Sometimes I thought of the days, long before, when we sat by the bedside of the old Master. He had known he must soon die for certain; the end was fixed; and, for me at least, it was more terrible because he talked only of his visitors' concerns – he, who lay there having learnt the date of his death.

Roy knew me too well to do the same. He was more natural and spontaneous than the old Master; he took it for granted that I was strained, that he was strained himself; he left it to instinct to make it bearable for us both. And, of course, there was one profound difference between his condition and the old Master's; Roy did not know for certain whether he would live or die.

As a rule, he called at my office in the afternoon and stayed with me until he caught a train at night. In that office he looked down into Whitehall, and told me simply that he was getting more frightened. He told me of his different kinds of fear: of how one wanted to stop short, throw the bombs away, and run for home. He smiled at me.

'It's peculiarly indecent for me to bomb Stuttgart, isn't it? Me of all men.' (He had worked in the library there.)

I nodded.

'They'll want me to bomb Berlin soon. Think of that.'

Then he said:

'But you don't believe in bombing anyway, do you?'

'No,' I said.

'You don't think it's any use? It won't win the war?'

'I don't believe so.'

'You're pretty sure?'

'Reasonably.'

'What does he think?' Roy pointed to the door which led through to the Minister's room.

'The same.'

'Just so,' said Roy. 'He's a wise old bird. So are you, aren't you?'

He smiled brilliantly, innocently, laughing at himself and me. He said:

'There's never been a place for me, has there?'

On those afternoons I heard something about his crew. He had become interested in them, realistically, affectionately, with amusement, just as with everyone he met, just as with the inmates of No. 32 Knesebeckstrasse. They were nearly all boys, and the oldest was twenty-six, seven years younger than himself. 'I'm getting too old for this game,' said Roy. There was a Canadian among them. Most of them were abnormally inarticulate, and Roy mimicked them to me. Some were extremely brave. 'Too brave for me,' he said.

I often speculated about what they thought of him. So far as I could gather, they did not consider him academic, donnish, or learned; it had always surprised people to discover his occupation. But they also did not think him intelligent or amusing. They liked him, they respected him as a pilot, and thought he was a kind, slightly eccentric old thing. I suspected he had gone in for some deliberate dissimulation – partly to stay anonymous, partly to shield them from what he was really like. For instance, they certainly did not know that he was a notorious lover of women. They just placed him as an uxorious married man, devoted to his daughter and inclined to show them photographs of his wife and baby.

He told me that with a smile. It was often, I reflected, odd enough to send a shiver down the spine, when one heard a friend described by other people.

It was as though each of us went about speaking a private language which no one else could understand; yet everyone caught a few words, uttered a cheerful, confident, dismissive judgement, and passed on. It reminded me of the fellows discussing Roy before he was elected. If one heard people talking confidently of another's character one realized once for all that human beings were inescapably alone.

Actually, the opinions formed by Roy's crew were quite explicable. He was devoted to the child, with a strength of feeling that at times astonished me. And he was content and comfortable with Rosalind.

During one of his visits to my office, both he and I were set to write letters that were difficult to put together. For I had heard from Joan the day before that Humphrey Bevill had just died in hospital. He had been decorated again for one of the small boat actions; then, a week or so past, his boat had been sunk and he had spent some hours in the water. His fantastic courage was a courage of the nerves, and he was as frail as he looked. He had died from exposure and loss of blood, when a normally tough young man would have recovered.

'Poor boy,' said Roy. 'It must have been dreadful to go out and fight – and then come back in an hour or two. Everything clean and normal. It makes it much harder.'

He said that he felt it acutely himself. In the daytime he would be at home in peace, all tranquil. At night they would be flying out in fear. Next morning he came back home again. It would have been easier if all his life were abnormal, disturbed, spent nearer the dark and cold. It would have been easier in trenches in a foreign country. Here the hours of danger were placed violently side by side with days of clean sheets, in familiar rooms with one's child, one's wife, and friends.

'Poor boy,' said Roy. 'He couldn't have had a happy life, could he?'

We each wrote separate letters to Lord and Lady Boscastle.

'It's hard to write,' said Roy. 'It will break up Lord B. It's a mistake to be fond of people. One suffers too much.'

We had no doubt that Lord Boscastle would be terribly afflicted, but even so we were amazed by the manner of his grief. I heard of it from Lady Boscastle, who wrote in reply to my letter of condolence. Herself, she was taking bereavement with her immaculate stoicism – but she seemed overborne, almost stunned, by her husband's passion of inconsolable misery. He shut himself up in Boscastle, would acknowledge no letters, not even from his family, would see no one except his servant. He had only spoken once to his wife since he heard of Humphrey's death. It was a rage of misery, misery that was like madness, that made him in sheer ferocity of pain shut himself away from every human touch.

Lady Boscastle was out of her depth. She would have liked to help him; yet, for once in her life, she felt ignorant and inept. She had never been possessed as he was now; for all her adventures, she had never been overmastered by an emotion; she had never abandoned herself to love, as her husband did, with all the wildness of his nature, first in love for her and then for his son. She could not meet such a passion on equal terms. For the first time in their marriage, she was not mistress of the situation.

When Roy next came to see me, it was a warm, sunny day at the end of February; the other side of Whitehall was gilded by the soft, misty, golden light.

I told Roy about Lady Boscastle's letter.

'She's too cold,' he said. He had never liked her as I did, though he felt a kind of reluctant, sparring admiration. 'She'll survive. But he'll live with the dead.'

Roy looked at me, and spoke with extreme gentleness and authority:

'You mustn't live with the dead too much. You could.'

He had seen me live on after my wife's death; he was the only person who had seen me close to.

'If you lose me as well,' said Roy, 'you mustn't mourn too long. You mustn't let it haunt you. You must go on.'

He was pale, quiet, burdened that afternoon. He and his crew had moved a few days before to another aerodrome. 'They don't want us to see our losses. They need to keep us cheerful,' he said.

He went on:

'If we started with thirty aeroplanes' (he never used the current terms, but always with great precision brought out the outmoded ones, such as 'aeroplanes') 'and we notice that two don't come back each night, they think we mightn't like it much. Because we've got to make thirty trips before they give us a rest. Even if the losses are only five per cent – we might start working out our chances. They're not good, are they?'

It was such a beautiful afternoon that we went for a walk in St James's Park. The sky was a light, radiant blue; but, although it was only early afternoon, a mist was creeping on to the brilliant grass.

'Excellent,' said Roy. 'I like to see that.'

I misunderstood him.

'It is a lovely day,' I said.

'Not so aesthetic,' said Roy. 'I meant – as long as this weather lasts, we shan't have to fly.'

He walked by my side, over the soft winter turf.

'Some nights,' he said in a moment, 'I'm pretty certain that I'm not coming back. I want to ask them to let me stay at home. I need to be safe. I feel like saying that I can't go through it once again. Those nights, I feel certain that I'm going to die.'

He added:

'Somehow I've come back, though.'

We walked along through the calm, warm, fragrant air. Roy turned to me, his face quite open.

'Dear old boy, I am afraid, you know,' he said. 'I am afraid of my death.'

CHAPTER 38

An Evening without Incident

ON Roy's next visit, nothing of importance happened; he said nothing which struck me at the time; it was a placid evening, but I came to remember it in detail.

He was shown into my office about half past two on a Saturday afternoon. I should not have been there, but I was preparing a draft for the Minister. Roy saw that I was writing, cocked an eyebrow, and with exaggerated punctiliousness would not come round my side of the desk.

'Too secret,' he said.

'No. Just a speech.'

Roy was light-hearted, and his mood infected me. He had the next four days free, and when he left me that evening was going on to Cambridge. He was so calm and light that I could not stay in a grey, ordinary, workaday mood. I had nearly finished the speech, but I recalled that the Minister had one or two idioms which he always got wrong: 'they can't pull the wool over my ears', he used to say with great shrewdness. I was fond of him: it occurred to me that those idioms should be inserted in the speech. I told Roy what I was doing.

'I thought you'd become much too responsible.' He smiled with cheerful malice. 'Remarkable occupation for a high Civil Servant. You should model yourself on Houston Eggar. I'm afraid you'll never catch him up.'

When we went down into the street, Roy said that he needed some books for the next four days. So we took a bus, cut down Charles II Street, and reached the London Library before it closed. Roy bent over a rack of recent books; his nose looked inquisitively long, since the peak of his cap cut off his forehead. He talked about one or two of the books. 'Very old-brandy,' he murmured. Then suddenly, with an expression serious and concerned, he pointed to a title. He was pointing to a single word – FISH. 'Lewis,' he said, in a clear, audible tone, 'I'm losing my grip. I've forgotten the Soghdian for fish.' He looked up, and saw a member, fat, stately, in black hat and fur-lined overcoat, walking out with books under his arm. 'I wonder if he knows,' said Roy. 'I need to ask him.'

Roy stepped lightly in front of the fat man, and gave him a smart salute.

'Excuse me, sir,' he said, 'but I have forgotten the Soghdian for fish. Can you help me?'

'The what?'

'Soghdian.'

'I'm afraid not.'

'One ought to keep one's languages up,' said Roy: his gaze was solemn, reproving, understanding. 'It's terrible how one forgets them. Isn't it?'

Hypnotized, the member agreed that it was. Roy let him go.

On the bus to Dolphin Square, the word returned to Roy. He professed extreme relief. The bus racketed and swayed round the corner by Victoria. Roy said, calm and matter-of-fact:

'If I live, I shall go back to the Soghdian, you know. I may as well.'

'I think you should,' I said.

'I shall become extremely eminent. And remarkably rude. '

'I wish you'd study that whole Central Asian civilization. It must be very interesting – how did it keep alive? and why did it die?'

'You always wanted me to turn into a journalist,' said Roy. 'I'm too old to change now. I shall stick to something nice and sharp.'

In my flat, we made a kind of high tea, since Roy was catching a train just after seven. But it was a high tea composed of things we had not eaten for a long time. I had a small hoard of foods that once we ate and did not know how good they were – butter, strawberry jam, a few eggs. We had bought a loaf of bread on our way; we boiled a couple of eggs each, and finished with several rounds of bread and butter and jam.

'Excellent,' said Roy. 'This is good stuff.'

We had eaten well together in many places, but it was a delectable meal. Afterwards, we made another pot of tea; Roy lay on the sofa, smoked a cigarette, asked me about my love affair.

For I had fallen in love in the middle of the war. It had given me

days of supernatural brilliance among the pain, anxiety, and darkness.
For hours together, I had been ecstatically happy and blind to everything else.

'You should let me vet them,' said Roy. 'I still don't like the sound of her.'

'She wouldn't do for you,' I said.

'You like women who wouldn't do for anyone, old boy. Such as Lady B.'

'Life wouldn't have been dull,' I said, 'with Lady B.'

Roy smiled mockingly, protectively.

'You've not tired yourself out, have you?' he said. 'So much has happened to you – and yet you still don't need life to be dull.'

He teased me, gave me advice, made me promise to arrange a dinner with both him and the young woman. Once I turned and caught him watching me, a half-smile on his lips, his eyes intent.

Then he said:

'We haven't had a walk for a long time, have we? Walk with me to the station.'

It was several miles, but I was glad to. We were both active that day. As soon as we got into the open air, we felt the prick of a Scotch mist, almost a drizzle. I asked if he minded about his buttons.

'Never mind them,' he said. 'Rosalind will clean them tomorrow. She likes to.'

The drizzle persisted, but the moon was getting up behind the clouds, and the last of the daylight had not quite faded. Along the embankment to Westminster it was not oppressively dark; the derelict houses of Millbank stood blacker than the sky, and on our right there was a sheen upon the water. The tide was running full, and brought a smell from the sea.

'It's a good night,' said Roy.

We left the river at Westminster, strolled down Whitehall, and then went back to the Embankment as far as Blackfriars Bridge. Trams clanked past us, sparks flashing in the dusk. Now and then a torch shone a beam on the wet road. Roy recalled jokes against us both, predicaments we had run into when we were younger, the various attempts to domesticate us.

'They got me at last,' he said. 'They got me at last.'

He talked fondly of his daughter.

'I wonder what she'll be like,' he said. 'She won't be stupid, wil she?'

I smiled.

'I hope not,' said Roy. 'I've got a feeling she'll be anxious to please. If so, there'll be trouble for someone.'

He took my arm, and went on in a light, clear, definite tone:

'They mustn't teach her too much. They mustn't teach her to hold herself in. I'd like her to be easy. She's my daughter. She'll find the dark things for herself.'

Arm-in-arm, we went up Ludgate Hill towards St Paul's. Roy was talking with affection tender and disrespectful, about one who 'held herself in' – Lady Muriel. She must not be let loose on her god-child; he teased me about all her efforts to make me respectable in a way fitting to my station.

'Yet you dote on her,' I said.

'Ah, she needs so much love.'

'And Joan?'

He never laughed much about Joan. Of all the people we knew intimately, she was the only one he never mimicked. Even that evening, when he was so free, when his feelings flowed like quick-silver, he paused.

'And Joan?' I repeated.

'She needs more still,' said Roy.

We passed the cathedral; the rain was pattering down, but by now the invisible moon was high enough to lighten the sky, so that we could see the waste land close by; we stopped on the city side, near what used to be Bread Street, and gazed at the empty expanse under the gentle rain.

'Not pretty,' said Roy.

'No,' I said.

Then we discovered that we had cut it fine, if he were to catch his train. We walked fast the rest of the way to Liverpool Street. 'Good for you,' said Roy, as he made the pace with a light step.

He was smiling as we entered the station. 'I'll send you a book,' he said, with a flick in his voice, as though he were playing an obscure joke.

He had only two minutes to spare. The train was at the platform, the carriage doors were being shut, men were standing in the corridors. Roy ran towards it, waving back at me. He was the most graceful of men – but I thought then, as I used when he ran up to bowl, how he suddenly ceased to be so as he ran. His running stride was springy and loose but had a curious, comic, rabbit-like lollop. He got a place in the corridor and waved again: I was smiling at the picture of him on the run.

CHAPTER 39

Grief

THE following Friday afternoon, I was in my office reading through a file. The telephone bell rang: it was a trunk call. There were mutters, faint sounds at the other end – then Arthur Brown's rich, steady, measured voice.

'Is that you, Eliot?'

'Yes.'

'I have bad news for you, old chap.'

'Yes.'

It did not need saying, but the kind, steady, deliberate voice went on:

'Roy Calvert is missing from last night. His wife has just been in. I'll see that she is properly looked after. She's taking it very sturdily.'

'Thank you, Arthur.'

'I'm more sorry than I can say. I suppose there is a little hope, but I cannot hold it out to you.'

I did not reply. I could not reply. I had been swept by the first paralysing shock of death.

'If he is dead,' Arthur Brown's voice came firmly, 'we have lost someone who will never be replaced.'

For nights I could not sleep – or when I did, awoke from nightmares that tormented me as Roy's had once tormented him. I thought of his nightmares, to get away for a second from my own. For mine, in those first nights, were intolerable with the physical imagination of his death. Sleeping or waking, I was lapped by waves of horror. A word would bring him back – 'stuffed' or 'Welsh' or often one that was not his special use – and I could not shut out the terrifying pictures of the imagination: the darkness, the face in the fire, the moments of unendurable anguish and fear, the face in the fire, the intolerable agony of such a death.

Nothing could guard me from that horror. It was impossible to harden oneself to such a death.

While that physical dread swept over me night and day (sometimes

336

another pain attacked me: the night he died, I was dining happily with friends at Claridges), I could not bear to see anyone who wanted to give me hope. I could not bear to see anyone who knew him. I got through my committees somehow. I did my work. For the rest, I went about alone, or searched for company. Any company that would not bring him back.

This was the second time I had known intense grief through death. I could understand well enough the mad, frantic, obsessed concentration on his grief into which Lord Boscastle threw himself after the death of his son. I could understand well enough how some in grief squandered themselves in orgies.

After a fortnight of those days and nights, the first shock lessened. I had still spoken to no one about him, though I had managed to write a note to Rosalind. I was not ready for it yet. But I found myself searching for recollections of him. Time after time, I went over each detail of that last evening: it had seemed so light and casual when it happened, far less significant than a hundred other times we had talked together. Now I knew it off by heart. I kept asking myself questions to which there could never be an answer: just because of that they were sharp as a wound. What was the book that I should never receive? When he talked of his daughter, was he giving me instructions? Did he fear that this was his last chance to do so? Had he been fey that evening? Was he acting so lightly, to give me peace?

Then came the final news that he was dead. It was not an added shock. It meant only that I could indulge myself no longer. It was time to see others who were stricken. I would have avoided it if there had been a way: there was nothing for it but to go among them, and listen.

I sat through a night in Curzon Street with Lady Muriel and Joan. Joan was prostrate and speechless, her face brooding, white, so still that it seemed the muscles were frozen. Of those who loved him, perhaps she suffered most. Lady Muriel was like a rock. In the first shriek of pain, her daughter had told her everything about her love for Roy. Lady Muriel had forgotten propriety, had forgotten control, and had tried to comfort her. Lady Muriel had never been able to speak from her own heart; she had never seen into another's; but when one of her children came to her in manifest agony, she lavished

on them all her dumb, clumsy, overpowering affection. It was better
for Joan than any subtler sympathy. For the first time since her
childhood, she depended on her mother. She gained a deep, primitive
consolation. Like all of us, she had laughed at Lady Muriel; she had
produced for Roy's benefit some of the absurdities, the grotesque
snobberies, the feats of misunderstanding, which Lady Muriel in-
corribly perpetrated; but after she was driven to tell her mother
how she suffered, Joan felt again that Lady Muriel was larger than life
and that her heart was warm.

I thought that, of the two, Lady Muriel would be more crippled.
For Joan was very strong; she had not a happy nature, but underneath there was a fierce, tough vitality as unquenchable as her
mother's; and she was still young. She would never be quite the same
through knowing Roy – but I believed she was resilient enough to
love again with all her heart.

It would not be so for Lady Muriel. It had taken an unusual man
to tease her, to see that she was not formidable, to make her crow
with delight. To find a friend like Roy – so clear-sighted, so utterly
undeceived by exterior harshness – was a chance which would not
come again. With age, disaster, and loss, she was becoming on the
outside more gruff and unbending. She would put everyone off,
more completely than in the past. It would only be Joan who came
close to her. Yet that night, her neck was stiff, her head upright, as
she said good-bye in the old formula.

'Good evening, Mr – Lewis. It was good of you to come and
see us.'

I went to see Rosalind in Cambridge. She had hoped right up to
the end. She had seemed callous and thoughtless to many people;
but I noticed that, in a few weeks, the hair on her temples had gone
grey. I mentioned it.

'It doesn't matter,' she cried. 'He won't see it, will he?'

She sobbed most of the time I was with her. She was trying to
recapture every physical memory of him. She wanted to think of
him, feature, skin, and muscle, until she could recreate him in the
flesh.

It was pagan. It was what all human beings felt, I thought, when
someone dies whom they have loved in the body. Above all with
sexual love – but also with the love one bears a son or anyone who is

physically dear. If one has been truly bereaved, all resignation is driven away. Whatever one's mind says, one craves that they may live again. One cannot help but crave for resurrection and a life to come. But it would all be meaningless, a ghastly joke, without the resurrection of the body. One craves for that above all. Anything else would be a parody of the life we cry out to have restored. Rosalind did not believe in an after-life, did not believe in resurrection, either of the body or anything else; she believed that Roy had gone into annihilation. Yet with every atom of her whole existence, she begged that he might come to her again in the flesh.

We all found a kind of comfort in anything to do with his memory: as though by putting ourselves out, by being busy, by talking of him and making arrangements, we were prolonging his life. So Arthur Brown spent days organizing the memorial service; and I occupied myself with the obituaries. It seemed to push back the emptiness – and I became obsessed, beyond any realism, beyond any importance that they could possibly carry, that the notices should praise his work and should not lie. I wanted them to say that he was a great scholar, and try to explain his achievement. For the rest, let them say as little as could be. It was hard to tell the truth about any man; the conventional phrases, the habits of thought which came so glibly, masked all that men were like. For Roy to be written about in the 'stuffed' terms which he had spent so much of his life mocking – that I found painful out of proportion. He had spoken of himself with nothing but candour: with none of the alleviating lies which helped the rest of us to fancy ourselves at times: with a candour that was clear, light, naked, and terrible. It would be a bitter irony to have that tone silenced, and hear the public voices boom out about his virtues and his sacrifice.

I broke my silence about my own feelings in order to get Arthur Brown's help. He saw the point; he saw also that I was desperately moved, and exerted himself for my sake as well as Roy's. The chief obituaries finally appeared as curiously technical, bare, and devoid of human touches; they puzzled and disappointed many people.

Perhaps because I was silent about Roy's death, I did not receive much sympathy myself. One or two near to me were able to intrude – and I was grateful. Otherwise, I would rather have things as they were, and hear nothing.

Lady Boscastle wrote to me delicately and gracefully. And, to my astonishment, I had a note from her husband. It was short:

My dear Eliot,

They tell me that Roy Calvert is dead too. When I last saw you, those young men were alive. I had my son, and you your friend. I have no comfort to offer you. It is only left for us to throw away the fooleries of consolation, and curse into the silly face of fate until our own time comes. – B.

I was given one other unexpected sign of feeling. One night I was sitting in my office; the memorial service was taking place next morning, and I was just about to leave for Cambridge. The attendant opened the door, and Francis Getliffe came in.

'I'm very sorry about Calvert,' he said without any introduction, curtly and with embarrassment.

'Thank you, Francis,' I said.

'The memorial service is tomorrow, isn't it?'

I was surprised at the question, for Francis was rigid in never going inside the chapel. He and Winslow were the only unbelievers in the college who made it a matter of principle.

'Yes.'

'I'd come,' he said. 'But I've got this meeting. I daren't leave it.'

Francis had been found unimportant jobs, had been kept off committees, since he opposed the bombing campaign. He was just forcing his way back.

'No, you mustn't,' I said. 'It's good of you to tell me, though.'

'I didn't understand him,' said Francis. 'I'm sorry we didn't get on.' He looked at me with a frown of distress.

'He must have been a very brave man,' he went on. He added, with difficult, friendly concern: 'I'm sorry for you personally, Lewis.'

CHAPTER 40

Memorial Service

I WAS lying awake the next morning when Bidwell pulled up the blind. The room filled with the bright May sunlight; above the college roofs, the sky was a milky blue.

'It's a sad old day, sir,' said Bidwell.

I muttered.

'I wish I was bringing you his compliments, sir, and one of his messages.'

Bidwell came to the side of the bed, and gazed down at me. His small cunning eyes were round and open with trouble.

'Why did he do it, sir? I know you've got ways of thinking it out that we haven't. But I've been thinking it out my own way, and I don't feel right about it now. He'd got everything he could wish for, hadn't he, sir? He wasn't what you'd call properly happy, though he'd always got a joke for any of us. I don't see why he did it. There's something wrong about it. I don't claim to know where. It won't be the same place for me now, sir. Though he did give me a lot of trouble sometimes. He was a very particular gentleman, was Mr Calvert. But I should feel a bit easy if I knew why he did it.'

When I went out into the court, the smell of wistaria – with pitiless intensity – brought back other mornings in May. The servants were walking about with brushes and pans; one or two young men were sitting in their windows. For a second, I felt it incredible that Roy should be dead; it was so incredible that I felt a mirage-like relief; he was so full of life, he would soon be there.

Then in reaction I was gripped by savage resentment – resentment that these people were walking heedlessly through the court, resentment that all was going on as before. Their lives were unchanged, they carried no mark, they were calling casually to each other. I felt, with a sudden chill, the irrevocability of death.

The bell began to toll at a quarter to eleven. Soon the paths in the court were busy with groups of people moving to the chapel. From my window, I saw the senior fellow, Gay, who was eighty-six, hobbling his way there with minute steps. Lady Muriel and Joan followed him, both in black; as at the old Master's funeral, they walked with their backs stiff and their mouths firm.

I took my place in the fellows' stall. The chapel was full, as full as it had been for the funeral of Vernon Royce. Roy had been a figure in the town, and there were many visitors from other colleges. There was also Foulkes, in uniform, and a knot of other Orientalists, sitting together. All the fellows had come except Getliffe, Luke (who was in Canada) – and old Winslow. Stubborn to the last, he had decided he would not set foot in the chapel – even to honour the memory of a young man he liked. It was like his old proud, cross-grained self.

There were many women in the chapel. Rosalind was given a stall by the Master's; she was veiled and weeping. Lady Muriel and Joan sat just under her. Mrs Seymour was placed near the undergraduates. There were other, younger women, some of whom I knew slightly or had heard of from Roy. One or two I did not know at all – one struck me in particular, for she was beautiful.

'There seem to be several widows,' I heard someone in front of me whisper. He came from another college. I did not mind. I was ready for them to know him as he was.

For days past there had been a hidden bitter dispute in the college about who should officiate at the service. By all tradition, convention, and precedent, Despard-Smith had an unshakeable claim. He was the only fellow in orders; he had taken every memorial service for the last thirty years; he assumed that as of right he would preside at this one, as he had done at the old Master's.

But Arthur Brown did not like it. He had heard that last conflict between the old man and Roy. He knew, and so did most of the fellows, that Despard-Smith had been an enemy of Roy's, throughout his time there. Brown also knew that Despard-Smith was one of the few people alive who did not come within Roy's charity.

Brown was the last man in the college to make an unnecessary disturbance; he was willing to put up with a great many nuisances for the sake of a decent and clubbable life; and no one had more respect for precedent. But he could not let this pass. It was not fitting for Despard-Smith to speak in memory of Roy. Brown used all his expertness, all his experience of managing awkward situations, all his bility to get hints dropped and friendly representations made: but nothing came of it. Despard-Smith took it for granted that he would celebrate the service. Brown caused it to be suggested by other fellows that Calvert had intimate friends, such as Udal, in the church. It would give great pleasure if one of those officiated. Despard-Smith said that it would be reprehensible on his part to forsake his duty.

At last Brown fell back on the extreme obstinacy which he always held in reserve. He decided to 'have it out' with the old man. For Brown, who disliked any unpleasant scene, it was an ordeal. But I had no doubt that he spoke his mind with absolute firmness. Even then Despard-Smith would not give way. He could not abrogate his moral responsibility, he said. If his taking the service gave too much offence, then there should be no service at all.

All that Brown could secure was a compromise about the actual oration. Despard-Smith was willing to be guided by Calvert's friends upon what should be said. He would not pledge himself to use any specific form of words. But, if Brown gave him the notes for an address, he would use them so far as he felt justified.

So that morning Despard-Smith took the service. He looked younger than usual, buoyed up like other old men when a young one died – as though full of triumph that he was living on.

He did his office with dignity. At his age he was still spare, bleak, and erect. He viewed the crowded chapel severely: his voice had not lost its resonance. Some of the women cried as he spoke of Roy. Lady Muriel and Joan were dry-eyed, just as they had been at the old Master's funeral. Just as at that service, Despard-Smith got through his work. Brown frowned, heavy-faced, his high colour darkened, throughout the address.

I was glad when it was over. The old clergyman told us, as he had told us before at other memorial services, that there was no sorrow in death for him who had passed over. 'He has gone in great joy to meet his God. There should be no sorrow for the sake of our dear colleague. It is we who loved him who feel the sorrow. It is our lives which are darker, not his. We must try to conquer our deprivation in the thought of his exceeding joy.'

That was common form. So was much of what he said about Roy's life in college – 'very quiet in all his good actions, never seeking

343

power or fame or worldly pleasures, never entertaining an unkind
thought, never saying an unkind word'.

He had said almost exactly the same of Vernon Royce: I remembered catching a flash in Roy's eye as he heard that last astonishing encomium.

Then Despard-Smith put in something new.

'Our dear colleague was young. Perhaps he had not yet come to
his full wisdom. If he had a fault, perhaps it was to be impatient of
the experience that the years bring to us. Perhaps he had not yet
learned all that the years must tell us of the tears of things. *Lachrymae
rerum*. The tears of things. But how fortunate he was, our dear colleague, to pass over in the glory of his youth, before he tasted the
tears of things. There is no sorrow in such a death. To have known
only the glory and happiness of youth, and then to cast away life for
one's country. "*Dulce et decorum est pro patria mori.*"'

The old man realized he had departed from his brief. He was a
man who stuck to his contract; he adjusted his spectacles, fumbled
with his notes, and began to read Arthur Brown's version. It was clear
and simple. Despard-Smith read it monotonously, without much
meaning or inflexion until the end. Brown had put down Roy's great
successes. And he had written: 'He could have stayed in safety. But he
chose otherwise. The heart knows its own bitterness.' Brown meant
it as a comment on Roy's whole experience, but Despard-Smith
read it as mechanically as the rest.

The service ended. The fellows filed out first. Arthur Brown
pressed my hand without a word. I wanted to escape before the others
came into the court. I went across quickly to my rooms in the bright
sunlight. The cold wind was getting up.

I had a few last things to do. Our belongings in college had been
mixed up together. I happened to have a safe in my room, and there
he had stored some of his manuscripts. I unlocked it, took out one or
two of his papers, read through them, considered how they should
be disposed of. Then I went down to the college cellar, under the
kitchen. For years we had shared a section of the cellar together; we
did not buy much wine, but there were a few dozen bottles of mine
on the top racks, a rather less number of his below. His racks were
labelled in his own hand.

Inexplicably, that sight wounded me more than anything at the service. I had been prepared for much: but to this I had no defence. I could not bear to stay there. Without any plan or intention, I went up into the court, began walking through the streets.

It was dark in the sunshine, and difficult to see.

The may on the trees was odorous on the cold wind. I felt beside me, closer than anything I saw and yet not close enough to take away the acute and yearning sadness, the face of a young man, mischievous and mocking, the sleeves of his sweater tied round his neck, as when we walked away from cricket in the evening light.

MORE ABOUT PENGUINS

Penguinews, which appears every month, contains details of all the new books issued by Penguins as they are published. From time to time it is supplemented by *Penguins in Print*, which is a complete list of all available books published by Penguins. (There are well over three thousand of these.)

A specimen copy of *Penguinews* will be sent to you free on request, and you can become a subscriber for the price of the postage. For a year's issues (including the complete lists) please send 30p if you live in the United Kingdom, or 60p if you live elsewhere. Just write to Dept EP, Penguin Books Ltd, Harmondsworth, Middlesex, enclosing a cheque or postal order, and your name will be added to the mailing list.

Note: *Penguinews* and *Penguins in Print* are not available in the U.S.A. or Canada

CORRIDORS OF POWER

C. P. Snow

Roger Quaife wouldn't have been seen dead on an Aldermaston march. His was a lonelier ban-the-bomb campaign – waged from his seat in the Cabinet and his office at the Ministry. His weapons were persuasiveness and a consummate skill in top-level diplomacy. And the stakes were far higher than a pair of blistered feet.

C. P. Snow sets his story in a world he knows well – the corridors and committee rooms of Whitehall.

Rarely has the manipulation of political power been handled with such authenticity and intimacy.

THE AFFAIR

C. P. Snow

The Affair is one of the best designed novels in C. P. Snow's
Strangers and Brothers sequence, in which Lewis Eliot records
the world of men both through his own experience and that of
others. It tells, with impartial and friendly insight, the details of
a miscarriage of justice in the same Cambridge college which
served as a setting for *The Masters*.

The dismissal, on the grounds of scientific fraud, of an un-
popular young don who is probably a fellow-traveller, seems to
be regretted by nobody. But a doubt creeps in, and gradually the
fellows of the college are divided into two camps, neither of which
possesses a monopoly of rightness. The victim in this little *Affaire
Dreyfus* scarcely engages our affection, but the great scope of
Snow's vision nevertheless swings us to the side of justice.

The Affair was successfully produced as a play in London's
West End in 1961.

THE NEW MEN

C. P. Snow

This novel is concerned with a real historical event, the discovery of atomic fission, and its immediate consequences. The events, some of the most decisive of our time, are seen through the eyes of people living close to them. The stories of these men and women – the stoical and subtle Martin Eliot, his wife, Irene, his scientific colleague Walter Luke, and the ageing Cabinet Minister Thomas Bevill, other scientists, politicians, civil servants – are told with human realism and excitement. All their activities, in the middle of great impersonal happenings, are rooted in everyday flesh and bone; and at the core of the novel is the relation, difficult, profound, tenacious, between the two brothers Lewis and Martin Eliot.

'*The New Men* is a fascinating book because it seems so near to important reality. This was the way scientists thought and behaved, this was the politicians' reaction, or so C. P. Snow persuades us' – *Times Literary Supplement*

C. P. SNOW

C. P. Snow has firmly established his reputation as a novelist with his ambitious sequence of books, *Strangers and Brothers*. These novels, each of which is complete in itself, relate the experience of one man – the narrator, Lewis Eliot. Sometimes he describes his direct experience, as in *Time of Hope* and *Homecomings*: sometimes the experience is gained through viewing the lives of others, as in *The Masters* and *The Conscience of the Rich*. Altogether the sequence forms an impressive study of both the great public issues and the private problems of our age.

ALSO AVAILABLE

George Passant. The story of George Passant, a Midland solicitor's clerk. (1925–33)

Time of Hope. Lewis Eliot's early life, in the Midlands and at the bar. (1914–33)

The Conscience of the Rich. The story of Charles March, scion of an Anglo-Jewish banking family. (1927–36)

The Masters. The struggle for the mastership of a Cambridge college. (1937)

Homecomings. The middle life of Lewis Eliot and his second marriage. (1938–51)

The Sleep of Reason. Eliot's return to his home town, and his part in a sinister murder. (1963–64)

Last Things. Sir Lewis Eliot's heavy responsibilities fall at last onto the shoulders of his son.

and
The Search